EARTH (ISH)

Other Books from Splinter Press

Song of the Sands by Spencer Sekulin
Between Tungsten and Gold by Taryn Skipper
Sorry, Humans (Especially Greg) by Faralee Pozo

In the Splinterverse

Splinter's Edge by Boydell Bown
The Dissection and Reassembly of Cohen Hoard by Elesa Hagberg
Mere Mortal by AJ Stevens

An anthology from Splinter Press

SPLINTER PRESS

Earth(ish): Tales from the Splinterverse

An Anthology

Cover art by Rebecca Sorge Jensen

Published by:

Splinter Press,
Spanish Fork, Utah

splinterpress.com

ISBN-13: 978-1-960108-23-4

Contents

Date: 2590-04-17 02:41:11 PRT
From: Green Kinsha
To: Torts El-Sayed
Subject: Welcome

Congratulations, Mr. El-Sayed, and welcome to the Anachronauts Rebellion Group as our new supervisor. I wasn't aware we needed a supervisor or that they were hiring from outside the organization, but I suppose you're in charge now, so you should probably know how this all works. I've been chosen as the one to introduce you to our cause. Here's a quick rundown.

You know our home is just a copy of Earth, right? A pocket universe, a splinter, etc. If you don't know that, review your intro packet. It should have arrived on your doorstep/mailbox/wheelbarrow this morning. Most people already know, but maybe that information didn't make its way to the backwater you're from. Not sure how it got leaked to the general public, but after all the screaming and looting and ill-advised eloping, most people seemed to forget about it.

But we researchers don't forget.

We discovered this moonbase near a nexus point—a crossover between splintered worlds—and have rented out a corner for research. And we've found out quite a bit, most of it completely bonkers.

First, we know this isn't the only "splinter" out there. In fact, there are twenty-three others that we know of, all without stars just like us. All these splinters were opened at different time periods in Earth's history, and each one has progressed very differently from our own. Almost no other Earths have space Cat overlords, for example. Go figure.

The immortal beings who created these splinters (no,

they aren't gods, they're just jerks with too much power and time on their hands—we think they're from Qoretech) can't seem to leave the splinters alone: weather experiments, unsanctioned portals, government and technology manipulation, and unholy experiments. As if those humans didn't have enough to deal with already. Someone should probably do something. Not us, of course. We just observe. And write reports. (Gentor insists we are wasting our time. But Gentor is a dodo). (Wait. Not a real dodo. Those only exist on the Agartha splinter).

By the way, here are this week's reports for you, with information we gathered that came through the nexus. for simplicity considering all the timelines we are dealing with, the reports are timestamped in Prime Relative Time (PRT). We've also started collecting some first-hand (or third-hand) accounts from people living in each of the splinters, and those accounts (like the first one here) are attached. In my opinion, these direct accounts are key, leading us to finding real answers.

If you have any questions, feel free to find someone else to ask. I'm on break.

—Green Kinsha

QUEEN OF THE NIGHT

By AJ Stevens

IC-1, Earth, 2516 CE

"Commencing countdown for splintering S15." Rosalind Alves glanced at the rest of the mission leaders in the gallery.

"Go ahead, Jump, Director Alves." The Mission Director gave her a nod. She started the timer.

"Sixty seconds to splintering," an automated voice announced.

The thrum of the antimatter generators powering up pulsed through Rosalind's skeleton and made her teeth ache. She leaned in close to Zeke's clone lying on the travel deck. Even though he was in stasis for the journey, she squeezed his hand.

The deck lit up. "Forty seconds to splintering."

Rosalind tucked a folded paper in the clone's hand and backed away. The higher-ups in the gallery went on chatting.

"A thousand credits says nobody on S15 lasts the year," Vixus said with a sneer, punching his final coordinates into the time interface.

Rosalind ground her teeth and rolled her eyes. Normally, she ignored Vixus and his jibes. But today he was harder to shut out. Today it was Zeke he was betting against. "You're on."

"Twenty seconds to splintering."

She waved Vixus through the exit before pulling the blast door shut behind them and sealing Zeke inside the travel chamber.

The chamber pulsed brighter as the platform glowed a painful white. Rosalind watched until her eyes watered.

"Three . . . two . . . one."

The world went white and silent.

* * *

Li Lunar Proxima Depot, Earth, July 20, 2040 CE 1:59:57 AM GMT

A pulse vibrated through the commander and, for a moment, he saw two Earths. They snapped apart and then slowly fused back into one. He stared out the viewport and blinked hard.

"Whoa. What was that?" His engineer backed away from the controls, palms up. "I didn't touch anything. I swear."

"What was what?" the commander asked, turning to her.

"The controls all went crazy, spinning and flashing," she explained.

He glanced them over. "Looks normal to me."

"Well, *something* happened."

The commander looked back out the viewport at the solitary blue planet. "What happened is we've been on this space station too damn long."

* * *

Quietus, July 20, 2040 7:59:35 PM MDT

Nyx Jensen gripped the steering wheel tightly and slid her sunglasses down over her eyes. She was driving right into the setting sun. She could barely see ahead of her and was afraid to look behind her.

She pressed the accelerator and looked over at her little sister, hunched in the passenger seat. "It's okay, Yo. We'll be okay. That's the last time he hits you."

"He'll send the cops after me, Nyxie. You know he will," Eyos said, setting her jaw and staring out the window.

"Let him," Nyx replied, eyeing the bruise purpling Eyos's left eye and cheekbone. "No way they take you back to him."

"What if they charge you with kidnapping?" Eyos asked, her face grim.

"A girl can't take her sister for a ride? Please." Nyx gave a dismissive wave of her hand. "Let me worry about that, you worry about being the drive dee-jay."

Eyos obediently synced her phone and began scrolling her music. Their father was a hundred miles behind them, and if he came knocking, there was always the Beretta in the glovebox. Nyx breathed out slowly as the music came on. *One step at a time.* Eyos was safe, and that's what mattered for now. She turned her focus back to the road and to staring just beneath the sun.

Only . . .

There was something wrong with the sun.

It had a hole in it.

Nyx lifted her sunglasses as the hole swallowed the sun and bled across the sky. As if the Earth was flying into a tunnel with reckless abandon. She brought the car to a stop in the middle of the lonely Wyoming highway and got out. The sunlight receded in a perfect half-ring, eating its way across the sky toward the horizon behind her, and then blinked out and was gone.

"What . . . In . . . The . . . Hell." Nyx spun forward and backward, searching the sky.

"Is it an eclipse?" Eyos asked, eyes wide in the lights from the dash.

Nyx looked up into the void, a blackness so deep it pressed heavily down on her. She sank back in her seat and closed the door against the sudden chill. "I don't know, Yo, but I don't think so. Let's get to my place fast."

* * *

Zeke stirred.

Prairie grass prickled his cheek. He pushed himself to his hands and knees and sat back on his heels. He would never get used to that. It was worse than dying.

A paper crinkled in his right hand. He flipped on his headlamp and unfolded the note.

Good luck.

I'll be watching over you.

—Rosalind

With a little smiley after the *d*.

He shook his head. It was just like her to violate protocol to boost his mood. He tucked the note in his jacket pocket and stood. His gear was sprinkled around him in a wide circle roughly the width of the travel deck. He disconnected the portable memory unit from the subdermal chip at the back of his neck and stowed it in one of the packs. It had done its first job, and he wouldn't need it again until the mission was over. He carefully wrapped his scarf over the glow of his chip before extracting his first bubble probe. The plasmaglass sphere hummed to life at his touch, and he carefully launched it into the night. He gave the probe a moment to establish a timelink before gathering his gear and checking his geolocator. Data from the probe populated its screen.

Damn Vixus. He was two hundred miles off the designated site for the observation post. He would have to find a ride, which meant talking to locals. It was early in the mission for that, no time for integration training. Hopefully, his research had paid off, and he wouldn't stand out. It was against regulations to alert the locals to the mission or interfere with their fate. Zeke smiled wryly: as if this whole business wasn't interfering with fate.

It didn't take him long to find a road. He trudged along it westward, left arm out with the thumb up as he'd seen in the records and vaguely remembered in real life. He'd been an old man last time he existed in 2040, and not the type to hitchhike.

It was more than an hour before he heard the first engine behind him, and by that time he was feeling the cold even through his many layers. He stood in the middle of the road flashing his light and waving it. The car didn't slow; Zeke cursed and shouted as it approached. Just as he was about to jump off the road, the brakes squealed as they engaged with sudden force and rubber burned. The wide eyes of the frightened girl behind the wheel locked on his just before the SUV plowed into him.

He grunted with the impact and stumbled backward. He heard the dull thwack of his skull against the pavement and saw stars before the darkness came.

Just perfect.

* * *

Just perfect.

Nyx stared out at the body lying in the pool of her headlights, then turned slowly to look at Eyos.

Eyos sat up tall, peering over the dash and gaping. "Is he dead, Nyxie? What do we do?"

Nyx glanced up at the unholy dark above and tried to still her shaking hands.

"I guess I'd better check." She put the car in park, then leaned over to the glove box to retrieve the Beretta before opening the door and climbing out. *Where had he come from?* Something didn't feel right about this. She leveled the gun at the motionless figure and slowly approached, her breath frosting in the frigid air while her heart thundered in her chest. Near his head, she squatted down beside him and felt for a pulse. *Not dead.*

Nyx dropped her head and rested both hands on her knees, gun dangling, as she breathed a sigh of relief. The car door opened, and Eyos popped her head out. "So?"

"Stay there." Nyx stood, tucking the gun in her waistband. "He's alive, just unconscious."

"We can't drive off and leave him, Nyxie."

"I know." Nyx walked back to the car and leaned in to retrieve her phone. "I guess we call the police and get him an ambulance."

"No." The man groaned and sat up. "No police."

* * *

Zeke rubbed his head and climbed to his feet, wincing as he tried to put weight on his left foot. At a motion from the driver, the passenger door slammed shut. The girl on the driver's side eyed him cautiously, one hand on the door, the other behind her back.

He shone his light on her, and she flinched. *Okay. Not a girl, a woman.* Her short black hair angled sharply from the back of her head to her shoulders, and a tattoo of a beautiful, winged woman cloaked in black graced most of her right shoulder and arm.

"Please, miss. I need a ride to Jackson Hole. It's freezing out." He limped to the vehicle and placed his hands on the hood of the car.

"Not my problem. Get out of my way." Her ice blue eyes flashed a challenge, but she seemed more afraid than angry.

"At least drive me to the nearest town so I can get a taxi. I can't exactly walk there anymore, thanks to you."

"Me?" The woman scoffed. "You were wearing black, standing in the middle of the road on the darkest night I've ever seen. Not *entirely* my fault. Besides, there aren't exactly a plethora of taxis in rural Wyoming, dude."

"I can pay you," Zeke offered, though he had no current money.

"I don't like to repeat myself, asshole." She lifted a gun and pointed it at him. "Now get out of my way."

* * *

Nyx shivered in her tank top but held her ground. The man wasn't much older than she, maybe twenty-three, and he was handsome as hell, but she wasn't about to get Ted Bundied at the end of the world.

Or whatever this was.

"Listen," he said. "I can see you're scared. I'm scared too. I need your help."

Nyx's heart twinged, and she glanced at his injured foot. "Sorry. I can't. I can't help you. I have other people who need my help. I don't know you. Someone else will be along—maybe they can help." She moved to duck back into the car.

He held his hands up and wobbled a little on his feet. "Please. I'm one of the good guys. I won't hurt you, and I can return the favor once I get to Jackson."

"I don't need help."

The man smiled gently—he wasn't buying her tough girl attitude. "Everyone needs help. And this . . ." He waved at the darkness around them. "This is extinction level. Trust me. Whatever you are running from, whoever you are trying to save, none of that matters if you don't survive this."

She chewed her lip and glanced in at Eyos. "What do you mean?"

"I won't just help you, I can *save* you. I have a safe place; take me there, and decide for yourself. I'm a researcher. I've been preparing for this."

"You've been preparing for the sun to vanish?" She cocked an eyebrow at him.

"Yes?" He shrugged helplessly.

"Is that a question?"

The man hesitated, then seemed to come to a decision.

"Here." He pulled open one of his many bags and tossed a package at her. It landed on the car roof. "It's a lightweight thermal suit. It will keep you warm up to negative four hundred degrees. You could survive on the moon in that."

"What moon?" She waved at the black sky. "Listen, man, I'm going to Salt Lake, not the moon. It's cold, but it's not that cold. Thanks anyway."

"It's going to get colder."

As if on cue, it started to snow. In July.

Nyx looked at the suit and back at the man, then in at Eyos, who shrugged. "Got one for my sister, too?"

* * *

"Jackson Hole is pretty far out of my way," the woman said, tucking her shoulder-length black hair back behind her ear as Zeke loaded his gear in the back of the SUV.

"Look miss, I have four of those suits, and I'm giving you one now and one when we get there. I'll even show you how to use them. Driving a few hundred extra miles for the difference between life and death is a small price to pay."

She scoffed. "Yeah, if they work, and if the sun doesn't rise tomorrow as it has for the past four billion years."

"It won't," Zeke replied, opening the back door.

"Oh, no, no, mister. Up front, where I can keep an eye on you. Eyos, hop in back."

The girl in the passenger seat grumbled and climbed out. Zeke got a good look at her for the first time. She was maybe twelve, with blue eyes and a long black braid that fell past her waist. Well, one blue eye and one swollen shut and purple with bruises.

Zeke swore and closed his eyes, breathing deep in and out once. Then he turned to the girl. "You okay, kiddo?"

She blew her bangs from her eyes and gave him a small lop-sided smile. "Eyos, not kiddo. And yeah. You should see the other guy. Took his sweet SUV, took his gun, and made his daughter drive the getaway car."

"Your father, then? Because you two are definitely sisters." He held the door for her and gestured her inside.

"Yeah. My father. He's a real peach." She slid into the back seat.

Zeke furrowed his brow, trying to sort that one out, but failed and shook his head. "Well, unless he rescues a stranded researcher and gets his own thermal suit, odds are you'll never have to worry about that peach again."

Zeke shut the door and sat in the passenger's seat. The woman climbed in behind the wheel and handed the gun to Eyos. "If he breathes wrong, you know what to do."

Zeke smiled and offered his hand to the woman. "I'm Ezekiel. You can call me Zeke."

"Okay, Zeke. No chitchat. Spill. I want to know everything you know. You have four hours." She shifted the car into drive.

Zeke turned and studied Eyos. It had been a long time since Zeke had felt much of anything beyond the drive for knowledge, but the black eye and busted-up lip on someone that small woke something in him. Something from way back in his first life.

Damn Vixus. Damn the regulations. Damn it all.

He turned to the woman. "You two should stay in Jackson Hole. Don't go back to Salt Lake City."

* * *

"Why?" Nyx asked, trying to keep her mounting curiosity from her voice. "What's in Jackson? What's happening?"

The man, Zeke, sighed. "I can't tell you that."

Nyx rolled her eyes. "Well, what can you tell me?"

"I can tell you that the sun isn't coming back. Ever. It will get very cold, very quickly. Yellowstone is a large area of geothermal activity. It will be one of the few places nearby capable of maintaining any kind of heat or generating energy. And the sooner you get there, the better."

"What happened to the sun? Did it burn out?" Eyos asked.

"I can't say exactly. But we can't see it, and its light and heat can't get to us."

Nyx looked at the black void beyond her headlights and shivered. "What about the moon?"

"I'm afraid the same with the moon."

"So the tides will stop?" Nyx asked, shaking her head in disbelief.

"It's complicated. If the moon's gravity is gone, in a week or so, the oceans will be as smooth as glass. If not, the tides will continue. Either way, the oceans will eventually freeze over."

"That's unbelievable, you know," she said. Hell, if she hadn't just seen the sun blink out, she'd assume he was crazy. "What are you? An astronomy student? How have you been preparing for this?"

"I'm a physicist."

Nyx scoffed. "You aren't old enough to be a physicist with this much research behind you."

"Oh, yes I am. Believe me." He was earnest, and his eyes seemed wise and kind. Not that Nyx believed you can tell much about a person by looking into their eyes. Her father had kind eyes . . . most of the time.

"How did you come to be in the middle of Nowheresville, Wyoming?" she asked.

"A slight miscalculation. My co-worker dropped me off at the wrong place."

"You have to know what a messed-up answer that is, Zeke."

* * *

The little girl dropped off to sleep about an hour later. Even the end of the world wasn't enough to keep her awake. Zeke rode in silence with the slightly older girl pretending to be a hardass.

"How old are you?" she asked.

"How old are *you*?" he asked right back.

"Old enough to know you're avoiding the question. I'm twenty."

"And how long have you been looking out for Eyos there?" he nodded toward the back.

She gave him a sidelong glance. "Most of my life. Since my mother died."

"You should stay in Jackson Hole," he repeated. "So you can keep looking out for her."

"Why can't I look out for her in Salt Lake?"

"Trust me, you can't." He shook his head.

"Trust you? I don't know you, man. You could be an axe murderer."

He shrugged. "I've never murdered anyone . . . with an axe."

That got a small smile from the woman, though she hid it quickly.

* * *

The SUV glided through the darkness, a small island of light, and Nyx was grateful for the 4-wheel drive as snow started accumulating on the road. It was nearly midnight, and they were almost to Jackson. She studied her passenger as she drove. His clothes were odd. And for some reason, he'd been wearing boots and a parka in the summer. He was working on a small handheld that was unlike any she'd ever seen. Maybe he *was* a researcher.

"You're not from here, are you?" she asked.

"No. I am not."

"Where are you from?" Nyx pressed.

"Nowhere you've heard of," he replied.

"Ah. Another non-answer. Lovely."

"Turn right up ahead," he said.

"I thought we were going to Jackson Hole."

"Not all the way. Turn right please." He pointed, jabbing his finger right.

Nyx slowed and turned off Highway 26 onto an unmarked road. About fifty feet further, she brought the car to a halt in front of a large gate. Zeke climbed out and punched some numbers into the keypad. The gate slid open, creaking on its heavy hinges as Zeke climbed back in.

She gave the man a side glance. "Ohhh-kayyy. Let's just take the strange dude through the creepy gate into the Yellowstone wilderness."

He chuckled. "It's about thirty miles more. If you want to leave after you see it, you can leave."

"Ah yes, taking the word of an absolute stranger is always good advice." But she glanced at the blackness around her and the sleeping form of Eyos in the back and pulled through the gate despite her misgivings.

* * *

The road wound upward through the mountains. Both the snow and the trees got thicker as they drove. The woman seemed unperturbed by the snow, competently steering the vehicle slow and steady. She had clearly done this before. Zeke was suddenly glad she was there, glad he hadn't had to sort out how to drive. The road ended some forty minutes later at a fenced-off clearing in front of a vault-like door into the mountain. It was exactly as Zeke remembered. A guard approached from the gatehouse carrying a rifle.

"Are we there?" Eyos asked, sitting up. Zeke looked back at her. *Damn the regulations.* He could hardly just leave them now. Even if they stayed in Jackson Hole, they wouldn't survive for long.

"I got this," Zeke said, climbing out before the woman could protest. Zeke met the guard in front of the SUV, bathed in the glow of the headlights.

He stretched out a hand. "Hello. I'm Ezekiel Torres."

The guard lifted a skeptical eyebrow, so Zeke pulled out his ID and handed it over. He was much younger than the man in the ID, but it was still him.

"Thank goodness for Botox, am I right?" He smiled.

The guard did not smile back. He fit the ID into a slot in his reader and scowled at the read-out.

"I need your DNA sample as well, Mr. Torres. Your Oasys employee card is insufficient alone."

"Of course." Zeke submitted to a finger prick and waited for the machine to confirm that his DNA was indeed a match.

The guard studied the screen and then shook his head, waving at the car before handing it back. "Sorry, Mr. Torres. I can only admit you."

"I completely understand." Zeke grabbed the guard and pulled him into a guillotine choke, squeezing until the man went limp.

* * *

Nyx clamped both hands over her mouth.

"Bad ass," Eyos said from the back seat.

Zeke hauled the guard through the snow and back into the guard shack and punched a button. The gates swung open. He climbed back in the passenger seat, but Nyx just stared.

"Go on." Zeke waved.

"Is he . . . dead?" Nyx asked.

"Not yet," Zeke replied.

Nyx's heart thundered in her chest. "Why did you do that?"

"He wouldn't let you in." Zeke shrugged.

"What kind of 'researcher' knows karate?"

"Jiu jitsu," Zeke corrected. "And this kind."

Nyx edged the SUV forward, and the gate swung shut behind them.

"What is this place?" Nyx parked the car beside the vault door.

"This," Zeke said, climbing out, "is a state-of-the-art, self-sufficient underground bunker for the rich and powerful to survive a nuclear war."

"And, uh, how do you know about it?" Nyx followed him out of the car, wrapping her arms around herself.

"Well. I designed it." He flipped open the keypad by the door.

Nyx stopped in her tracks. "You're shitting me."

"Nope." He punched in an access code and submitted to some kind of eye scan, then the vault door swung open. Lights popped on sequentially from the door illuminating a tunnel deep into the mountainside and warmth flooded out. "Welcome to Oasys."

Eyos skipped in before Nyx could stop her, her braid swinging behind her. "This is siiiick, man."

It was everything he said. They climbed down past a hydroponic farm. Zeke showed them the water recycling facility. Natural heat, powered by a mix of nuclear and geothermal energy, wrapped around them as they walked. Nyx, and her heart, finally started to thaw.

Zeke opened the door to a small studio-style apartment. "At least spend the night and think about staying. I'll need help getting it all up and running, and you're in no condition to drive."

"What do you mean you'll need help. What about everyone else?"

"There is no one else. Just a guard whose only job is to keep people out".

Nyx hesitated. "Why are you doing this? Why us?"

Zeke glanced in at Eyos, already snuggling into a bed, and lowered his voice. “I had my own Eyos. Long time ago. I couldn’t save her.”

Nyx bit her lip, considering. “I guess I could use some sleep.”

A light knock at her door woke her. She grumbled and glanced at her watch. 8:05 AM. *Shit.* She had not meant to sleep that long.

She sat up and unrumpled her clothes, then stumbled to the door, opening it a crack.

Zeke stood there looking like he’d been up for hours.

“I’d like to show you something,” he said.

Nyx slipped her shoes on and followed him out the door and up the tunnel to the exit. Zeke swung the door open and gestured her outside.

Nyx couldn’t move. She could see from where she stood that the sky was as empty and black and devoid of light as it had been last night. Stepping into that void would make it real, and she didn’t want it to be real. A coldness gripped her heart so tight she couldn’t breathe.

“It’s going to be okay,” Zeke said. “Stay here and help me get things going, and your spots in the Oasys are ensured. More people will come, we will expand, but most importantly, we will survive. You and Eyos will survive.”

Nyx nodded, shaking off the despair that crowded her thoughts. She couldn’t give in to hopelessness; she had to think of Eyos. “We’ll stay.”

“Don’t tell me you’re afraid of the dark,” Zeke said, stepping into the blackness and looking up with his hands in his pockets. “It’s no big deal.”

It seemed like a big deal. It seemed like the only deal. “I’m not afraid of it. I just don’t understand it.”

“I’ll help you. For starters, I just need one thing from you.”

“What’s that?” she asked, edging forward.

“Your name.”

She smiled. “It’s Nyx.”

Zeke chuckled, glancing at her tattoo. “How fitting.”

“Oh?”

“In a world of eternal darkness, I was rescued by none other than the Queen of the Night herself.”

Nyx followed him into the dark, staring up at the starless sky. “I suppose.”

From over the years, her mother’s bedtime words to chase off nightmares and monsters echoed in her mind.

You girls have nothing to fear, for Nyx rules the night, and Eyos brings the dawn.

Date: 2590-04-09 17:23:33 PRT
From: Green Kinsha
To: Anachronauts
Subject: Sunset
Re: Queen of the Night

I read a lot of personal accounts. A lot. That's pretty much all I do; sit at this tiny desk in this grimy corner of this backwater moonbase and read accounts. (It's not what I thought I'd be doing when I ventured into the empty blackness of space, but it pays the bills. Mostly.) And this is the first account I've seen that documents the precise moment of splintering. You'd think everyone would be writing about it—the moment the stars went out, and their whole world changed—but I guess people are too busy being terrified to write in their diary.

Which is why this account is so special, even considering the fact that it gives us essential information on Quietus. How that world keeps spinning is a mystery I'm determined to crack.

And I suppose now we know where the Oasys Foundation began. Yeah. THAT Oasys Foundation. The one that the Ceruleans broke off of. I haven't yet figured out how to use this knowledge against them, but they've guarded their origins so fanatically there must be a reason. Maybe Ren can see some patterns that I don't?

Did you know I met Ezekial Torres once? Nice guy. Hair like obsidian waves. I have a meeting with the Space Cat Council at 03:30, so that's all I have to say.

Green Kinsha Out.

INTO THE VOID

By Ethan Whitaker

"Silvia Eldritch! This is the YCR. Open up!" a familiar, demanding voice bellowed from the other side of the door. Silvia guessed it was the chief of the Yellowstone City Rangers, Doug Reckman. They pounded on the door to Silvia's hideout, but the barricade she had set up would hold, for now. She turned her attention back to the window she was leaning against.

Silvia watched the denizens of Yellowstone City walk its cold, quiet streets. There were always a fair amount of people milling about at any given hour, ever since the very concepts of night and day were consumed along with the sky. Everything had simply stopped that day ten years ago—everything except for the geysers that is. From her vantage point at the second-story window of the ruined hotel she was attempting, and failing, to hide in, Silvia could see one such geyser erupting about two miles away. Its cascading, geothermal water glistened in the artificial light. Tiny spherical machines buzzed around the geyser, harvesting the hot water, barely visible as tiny black specks from this distance.

Silvia nearly forgot about the incessant banging on the door, but as the knocking turned to slamming, she was reminded that she was still on the clock. Sighing, she grabbed the bulky backpack off the ground next to her. Silvia took one final moment to drink in the sight of the city, her home for the past decade, close to a third of her entire life. The technologically warmed air and protective glass dome provided her and the people below a small comfort to contrast the forever blackened sky.

"Eldritch! This is your final warning, open this door now! You are under arrest for—"

"Burglary, resisting arrest, assaulting a ranger," Silvia interrupted. "Yeah, yeah, I get it. Can we just get this over with already, guys?" While she spoke, she swung the window open and slid one leg out. There was no response from Reckman. Instead, the urgent banging on the door turned into something ramming against the door.

Yep, break's over. Time to go! She quickly lowered herself down, found a foothold in the brick, and dropped the rest of the way to the street below. Above, she heard the splintering of wood as her barricade gave out, and the door was flung open. That sound was followed by an ear-splitting *crack* as the flashbangs she had rigged at the door went off. She smiled; it was such a wonderful feeling to have a trap go off without a hitch. Her smile faltered as two rangers who were watching the entrance to the hotel spotted her and headed her direction, shouting.

Okay, maybe one hitch. Silvia took off down the street; no doubt the rangers behind her were following suit. She took a sharp turn into an alley just before the snapping of gunfire filled the air. Silvia's stomach dropped, but she kept running, turning every corner she hit. She had been in trouble with the law on many occasions, but they had never just started shooting at her before. Though she supposed she should've expected this, given the man she had just stolen from. Regardless, Silvia knew she had to lose these two trigger-happy rangers before she could continue the plan and blend into the crowd at Old Faithful Square. What would be the point of trying to help one group of people just to cause harm to another in the process?

She turned into a dead end. This was no mistake, as she knew firsthand that the wall here was the easiest way to the rooftops. The rangers had lost her for the moment, but it wouldn't be long before they found her again. Silvia hastily made her way up the wall, the slapdash brick placements of the building providing ample footholds. She hoisted herself over the lip onto the roof and hunched down a short distance from the edge. The sounds of the rangers turning into the dead end echoed up to her. She held her breath. The rangers briefly argued, blaming each other for taking a wrong turn somewhere, and their echoed footsteps got quieter as they backtracked into the winding alleys.

Silvia stood up straight and let out a relieved breath. But her relief was short-lived as there was a strange mechanical warbling noise coming from behind her, getting louder. She glanced back and saw a small cluster of flying drones buzzing above the rooftops, headed straight for her. They were tiny, metal spheres with camera lenses poking out the front and no visible forms of propulsion.

Enforcers? Really? Voids, you've got to be kidding me!

Silvia tore across the rooftop. She reached a ten-foot wall up to a higher roof and clambered up it, just managing to get on all fours onto the higher roof when a volley of bright blue bursts of energy snapped against the wall, barely missing her. She shuddered as she scrambled to her feet. That was way too close; if she was any slower, she would be spasming on the ground. There was no time to worry about that right now. From what Silvia had been told, it took those things about twenty seconds to recharge their weapons before they could fire again. She had to shake them off her tail before that happened. Thinking fast, she slowed as she reached the edge of the rooftop. There was a ladder down to a fire escape staircase. She slid down the ladder and rocketed down the stairs, putting her hand against every window on her way down, hoping to find—

The fourth window she tried pushed open. Silvia dove into the pitch black room and clicked the window closed just before the Enforcers curved down into the alley. She pressed herself against the wall next to the window, listening as they passed her hiding spot and moved lower. Silvia risked a glance out the window. The black spheres moved in unison as they hovered down to street level. Then they scattered, moving to search procedures. Silvia had to duck back out of line of sight when one drone worked its way up and scanned the windows of the building she was in. Eventually, all the drones moved off to search the surrounding area.

After waiting a few beats, Silvia let out a shuddering sigh. She knew she wasn't out of the woods yet; the drones would almost certainly return to this area to do a more thorough sweep, but she had given herself a brief moment to breathe. She reached into her pocket and pulled out a small, square piece of nylon. With one slight tug, the palm-sized bundle unfurled into a full-sized jacket with a hood. It was dual-sided, maroon on one side and a dull brown on the other. She swung the backpack around to her front and pulled the jacket on, maroon side facing out. Hoping that her disguise would be enough, she pulled the hood up and carefully opened the window. She checked to see if the alley was clear, then climbed out to the stairway and made her way down.

The walk to Old Faithful Square was a stressful one. An Enforcer would occasionally pass by overhead, forcing her to hunch and wrap her arms around the backpack to keep it out of line of sight. Thankfully, none of the drones clocked her as she finally made it to the edge of the crowd surrounding the square. She slowly pushed further into the crowd, making her way towards the center. She thought she could make out the faint glow of a holo-timer peeking through the people in front of her.

As she grew closer to the center, she saw that she was correct. At the center of the square sat a circular patch of dirt with a hole in the direct center, the titular geyser itself. A large holographic timer, made to look like a clock, was superimposed onto the dirt surrounding the geyser, slowly ticking down. Based on the timer, there was a little more than two minutes before Old Faithful's next eruption. She reached the inside edge of the crowd standing behind a circle of ropes. Silvia risked a glance behind her. There were a smattering of Enforcers hovering around fifteen feet in the air, scanning the crowd. Their programming was smarter than Silvia had assumed; it made sense to check nearby crowds for any sign—

One of the drones swiveled and caught sight of her face—she quickly turned back around, but the damage had been done. The drone that spotted her let out a warbling siren noise, and all the drones locked onto her and started closing in. *Idiot!*

This was bad, very bad. She had nowhere to go. She couldn't hide in the crowd without risking someone getting blasted. Her mind raced, scrambling to think of something, anything to get her out of this. She needed some way to put distance between herself and the drones, something to hide behind while also keeping bystanders out of the line of fire. But what could do that? The only things around her were the crowds.

No . . . they're not the only things. She glanced towards the geyser; there were thirty seconds left on the timer. A terrible, stupid idea came to Silvia, and she continued to tell herself how stupid it was even as she surged to the front of the crowd and vaulted over the rope. She sprinted as fast as she could towards the geyser. People gasped and shouted out. The Enforcers immediately pursued they were thirty feet behind and closing. There was a buzzing sound, and the hairs on the back of Silvia's neck stood on end. She dove to the left, hitting the ground and rolling. A moment later, electricity shot up dirt all around her, but she wasn't hit. She got to her feet and ran. There were twenty seconds left on the holo-timer.

Legs aching, lungs burning, Silvia pushed herself faster. Silvia reached the mouth of the geyser as the timer hit ten seconds and leaped over it. Hitting the other side on her feet, thankfully, she kept going, putting as much distance between her and what was about to happen. She glanced behind her. *Five . . . four . . .* The Enforcers were closing in, beelining straight for her. The air buzzed once again, and they just passed over the geyser mouth when—

One . . . Zero!

The geyser erupted with a torrent of glistening, scalding water that took Silvia's breath away. The steam boiled around her, providing a harsh contrast to the eternal cold. She was sprayed by a smattering of stray droplets, which burned through her jacket but left her unburned. After the initial burst of steam, Sylvia hazarded a backward glance. Just as she had hoped, the cluster of drones got caught in the eruption. Nearly a dozen of the infuriating metal spheres were hit directly by the powerful torrent and were blasted out of the sky, thumping down to the nearby dirt, destroyed. The drones that weren't blasted got swarmed by water collection drones that surrounded the eruption, forcing the Enforcers to pull back.

Silvia leaped over the ropes on the other side of the circle, narrowly avoiding the bulk of the falling, scalding spray. Stunned members of the crowd pulled back and allowed her to move through. The Enforcers would have to find a roundabout path around the geyser, or wait upwards of five minutes for the eruption to end. Silvia briefly mused on the idea of high-end technology being bested by the powers of nature. Quietly laughing to herself with jokes she knew Ben would hate, she made her way out of the square.

Finally leaving the crowd, Silvia blended into a small group that was headed away from the square. She removed her jacket and flipped it inside out to the brown side. Putting the flipped jacket back on and resituating the backpack slung around her front, Silvia started east, choosing to take a more roundabout path home.

As she walked, and as the adrenaline started to fade, Silvia realized just how tired she was. Her feet hurt like hell, and every muscle in her body was taut. Unfortunately, she couldn't stop yet. Once she got home, maybe she could consider taking a breather.

After a few minutes, Silvia risked a glance behind and above her. Nothing was chasing her. She stopped and took a moment to look up at the void. Above her, there were mostly just water collectors making their way to their designated storage facilities. A few Enforcers were scanning streets far away from where she was, but none of them were headed in her direction.

Somehow, after surviving three close calls back to back, she'd done it. She let out a shaky laugh. *Voids, I have to get a new hobby.* Pleased with herself despite everything, Silvia continued walking, now headed directly southward. Her body ached, but she reveled in it, for it signified all the work she had put in. Finally, her job was done. Finally, she could go home.

❦ ❦ ❦

On the outskirts of Yellowstone City, right up against the large glass dome that separated them from the hungry dark, sat a shanty town that circled the entire city. It was much colder in the shanties; the artificial heating systems on the outskirts were slowly failing, and the people in charge didn't see much point in repairing them. The roads of the South Shanty were bustling with activity as Silvia made her way home. Beggars—wrapped in as much cloth as they could find—lined the streets on both sides. They called out to Silvia and everyone else who passed by, pleading for warm water or food. Silvia passed them, ignoring the pleas out of necessity rather than a lack of sympathy. Despite the fact that she had lived here for a decade, Silvia still felt the same level of sorrow for those she couldn't help.

Ahead of Silvia, a man dressed in all black shouted out to the moving tide of people, his voice drowning out the unfortunate souls around him. "Cast aside your worries and needs, my brothers and sisters! Join me in prayer and celebration! For the Mother of Darkness is here to save us from ourselves!" The man—who Silvia now noticed had a shaved head and a blindfold—pointed to the sky beyond the dome. "Her eternal hunger has claimed the very stars, and now she has chosen us to bask in her divine beauty! Accept the bitter cold and join me as we are welcomed in her dark embrace!" Silvia kept walking, tuning out the man's feverish zeal. The Order of the Hungering Dark were gaining more and more followers as the years went on, so seeing their preachers in the streets was becoming a common occurrence. Silvia shook her head; she couldn't understand how someone could see the end of the world to be this beautiful, wonderful thing, when all she had seen was pain and misery. But then again, she supposed she could understand the need to make sense of it all.

As she passed more and more of the downtrodden people of the shanty, all pleading for help, crying out for a chance to simply live, her sorrow bled into rage, as it always did. A deep burbling rage towards all those leeches that lived in the undercity filled with warmth, food, and water. They could live their lives in blissful ignorance of what they took from everyone else, completely ignoring the fact that the sky was gone, simply because they didn't have to be reminded of it.

Finally reaching her destination, a two-story, ramshackle building near the center of South Shanty, Silvia opened a ramshackle door that scraped loudly as it opened. Stepping within, Silvia's ears were flooded with the familiar sounds of the injured and ill coming from inside. The infirmary, if you could even call it that, was lined with cots on either side, all filled with people. They didn't have enough cots to house everyone, so the people with the most minor ailments had to sleep on the ground. Both floors of the building were equally packed with people, the upper floor being a "quarantine" of sorts. The infirmary was probably the biggest building in the shanty, and yet it still wasn't nearly enough space.

As Silvia walked through the rows of groaning people, a side door opened, and Trisha walked out. The short woman's long, greying hair swung behind her as she locked eyes with Silvia and froze, surprised.

"Silvia? Voids, we thought you were dead! You were gone for nearly a week!" Trisha said, walking up and grabbing Silvia's arms.

"Yeah, sorry, Trish," Silvia said. "I had . . . business to take care of, and it took a lot longer than I thought it would."

"Well, you could've at least told us what you were doing! We were worried sick!"

"I . . . I couldn't tell you, and I still can't. It's for your own safety," Silvia replied, slinging the backpack around to her back. Trisha frowned at that response, then she began towing Silvia into the side room. She must've noticed how exhausted Silvia was; Trisha had an annoyingly good eye for that sort of thing. The side room was a makeshift break room for the infirmary's three caretakers. There was a single couch where Silvia, Trisha, or Ben could crash if needed, and a small fridge in the corner that barely worked.

"Well, whatever you were doing, you look half dead!" Trisha said as she moved Silvia towards the couch. Silvia decided not to mention how true that observation was, though she did resist Trisha's attempts to make her rest, knowing that the moment she sat down, she wasn't getting up for a long time. There was still work to be done.

"I can't rest yet, Trish, I brought something, something big," Silvia said, as she set her backpack down on the couch and started to zip it open. Before Trisha could say anything else, Silvia began removing the bag's contents. She pulled out pill bottles, clean syringes, bandages, and assorted other medical supplies from the bag. Trisha stared, eyes wide, her mouth moving but no words came out. Eventually, as the last of the bag's contents were removed, Trisha found her voice.

"Wha-how—where did you get all this?!" Trisha sputtered in complete awe.

"I . . . bought them," Silvia replied.

"Silvia, you don't just find this stuff at shops around! The only people who have medical supplies nowadays are—" She cut off, looking sharply at Silvia and gasping. "You didn't!"

"I don't know what you're talking about, and even if I did, I doubt anyone would notice this amount was gone—it's only a single backpack's worth," Silvia said, knowing damn well that was a lie. Trisha wasn't likely to be convinced either.

"But if they do, do you know how much danger you've put us in?!" Trisha said loudly. Silvia hissed and motioned for her friend to keep her voice down. Trisha breathed deeply and nodded, continuing in a softer tone. "This could endanger the lives of everyone here!"

"No," Silvia said. "The only life I've endangered is my own, because nobody but me knows where these came from. If anyone comes around asking, you'll tell them that I said I bought these supplies, because that's exactly what I did say, right?" Silvia emphasized the point, making her point very clear. Trisha didn't reply for a long moment; she was obviously worried and wanted to object. But eventually, Trisha simply nodded.

Silvia breathed heavily and nodded back. "Good, now let's put these to good use." Silvia turned and grabbed some surgical masks from the pile, putting one on and handing another to Trisha.

"Where's Ben at?" Silvia asked. As if on cue, the door opened and Ben, a tall, bald man, walked in and froze.

"Silvia? Where did you get all that?" He asked, his voice deep, yet gentle. Silvia sighed, grabbed a specific assortment of pills and bandages, and walked past the tall man.

"Trisha will explain, I have work to do." Then Silvia continued into the infirmary.

Silvia knew who she wanted to see first. She found Adam huddled in a corner on the first floor, as always. He was a scrawny young boy, barely eight years old, with dark skin and bright green eyes. Adam had a very bad vitamin D deficiency. That wasn't uncommon; the disappearance of the sun practically guaranteed that everyone was vitamin D deficient. Unfortunately, it took a much greater toll on Adam due to being severely malnourished. Silvia and the others weren't sure how much longer he had left. And yet, as Silvia walked towards Adam, who was sitting on the floor sketching as he usually did, she found it hard to believe he was as sick as he was. He looked from his drawing up to the elderly woman lying in a makeshift bed next to him. The woman coughed, then noticed Adam was staring at her. She looked at him curiously. Wordlessly, Adam picked up his drawing and showed it to the woman, flashing that radiant smile of his. It was a sketch of the old woman, but healthy, happy, beautiful.

The woman looked surprised, then let out a weak, yet delighted giggle. Adam's smile brightened even further, and he handed his drawing over to the woman. He glanced over and saw Silvia approaching. He gasped, then hurried over, as fast as he could in his condition, and hugged her around the waist. He pulled back and signed with his hands, "Where have you been?"

Silvia smiled and set down a tray she had been holding so she could reply.

"Work stuff—it's a secret," she signed. Silvia's sign language wasn't perfect as she had been taught by an eight-year-old, but she was picking it up fast. She was always a quick learner. Adam pouted, but didn't ask for clarification. *Smart boy.*

"I brought something for you. Do you want to see?" she asked. His eyes widened, and he nodded eagerly. Silvia plucked a small bottle of supplements from the tray she had been carrying, popped it open, and handed a few of the capsules over to the boy.

"These will hopefully make you feel a little better," Silvia signed, then passed him a glass of water. Adam beamed, downed the pills, then hugged Silvia again. She held him for a long moment, feeling his gratitude, then she pulled away and stood up.

"I have to go help some of the others now, okay?" she signed.

"Okay . . . but come back later. I wanna show you some of my new drawings!" he signed back. She smiled and nodded. Adam paused, then signed, "Thank you."

Silvia patted him on the shoulder, then turned to get back to work.

* * *

A few hours later, Silvia collapsed onto the couch. She was beyond exhausted, her entire body like tungsten. First, all the running and climbing, then giving treatment to over a hundred people in the span of a few hours. The human body isn't made for this, especially not mine. Voids, do I miss alcohol. Despite her pain and fatigue, she couldn't help grinning. Seeing all those hopeful faces as she passed out medicine and clean bandages made the entire ordeal worth it. She felt joy, pride, and . . . worry? Those supplies won't last long; hell, we used nearly half of them in one day. The small, wary part of her mind said. We'll eventually have to get more, and the only way to get more is to steal it again. How many times will I be able to get away with this?

That tiny part of her mind was quickly snuffed out by something much stronger, something that guided her throughout her entire life. Her spite. *It doesn't matter how many times I have to do this, how much I have to steal from those pompous leeches in the undercity, I'll do whatever it takes for these people. And if I die in the process? So be it.* Filled with resolve and a lingering feeling of worry, exhaustion finally took hold, and Silvia drifted off.

* * *

Shouting. Silvia jolted upright, her instincts getting her on her feet even before she fully awakened. When her brain confirmed that it was, in fact, awake, she was already opening the door of the break room. It sounded like many gruff voices arguing, but she couldn't make out the details. Trisha spotted Silvia and hurried over to her.

"Trish, what's going on?" Silvia asked.

"It's The YCR! Like, all of them! Ben is outside trying to figure out what they want," Trisha replied, panic in her voice.

What? But . . . the only reason they would all be here is—

Ben's high-pitched, relaxed voice was cut off by a louder, clearer one.

"Enough excuses! We know Silvia Eldritch is here! Let us in NOW!" It was Chief Ranger Reckman's voice. How did they find her this quickly? She had taken every precaution to make sure she wasn't followed, taken several detours, changed the jacket . . .

Silvia gasped and glanced back into the breakroom where the jacket was draped across one of the couch armrests. It had several pockmarks scattered all over it from when she was splashed by the geyser. *Silvia, you are a moron.* A stray drone, probably manually controlled, must've identified her from the damaged jacket and followed her home after she thought she was in the clear.

What could she do? She couldn't hide; as persuasive as Ben could be, there was no way he could get the YCR to leave. They would find her, and everyone else would be in serious trouble for harboring her. She couldn't escape, not this time. They probably had the place surrounded, and Silvia had barely escaped earlier today, she didn't like her odds at doing it a second time. That left her with only one option, it wasn't a good one, but it was the only one that could get everyone out of this situation safely. Well . . . everyone except her.

Determined, Silvia marched towards the front door. Before she could reach it, a hand grabbed her by the arm. She turned to see Trisha staring at her wide-eyed, silently pleading for her not to do what she was about to do. For a moment, Silvia wanted nothing more than to stay, to hide, both because of Trisha's sorrowful look and her own survival instincts. But she couldn't ignore the sight of all the people in need behind her friend. As much as she wanted to stay, Silvia knew the best thing she could do to keep them all from getting hurt would be to leave. Silvia put a hand on the older woman's shoulder.

"Take care of them for me . . . and tell Adam that I'm sorry we couldn't talk again." With that, Silvia turned back towards the door. She could hear Chief Reckman still shouting for her.

She took a deep breath, then bellowed, "Yeah, yeah I'm coming! Voids, guys, they say patience is a virtue, you know." All the voices outside went silent, as if they were suddenly consumed by the void. Silvia opened the door and was nearly blinded by all the lights shining on the building. She immediately held her hands up and was swarmed by barking rangers. She was quickly, and painfully, taken to the ground and handcuffed. When she was pulled back up to her feet, she was face to face with Chief Reckman, a large bald man with an admittedly impressive mustache.

"Silvia Eldritch! You are under arrest for burglary, resisting arrest, assaulting a ranger, and vandalism." The smug grin on his face told Silvia that he had been eager to say that. She simply clenched her jaw. That's when she saw that Ben was also handcuffed and was being pulled away. She turned back to Reckman, seething with anger.

"Let him go!" she yelled. "He had nothing to do with this!"

Reckman smirked.

"He is under arrest for harboring a criminal. I'm afraid he has everything to do with this."

Silvia tried to step closer, but the two rangers pulled her back painfully. There was a brief moment where Silvia and Ben locked eyes. In those few seconds, everything seemed to slow. She could see in Ben's expression that he knew what he was supposed to do—they'd gone over this exact scenario several times. But his eyes were hesitant, sorrowful. Silvia felt a pit in her stomach. She hated that she was putting Ben through this. Despite that, she steeled herself. She deliberately flicked her gaze to the clinic, then back to Ben's eyes. Then she fixed him with a stare that clearly conveyed *You know what's at stake.*

Ben closed his eyes, looking defeated. When he opened them again, he put on an expression of outrage. "We trusted you! We welcome you in, give you purpose, and this is how you repay us?!" Ben yelled with a level of vitriol that seemed to surprise even himself, as if part of that was more real than either of them expected. Silvia glanced down, wracked with guilt.

"Oh shut up!" Reckman barked. "It's your own damn fault. You should already know you can't trust anyone nowadays!"

Silvia looked back up at Reckman. "Please . . . They didn't know anything about me or any of this . . . I swear I'll confess, cooperate completely, just . . . leave them all alone," Silvia pleaded. Reckman glanced around at the other rangers, then shrugged.

"Fine, the quicker we get out of here, the better; it's freezing out here." As the collected rangers started to move, Reckman pointed at Ben. "Bring him in too, I have some questions for him." Both Silvia and Ben were about to object, but Reckman cut them off sharply. "Not another word! I do not care!"

With a command to head out from Reckman, the group of rangers escorted Silvia away from her home, her purpose, towards what probably would be lifelong imprisonment.

* * *

It was bitingly cold the day her sentence was carried out, the only warmth from a few portable warming units that were brought for the occasion. Silvia and a small group of officials and rangers were packed into a small, circular room with an adjoining airlock, featureless save for the two thick metal doors on opposite sides of the room. The one behind the officials led back into South Shanty, Silvia's former home. Through the one behind Silvia, only unending darkness waited.

"Silvia Eldritch, as punishment for your crimes against Yellowstone City, you have been sentenced to exile in the voidlands," High Judge Christina Vienna said, the stern woman's slow drawl shaking Silvia from a momentary haze.

Exile. It was a death sentence. Perhaps Silvia should've expected as much. They could've simply executed her and been done with it, but being cast into the voidlands made a far more potent example out of a person, she supposed. Silvia glared just past the High Judge at the younger, blond man standing behind her. Clark Trennan, the very man she had robbed. He didn't even look at her; he just typed away on a tablet, almost . . . bored. He'd seemed so excited, animated even when he called for her exile in court. But now he couldn't even be bothered to look at the person he'd just sent to die.

High Judge Vienna finished describing the details of the sentence. Silvia hadn't been paying attention, but she knew everything she needed to know. A technician finished setting the seals of the voidsuit she was wearing. The Yellowstone City higher-ups didn't want the people they exiled to simply walk out and freeze to death immediately. Silvia guessed they wanted to take the children's story approach and imply an unknown, more sinister fate for those who misbehaved. So, she was provided a voidsuit: they were easily manufactured and could be reliably retrieved from her corpse by a scouting team. Additionally, she was given a flimsy wrist-mounted flashlight and enough air to last her about a week. So at the very least, she probably wouldn't die from asphyxiation. *Yipee.*

Silvia's mind raced. Was there really no way out of this? For a moment, she considered desperately fighting her way out. But . . . for the first time in her life, she had to accept there was no escape. Even if she somehow managed to get away, they might hurt her friends just to find her again. So she clenched her fists but simply stood there as the scrawny technician sealed her helmet into place. At the same time, two rangers opened the inner airlock door and motioned for her to step inside.

She hesitated. Then, feeling numb, she walked into the airlock. The door behind her shut with a heavy thud. Everything went dark, and all Silvia could hear was a loud hissing as the exterior door unsealed. Then she heard what she thought was the door slowly scraping open, but she still couldn't see anything. Taking a shaky breath, Silvia flipped on her flashlight and pointed it forward. It illuminated the doorway out into complete darkness. Her stomach lurched. Nothing about her sentence felt real. She understood the implications the moment the gavel had come down. But now, staring directly into the jaws of hell itself, she realized that nothing could've prepared her for just how afraid she would be.

Her mind swam. She could barely think. She closed her eyes tightly as a wave of nausea flowed over her. Then, strangely, her shallow breathing became sharper, heavier, as the deep pit of dread in her belly began to boil over into rage. She was enraged at Clark Trennan and all the other high and mighty aristocrats who only cared for themselves. Enraged at herself for messing up so badly. But in that moment, she found she was most angry at the void, for putting them all in this nightmare.

No . . . no! This isn't me; I don't swoon and pass out from a little darkness. I'm Silvia Eldritch, damnit! And I will face this like I face all of my problems—head on!

Silvia's eyes snapped open, and she stared down the eternal night. She let out a few heavy breaths, then with a huff, she stepped into the void.

* * *

Path illuminated by her wrist-mounted flashlight, Silvia marched through the remains of a dead forest. She didn't know where she was going, she didn't think it mattered, but she couldn't just sit around and wait for death. She had to keep moving. She had been walking for hours, but everything looked the same, just more frozen trees and the occasional corpse. Most of the time they were animal bodies, but Silvia did stumble upon a few frozen-over people. She couldn't bear to look at them for more than a second.

It was raining, had been for an hour. It wasn't water, Silvia knew that wasn't possible. She remembered something Trisha had told her, about it being cold enough out in the void for oxygen to condense and fall as rain.

Thinking about Trisha slowed Silvia's progress. How would the infirmary last without her? From the little she'd heard, it was unclear whether or not Ben would be released. If that was the case, Trisha would be on her own. Silvia couldn't help but imagine Trisha trying desperately to prevent what, without proper supplies or assistance, would be inevitable. So many people like Adam who, if the sun was still here, might've been perfectly healthy, gotten all the vitamins they needed. Now, they were going to die, because some rich guy in power just couldn't bring himself to share.

Silvia stopped at a mid-sized rock and sat on it. She needed a break. A break . . . from what? Marching blindly into nothingness? It didn't matter; she was going to die out here no matter what.

Stop, just . . . stop and breathe. Silvia had barely noticed that she was hyperventilating. It took a considerable effort to push away her anger and anxiety. She sat there for a few minutes, slowly getting her breathing under control, trying to focus less on what happened before, and instead focus on the here and now.

Only in that moment did she realize just how quiet it was out in the void, the only noises coming from the rain on her helmet and the hiss of her oxygen. Silvia shone her light upwards, looking for anything to distract her. Lifeless trees hung around her, their frozen branches entangling with each other. Despite the eerie trees and darkness all around her, she found the scene strangely serene. Yes, the voids were completely inhospitable, only holding death in each direction, but they were also peaceful. Nothing was coming for her; there were no expectations, no burdens. Out here . . . it was just her.

Part of her knew this shouldn't be comforting to her—she had always thrived on difficulty and constant action. But she hadn't realized just how much that had taken a toll on her. *Voids . . . I haven't gotten a chance to relax like this in . . . well, ever. Funny how it took me until my literal death sentence to finally take a load off.*

As the minutes passed, so too did her strange comfort. The deep dread and burbling anger returned, but at a more tolerable level. What use was there in blowing up or losing it out here? The void certainly didn't care.

Anxious to start moving again, despite the fact she still had no idea where she was going, Silvia stood and continued deeper into the dark.

After another few hours of walking, Silvia found she wasn't scared of the environment at all anymore, nor did she feel the same sense of serenity from before, or even the anger. She grew mostly indifferent. Everything looked the same, grey and lifeless. She preoccupied herself with trying to find shapes in the branches above her as she walked. It did help take her mind off things for a little bit. One cluster of trees kind of looked like a heart when viewed at the right angle; a lone tree looked like a shark if you squinted hard enough; and wasn't that tree behind her—

A tall, imposing figure loomed just behind her, wearing a voidsuit very similar to her own. Startled, Silvia screamed and punched the person. She stumbled and fell on her back.

She raised her hands defensively. "S-stay back! I swear to god I'll hit you again!" she yelled, her voice amplified through a speaker at the front of her helmet. She shone her flashlight onto the figure. He was holding his side where Silvia had hit him. *Attack! Quick! Before they recover!*

Silvia got to her feet, then approached, poised to strike. The man's eyes widened, and he backed up, holding his hands out in what Silvia could tell was supposed to be a calming gesture. Silvia stopped, but kept her guard up. She got a better look at him through his helmet. He had a large, bushy beard and dark red hair. He had square features and looked to be in his late forties or early fifties. He was also massive, nearly seven feet tall.

"Who are you? What are you doing out here?" Silvia asked. The man didn't respond. Instead, he pointed at his own oxygen tank, then to hers. Silvia frowned, then, trying to still keep an eye on the large man, checked her oxygen tank. It had been dented, probably when she fell after she punched him, and a tiny stream of oxygen was hissing out, immediately condensing in the cold. Silvia cursed and began to panic. How long would it be before she ran out completely?

The man made a grunting noise, she turned back to him and saw he was holding out a roll of duct tape. Hesitant, she approached the man and carefully took the tape from him. Once he handed her the tape, he kept his hands up. Silvia backed away a step, then tore off some of the tape and placed it gingerly against the leak on her tank. A tiny readout in the bottom right of the helmet visor showed that she was still leaking oxygen, but at a much slower rate. She probably had a few more days before she ran out. Still not good by any means, but better than immediate asphyxiation. She turned her attention back to the man.

"Thank you. Uh . . . sorry for punching you," she said. The man simply nodded and dropped his hands to his sides.

"You didn't answer my questions before," Silvia continued. "Where did you come from? Is . . . is there another city nearby?" Silvia asked, getting her hopes dangerously high.

The man didn't reply; instead, he turned, then started walking away. *Oookay?* Silvia wasn't sure if she should follow this silent stranger. Then again, what choice did she really have? It was either risk getting murdered or guaranteed death. Decision made, she followed the man through the woods. After a few minutes of walking in silence, Silvia started walking alongside the man and tried to engage in conversation.

"Sorry again about earlier, but you kinda snuck up on me. I'm Silvia, by the way. And you are?" she asked. He didn't reply, just kept walking.

"Uh . . . where are you headed? Do you mind if I follow you?" Again, no response. He didn't even acknowledge her. *Yeah . . . this is seeming more and more like crazy murderer. I should probably—*

The man glanced over in her direction and jumped slightly, startled, as if he had just noticed her right next to him. He stopped, and his eyes narrowed at her. She knew that expression all too well, the "mind your own business" expression. But why had he jumped? Had he not heard her next to him talking? Oh. Oooohh. It suddenly made sense, the man was probably deaf. Silvia walked in front of him.

"I'm sorry. You're deaf?" she signed to him.

She found it surprisingly awkward to make signs in the bulky gloves of the voidsuit. But the man's eyes went wide, and he eagerly started signing back. "You can sign? Oh thank god! I haven't talked to anyone in so long."

Silvia nodded and grinned. They continued walking.

"What's your name?" Silvia asked. The man spelled out his name for her. Victor. She smiled and spelled out her name for him.

"Thank you for saving my life earlier. And sorry for punching you," Silvia continued.

"Don't worry about it. My bad for scaring you," Victor replied. Silvia shrugged.

"It's all right. Where are we going?" she asked.

"My home close to here."

"Wait, close to here? So there is another city nearby?" Silvia asked, growing excited.

"Not exactly. You'll see."

Silvia was about to ask for clarification, but she stopped. Was that . . . light ahead? Yes, it was; there was a faint, pale-green light poking through the skeleton trees in front of them. Silvia started walking a little faster, curious.

The light grew brighter and brighter until Silvia left the treeline, passed through a thick fog, and saw a wide, open clearing. Silvia froze, unable to believe what she was seeing.

A massive tree, probably a hundred feet tall, stood solitary in the direct center of the clearing, and it was glowing. Voids, it was glowing! The tree gave off a bright pale-green light. It was almost painful to look directly at the tree after so long spent in the dark. It was amazing enough to find a tree that wasn't dead, let alone this one. Its branches were covered in leaves that also glowed with light. Silvia started slowly walking towards the tree, awed. As she got closer, she realized that she wasn't getting rained on anymore. Confused, she looked up and saw that the entire clearing was covered in a dome of what looked like mist.

Victor walked past her, and her eyes nearly bulged out of her head. He had taken his helmet off! He glanced back at her and chuckled, then continued walking towards the tree. Hesitantly, but having nothing to lose, she reached up and undid the seal of her helmet, removing it. It was . . . a little chilly, but that was it. She breathed in, and was surprised by how fresh the air tasted. She looked around at the ground, thinking there had to be hidden heating units, but all she saw was grass. Wait . . . grass?! She immediately crouched down, pulled one of her gloves off, and dug her fingers into the ground. It was real. Real grass! It had been years since she'd felt real grass. Tears began to form in the corners of her eyes.

There was a soft noise to her left, she turned and saw . . . birds. Two small, blue-feathered birds sat on a tree stump a few feet away. The tears she had been holding back started to flow freely. In an instant, she was a child again, running through the fields near her home, chasing birds. She remembered the non-artificial warmth of the sun on her skin, the sounds of her mother calling after her, completely ignorant of what would happen in the next decades.

Silvia pulled herself from her memories, wiping the tears away. She was overwhelmed; it had been so long since she'd seen anything like this. She stood and noticed Victor was waiting for her. She hurried to catch up to him. It was warmer the closer they got to the tree. Silvia pulled the gloves of the suit off so she could sign a little easier.

"What . . . what is it?" Silvia signed, gesturing to the tree.

"I've been calling it 'Lifebringer,' It appeared two years ago," Victor replied. That seemed a fitting moniker, especially now that Silvia started to notice other animals besides just birds. She passed a few foxes, a deer, she even thought she saw a grizzly bear on the other side of the clearing.

"Wait, if Lifebringer appeared two years ago, how are there this many animals here?" she asked. Victor just shrugged.

"What's up with the dome? Or do you not know that either?" He shrugged again. She had so many more questions, but was starting to realize that he didn't seem to know much more than she did.

Lifebringer was ringed about a hundred feet away by a small assortment of cabins, each one a slightly different size and design. Closer to the tree, Silvia noticed a deep, rhythmic pulse emanating from the tree, as if the tree was breathing. Subtle waves of warmth and . . . something else she couldn't quite place. Silvia turned to Victor.

"Did you build all of this?" she asked.

"No, me and my community, before the sun vanished."

"Where is everyone else?" Silvia asked. Victor didn't reply but grew noticeably somber.

She realized what that meant. "Oh . . . I'm sorry."

"It's all right. You didn't know." He paused, then answered the question Silvia was afraid to ask. "I planned for the end of the world, set up my cabin with new technology, just in case. Everyone else was very traditional, thought I was crazy. They died. I didn't."

Silvia felt his grief in the air.

"I'm so sorry," she signed. Victor closed his eyes and breathed deeply.

"It happened. No use crying over it now," he signed, then he continued walking towards one of the cabins. Suddenly curious about something, Silvia jogged towards Lifebringer. Before she could get very far, Victor grabbed her arm and stopped her. She looked back at him, and he let go of her arm.

"Hey, you're fine to go closer to it. Just . . . be careful," he signed.

She nodded, a little impatiently. "Yeah, okay, I just want to get a closer look." Then she turned and started towards the tree again before Victor could reply. She stopped just in front of Lifebringer. A small family of wolves lounged against the trunk nearby, though they didn't pay her much attention. It was quite hot this close to the tree. She was already starting to sweat. The warmth . . . It felt just like the sun that day, all those years ago.

Right next to Lifebringer, the pulses were much stronger, almost to the point of pushing Silvia back with each wave. That other sense with the pulses, they were . . . memories. Her memories. Each breath of the tree filled Silvia's mind with flashes of moments long gone. The fields as a child, her first kiss with the shy boy from school, working with Trisha and Ben. But there were also flashes of moments she didn't recognize, fuzzy, hard to make out. Before she even realized what she was doing, Silvia tentatively reached out and placed her hand against the trunk of the tree.

There was a flash, then waves of noise, emotion, memories, and so much more washed over Silvia all at once. She felt a pain in her chest—something was wrong, her heart wasn't beating right. No . . . it was . . . it was like she had multiple hearts that were all beating out of sync with each other. Five? Ten? A hundred? She couldn't tell how many hearts she had. There were more flashes of . . . memories? Ones she recognized, but others she didn't. She heard hundreds of voices all at once, some of them she knew—most of them were hers. But they all blended together. She couldn't make any of it out. This wasn't like the pulses. It was like every moment of everything that

has and could have happened was happening all at once. The Silvias weren't one person anymore, she . . . they were every possibility. They were simultaneously in sunlight, and dark void, their father was alive and dead, they were imprisoned, exiled, and neither. It was way too much stimulation, and they were panicking, a collection of Silvias all falling through realities, all screaming. They didn't know who they were anymore, which Silvia they were. They didn't know where they were. *I am Silvia Eldritch, and I live in Yellowstone City,* a part of her brain reminded her. *I have my hand against Lifebringer. It's showing me all this somehow. Focus: just pull my hand—*

Her hand disconnected from the tree, and she collapsed backwards. She was hyperventilating. It took her a moment to realize where she was and what she was doing. She only had one heartbeat, but the pain in her chest told her something was still wrong. The time touching the tree had confused her body, it seemed.

Thankfully, her heart corrected itself and started beating normally again, and she somehow managed to calm her breathing. Victor ran to her side and offered a hand to her. She took it, letting him help her up.

"More warning would've been nice," she signed, a little frustrated.

"It was calming for me, if a little weird to get used to. I thought it would be the same for you," he replied. Silvia couldn't imagine how something like . . . whatever that was could be calming. Silvia glanced around, still a little dazed, when something dawned on her. She started signing frantically, excitedly. Victor seemed confused and signed for her to slow down. She took a deep breath to calm herself, then started again.

"All this grass out here, it's real, right?" she asked.

Victor nodded. "Yes, and every 'day' when I wake up, the field is covered in dew, not sure why or how." .

"But plants also need sunlight right? That means . . . Lifebringer must be producing something similar to sunlight right?" she asked, growing even more excited. Victor seemed confused, but nodded again.

"I . . . suppose?"

Silvia's mind went back to the infirmary, filled with people who needed supplies, needed warmth, and most of all, needed the sun. She thought of Adam, a boy who never got the chance to see the sun. All that time, they had only delayed his pain, prolonged the inevitable. But now . . . she had a solution, burning bright only a few feet away from her. She had a way to save him, to save everybody she cared about. Everything she had just experienced with touching the tree got tossed aside while a crazy, stupid scheme entered Silvia's mind. A heist to end all heists. Part of her scolded *I thought we were done with this sort of thing.* Another part knew damn well that was never true. She grinned in a way that seemed to worry Victor.

"Victor," she signed. "How would you feel about making this a community again?"

Date: 2590-04-09 19:26:42 PRT
From: Ren Stornman
To: Anachronauts
Subject: Naturally occurring Nexuses
Re: Into the Void

Look, Nerrid, I know you don't agree with my proposed sources for naturally occurring nexuses between splinters, but something is obviously going on here. The energy described in this account is more than just heat and oxygen to drive back the Void.

The presence of animals is extremely telling. If the details are to be believed, the timing doesn't work out for them to be native. They MUST have come from another splinter. If we can determine which one, we could run some direct tests on that side and get some insights into how these nexuses are formed.

It would also give us alternate access to Quietus that doesn't involve bribing the Immortal agents at the base in Yellowstone.

Think about it.

Oh, and Kinsha, if it's essential information on Quietus you're looking for, I think this account qualifies.

—Ren

Date: 2590-04-10 01:34:21 PRT
From: Ms. Six
To: Anachronauts
Subject: Nexuses (Nexi?)
Re: Commercial Break

Wait! Ren, are you suggesting that the Lifebringer Tree mentioned in your attached account is a natural nexus point? How? How? HOW? I can't believe you dropped the Lifebringer bomb in our laps and just left it at that. Kinsha nearly had a heart attack. It's exactly this kind of thing that makes people call you a robot.

Anyway, I'm just getting preliminary data on Mercantis, and it is very promising for further examination. There may be some important info here. The splinter is dominated by GovCorp and their incessant marketing-based economy. Death by advertisements (shudder). The Alliance Space Agency has just made an interesting discovery. Plus, there may be tacos. None of the data reports the presence of tacos, but none of it reports not having tacos either. I'm heading time-side to investigate. I'll send you what I find. Well, not if it's tacos, I'll just eat those.

COMMERCIAL BREAK

By Matthew Cushing

Ellie searched for an adventure. Craved one. It had been months since a story captivated her. Let her escape.

She browsed the titles of books that spilled from her bookshelves, crowding the walls of her cramped, concrete studio apartment. Perhaps a space opera. Or maybe an old crime thriller about the 1930s no-nonsense detective Malone. Her fingers brushed the spines, hovering over the imprinted titles, feeling the shape and texture of the words as much as reading them. So many delightful tales from which to choose.

But she was behind on her quota. Again. And diving into a book would only put her further behind schedule. Her stomach twisted, and she wanted to spit. Just the thought of having to watch commercials—forced viewership in order to receive her GovCorp-provided pension—pissed her off. And few things did anymore. At ninety-five, she'd earned the right not to care about government funding or leading economic indices or trade deficits.

Retirement should be relaxing. She'd done her part decades ago.

But that was then.

Now, if she didn't meet her daily eight-hour quota of watching commercials, she'd lose her food stipend, her health insurance, and even her home. Pain crept from her temples up and around to the back of her skull, pulsing to the thump of her racing heart.

She had to calm herself before she blew another gasket. High blood pressure had always been a problem, and getting worked up—which thinking about the soulless GovCorp often caused—just made it worse. The last time her anger boiled over, she'd had a minor stroke. The doctor warned her that next time might be the last time, and not in a good way. At least that's all she remembered from the forty seconds he spared to talk with her. Damn GovCorp doctors. Her head throbbed harder.

She closed her eyes and recited prime numbers. Better than counting to ten. It made her mind work. Deep breath in, hold it, and a long, slow exhale. Again.

She hobbled over to her chair and plopped down, cursing under her breath. She snatched the forsaken Halotainment device from its charger and blew the dust off. Just holding it filled her with disgust.

The halo slipped over her head, resting on the bridge of her nose like glasses, but instead of lenses, clusters of transmitters projected images directly onto her retina. Little arms extending from the temples reached into her ear canals and rested against her tympanic membranes to control the sound. Nothing provided a more immersive experience than having content fed directly into the brain. The halo noted when the eyes closed—even for a blink—and paused the content accordingly. No moment missed. And only those seconds in full, overwhelming immersion counted towards her quota.

Ellie accessed her content stream, and the blast of information thrust her back into her chair. Her aged retinas and eardrums struggled to keep up with the torrent of information. A lifetime of personal use—a life well-lived—had worn them out. More pain than content reached her brain. But she had to watch.

Advertisements for everything from antacids to xylophones to hot dogs to computer cores, one after another after another after another, flooded her senses. She tried to let her mind wander, but the halo monitored her attention and paused the countdown on her quota. Ellie pushed the pain aside, refocused, and absorbed as much as she could. Her quota slowly decreased. Too slowly.

A knock at the door paused the halo, and Ellie ripped it from her head. Throwing it across the room into the bin crossed her mind, as it did every time she used it, but a replacement would arrive, and her quota increase to cover the cost. She tossed it onto its charger and hauled her slight frame out of her armchair.

After a moment to catch her balance, she shuffled to her front door.

"Yes?" she called as she peered up at the small vid screen embedded in the back of the door. Two suited individuals stood outside. Based on their builds, one was a petite woman, while the other was an average-height, thick-chested man. Full-face masks concealed their identities—whether from the public or from themselves, Ellie didn't know. The digital oval masks presented white stick-figure expressions on a black background. GovCorp agents. Damn.

"We're with the Office of Citizen Benefits. We need to speak with you."

She couldn't tell which person had spoken, though the mouth line on the woman's mask briefly switched to a circle.

"About what?" Ellie hoped this was a random check, but her eye caught on the infernal Halotainment device, and she knew this was about her quota.

"Please open the door," the woman said. "If you don't, we will open it for you. This is a government-provided facility. You can't keep us out."

That was true. This place was all her government pension allowed—the benefits slowly downgraded over time. Her temples throbbed. "Can you show me some ID?"

The large man stepped up and crowded the door. "How's this?" He slid his government badge into the lock. The door swung open, and Ellie hopped back in surprise. The sudden involuntary movement sent a stab of pain shooting from her knee through her hip and up her spine. She sucked in air to keep a litany of verbal curses from escaping her lips. It only partially worked.

"Dammit!" she barked. She grasped her lower back and stumbled to her chair, latching onto the backrest to keep from falling. With an effort and a grunt, she turned around and sat down with another jolt of pain.

The two agents entered as though they owned the place—which she figured they technically did—closing the door behind them and strolling to the couch. They settled opposite her without a word. The woman perched on the edge of the seat while the man leaned back and sank into the cushions.

"Ooh, comfy," he muttered as he looked around the room.

"Well?" Ellie asked.

"I think you know why we're here," the woman said. She referenced her datapad. "Our records indicate you are behind on your monthly quota of Halotainment commercial marketing time as stipulated in your government benefits contract. This is the third month you've run a deficit. Since you haven't responded to our correspondence, we're here to discuss alternate plans."

Alternate plans was a euphemism for fewer benefits—less food and less care. It had happened before, and Ellie barely got by on what she had.

Vultures. After the Great Darkening and the collapse of the republic, this new GovCorp focused only on making money and providing a solid return on investment to its billionaire shareholders. Citizens were nothing more than commodities. The elderly even more so since they no longer worked. Lazy old people—that's what President Prattleton called them during the last election. All the work she'd done, all the value she'd created during her distinguished scientific career, meant nothing. Unless she watched these stupid commercials. Or got a job. At her age? Ha!

"It's just that the halo gives me headaches," Ellie explained, "and my ears ring for hours afterwards. Even at the minimum-allowed volume, it is too much. I watch as much as I can, but it makes me ill. I can only endure so much." She wasn't sure a plea for compassion would work with the government thugs—it seemed they wore a mask on their hearts as well—but she'd try it. "Look at my health statistics. Each time I use the halo, my heart rate increases and my blood pressure skyrockets. I don't want another stroke."

The woman reached over and patted Ellie's leg as though it were a dog. "Now, Ms. Newton-Woode, no need to be alarmist. Our medical professionals keep a close eye on everyone's vitals at all times, and your numbers are well within safe limits."

This woman couldn't be serious.

Just yesterday, Ellie's blood pressure had spiked to over 240 systolic. She wasn't a medical doctor, but she knew what high blood pressure was and at what level she could stroke out.

"But," the woman continued, "if you'd like to reduce your monthly quota of Halotainment, we could look at moving you to Horace Towers. An efficiency has recently opened up, and we could get you in immediately."

Jesus, not Horace Towers—better known as 'Hospice Towers.' People only moved in. Moving out required a body bag. An apartment in Horace Towers was often the last, undignified step in a long line of mistreatment and neglect.

The man leaned forward. "Yeah, it'd only take thirty, forty minutes to move what you've got here to over there. It's already got furniture."

"You'd have to leave your books, though," the woman said, again patting Ellie's leg.

Ellie wanted to scream. They'd take her books over her dead body. And maybe that was their plan. Too many elderly people lived longer lives, needing more help from a government more interested in money than empathy.

She counted primes and caught her breath. Slowed her heartbeat. She'd had enough of this crap. GovCorp was just another bully, and she knew how to stand up to bullies. She was older than she used to be, sure, but if they came out on top, so be it. She was ready. At peace with her life.

"How about this?" Ellie countered. "Why don't the two of you get out of my apartment, and you can keep your kneecaps." She pulled a small silver revolver from the gap next to her seat cushion, though the gun looked enormous in her delicate, arthritic hand.

Tension electrified the room as the agents' backs clenched, sitting them up ramrod straight. A high-pucker moment. Ellie wished she could see the expressions on their faces, but she could only imagine the shock hidden behind the emotionless masks.

The man reached toward her. "There's no need for—"

Ellie cocked the hammer. She knew these agents had seen it all before. Her threat might not faze them at all. But maybe it would. It might make her day.

"I may be old," Ellie said with a chuckle, "but I got the drop on you two. Now, go on and get out." She motioned the gun toward the door. "And you keep your 'alternate plans' to yourselves. I'll get my account sorted. Don't you worry."

"You'd better," the woman said, "or we'll be back."

Ellie motioned with the gun a few more times. "Out!"

The agents sighed and exchanged a glance. With a nod to each other, they rose and headed toward the door. A few feet from exiting, the man turned and reached out, a business card extended from his fingertips. His mask-mouth turned into a circle, "This home consultation has been brought to you by Mr. Chili's 'Stay Chill' brand pepper spray, the official pepper spray of GovCorp. Your shopping ID has been awarded a ten percent discount on your next purchase. Remember, 'everything stays chill with Mr. Chili.'"

Ellie didn't move. She couldn't. Her brain struggled to process what was happening. Was this goon ending their visit with a sponsor plug? At gunpoint?

He placed the card on a small table, and the two agents left, closing the door behind them.

Ellie exhaled. That was too close. She did not want another visit from them. It wouldn't be as civil. She'd have to get her account up-to-date if not paid ahead to keep them from coming back. Or she'd have to buy bullets.

"Assholes," she muttered as she pulled the halo down over her head. It was going to be a long, painful night.

📺 📺 📺

Dr. Darnell Brightly, Deputy Director of the marginally functioning and underfunded Alliance Space Agency, burst through the swinging doors and strode down the short hallway into the overbright, converted retail space currently serving as his new laboratory. He paused just inside the bustling room.

Weeks prior, a skeleton crew operating the aged Vera Rubin telescope had identified an interstellar object—named 63I/SENTINEL after the observatory's last remaining program to monitor the night sky—entering the solar system on a course to Earth. It had set the world abuzz. Since the Great Darkening forty years ago, when all the stars mysteriously vanished, nothing had appeared in the night sky beyond Sol's known system objects. So where was this unexpected visitor from? Talking heads of various ilk and dubious expertise claimed 63I/SENTINEL to be everything from alien invaders to space trash to the hand of God ready to smite the Earth.

Whether angels, aliens, or something in between, Brightly was charged with discovering the truth.

"Your attention," he stated, projecting his voice so all in the expansive room could hear. His hastily gathered staff of professional and private astronomers, engineers, and astrophysicists—the few left in the western world with the requisite skills and knowledge—looked up from their workstations in unison.

"I just left a briefing with President Prattleton and the Secretary of Marketing. People around the world are going absolutely nutty thinking the world is about to end. They are fighting in the streets, robbing neighbors, stealing cars, and looting stores. It's as bad as after the Great Darkening, and in some cases worse." Brightly paused for effect. "We need to find out what is headed our way and give them answers."

Since first discovering the incoming object, his team had reoriented every private, commercial, and scientific telescope looking for answers. But the few Earth-based facilities once capable of seeing that far had all been shuttered due to GovCorp's focus on profitability, and the old orbiting telescopes no longer worked. The only image they had was from the Vera Rubin Observatory, and it only showed a bright speck on a black background.

The object was still too far away for meaningful analysis from Earth. His team needed measurements from up close. It had been a minor miracle when the archives identified a probe near the edge of the system and right in 63I/SENTINEL's path. The probe—called Marlowe—had launched over fifty years ago to investigate an orbital anomaly beyond the Kuiper Belt thought to be the mysterious Planet Nine. Marlowe had just begun its long journey to the outer solar system when the Great Darkening sent society into chaos. The program had been shut down as a cost-cutting measure, but the probe was still streaking toward its destination. It was loaded with specialized sensors and instrumentation operated by a prototype command intelligence that could quickly and independently study, analyze, and assess a celestial object for everything from ecosystems and biological inhabitants to technological capabilities to soil composition and natural resources. It was perfect for studying 63I/SENTINEL.

They just couldn't get it to work.

The ASA's archive on Marlowe was spotty at best, much of the information lost during GovCorp's takeover and the purge of non-profitable programs. Beyond the mission objectives, little was known about how Marlowe actually worked. Instruction manuals couldn't be found, and code samples—which only covered a few basic functions—were indecipherable by Brightly's team of scientists.

Every command sent returned an "Invalid Command Format—Resubmit" message.

"Has Marlowe responded to anything yet?" Dr. Brightly asked.

"Not since it's come back online, sir," Wallace, the lead engineer, replied. He stood and approached Dr. Brightly. "We're trying random commands, but the probe is replying with the same message to everything we transmit. There's been no change."

"You've been working on it for days, Wallace." Dr. Brightly threw his hands in the air. He never considered that accessing the probe would be an issue. If they couldn't activate it soon, their window of opportunity would close as 63I/SENTINEL sped past Marlowe on its way to Earth. The entire project would fail. "You're our communications expert. What do we try next?"

"I have no idea." Wallace scratched the back of his head, causing his brown mop of hair to fluff out in the back, filled with static electricity. "And neither does anyone else." Murmurs of agreement and disbelief echoed throughout the lab.

Dr. Brightly crossed his arms and closed his eyes, tuning out any distractions. What type of transmission would the probe recognize and respond to? The damn thing was so old, he had no clue who programmed it or how. What language was it coded in? And would anyone be able to get the probe working?

"We need to find out more about Marlowe's original code base." Dr. Brightly rubbed his temples. "Wallace, contact Personnel for everything they have on the team that built this thing. I want to know every detail about them. Who they were, their education, their histories, and their expertise. We need to find anything about Marlowe they may have left behind." It was a long shot, but Brightly didn't have a better idea.

An hour later, a woman burst through the laboratory doors, holding a single piece of paper high in her hand. "I found one!" She headed toward Dr. Brightly without slowing down.

"One what?" Dr. Brightly asked.

"A member of Marlowe's original programming team." She bounced with excitement. "And they are still alive."

📺 📺 📺

A commercial for industrial wood stain assaulted Ellie's eyes and blasted her eardrums. She mumbled the tagline along with the voiceover, having watched this particular ad over fifteen times. Watching the stupid commercials for hours was punishment enough, but enduring the same ones over and over with little variety crossed into cruel and unusual territory. Any relevance the products had to her life had long since passed. She would never need a five-gallon tub of wood stain, no matter how conveniently packaged or cheap the shipping.

Two hours remained on her daily quota, and at mid-afternoon, she decided to break until that evening. She could take a pill for her pounding head, eat, and maybe read a few chapters of the engaging crime novel sitting on her nightstand. The badass cop had just blown away three perps with his giant hand cannon, and she wanted to know what happened next.

The thought of a few hours of enjoyment and escape calmed her frayed nerves. Deep breaths slowed her heart rate and lessened the pounding in her temples.

Until a knock at the door spiked everything again.

After her last visit, she knew this was coming. She hobbled over to the screen on the door. Two men waited in the hall. Their suits suggested they were from GovCorp, but their mannerisms did not. Neither wore the ubiquitous digital masks to hide their identities. And was one of them whistling? If they were here to kick her out, they were enjoying it way too much.

"What do you want?" she asked through the door speaker. The whistler stopped and leaned in with a smile.

"We'd like to speak with you," he said. "It should only take a moment."

"Why? Who are you?" Ellie was pretty sure they were with GovCorp, but better safe than sorry. The last thing she needed was scammers breaking in and stealing her books. Many were priceless first printings.

"I'm Dr. Brightly," the whistler said, then pointed to the shorter man next to him, "and this is Wallace. We're with the ASA."

The Alliance Space Agency? What the hell did they want? Ellie hadn't worked on space projects for nearly fifty years. They must be looking for someone else.

"Are you sure you have the right apartment?" Ellie asked.

Dr. Brightly's smile faltered. "This is apartment 6244 of the Liberty Apartment Bloc, is it not?"

"Congratulations. You can read an address," Ellie said through the door. "But who are you looking for?"

The two men whispered together for a moment. Dr. Brightly asked, "Are you Eleanor Newton-Woode, age ninety-five?"

Damn. Yep, they were here for her. She cracked open the door and hustled out of the way, in case these were also the barge-in-twist-your-knee kind of government agents. She shuffled back to her chair and sat with her back towards the entry.

The door clicked shut, and quiet footfalls accompanied the two men to the couch. They sat with upright posture, both on the edge of the cushions. With a nod to his colleague, Dr. Brightly opened a datafolio and scanned the information. Was that her file?

"Just to confirm," Dr. Brightly said, "you're the Eleanor Newton who worked on the Marlowe project back in the thirties?"

"Mm-hmm," Ellie said. "The 'Woode' was added in 2052 when I got married, though that only lasted a few years."

"Your husband passed?" Wallace asked.

Ellie stared at him and took a measure of his eyes. He blinked and looked away.

"That's right," she said impassively. "Cancer's a bitch."

The young man swallowed hard. She returned her attention to Dr. Brightly.

"Yes, well, uh," he scrolled rapidly on the datafolio, "we're most interested in your time working on the Marlowe probe. You were on the programming team for the command intelligence?"

Ellie chuckled. "I *led* the programming team for the command intelligence." Her mind dredged up old memories of whiteboards filled with psychological calculus, logic quantums, thousands of process objects, and millions of lines of machine code—all in a custom programming language she had helped develop to maximize efficiency with the probe's prototype components. "There were five of us who programmed the command intelligence. Everyone else worked on ancillary processes or system integration."

Wallace scribbled notes on his own datafolio.

"Why don't you just record this meeting?" Ellie asked him. With a grin, she added, "I am." She pulled a small recorder from her sweater pocket. "Streaming directly to my data vault." She returned the device and patted her pocket. If they were going to intimidate her or force her out of her apartment, she wanted a record.

Dr. Brightly coughed. "Yes, well, we just need to know if you remember how to communicate with the probe."

"Of course I remember," Ellie replied. "I'm old, not senile." At least she didn't think she was. Programs and schematics slowly bubbled up from the depths of her brain, accessing information from a different era of her life. An era when she was a leader in her field, a prodigy in neural networks and computer algorithms. When everyone in space exploration knew her name and wanted her help. When people treated her with respect. So different from today, as an afterthought in a high-rise and a number in a database—a data point for marketing statistics. How times had changed.

"Why all the questions about Mar—," she cut herself off. She should have connected it sooner. 631/SENTINEL. She vaguely remembered something about it from the news. GovCorp wanted to learn more about it, and Marlowe was outfitted with exactly the systems needed to conduct a thorough analysis. She was impressed they had even remembered the probe.

"We can't get the probe to do anything," Wallace blurted.

Dr. Brightly glared at Wallace before returning his attention to Ellie. "We receive the same message each time, so we can't adjust the probe's course to approach and scan the—"

"This new object entering our system," Ellie finished for him.

An interesting problem. But why did they need her? A feeling of ominous dread crept up her back, standing up the hairs on the back of her neck.

"Why are you here?" she asked. "You're not just looking for a few quick tips, are you?"

"No, ma'am," Wallace said. "We have no historical information on how the probe works. We need your help to retask its command intelligence," Dr. Wallace said. "The mission will fail without your involvement."

Ellie about choked.

How dare they come here and ask for her help! After treating her like a piece of meat for years, more worried about how she could still be of use instead of acknowledging her contributions and letting her enjoy the retirement she earned. The absolute chutzpah!

Her recitation of primes reached well into the triple digits before she stopped seeing red. Deep breaths calmed her, and she focused her mind. To do what Dr. Brightly wanted, a new command subsystem would need to be written and uploaded so Marlowe knew where to go and what to do. The languid mission to study Planet Nine would need to be replaced with a much faster study, as 631/SENTINEL would only remain in Marlowe's sensor range for a short time when the probe and object flew past each other. How long would they have? Which scans and surveys could be skipped? So many mission factors would need to be updated and taught to the command intelligence.

She was sure she'd remember all of Marlowe's processes and procedures once she dug into the code. She had developed most of them, after all. Her knuckles ached at the thought of writing new routines for hours on end. She massaged her fingers.

Her eyes lit on the halo device, and an idea blossomed in her brain.

Oh, she wouldn't do this for nothing.

Her mind raced toward a solution as it had done so many times in the past. A way to help them *and* help herself. Help others. A plan that, with some fortitude and theatrics, just might work. What did she have to lose? This was an opportunity. Another chance to make a difference—perhaps even be a real-life adventure like the stories she'd been craving so badly.

Just not as these scientists were expecting.

"I can help," Ellie said, nodding. "Under one condition."

Dr. Brightly's face lit up. He stood, his arms wide. "Anything. Name it."

She picked up the Halotainment device. "No more of this."

"Of course," Dr. Brightly said, smiling ear to ear.

"Ever."

His smile wavered for an instant. "Absolutely."

"For everyone over seventy."

Dr. Brightly's smile vanished as he blanched white. "I don't have the authority to do *that*."

"Who does?" Ellie asked.

"Only the President."

The ride in the presidential limocopter, provided by AirService International, had soured Ellie's mood. The garish AirService logo adorned every flat surface in the cabin. Cheap fake leather and gold spray paint gilding smelled of plastic and toxicity, matching Ellie's view of the president. Wallace, sitting across from her, seemed to nap while Dr. Brightly babbled non-stop, vacillating between the importance of learning more about 631/SENTINEL and the notable landmarks passing below. Ellie fixed an even expression on her face and tuned him out.

Her sciatica throbbed from the constant bouncing and jerking of the small aircraft's cabin, and she focused her efforts to not groan in pain. She did not want to be diverted to a hospital. This was a chance to address a gross inequity, and she would not squander it. Plus, the unknown object hurtling toward Earth, *blah blah*.

She massaged her thigh to relieve the ache stretching from her hip to her knee, wondering if she had remembered to take her evening medications prior to being whisked out the door.

With a turbulent jounce, a sharp grunt escaped her lips.

"Are you okay?" Dr. Brightly turned from his window to face her, genuine concern on his face, though Ellie wondered if it was for her health or for her help on his project.

"How much longer until we get there?" Ellie asked. She could withstand the pain for a while. She just needed to know how long to marshal her reserves.

"We're coming in now," Dr. Brightly said, looking out the window again.

Ellie's gut floated into her throat as the limocopter dropped toward the ground. She glanced past Dr. Brightly to see the recognizable architecture of the Capitol, though the thirty-foot protective wall separating the governmental downtown from the rest of the city was new. It spoiled the majesty of the city, making it look more like a prison than the headquarters of the Western world.

A patch of grass in the distance grew as the aircraft circled downward, and with a thump that shot from the wheels of the craft through Ellie's chair and into her spine, they landed. An officious-looking young woman wearing a sharp navy pantsuit, a tight bun, and a tighter expression waited a few steps from the craft.

Under the whoosh of rushing air from the propulsion pods and the screaming whine of the turbines, Dr. Brightly made the introduction. At least that's what Ellie thought he was doing, as she couldn't hear a word. She simply nodded and followed the others toward the nearest building, leaning on her cane and quickly lagging behind. Though the grass looked thick and lush, the ground was lumpy, and she didn't want to twist an ankle or fall.

Dr. Brightly and the woman didn't notice and hurried ahead. Why was everyone in such a rush? Ellie took a deep breath and paced herself. Only Wallace waited for her, offering his arm. She waved it off.

"I'm coming, I'm coming," she said as she shuffled past him. Once the grass of the landing field transitioned to concrete, she found her footing. The group met up just inside the door of the immense White House. A shiny marble corridor led past dozens of rooms and offices as throngs of well-dressed officials and assistants bustled in and out of doorways.

"President Prattleton is very much looking forward to meeting you," the officious woman said, not looking up from her datapad. "He has only five minutes but is eager to discuss your proposal for helping with our deep-space probe."

Their deep-space probe? Ellie stifled a laugh, though a snicker may have escaped her lips. This administration—and several before it—had forgotten all about Marlowe and its search for Planet Nine. It had come from a time when science and space exploration meant something. From Ellie's time.

"Let's get to it, then," Ellie replied and headed down the hall, reading the nameplate next to each door. Office of Communications. Office of Legislative Affairs. Ellie had toured the seat of executive power decades ago and now searched for one room in particular. The group quickly caught up and moved past her, and when they turned right toward the President's office, Ellie turned left toward the room marked Press Corps.

"I don't think that's the way," Wallace loudly whispered, hanging back from the others.

"Don't you worry about it," Ellie said with a wink. "And keep them occupied for a minute," she said, pointing her cane at Dr. Brightly and the woman deeply engaged in conversation as they continued down the hall.

"Ma'am. Ma'am!" Wallace said, reaching for her.

She ducked under his arm. "This will only take a moment." And then she'd either be in handcuffs or on her way to Dr. Brightly's lab. She entered the press room with purpose.

Reporters lounged in the stadium of seats and along the walls, talking in small groups, typing on datapads, or dictating into holo-devices. Though she had hoped to interrupt an ongoing press briefing, catching them on break meant no staffers were in the room to stop her.

Ellie walked to the front and climbed the three steps onto the stage, her cane thumping loudly on the wooden riser as she made her way to the podium. She hooked the handle of her cane over the side and grasped the top of the lectern. Barely able to see over the top, she cleared her throat, and all eyes turned her way.

"I'm Eleanor Newton-Woode," she said, channeling her energy into her voice. The microphone was not on, but her voice projected loudly and clearly. "I'm a software engineer—well, I used to be—I led the programming team for the command intelligence and was the person who wrote the sensor program for Marlowe, a deep-space probe nearest to this interstellar visitor entering our system. I've agreed to help bring Marlowe back online, and in return, President Prattleton has graciously reviewed and reversed his administration's approach to elder care."

Gasps filled the room as eyebrows shot up foreheads, and butts rushed to seats.

"The president recognizes the contributions to society that the elderly have made during their working careers," Ellie said over the clamor. "From store clerks and construction workers to farm laborers and artists, everyone has contributed to the advancement and maintenance of our society. And with this policy change, all labor and marketing quotas will be eliminated for anyone over seventy, and all government-provided benefits, including housing, food, and medical care, will be standardized at the highest level."

President Prattleton burst into the room at full sprint, screeching to a halt just inside the door, his Press Secretary and the officious woman close behind. Cameras spun in his direction, and he quickly smoothed his hair and tugged the wrinkles from his jacket as he strode toward the podium, a practiced, plastic smile on his face.

Ellie continued with a warm gesture toward the president.

"And here he is now, the honorable President Prattleton! Please, Mr. President, explain the details of your new elder care plan that will help millions of citizens—and voters!" Ellie tried to make eye contact with each reporter in the room. She had to sell this. "The President assures me that GovCorp and all its sponsors are fully in support of proper elder care, because we all get old, don't we?" Ellie winked and turned toward the President, now at her side. She snatched her cane from the lectern and grasped the President's arm, pulling him down to her level.

"Do this or you'll get no help from me," she whispered in his ear, then patted his arm as he recovered at the lectern.

"Yes, well," Prattleton stumbled, dumbfounded. "The details are still being finalized, but we believe . . ."

Ellie stopped listening, her gambit played. Either it would work or it wouldn't. She hobbled off the stage, her cane again thumping loudly with each step, and strode up to Dr. Brightly standing at the side of the room in stunned bewilderment. She rapped the end of her walking stick across his shin, startling him into consciousness. He looked down at her.

"Alright, let's go unbugger your probe," she said, and headed back to the limocopter.

Ellie's cane dug into the plush pile carpeting of the no-longer-exclusive Central Park Retirement Estates' lobby. Since her deal with the president, a seismic shift had occurred in the treatment of the elderly. Just as she had hoped. News reports from every city across the Alliance described ritzy and nearly empty retirement and convalescent complexes reaching capacity as thousands of ecstatic elderly denizens filled the rooms and received the care they deserved.

Finally.

A group had gathered in chairs and on couches, watching the news on a wallvision screen.

In a breaking announcement, the ASA reported they had activated the old Marlowe probe and had new, groundbreaking information on the origin of 631/SENTINEL. The findings were momentous and historic. The world would never be the same. Leaders of all Alliance nations had gathered in the Capitol to reveal . . .

"Bah!" Ellie swiped her hand toward the screen. Her sciatica was killing her, and she needed rest to keep her blood pressure down—per her new doctor's orders. She headed for the elevator and her suite on the ninety-first floor overlooking the park.

She'd done her part fifty years ago and now done it once again. Fate-of-the-world events were for the young. She had books to read.

END NOTE

I think this account shows the possibility of supra-Terran nexuses! I just returned from scouting the planet (alas, no tacos) and found the results of the Marlowe probe's investigation of this "interstellar" object (impossible, right? Because no stars means no space between stars). I had to slip into the Alliance Space Agency (and Flopdoodle says I'm not spy material. I still got it, Flopsy) and see for myself. Impressed it was still running over a hundred years later.

Oh! Also, all the Immortals that should have existed in this splinter have been deleted. I know because I was trying to find one. Presumably they at least remember how to make a taco. But no. Deleted one and all without a trace. Even the Morreaus. Who has the power to do that? I guess maybe the Cats. But why?

Hail our Feline Overlords!

—Ms. Six

Date: 2590-04-10 09:21:01 PRT
From: Ms. Six
To: Anachronauts
Subject: Climate Crisis
Re: Standing in Line for the First Ship Off-Planet

This account is spotty at best, but it confirms Flopdoodle's suspicions that the Immortals were conducting climate experiments. The accelerated melting of the polar ice caps in this splinter is only explicable through the use of a thermal magnifier. Since that kind of weather tech only exists in the Thunderstruck splinter, its appearance here points to Immortal interference, probably via QoreTech. This leaves local humanity in a crisis as the planet heats up and they lose their water to space.

STANDING IN LINE FOR THE FIRST SHIP OFF-PLANET

By Kara Reynolds

In her role as Head Project Manager of Earth's Exploration and Colonization Task Force, Captain Liana Sinclair had decided that the leadership team would wait in line to board the ship, just like the rank-and-file crew members. Now, after two hours of standing in the sun, filter mask digging into the skin around her nose and mouth, Liana was regretting her decision—good optics or no.

She tugged at her uniform, trying to manufacture a breeze without making it obvious how uncomfortable she was. Her husband, Troy, fanned the back of her neck as he chatted with the man in front of them, who also wore the baggy one-piece Task Force uniform. Thanks to Troy, Liana had learned that the man's name was Manuel, and that he was a xenobotanist—or would be, if the ship actually found a suitable planet for colonization on its voyage.

Unlike most people in line, Manuel was alone. Most people had friends and family with them, trying to squeeze in last goodbyes before the Task Force members boarded. Liana had a feeling this was why it was taking so long to get on the ship. When she'd calculated the boarding time, she'd assumed everyone would say proper farewells before arriving at the ship. She'd failed to take into account the human element.

Liana, for her part, had said her real goodbyes to Troy last night. They'd both agreed it would look better—optics, again—for the Head Project Manager to stay composed while waiting to board. Last night, there had been tears, kisses, and (because Liana couldn't just turn off who she was), last-minute instructions on how to keep their eight-year-old son, Hardy, healthy. Today, Liana was intent on keeping her composure.

Troy kept chatting, like they were waiting in line for their water shares on any ordinary day. Manuel had said something about pinto beans and hoping to find a world where they'd be able to grow them, and now he and Troy were exchanging dip recipes.

Liana tightened her grip on her tablet. Being outside was horrible. The heat, the unfiltered air. The loosely packed dirt they stood on got all over their boots and the ankles of their uniforms as they moved forward in the line. The ship would be clean, air-conditioned, and oxygen-optimized. The new apartment Troy and Hardy would be moving to next week would also have air conditioning. Liana wished they were joining her on the ship instead, but there was nothing for it: Hardy's poor health automatically disqualified him from joining the Exploration and Colonization Program. Signing her cooling and water credits over to him and securing a new apartment was the best Liana could do. She'd said her goodbyes to Hardy last night, too, before putting him to bed.

She looked at the sun and squinted, trying not to see Hardy's face in her mind's eye. There was nothing she could do to shut out the memory of his cries last night, though. She attempted to pay attention to the people in line. Behind her and Troy was what appeared to be a large family, with two members of the group in the Task Force uniform. Beyond them, she saw people arguing, even yelling. There were several people along the line holding protest signs, with the popular slogan: "There's no place like home." It meant that they should stop looking for a new planet to live on, that everyone should stay on Earth and keep searching for a solution to the rising temperatures that didn't involve hoping there were other worlds beyond the starless skies.

Protestors were also not great for the optics. Liana looked away from them, continuing to travel down the line with her eyes. A uniformed young man wearing a floppy hat looked to be alone; Liana wondered if his parents were living. She would never have let Hardy wait in line by himself before leaving the planet for good.

Andrew tugged on the wide-brimmed hat his father had given to him that morning. He had encouraged his father to apply for the Task Force, too; his father was a mechanic, and the ship had plenty of positions for someone with his skills. But he'd refused. Said sending Earth's finest minds into space instead of keeping them on Earth to fix things was going to doom them all.

Andrew looked up and down the line of people waiting to board the ship. He estimated that he was ahead of three-quarters of the people in line. The order in which they boarded made no difference; everyone in line had an

We
ALL
go
OR
NoONE
Goes

assigned duty, a cabin space, everything they'd need once they got on the ship. What mattered to him, as a Security Officer, was the safety of everyone on the ship, and that began now. Although, there didn't seem to be much for a Security Officer to do at the moment. Even the people holding protest signs were just standing.

Andrew moved his gaze to another group in front of him. A guy in uniform, maybe twenty-five, certainly not more than a few years older than Andrew, was surrounded by people. Two women, the right age to be his parents, each hugged one of his arms. A few other twenty-somethings, likely friends or siblings, hung around, talking to each other and the uniformed guy.

There were some scattered signs among the people in front of them; he couldn't see what they said, but he assumed they were protesting the ship. He was glad his father hadn't joined him with a sign of his own. Immediately in front of him, a blonde girl with a long ponytail and a uniform bounced on her toes, probably trying to see around one of the signs. A girl with an identical ponytail, but no uniform, stood beside her. Neither of them looked happy, which was reasonable given that they'd be saying goodbye soon, but they didn't look like security threats, either. Andrew huffed into his filter mask.

Estrella bounced on her tiptoes, trying to see the front of the line, but there were too many protest signs in front of her to get a clear view. "I don't think it's moved in the last ten minutes," she told her sister.

The people in front of them were arguing, a young man in a uniform against two women with tearstained faces. Estrella was glad she'd said her goodbyes to her parents in private. It was easier that way; she could pretend she was leaving their apartment and going to work, like any other day. Étoile, however, had insisted on coming with her to wait in line to board the ship. There would be no pretending their goodbye was anything but final. Still, Estrella hadn't felt like she could argue with the last request her sister would make of her.

Étoile crossed her arms, covered in a thin long-sleeved shirt to protect against the sun. "Stop bouncing. We'll be out here for hours," she said. "You'll be completely dehydrated before you even get on. You'll spend takeoff in a bed in sick bay. I've got a headache; you will too if you don't already."

Estrella ignored her warnings. Why would she, a healthy twenty-six-year-old, spend takeoff in sick bay? She wasn't fragile. No one in line to board the ship was; they were specially selected for their fitness. Sharp minds. Even tempers. And something else, something that apparently Estrella possessed and Étoile did not, though they were identical twins. The unfairness took up space in her lungs, making it hard to breathe.

Étoile pulled at the hem of her t-shirt, layered over the long-sleeved shirt. She had hand-painted a rainbow across the front and added glitter to make it sparkle. Estrella watched the little flecks appear and disappear as Étoile moved the shirt to cool herself. She wished she could do the same, but she thought it might look undignified for someone in the Task Force uniform to look so obviously uncomfortable.

"Will you paint a picture of the stars for me? You know, if they even exist." Étoile had apparently lost interest in pointing out her sister's weakness, and had shifted back to their earlier discussion.

"How will I see them? You know there aren't exactly windows on the ship," Estrella replied. "It's not like the old movies. Windows are potential weaknesses in the infrastructure."

"I know that," Étoile snapped. She stopped fanning herself. The sparkle disappeared. "But there will be a display or something somewhere that will show them. And you can paint from that."

"And I will get it to you . . . how, exactly?"

Étoile's eyes widened, and Estrella instantly regretted what she'd said. There would be no idle communication between the ship and those left planet-side. Only the ship's higher-ups would be able to receive updates from Earth and transmit a message back to Earth if a suitable colony planet was found. Even if by some miracle that happened, the time-dilation involved in space travel meant that Étoile and her parents would be long dead before Earth could send more colonists. Étoile would never see the stars, whether Estrella painted them for her or not.

When they'd applied for the Exploration and Colonization Task Force, they'd imagined going together. Estrella remembered the disappointment when Étoile received her application rejection, which turned to sinking horror when her acceptance arrived an hour later. They'd argued for so long about what to do that their parents had intervened, just like when they were children. Yes, things would be a little easier for Étoile, with Estrella gone; Estrella had designated her sister as the recipient of her monthly water and cooling credits. Being able to provide comfort for those left behind was one of the incentives of joining the exploration ship.

Estrella had used almost an hour of water credits the day she accepted her Task Force role, crying in the shower so her sister wouldn't hear. Étoile had also taken a long shower that day.

♠ ♠ ♠

Troy and Manuel had moved on from pinto beans to Troy's work on constructing the ship.

"Welding," Troy explained. "Very exacting. I got double cooling credits for every hour I spent with the torch."

Manuel nodded, looking very serious. "Your home must have been so comfortable during those months."

Liana shook her head. "We traded them," she said, startled to pull herself into the conversation. "Our son has asthma. He needs higher quality filter masks and the first-tier home ventilation system."

"A son!" Manuel clapped Troy on the shoulder. "How old?"

"Eight." Liana surprised herself by answering again. "His name is Hardy." She gripped her tablet tighter.

Manuel's eyes narrowed. "And with you leaving, is he the designated recipient of your credits? Will the extra water and air help his condition?"

Her mouth was dry. Troy had suggested bringing water for the wait in line, but she didn't want to take any more from them. She nodded.

"She got a bonus," Troy cut in. "For being on the leadership team. Hardy and I move to a new-construction building next week. Top of the line ventilation, tinted windows, the works."

"I have two daughters," Manuel said. "They are splitting my credits."

"Where are they?" Troy asked. "Not able to make the farewell?"

The tablet slipped in Liana's sweaty grasp; she shifted it to the other hand and wiped the offending palm on her pant leg.

"They live close to the Canadian border," Manuel said. "I visited them last week to get their upload for the AI program. We said our goodbyes then."

"Liana didn't want Hardy outside for too long, even with the filter mask," Troy said. "Said it'd be bad for his asthma. She said goodbye to him last night. My sister's with him today."

Every crew member had been provided a tablet with an AI simulator program. You recorded your loved ones talking, saying a number of template sentences as well as unscripted speech. The program then used the videos to create realistic versions of the people that the crew members could talk to on the journey. Hardy had loved making recordings for "robot Hardy;" it had been easy to get all the required video hours from him. She had more videos and photos on her personal tablet. Hopefully enough to last a good long time.

A grunt from behind him caused Andrew to turn. A man in uniform was doubled over, clutching his stomach. He didn't appear to be a threat to others. Andrew cleared his throat. "Sir, can I help you?"

"Probably just nerves," the man said, a little muffled through his filter mask. His knuckles whitened as he clutched his stomach harder. Andrew noticed the reddening skin on the top of the man's head. This man was decades older than him, with most of his hair already gone, nothing additional to protect against the sun.

Andrew hesitated, then pulled his hat off. "Why don't you try this?" he offered. "In case the sun exposure is affecting you more than nerves. My father gave it to me; it's old, but soft."

The older man straightened up with a grimace and took the offered hat. "Well, thank you," he said. "I can give it back to you on the ship."

"Thank you. I'd appreciate that." Andrew's shoulders relaxed a centimeter. Yes, he had his father on his tablet's AI upload. He could talk to him, or at least his likeness, and the AI generator would replicate his personality. Still, the tangibleness of the hat made it a better receptacle for the memory of his father, who hated AI. He held his hand out to the older man. "Andrew Lewandowski. Security Officer."

"Kevin Fry. Psychologist." They shook hands. "Security Officer sounds like an enjoyable position for someone your age."

"They told me it was more like keeping people safe from the ship. Cleaning up a spill so people don't slip, or cordoning off an area that needs a repair. I don't think I'm going to have much else to do. Everyone's been screened, right? It's not like we're taking violent criminals on the ship."

Kevin shrugged. "No. But still. You never know how people will react to ship life. Things could change." He exhaled heavily.

Andrew wondered if Kevin's exhale meant the man's stomach still hurt.

He rested his hand on the back of his neck. The skin felt hot.

The line moved forward. *Shifted* was probably a better word, given the minuscule distance they moved.

"How are you feeling about our imminent departure?" Kevin asked.

"I wish they'd asked us to line up in the middle of the night," Andrew said.

Kevin chuckled. "I agree." He turned awkwardly, and his backpack slipped to the ground. There was a water bottle in an outside pocket; he pulled it out and handed it to Andrew. "Thirsty?"

Andrew nodded. The water was warm, but felt amazing spilling across his tongue, sliding down his throat. "Thank you."

He handed the water bottle back; Kevin took a sip before returning it to the backpack. He looked over Andrew's shoulder. "You don't have anyone with you?"

"I said goodbye to my friends last night." Andrew hesitated, but didn't see much of a point in trying to hide information from a psychologist. "My dad refused to come," he admitted. The echoes of their argument that morning still hurt. Andrew could feel the phantom tingles of the goodbye hug he'd imagined that never materialized. He'd gotten the hat shoved at him instead. "He hates the exploration program, and he hates that I signed my credits over to him."

"He wished you'd stay instead, and use the credits yourself?"

Andrew nodded. "But if there's a chance there's something out there, I want to help find it. And there's nothing here for me, really."

"No," Kevin agreed. "There's not much of anything for anyone."

"You don't have anyone with you, either," Andrew pointed out.

"That's right. I said my goodbyes already."

There was a part of Andrew that wanted to ask who Kevin had said his goodbyes to, but he thought it might be a rude thing to get into if you weren't a psychologist. If Kevin wanted to tell him, he would, right? As a Security Officer, Andrew's job was to keep the peace, not stir things up. He was feeling stirred up enough for two people, thinking about his dad. Better to let Kevin keep his silence.

The line moved. Estrella and Étoile stepped in unison to fill the gap. The group in front of them was still arguing, more loudly now. The man in the Task Force uniform had started crying, too. Estrella swallowed. Nothing made her cry faster than seeing someone else crying, even a stranger. The feelings hit her like a knife in her heart, a burning in the back of her throat. Why that always manifested as water from her eyes, she didn't know. And yet somehow, the water usually made the burning go away.

Estrella looked at Étoile. The filter mask cut into the skin over her nose. The soft skin around her eyes was red, which could have been from the particles in the air, but Estrella had a feeling it was more than that. She knew how private her sister was, how she hated showing other people her true feelings. Estrella tried to give her an out. "You don't have to stay in line. I'll be fine."

"We're never going to see each other again. Of course I'm staying the whole time."

The words hung in the air between the sisters. Estrella chewed the inside of her cheeks to keep her tears at bay. She didn't think she'd be able to stop if she started.

"Do you think you'll be able to paint, stars or not?" Étoile asked the next time they shuffled forward. "Will you have any free time?"

"I think so," Estrella said. She hoped that was true. She'd received an email from the head project manager for the Task Force, Liana Sinclair, outlining their schedules and breaks, but also warning them that in the case of a disease outbreak or a disaster resulting in injury, it would be all hands on deck.

"I hope you do," Étoile said. "I'd hate to think of you up there, working all the time, not even enjoying your new life."

"I'll just talk to your AI upload all the time," Estrella half-joked. She had uploaded Étoile, their parents, and her mentor from medical school.

"I hate those things. They're just going to be an excuse not to talk to the other people on the ship." Étoile blinked. "You should delete mine. Talk to an actual person."

Estrella recoiled at the thought of deleting the last link to her sister. "I'll talk to plenty of people. Doctors always do."

Étoile scoffed. "Not that kind of talking. Actual conversations about things that matter."

"People's health matters."

The line moved. Étoile stayed put. "You're being obtuse on purpose."

"I am not."

"Yes, you *are*. Stop pretending like you don't know what I'm talking about."

Estrella fought the urge to roll her eyes. She didn't want to tarnish her last hour with her sister with childish behavior. "Why don't you just say what you actually mean, then?"

"You must be an excellent mother," Manuel said to Liana, who startled so hard she almost dropped the tablet.

"What?" she replied, trying to cover her discombobulation. She hugged the tablet to her chest.

"You gave up your last minutes with your son so he wouldn't suffer physically," Manuel went on. "Such sacrifice."

Liana tried to get rid of the burning behind her eyes by blinking. It mostly didn't work.

"Of course she's an excellent mother," Troy said, coming to her rescue. "I mean, Head Project Manager? That's what she's like at home. Organized, knows where everything is, where everyone needs to be at all times. Keeps track of everything Hardy needs, keeps him healthy. I'll do my best, but it won't be the same." He rested his hand on her shoulder and squeezed it through the thin fabric of the Task Force uniform. His thumb moved in circles on the spot where her neck met her back.

It wouldn't be the same, which was the whole point of her going. Troy and Hardy would be in a better apartment. Hardy would be able to breathe more easily. Troy was definitely the more fun parent. Liana told herself that those things were more important than rigid medication schedules and routines.

There were fewer than twenty people ahead of Manuel now. Troy kept his hand on Liana. She tried to focus on the pressure. Inside her newly-issued boots, her feet were sweating. That was something else to focus on. Anything but the pain in her throat and her eyes.

"We are all keeping humanity going, in our own ways," Manuel said, after the line moved yet again. "Whether we stay here or leave. Whether we settle a new world or keep the old one safe for those around us just a little longer."

Liana caught the inside of her cheek with her teeth, bit down. Felt the pain. It wasn't enough.

"It will matter," Manuel said. "Our sacrifice."

"It has to." Liana choked on the words as they filled her filter mask. She pulled it away from her face and coughed before settling it back into place. "We don't have anything else to give."

"It's going to work," Troy said. "I can feel it. Through the rift, there's other worlds. There will be a place for us to go."

"But until then, you will suffer," Manuel murmured. "You, and your Hardy, and my daughters. You will stay here, and the temperatures will rise. The water will disappear."

"We'll be fine," Troy said. "That's decades away, maybe even a century. Our new apartment and Liana's credits will keep me and Hardy going for a long time. Humanity will keep building ships, and when your Task Force sends us the coordinates of our new home, we'll be ready." His grip on Liana's shoulder started to hurt, the only sign that he was having trouble maintaining his composure, too. The pain was reassuring.

At the head of the line, a copper-headed woman with no filter mask clung to the arm of a girl with the same color hair who wore the Task Force uniform.

The girl tried to move forward, but couldn't with—it must have been her mother—hanging on. Liana couldn't look away as the girl shoved her mother off and ran onto the ship. The woman remained on the ground, sobbing.

"So, you probably won't have much to do on the ship either," Andrew said. "Since mental health screening was part of the application process and all."

Kevin massaged his stomach. "I'll have plenty to do, especially at the beginning of the voyage."

"Why's that?"

Kevin pointed up and down the line. "Look at all these people. They all have different voices telling them to stay, conscious or unconscious. Some of those voices are going to rear up and make themselves known once it's too late to go back. Or they have voices telling them to leave, which is its own set of issues. Either way, I'm anticipating a ship full of people needing to talk about their choices."

Andrew thought about it. "Don't you think they'll just talk to the AI uploads? If they miss their family or friends or whoever?"

"That's definitely part of why the Task Force provides them," Kevin agreed. "But I think everyone will find quickly that they're a poor substitute for the real thing."

"That's what my dad said. Only he called them 'fake-ass nonsense' instead of poor substitutes." It was kind of funny when he said it out loud. And his father was right; an AI upload would never replicate his father's hatred of AI, which was a huge part of his personality. It would probably smile too often.

"But he agreed to participate in the upload process anyway?" Kevin asked. "Answered the interview questions, provided the video, all that?"

Andrew nodded. Kevin clapped his hand on Andrew's shoulder. "He loves you." Andrew nodded again. "And you're leaving him."

Andrew blinked.

Kevin shook Andrew a little bit before releasing his shoulder. "When those two voices start having a war in your head, come talk to me, okay?"

"All right."

The line moved forward. Kevin took the hat off and handed it back to Andrew, who gripped it tightly instead of putting it back on right away. The sun still burned, but the feel of the fabric clenched in his fist felt better than the shade.

A woman peeled off from a group ahead of them and walked rapidly away from the line, wiping at her eyes. Andrew could hear her sobs, even with the filter mask muffling them. He watched her break into a jog, then disappear around the corner to the shuttle loading zone. He wondered if she had a Kevin to talk to. He wondered if Kevin had a Kevin to talk to.

"So, who did you say goodbye to?" he asked. Maybe a Security Officer was justified in stirring things up a little, if it gave someone an opportunity to talk. Maybe a little stirring up was needed to get to the peace.

Étoile glared at Estrella. "After you enter this ship, your life isn't on Earth anymore. Any future humanity might have is on this ship. So you better act like *humans* and not like robots who wish they were still on Earth."

"What does that even mean?" Their voices were raised, but given the volume of the conversations around them, Estrella figured no one noticed.

"You can't just go up there and spend your days taking care of sick people and your nights talking to your AI uploads. You have to be a human. You have to make art. Music. Friends. Fall in love. Get in a fight. Otherwise, what is even the point of sending all of you? We might as well send the AI." Étoile grabbed the arm of the uniformed man standing behind her. "You, what's your name?"

"Andrew Lewandowski. Security Officer." Andrew's glance shifted back and forth between the sisters. "Everything all right here?" The older man standing behind him tilted his head as he looked at Estrella.

"Andrew, this is Estrella Lyons." Étoile gestured at her, and Estrella wished she had a filter mask that covered her entire face. "She's one of the ship's doctors. But she's also an identical twin, named after the stars no one alive has seen, and when you all get off this planet, I am holding you personally responsible to make sure that she looks at the stars and thinks about me."

Andrew's eyes narrowed as he looked at Estrella, who started stammering out an apology. Andrew held up his hand and turned his focus back to Étoile. "I will do that," he said, and even though she'd never spoken to him before, Estrella could hear the promise in his voice.

"And don't let her spend all her free time alone talking to her AI," Étoile added. "She has to have at least one friend by the end of the first week."

"Noted."

"Thank you." Étoile turned her back to Andrew and stared resolutely at the front of the line, blinking rapidly.

Estrella looked at Andrew once more, who gave her a firm nod and turned back to the man behind him. The line moved forward a few more steps.

Estrella was about to retort that she was perfectly capable of making her own friends when she noticed a tear slip under the strap of Étoile's filter mask. The fight left her, a physical weight blown away with the dust. Instead, she slipped her backpack off her shoulder and unzipped the main pocket. "Give me your shirt," she said to Étoile.

Étoile blinked at her before looking down at the hand-painted rainbow. "My shirt?"

"Now who's being obtuse on purpose? You've got the long one underneath, you'll be fine." Estrella snapped her fingers at her sister. "The line's moving again. Come on."

Étoile took a few steps forward while pulling her arms out of the t-shirt. She pulled it over her head and dropped it on Estrella's open backpack.

"Be careful! That's my favorite shirt," Estrella said. "My sister gave it to me. We're identical twins, except she's two centimeters shorter than me. We both like to paint, but she's better at it than I am. Maybe we could paint together sometime? Or look out at the stars?" She folded the shirt carefully and tucked it on top of the tablet with the AI uploads. The line shuffled forward, but she waited until the backpack was safely on her shoulders before moving.

"Yeah," Étoile said. "Something like that."

"Okay."

"But I'm only one centimeter shorter than you."

"Sure."

Now that it was almost her turn to check in, Liana could hear the people in front of Manuel arguing with the Task Force officer manning the check-in station about the amount of items they were trying to bring aboard. Liana felt like she should help him out, flash her badge, flaunt her authority. After all, she was the one who had set the packing regulations. Instead, she clutched her tablet more tightly. Let them fight. Let them fight all day, with their feet on familiar, dusty soil. Would she ever stand on a planet's surface again? Were the stars real, or just a theory by the same crazy scientists who were sending them out on this voyage? Was there anything out there, past the dark skies?

"Liana."

She looked up to see Manuel's back disappear through the hatch. The Task Force officer waved his hand at her and Troy. Liana took a step forward, lost her balance, leaned backward, expecting to fall on her backside. But Troy was right behind her, as always, and she thudded against his chest.

"I can't," she said.

"You can," he replied. He kissed the top of her head. "Liana Sinclair. Head Project Manager," he said over her head, to the officer. The officer threw a salute. "Captain Sinclair," he said.

Hardy had called her Captain Mommy for a week after Troy told him she was a superhero going into space. She was a superhero. They could not do this without her; her patterns, her critical thinking, her compartmentalization. The human race needed her.

Troy and Hardy did not. She could do more for them on the ship, with her bonuses and the credits, than she could at home. If she stayed, they would be together, suffering, Hardy never breathing quite right. He needed clean air more than he needed a mother. Especially a mother who loved her patterns, her compartmentalization—

"Captain?"

Her head snapped up. "Yes," she said. "Captain Liana Sinclair. Reporting for duty." And for humanity. And for the stars.

And for Hardy.

END NOTE

The locals’ response to the disaster is impressive. They haven’t let it tear them apart; they’ve united to save some portion of humanity. They don’t get into it in the account, likely because it was kept from the general population, but various scientific reports from the splinter confirm they have discovered a nexus point large enough to accommodate a ship (probably a Jovian nexus). We’ll need to keep an eye on the colony ships to see which splinter they arrive in. If they make it through. Which other splinters even have Jupiter? I guess my nexus hunt continues!

—Ms. Six

Date: 2590-04-10 21:45:11 PRT
From: Nerrid Flopdoodle
To: Anachronauts
Subject: books are everything
Re: Malone's World

Yes, okay, Ms. Six, I hear you, the nexuses are fascinating. We have a whole meeting scheduled about them next week, so you can stand down from the nexus alert system you've apparently set up specifically to torment me.

Anyway, Ms. Six (and I guess everyone else on this thread that doesn't know or care), you know I've been reading the "Malone's World" mysteries for a while now, as many as I can get my hands on out of Sprocket (like that one I sent last month about the refrigerated head—pure catnip!). But anyway, I found this one, and it seems to know too much about the splinter. Is it possible these stories are real, have been real all along? I swear I thought it was fiction, but now?

I think this may be the hint I've been looking for to understand what has been happening on Sprocket once and for all, find out why there is such a conspicuous lack of change here. But I also hope the revelations Malone discovers in this account won't mean an end to Malone's stories because I still need my fix.

—Nerrid

MALONE'S WORLD

By Paul Martz

Detroit, February 1933
Woodward Avenue and Clifford Street, Downtown

The days are short and the breadlines long. The clouds sag so low I want to cut them open and watch them bleed. I nose my Dodge Brothers Sedan up to the curb on Clifford and kill the engine. My office squats above a boarded-up soda fountain. That same bum's sleeping on the stairs. Hasn't seen a shower in weeks. How he sleeps with that radiator racket is anyone's guess. I drop a nickel at his feet and take the steps. Then I'm at my door.

FRANK MALONE, PRIVATE INVESTIGATOR

In my world, the paint's peeling, the coffee's cold, and the rent's always late. My desk chair growls under me—that's reality. I wouldn't trade it for nothing. Dreams are for suckers and street bums. Give it to me straight. Give me trouble that doesn't knock first.

Evelyn Daltry walks in. And she doesn't knock first.

If you're waiting for the part where my jaw hits the floor or she crosses her legs and I forget how to blink, don't hold your breath. She's not that kind of lady. Her coat is thin and her makeup thinner, and whatever she's carrying's heavier than both.

"The police have it all wrong," she says. "My brother didn't commit suicide. He was murdered."

"Tell me about your brother."

"Clarence Flammarion. That's my maiden name: Flammarion."

"I need more than a name, lady. Who were his pals? Who'd he drink with?"

"It's Prohibition, Mr. Malone. Clarence never drank."

"How'd he keep the lights on?"

She pauses. Not much, but enough. "I'm not sure what kind of work he did."

Then she jumps track faster than a rush-hour trolley. "There's something else. Clarence had a small device. Metal, shiny, fits in the palm of your hand. Unlike anything you'd normally see. He kept it close. It's missing."

Now she's got my attention. "Missing?"

"Yes. I need you to find it."

"What is it?"

"That's not important, Mr. Malone. Just . . . find it."

The way she says it sounds like the thing carries its own weight. I don't like the smell of this job already. Murdered brother, strange gadget. But the description sticks. A shiny little thing, fits in my hand, something that would catch my eye.

"There's one last thing you should know. Our grandfather recently passed away. His will bequeaths his entire estate to Clarence, with nothing for me. I contested that will before Clarence was murdered. I'm telling you now so you won't waste any time investigating me. As if I would murder my own brother."

"Clarence got any next of kin?"

"Me. I'm his next of kin."

"What's in the estate?"

"A large sum of money." She opens a leather purse and removes a checkbook. "What's your rate?"

She walked in wearing grief like a cheap coat. Now she says she's loaded because her brother bought the farm. Hiring me's a smart move, if she's got nothing to hide. It's also the perfect cover for a con. I don't know what to believe, not yet. But I charge a special rate when the stink of a setup hits my nose.

"Twelve bucks a day. If that scares you, you're in the wrong office."

She scribbles a check. "I hope this is sufficient, Mr. Malone."

The check's enough to cover the rent and leave a little extra for bourbon and bullets. But money that good never walks in without trouble trailing behind. I tuck it in my coat, hoping I live long enough to cash it.

Detroit Police Department, 1300 Beaubien Street, Greektown

Same tired bricks, same crumbling mortar. The building holds together out of spite, just so it can watch me squirm when I walk in. Four and a half years of wearing blues and busting my butt, then they kicked me to the curb. I only got one friend left here: Vinnie Calluto, the guy who let me keep my .38 revolver. The intake desk's a halfway house for screwups and spitballers, but it's where I find Vinnie. Must've drawn the short straw today.

"Look what somebody scraped off my shoe," he says. Real wise guy.

"Good to see you too, Vinnie." I lean in. "Give me the straight dope on a stiff. Guy named Flammarion."

Vinnie nods. "Imagine the butt-kicking he got on the playground with a name like that. Suicide, Frank. Open and shut."

He doesn't even look it up.

"Autopsy?"

"We don't autopsy stiffs in a bathtub with their wrists cut."

"Suicide note?"

He shrugs like it's not his business. "Nada. But he left the razor in the tub, nice and neat. Water was pink when they pulled him. Whole scene said don't ask questions."

I cock an eyebrow.

His voice slides down an octave. "You didn't hear it from me, but Homicide barely blinked. Case got pushed upstairs quick."

"You got a file?"

He hesitates, then pulls open a drawer like it might bite him. He slides over a file folder. "Absolutely not, Frank. You know the rules." He returns to the drawer, thumbs through the files one by one, careful not to make eye contact.

Home address is on the cover sheet. I jot it down. The property list goes straight to the point. Razor blade. Nothing like what Evelyn's after. Set of glossy prints. Guy in a clawfoot tub, wrists red ribbons. Steam still fogging the mirror in the background.

"Water still warm when they found him?" I ask.

"Yeah. What of it?"

"Do me a favor, Vinnie. Forget we had this talk."

He nods once. "What talk?"

A friend in the department's like a pocketknife. Useful for so many things. A knife for cutting through the crap. A can opener, if you're in a tight spot. Hope I don't need Vinnie for that last one.

I make for the door. Evelyn was right. Clarence's suicide was theater. The cops know it, same as me. Someone wants this whole thing buried fast. Well, I don't bury, I dig. And I'll start by digging into Clarence.

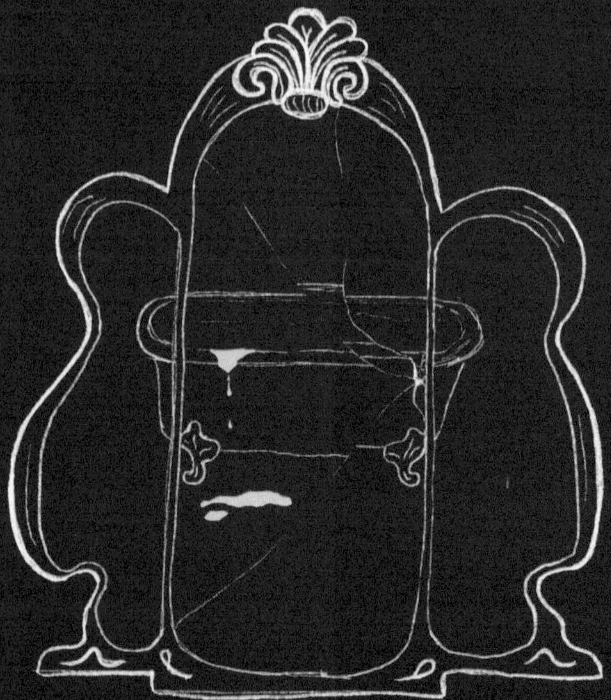

441 East Ferry Street, Midtown

Flammarion's apartment building is three stories of ugly bricks and bad luck. Midtown's got plenty of both, but this place makes the rest look like palaces. I enter and climb the stairs, then sweet-talk the lock with a bobby pin. I've had boogers harder to pick.

Looks like I'm late to the party. The flat's a wreck. Drawers yanked, cushions gutted, plaster chipped where some gorilla swung wild. If Flammarion's secrets are still here, they're scattered on the floor.

I step over a busted chair and paw through what's left of a desk. A pay stub would tell me how this guy paid the bills. Broken pencils. Old bills covered in spilled ink. No pay stubs. Then . . . a crumpled receipt from T. B. Rayl Hardware. Two hundred light bulbs. Who needs that many? Delivery address is Lodi Township. West, way outside the city. I pocket the receipt.

The bathroom looks nothing like the photos. This place was pawed through after the cops did their work. And whoever came later was no interior decorator. From the cracked mirror, three Malones eyeball me like I'm the next stiff.

The bedroom's worse: drawers turned inside out, bed ripped to the springs. In a pile of trash by the window, I find an old stereoscope viewer, one lens cracked but still working. A few cards lay scattered under a busted lampshade. I slot one in. The picture's got depth. Looking up at something big. Not the Brooklyn Bridge, but maybe just as old. A web of girders and steel ribs, high enough to reach the clouds.

I'm spinning my wheels. I've got that address in Lodi from the receipt, and it'll be night by the time I get there.

Before I leave the room, I catch a gleam by the nightstand. Fits my hand like a snub-nose when I pick it up, but it's no gun. It's old, been around a while, but still shiny. Has a whiff of Buck Rogers about it.

"Metal, shiny, fits in the palm of your hand. Unlike anything you'd normally see."

They trashed the place and walked right past what they came for.

I don't think long. I slip it into my pocket.

Outside his apartment, the stairwell smells of rotten eggs. Coal gas. That boiler's got a leak. I shove through the front door. Even the Detroit winter stinks better.

A Detroit Gas Company truck rattles at the curb. First surprise, they showed up. Second, the driver's climbing into the truck, not out. That should've clued me in. It didn't.

"Hey Bub," I say, ambling over to his truck. "That building's leaking enough gas to cremate Fatty Arbuckle."

He shoots me a look like I just spit on his shoes. "Beat it, dick."

Then the building blows. Glass, dust, and flame belching out the tenement windows.

My thick skull sums it up. Two plus two makes four.

I grab the guy by the collar. "Who sent ya?"

He gives me a shove and ratchets the gearshift. Too slow.

I pull the keys and kill the engine. The keys jut out of my fist like broken teeth. "Talk, or I'll unlock your face."

Sirens in the distance. I tighten my grip on his neck. "You want to talk to me or them?"

He shoots a glance toward the sirens, then back to me. "Barrett."

I don't stun easy, but that name lands hard.

The gas company chump snatches his keys, and he's gone by the time I make it back to my Dodge. My old sedan coughs, backfires, then roars to life. I peel out, smoke and flames in the rearview mirror. I'm already back on Woodward Ave before the hook and ladder rounds the corner.

Julian Barrett. The Detroit Public Works greaseball that's been skimming city contracts for years. A real piece of work. Back when I was on the force, I almost had him. But I leaned on one of his heavies a little hard. How was I to know the guy had a bad ticker? The police don't like dead witnesses. They canned me fast, real eager to sign that pink slip—and I bet pressure came from the city. Courtesy of Barrett.

How Barrett ties into Flammarion's death, I don't know. One thing's clear. He didn't want to leave any loose ends.

And me? I'm the loosest end there is.

I'll have to drop in on Barrett. A friendly chat. But that can wait till tomorrow. Tonight, I've got driving to do.

Rural Lodi Township

Night falls. The thick clouds turn black as motor oil. If this was Flammarion's racket, he burned through a lot of gas. Don't know what could be in Lodi that's worth the mileage. I follow Michigan Avenue straight into the sunset.

I find the address. The mailbox's nailed to a post that's seen straighter days. I kill the engine and get my flashlight. Give me hard pavement over frozen slush any day of the week. A skunk stinks the place up. Nature's way of telling me to get lost.

The fence is tall. The lock's a rusted Yale so old I wonder if my picks will fit. It takes a couple minutes. My fingers are numb from the cold. Then it pops like it was never locked at all.

Behind the fence is some kind of equipment shed. Run down. Not exactly postcard material. The lock on the door's even easier than the Yale. The tumblers barely pretend to resist.

Inside's got the oily smell of a machine shop. I take a slow step. The wood creaks under my heel. I pull out a flashlight and flick it on.

My flashlight beam lands on a globe, tall as me. At least I think it's a globe. It's mounted at an angle and made out of iron, a big round bird cage. But there's no bird inside, just a flat disk big as a table, with little trees and houses. Mounted on the wall next to it there's a smorgasbord of levers. Gears and chains everywhere. And the whole thing's ticking, like something screwed together by a watchmaker with a hangover. If this is a clue, it's like no fingerprint I ever dusted. I've got no idea what this is, or what Flammarion was up to. But it explains why a man like this worked alone.

Next to the big iron ball cage, a map drapes a work table, and it reads like something out of the Saturday horoscope. Sagittarius, Cancer, Deneb, Polaris. Next to the map, a half-empty box of light bulbs with enough wire to telegraph China. No clue why Flammarion needed so many light bulbs. Gears spin in my head, but the transmission's in neutral.

I pan my flashlight over a bookshelf behind the worktable. It's a regular Detroit Public Library. Dozens of leather-bound books with titles stamped in gold: *Celestial Mechanics*, *The Clockwork Cosmos*. I pick a book at random, flip through the pages. Column after column of numbers. And some old pictures, engravings. One catches my eye. I turn around and look at that globe again, then back to the picture in the book. Same thing. A celestial sphere. Whatever Flammarion did, it had something to do with the sky.

His desk's clean and orderly. In the drawer is some kind of brass gadget, all sharp angles and arcs. Something a sea captain would've used to chase stars, maybe. And this is just the front office.

Behind the library, there's a machine shop to make Henry Ford salivate. A lathe, a drill press, a milling machine. Takes me back to that summer I worked at the auto plant.

Back in the front room, I take a closer look at that rack of levers. They've all got labels. One says Intensity—Increase one way, Decrease the other, but it's in the middle, at Auto. Another lever's labeled Error Tolerance. I latch onto the worn handle. *Malone, do you really want to do this? Yeah, I do.* I swing it over to Zero. Nothing changes. That clock ticking keeps going like nothing's different. I don't know what I was expecting.

I could use somebody to make sense of all this. And I got a name in mind. But before I ring Evelyn's phone, I've got to do a little more shoveling. Not tonight. I've found enough links that don't make a chain. I'll drive back to town, get a drink, and call it a night.

I step out of the workshop.

Not a cloud in the sky. A full moon. And stars—sharp and too still.

The whole drive back to Detroit, I stare up at those stars. And I think about that lever I swung to zero error. I think about it a lot.

Suzie's, East Grand & Jefferson, Eastside

Nice thing about Prohibition, it's never too late for a drink. There's a speakeasy tucked behind the Salvation Army, and tonight it's jumping. Whiskey flows, smoke hangs heavy, and some joker's pounding a piano while crooning off-key. The place is jammed with guys and dolls jittering the floorboards six ways to Sunday.

Suzie's behind the bar, cigarette hanging from her rouged lips and a laugh sharp as a busted bottle. Lots of dames running gin joints today. Give them the vote and they take the whole town. She spots me at the door. I find a stool between a rum-soaked banker and a doll in sequins. By the time my butt lands, a whiskey's waiting, so fresh it's still got a Canadian accent.

I can smell a bum case, and this one reeks worse than the Detroit River in July. Flammarion was tinkering with the sky, something too crazy for words. And his flat? Barrett wanted Flammarion's flat out of the picture. Maybe it'll add up after my second drink. Or my third.

Women keep secrets better than men. Always a step ahead. So when Suzie tops off my fourth, I show her the shiny gadget I found at Flammarion's flat. "Hey, Suzie. You got any idea what this is?"

She glances once. "Beats me. Looks to be some kind a trinket." Then she's gone, weaving through the haze, pouring joy juice for the stool warmers.

"Your fortune?" The sequined doll next to me cuts a deck, stacks it neat. My head's swimming, and she shimmers every time I blink. Bet she's one of the gypsies that hawk two-nickel fortunes on Belle Isle.

She flips a card. "The Tower. Truth comes crashing down, da? All things break. And . . ." Another card. "The Moon. Shadow, trickery, forces you no see. Together, is secrets uncovered."

Her whisper brushes my ear, perfume cutting through the smoke. "What you possess, no trinket. Is key to reality. Opens the veil, lets you peek at what hides behind. Very careful how you use."

In a flash of sequins, she sweeps up the cards and melts into the crowd.

I give my head a shake to knock the fog back where it belongs. Then I settle my tab.

Outside, Detroit waits, cold, dark, and crooked. I crank the sedan. It complains, then starts. While the engine warms, my thoughts wander to Evelyn's missing toy. I take the gadget out of my pocket, turn it over in my hands.

I prod it, twist it. Then it rings like no bell I ever heard. Maybe it's the whiskey, maybe it's me. But the stars blink out, and the sky's black as pitch. A heartbeat later, they're back.

"Is key to reality," the sequin doll said.

The engine idles. So do I.

I pull onto Grand, headlights cutting the dark. Mysterious gadgets don't fit in my world. But Barrett does. How he's mixed up in this, I don't know. Tomorrow, I'll find out.

DETROIT PUBLIC WORKS, FORT & GRISWOLD, DOWNTOWN

The next day rises sunny and spotless, which only means the dirt's hiding somewhere I haven't looked. Probably DPW. Detroit Public Works is an architectural hemorrhoid squatting on half a block of Ford Avenue. A cockroach struts across the lobby like it's got an appointment with the commissioner. My Oxfords step in. Meeting cancelled.

Outside Barrett's office is a secretary with nails painted red and an attitude to match. She eyes me like I just tracked in mud from the gutter. "Got an appointment, Mister?"

Mister. That's rich. May as well call me Chump or tell me to beat it.

"The name's Malone."

She punches the intercom like it owes her money, eyes drilling through me. "Guy named Malone here to see you."

There's a long pause. I'm betting Barrett's chewing on the name and doesn't like the taste. Then the knob turns, and the door opens.

Barrett. Wingtip shoes, cheap suit, and a face grim as a judge with a hangover. "Malone," he says.

"Julian. Been a while."

We size each other up, two back-alley bulldogs wondering whether to growl or go for the jugular.

"Gonna invite me in?" I ask.

"Why don't you take a dive off the Ambassador Bridge, Malone? Our business is over."

"I got new business, Barrett. Guy named Flammarion."

That one lands. He steps back, wingtips clomping the linoleum. It's as much of an invitation as I'm getting. I walk in and shut the door behind me.

He sits. "I didn't expect to see you again. Not after your failed attempt to associate me with that . . . unfortunate misappropriations incident." His hand slips under the desk.

"Thumbing the muscle?" I ask. Same Barrett, same playbook. Never could resolve anything without a big goon for backup.

"What do you want, Malone?"

I slap my PI badge on his desk. "About Flammarion. The guy was found in a bathtub with his wrists cut. Funny thing though: when the cops arrived, the water was still warm."

He shrugs. "Glad to hear our men in blue respond so promptly."

"Public Works still got a contract with Detroit Gas? Bet you know a guy or two over there."

"Of course. The city maintains excellent relations with its public utilities."

"The stiff's apartment had a gas leak yesterday. Guy from Detroit Gas showed up."

He laces his fingers with the patience of a priest taking confession. "Responding to a leak, as Detroit Gas is known to do."

"Yeah. Funny thing about that gas guy. He wasn't arriving. He was leaving. In a hurry. And he almost drove off before the apartment blew."

"What of it?"

"Before he could scram, I leaned on him hard enough to find out who sent him. Said it was you. So there must be a good reason you knew some building in Midtown had a gas leak."

Barrett closes his eyes like I'm giving him a migraine. Trying to withdraw an alibi from his bankrupt imagination. Finally, his hamster wheel cranks out, "Who hired you, Malone?"

"My clients are confidential."

The door swings open, and it's not the cheerful front-desk hostess serving coffee and donuts. It's a walking ice box with a glare colder than the ice inside it.

"Pinky," Barrett says, voice slick as an oil leak, "Mr. Malone seems to be lost. Please help him find the exit."

Meat-hook hands clamp my shoulder. "You heard the boss." Pinky's voice grinds out gravel in a gearbox.

As he steers me toward the hall, Barrett adds his postscript. "Tell your client I don't know anything about a Clarence Flammarion."

The hall narrows. It's grimy, littered with cigarette butts and dirt. More ashtray than thoroughfare. Pinky's breathing rattles like a car with no muffler. I catch glimpses of his yellow teeth as he grumbles at the shadows.

The back door looms ahead, gaping wide and hungry. At the threshold, he closes his hand around mine.

"Fingers. Nice." His best attempt at English. He gives my little finger a hard twist. "Shame if they got broke."

When a guy half a foot taller shows you the door, mumbling to himself and making threats, the smart move is to keep your feet moving and your mouth shut. I wish I had those smarts.

"That's funny," I tell him, "I was just thinking the same thing about your face."

His arm whips around. A clean right hook to my eye, Max Baer style. Pain lights up the side of my head, and I stumble into the back alley. Behind me, the door slams like the lid on a coffin.

I drive back to my office with one eye swollen shut. But the information I got was worth the pain. Barrett showed his hand.

I never so much as breathed the name Clarence.

Woodward Avenue and Clifford Street, Downtown

My head still spins from Pinky's hook. I leave my sedan at the curb on Clifford and duck into the corner market for some ice.

"Whoa, Frank! Lose a fight with a trolley?" Sam the butcher, top-cut steaks, bottom-shelf wisecracks.

"I let it win. Didn't want to embarrass it in front of its trolley friends."

It's a half-block walk to my building, with the ice in a handkerchief pressed to my face. I open the entrance. Same bum on the stairs. He looks up at me as I take the first step.

"Did you see stars?" he asks.

I figure he means when I got my lights knocked out. "Did I ever."

He points out the window at the clear blue sky. "Don't twinkle right."

That one catches me. I think for a second, then climb the rest of the steps, but his words stick. For the first time since Barrett, the black eye aches less than the questions gnawing in my skull. At my door, I hear him mumble again. "Don't twinkle right."

I sit behind my desk. The ice is cold as a morgue slab, and just as useful for thinking. With a swollen eye and a few hours to kill, I try piecing things together. But nothing makes sense. Evelyn's inheritance, Barrett's little game, Clarence's fiddling with the sky.

Might be good to see what Evelyn thinks of her brother's apartment getting blown up. Normally, I'd call. But she's the bonus rate client. Clients like them, I visit in person. A little surprise.

I pull that gadget out of my pocket, light flashing off it. Bet Evelyn would like to get her hands on this. That fortune teller told me it was the key, something to do with reality. Well, Evelyn's not getting her little reality gadget, not just yet. I might need it as a bargaining chip. I lock it in the desk drawer.

1324 Winder Street, Springwells

Evelyn's Detroit neighborhood's the kind where every chimney smells like yesterday's stew, and every husband hides a flask behind *War and Peace*. Right on the edge, a razor that only needs one slip. Can't blame them for being scared. Middle class today, soup kitchen tomorrow. A streetcar rattles past like it's got somewhere better to be.

The sunset's a burning spill of gasoline. I turn onto Winder Street with the engine idling, eyes on the house numbers. I stop. Evelyn steps out, flanked by a couple of goons. One of them's Pinky, the same charmer that gave me the shiner this morning. She looks about as happy as a nun at a stag party. They shove her into a black DeSoto and peel out. I stay put till they're gone, just another parked car. Then I follow.

Springwells Street. West Jefferson. Corktown. Downtown. That DeSoto cuts through traffic like a knife.

I lose them at a streetcar crossing. An eternity before the intersection clears.

I gun the engine. Pass a truck. Corner by corner, traffic signals blinking past. Then I'm back on their tail.

They swing into a shuttered warehouse, right on the river. So close to Canada I can smell the rye fermenting. The only business here is booze and bodies. I don't like it one bit. I could use some backup. A can opener, in case I get into a tight spot.

I cruise to the next block, park next to a phone booth under a flickering streetlight. Digging through my trouser pockets, I come up with a nickel. Time to call a friend.

Former Great Lakes Grain & Storage Warehouse, Eastside Waterfront

Night drops fast, like a brick out of a third-story window.

The warehouse is a real beauty, if you've got a taste for cobwebs and crime scenes. Nice spot to ditch a body. You don't stumble into a place like this; you get brought here.

It's fenced off, but I don't look twice at the main entrance. The thug at the gate has a heater under his coat the size of a cannon. Around the corner, there's a hole in the fence just big enough for bad decisions. I slip through.

Inside smells like booze, mildew, and stolen freight. Hulks of old grain hoppers and conveyors slumber in the gloom. Sleeping giants I don't want to wake. The dark doesn't hide me, it sizes me up.

There's a clang up ahead. I freeze. Another, then quiet. Might be the building settling. Might be some goon banging his piece against an oil drum just to hear it ring.

Lots of traffic in a place like this after dark. Mostly booze from across the river, and mostly men who'd solve a problem like me with bullets instead of questions. I'm chasing Evelyn into a place that wouldn't bother burying me.

Cigarette smoke dances in the shadows. I catch the snap of cards hitting a table, one after another. Some hired gorilla playing solitaire until trouble shows up.

A hallway veers into the gloom, damp and narrow, and I'm fool enough to step in. I'm halfway down when a door opens. I flatten into an alcove, watch a slab of muscle lumber past.

My pal Pinky. Wouldn't mind paying him back for my black eye. He disappears into the murk.

The room he left's still lit, a pale rectangle bleeding under the door. After a few heartbeats, I step in close and put my ear to the wood.

Two voices. A man and a woman. I know them both.

Barrett.

And Evelyn.

I draw my .38, twist the knob, and kick the door wide.

Evelyn Daltry, lashed to a chair. Fear in her eyes.

"Glad you joined us, Malone." Barrett's standing with a pistol pointed at her chest. "Have a seat."

I could fill Barrett with holes.

But he'd take Evelyn with him on the way out.

The pause costs me. A paw lands on my shoulder. Pinky's back.

I twist the .38 toward his gut. He clamps my wrist, bones grinding. I squeeze, but he's already shoved my barrel skyward.

Bang! Plaster dust rains from the ceiling.

He wrenches the gun free and pops me one across the jaw. I drop into a chair. When I look up, Barrett's got his pistol on my nose, and Pinky's tying me tight.

"Should've had you killed two years ago," Barrett says.

"Do it now," I tell him. "Maybe you'll get it right this time."

He glances at Pinky.

Pinky cuffs the side of my head hard enough I see stars.

"Didn't take long to figure out who hired you," Barrett says. "Seems we share a client. Evelyn wanted me to handle her brother but didn't like it when I came for my fee. She thought you might scare me off." He laughs. It's cold and humorless.

I don't trust Barrett farther than I could throw him. But one glance at Evelyn, sniffling, bound, and looking anywhere but my way, tells me he's not lying. She played me from the start. Thanks to her, we're squeezed between Barrett's gun and Pinky's muscle. And there's no room for luck.

Barrett waves his pistol at Evelyn. "What'd you think, sweetheart? That you could get me arrested? That was a stupid move. I *own* this city. We had a deal. I handle Clarence, you tell me when the weather goes haywire."

He prowls back and forth. "I don't need you for this, lady. I'll do it myself. Where's the correlator? Talk."

"I told you!" Her voice cracks. "Clarence kept it with him all the time. And you blew up his apartment."

Barrett whirls on Pinky. "What did you dig up in Flammarion's flat?"

"We tore the joint apart, boss." Pinky scratches his neck. "No correl—correl . . ."

Barrett's face goes red, veins throbbing like they're about to burst. "Correlator, Pinky! Perceptual correlator!"

Evelyn sniffles, steadying herself. "If it wasn't in his home, then it has to be in Lodi."

No clue what a correlator is, but my money says I've got it locked in the desk drawer in my office. I feel like a grifter holding all the aces.

Barrett growls like a rabid dog. "If I want something done right, I've gotta do it myself. I'll check Lodi. If I don't find it, sweetheart, it's curtains for you."

Then his eyes cut to me. "And it's curtains for you either way, Malone."

Barrett's wingtips echo down the hall, and with the slam of the door, he's gone.

I catch Evelyn's eye. She looks away. I'd feel sorry too, if I got us into this mess. I got a few words for her. But now's not the time for a cozy conversation. Not with Pinky's eyes flicking back and forth between us.

He mumbles to himself as he lights his next cigarette off the butt of his last. Every twitch, every grumble is a loaded spring ready to snap.

It's a relief when something in the corner grabs his attention. He stands, charges, reaches behind a shipping crate. Closes his fingers around something small and wriggling. A squeak tells me it's alive.

"A little rat! I think I'll name it . . . Evelyn." He pets its head, then jabs it at me. Its claws scratch my cheek.

The rat bites, and Pinky bleeds. Serves him right. But Pinky hardly flinches. Then he grumbles, low and menacing. "Bad, Evelyn. Bad!"

He squeezes, and there's a sickening crunch. Warm blood hits my face.

Pinky frowns at the dead rat. "Lesson learned, right? Lesson learned . . ." His words degenerate into gibberish. The rat falls from his hands like a broken toy. I've got a hunch we might be his next playthings.

He finds his cigarette pack, but it's empty. He growls and crushes it with his blood-smeared hand.

"Don't go anywhere. I'll be back." He slams the door, turns the key. No knob on the inside. Even if my hands were free, we're not leaving. But I'm counting my blessings. With Pinky out, the air smells fresher already.

Evelyn examines my black eye. "You're hurt."

I tilt my head at the door. "A gift from our babysitter."

"I should apologize for getting you into this—"

"We got bigger fish to fry. Tell me what Barrett's looking for."

She closes her blue eyes, composes herself with a long breath. "We have been visited by time travelers. People from the future."

The way she says it, you'd think she was ordering coffee. The rope on my right wrist has some slack. I work it while she talks. "The future?"

She nods. "I can't explain it, not fully. But something they did in the past caused the stars to vanish."

I can brush that knot with my fingertip, pick at it with my nail. She's talking crazy, but it's crazy enough to make sense. "But the stars aren't gone."

"They only *appear* to be present. During the Civil War, my ancestors assembled a steel scaffold, something to alter perception and hide the absence of the sky."

The stereocard I viewed in Clarence's flat. *A web of girders and steel ribs, high enough to reach the clouds.*

"The scaffold is in a constant state of disrepair," she continues. "Perception and reality fall out of alignment. The stars blink in and out. The weather becomes unpredictable. Clarence maintained the system, kept it working despite its shortcomings. He replaced the light bulbs the system used to remember where the stars were supposed to be."

"Yeah. Okay. So what's the correlator? The thing Barrett wants." Pinky did a sloppy job on that knot. I'll have my right arm free in no time.

"By altering perception, the scaffold hides itself quite well. The perceptual correlator bypasses that illusion. I hired you to find it. I need it to keep the scaffold aligned. So does Mr. Barrett. If we can't find it, perception and reality will slip further apart."

I never expected I'd get a philosophy lecture in an abandoned Detroit waterfront warehouse. Most of what she says sails right over my head. But I catch her drift. That reality gadget matters.

"Just one thing I don't get. You hired Barrett to rub out Clarence. Why?"

Her eyes turn dark. "For four generations, money, power, and the secret of the sky have been passed from father to first-born son. And for four generations, every woman in my family receives nothing. No inheritance. I will not be looked over while my brother becomes the lord of the sky. Women have the right to vote, in case you haven't noticed, Mr. Malone. From now on, it's a woman's world."

A key grinds in the lock. The door opens. Pinky's back, a crooked cigarette hanging from his lips, every breath rattling like a cold diesel engine.

"Aw, poor Evelyn." He looms over her, raking her hair with his fingers, rough and unkind, a parody of affection. "The boss called from Lodi. Said he couldn't find no correlator."

He counts her fingers like he's inspecting machinery, slow and deliberate. "Eight, nine, ten. Let's start with this one." His hand clamps down on her slender finger like a vice. He bends it back, testing and twisting.

"No. Please, no!" Her voice goes shrill.

I've almost got the knot in the rope, but watching Pinky lean on Evelyn is tying a new knot in my gut. Never could stand to see a woman get worked over. Doesn't matter she played me. Doesn't matter at all.

"Talk, and you keep your pretty little finger. Stall, and I snap it off,"—it's bent back so far it don't look natural—"and then another, and another."

"I—I don't know where it is! I don't—"

Crack! Evelyn screams.

"She doesn't have it, you stupid ape. I do."

He turns to me with a sadistic scowl.

I give him the same scowl back. Then I give him my right fist—straight to his jaw.

His eyes flare to coals.

He lunges, and I twist just in time. His fist cuts the air where my face was a heartbeat ago.

My left hand's still tied to the chair. Works for me. I swing the chair low, hard, catching the monster under the knees.

The guy's built for pain. He hits the floor and rolls like he landed on a bed of feathers. He's at me before I can heft the chair again.

A punch catches me in the ribs. I suck wind and double over. Then a blow to my head. White sparks.

The floor comes up fast. I'm flat on my back. Pinky's weight pins me down.

I'm looking up the barrel of my own revolver.

Behind it—Pinky's cold glare.

"Big hero, huh? Bet you don't feel so big now." He pulls back the hammer with a click, hard and final.

I swallow hard. Case closed. Early retirement courtesy of a bullet to the skull.

A shout outside the room, then the sharp crack of gunfire.

Pinky turns, just enough. It's the opportunity of a lifetime.

I swing my fist with everything I've got. One clean shot to that slab of cartilage he calls a nose.

Blam! His shot goes wild.

"Freeze!"

Music to my ears. Standing in the door is Vinnie Calluto, badge out and heater leveled. Another flatfoot at his elbow.

My blow knocked Pinky out cold. Takes both officers to pull the ox off me.

I glance down. There's a clean hole in the floor. Missed me by an inch. Might as well have been a mile.

The flatfoot unties Evelyn, her little finger hanging crooked.

"Got your call." Vinnie cinches the cuffs on Pinky's dead-weight arms. "Thought I'd join the party."

I scoop up my revolver. "You didn't miss much. This brute's a lousy hostess."

Rural Lodi Township

Nice day for a drive. Clear blue sky, been that way for days. I park behind Evelyn Daltry's Ford Tudor and kill the engine.

The shed was ugly when I came here at night. Daylight and sunshine doesn't do it any favors, just shows off every sag, crack, and missing board. Might've been nice seventy years ago. Bet she's got some home improvements in mind with that inheritance coming.

Evelyn meets me at the door, cool as bourbon on the rocks. The lady's a criminal. Paid Barrett to ice her own brother. But that's the kind of woman I like. The kind who smells a raw deal and does something about it. She's a modern woman, Detroit steel in a skirt.

"Didn't expect to hear from you until parole." My way of asking how she dodged the charges.

"Did you really think I'd face prison, Mr. Malone?" She's got the cold blue eyes of a killer. "No one in the Detroit Police Department is enthusiastic about opening a closed suicide case, not when the only new evidence is hearsay."

Conspiracy to commit murder and accessory before the fact. Charges never even filed. She walks and so does Barrett. That's the way this city works.

"I knew hiring you was the right thing to do," she says. "If you had succeeded in pinning my brother's murder on Mr. Barrett, I would've won. But you didn't, and I still won. You expose Mr. Barrett's scheme to the city."

Barrett's angle. That's the one thing that doesn't click. "So how was Barrett skimming his cut?"

"When the system falls out of alignment, the weather turns bad. Barrett wanted advance notice so he could shift contracts, avoid blame, and profit from catastrophe. But after Clarence was dead, Barrett wanted more. He wanted me to delay correcting the drift, let the error accumulate, let the city suffer longer, so he could maximize his profits. And that, I would not do. Now that you've exposed him, City Hall has him on a tight leash."

This dame wasn't just running the sky; she was running the city.

"However, there is one fact that can't be denied. I never planned on being kidnapped and tortured." She holds up a hand with her finger in a splint. "You saved me, and for that, I thank you."

I couldn't sit there and watch him work her over, client or not. No man could. "My fee includes protection. All part of the package."

"Is that monster in prison?"

Assault. Menacing. Unlawful restraint. Piotr "Pinky" Zieliński was looking at five to ten at the Wayne County Jail. Life if they could've pinned Clarence's murder on him.

I deliver the bad news. "No warrant. Judge didn't even pretend to think about it."

She goes still, just for a beat. Time to change the subject.

"So. You're . . . running the sky?" I wave my hand around, at nothing, at the whole world.

"Mr. Barrett made quite a mess of this facility," she says, nodding at the shed behind her. "Restoring it to order has taken considerable effort. But there's very little I can do without the perceptual correlator. Did you . . . ?"

I fish it from my pocket, hold it out. Sunlight skips off it like a bright new day.

Her breath catches. "You really did find it!" She takes it slow, like it's something sacred, turning it over with care.

"Found it in your brother's flat. Don't ask me how Pinky missed it."

She smiles, like she's in on a joke I'll never get. "It has a way of being found by the right person."

"Not in my world." In my world, evidence sits on the cracked pavement where it's left. I find it, or I don't. That's it.

"But, Mr. Malone! This is a very powerful device, I can assure you." She stops, eyes narrowing, gauging me. "Perhaps I should show you what it can do."

That gadget pops open with a crisp chirp. She pokes at its glowing buttons. She knows its secrets. Then she turns to look behind the shed.

I expect leafless trees waiting for warmer weather. Instead, the day tilts. Light goes funny, the air ripples like heat over blacktop. Then the sky bends. Stretches, folds in on itself, and lays out flat. It's still blue, but it's no sky. It's a wall—or something like it. A boundary between here and somewhere else.

I've seen airplanes take to the clouds, a flu that empties whole houses overnight, rum runners who'd fill you with lead without a second thought, all of it packed into the same crooked city. But I've never seen nothing like this.

While I stand there staring, wondering if Pinky's blows cracked my head one too many times, Evelyn waltzes out of the shed, cool as ice, carrying a box of light bulbs.

"The shed was built in Lodi for a reason, Mr. Malone. It's a perceptual intersection point. The only place where one might access the scaffold that hides the absence of a sky."

She makes for that . . . boundary along a snow-packed trail, and I follow. She mounts a ramp to a platform and pivots to face me. Behind her, the faint outline of a door.

"Where's that go?"

"A maintenance corridor. Clarence used it to adjust the tracks that align perception." She holds up a light bulb. "And replace the reference points for the stars."

She touches the gadget to the door. A small panel glows and dims, glows and dims. Like a heartbeat.

Then she says, "Mr. Malone, would you care to see beyond the firmament?"

I feel the pull. I can only guess what's beyond that door. The gears that move the Sun. The wires that light the stars. The machinery that makes the world go round. I could look, see how it all works, take just one peek behind the curtain . . .

Or I could keep the world I've got. It might be broken. It might be corrupt. But it's mine.

"No thanks, lady. You can have it."

She nods. She had me figured before she even asked.

I turn away. Pretend I don't hear the door open. Pretend there's no low-frequency thrum, that the hair on my arms isn't standing up. Pretend the air isn't cooler near the door, like something beyond it remembers a different sky.

Then the door clicks shut. The light slides and shifts. And my world's back.

No boundary—just winter. Cold and heartless.

I slog through the slush to my sedan, turn the engine over.

Detroit lies ahead. Factories coughing smoke and speakeasies pouring bourbon. Breadlines for the hungry, longer by the day. Cold coffee, crooked suits, and a city that doesn't care if I never make it home.

But I'll find a bum on the stairs. I'll have a seat next to him. And I'll let him tell me about the stars.

THE LIGHTS IN OUR KEEPING

By Taryn Skipper

The stars went dark.
The seeds of dreams no longer gleaming.
Dead.

The stars burned out.
Unkindled embers of potential,
Snuffed.

The stars moved on.
Celestial ancestors who guide us,
Gone.

So our heads bow in miserable mourning.
But we'll live by the lights in our keeping.

The stars blaze bright,
In the campfires and under the hearth,
Glowing.

The stars so close,
In the eyes of our lovers and friends,
Dancing.

The stars below,
In the wishes undimmed by the dawn,
Sparkling.

So our heads bow in thanks for the morning.
And we live by the light of the sun.

Date: 2590-04-11 06:44:27 PRT
From: Green Kinsha
To: Anachronauts
Subject: What were they thinking?
Re: When the Light Goes Out

If the Malone stories are real, we need to send someone through that door to see how they manage it.

It’s not a Malone story, Flopdoodle, but if you’re in the mood for a good sniffle, this account is a real tearjerker.

Don’t say I didn’t warn you.

WHEN THE LIGHT GOES OUT

By Esther Davis

"She doesn't have a headstone."

"Honey, come inside," Cal said, a tinge of nervousness in his voice.

Jen didn't move, just continued staring up at the dark, lifeless sky, the lit vanilla-scented candle that she cupped in her palms one of the sole sources of light. "She doesn't have a headstone," she repeated, her voice dull.

"Jen dear, the Fog will be here soon."

The Fog. The other source of light. Already its tendrils waved on the horizon, a beautiful but deadly radioactive blue. Faint, yet growing.

Jen didn't move.

Cal inhaled sharply, then forced himself into a brisk march, leaving the relative safety of the doorway, and grasped his wife by the upper arm. "Come in. We can talk about this inside."

Jen made no move to stand from her seat on the overturned refrigerator. But she did finally look down from the black sky. "They each twinkled out, one by one. The stars. The children."

"Inside, Jen. Now!"

Cal's wife let him pull her to her feet, though Jen walked painfully slow, hardly more than a shuffle, as Cal practically dragged her into the house.

Once inside, Cal closed the door firmly, secured the three bolts, and taped the cardboard sheet back over the seams. No drafts. No irradiated fog. He was keeping *that* out. And what little he had left would stay in.

He felt stupid as he gave the painter's tape an extra rub to work out any wrinkles and secure it over the cardboard. This couldn't be making a difference. It was *cardboard* for crying out loud, not some lead-lined industrial sealant. And no one even knew if it was the Fog that caused all the deaths. But one of the surviving community members had recommended it. Had sworn by it. And, well . . . Cal wanted to believe that it did *something*. He had to protect his family. Somehow.

Jen wandered towards their upright piano. She set her candle on top, next to the unbeating metronome and a pair of cycling trophies. The candle saturated the room with a soft light while at the same time filling it with heavy shadows. That stupid cardboard covered the windows too, just like it did the door. So even if there were still starlight or moonlight or sunlight out there, it couldn't have gotten in.

Across the room, Cal watched his wife sit on the piano bench, where she stared blankly at the keys for a while. Then she touched the keys. Not playing any, simply gliding her fingers along the black and white key tops until her finger came to rest on a single black key. Jen let her finger sink, the note echoing through the boarded-up house.

"She could have had piano lessons," Jen said, her voice now a whisper. "And a pet dog, and friends at school. She could've had sleepovers and a favorite color. Skinned knees from running too fast, a bike that was just a little too big, a dress with popsicle stains on it . . . she could've had a million and one more bedtime stories, each paired with a hug and a kiss goodnight." Jen's chest rose and fell with a silent, heavy breath.

"Jen, I . . ." Cal stepped towards her, looking for words of comfort, but none came.

"But now . . ." Jen lifted her gaze and met Cal's eyes. The soft candlelight glistened on her tears. "But now she doesn't even have a headstone."

As the night drew on—or at least, what Cal's wind-up watch deemed night—Jen eventually wandered off to bed. Cal stayed up a bit longer, waiting in his office until Evan's weekly message came.

Cal scanned through his Morse code cheat sheet, grateful for Evan's slow pace that let him find each individual letter and scribble it down before Evan sent the next one. At least the oil lamp flickering on the desk gave better writing light than candles did.

They'd hijacked the old telegraph line a few months ago, running extra wires into their spare bedroom, back when Cal reluctantly agreed to become the local community's Receiver. *You'll pick up on Morse code eventually,* Evan had said. *It'll become muscle memory.*

Cal doubted that.

It was rather an impressive set-up though, considering it had only been, what, a year since the Cataclysm? No, it had been a few months less than that even. They'd been so busy surviving, tending to their physical needs, that they'd forgotten about other things. Things like headstones.

More beeping interrupted his thoughts, and Cal hurried back to transcribing.

1 S-U-R-V-I-V-O-R S-T-O-P

Another? That was always a pleasant surprise. It had been a while since Evan's crew had picked someone up. But only one? Cal was impressed they'd managed to survive this long on their own.

The messages came from the mostly abandoned capital. It was dangerous, but it was the only place all these old telegraph lines connected. The salvagers stopped there occasionally when they wanted to update the handful of small communities that had gathered across the valley after the Cataclysm. That way, they knew who needed supplies most, or could warn a community when new arrivals were coming, as it sounded like now.

Cal kept transcribing as the electronic beeps came through.

Y-O-U-N-G G-I-R-L M-A-Y-B-E 3 O-R 4 Y-E-A-R-S O-L-D S-T-O-P

Cal's *mind* came to a full stop. *A child?* His pencil dropped with a clatter. All the survivors had been adults so far. *All* of them, in every community, in every known corner of the world that they had even the slightest contact with. As far as they could tell, every single person under the age of seventeen had died the instant the Cataclysm struck, as if slain by a supernatural force.

A child?

The beeps were still coming in. Cal cursed, worried he'd missed too many already. He snatched up his pencil to resume transcribing.

-Z-V-O-U-S T-U-E-S-D-A-Y A-T T-A-B-E-R-N-A-C-L-E S-T-O-P

Rendezvous? Probably. Evan always managed to pick long words. It baffled Cal, who preplanned each reply to optimize for the least number of letters possible.

R-E-Q-U-E-S-T-I-N-G C-O-N-F-I-R-M-A-T-I-O-N S-T-O-P

The beeping went silent, waiting for Cal's response. He quickly ran through a mental checklist, making sure he could gather everything in time for a Tuesday meetup. The regular excess supplies to trade, of course. They already had a community gathering tomorrow, so he could take care of updating everyone then. And the bike trailer's axle had been repaired, so that was good to go, too. When there was a refugee, he usually towed an extra bike in the trailer alongside the supplies. Then the new arrival could bike back home with him. But if she were a child . . .

His mind flashed to the child tag-along bike, more like a passenger trailer than a bicycle really, that his daughter Millie used to ride in. Before she died.

Oh, Millie.

A lump formed in Cal's throat. He took a steadying breath. It was all right. They could use her tag-along bike. Millie would have been happy to share.

Cal scanned over his reference sheet and muttered the string of dashes and dots to himself as he clicked back a reply.

O-K

🚲 🚲 🚲

"I apologize for such short notice," Cal said from the stand, "but I need the trailer loaded today with any trades. Evan must have sent an advanced party ahead of his telegram. They'll be there by Tuesday, which means I need to leave tomorrow."

The gathered faces nodded back tiredly. The ninety-something-year-old widow, Cindy White, who now lived with the Smiths. The Lewises' nineteen-year-old son, Elliot, whose younger brother had died in the Cataclysm. Mr. Bartkowski, with his dark mustache and ever-serious face.

The meeting room was lined with small candles, cheap ones that they'd scavenged from the abandoned home goods stores. The candles gave minimal light and filled the air with an odd mingling of scents, but they did the trick. A couple of months ago, they'd voted as a community to save batteries for things like their biking head lamps. Not that there was any way to enforce that vote, but everyone at least pretended to follow it when they came to community meetings.

Each of the thirteen families had a representative for the community meeting. Except the Joneses, who were "sick" again and said to "just drop off a page with minutes." And the Webers. Harold had likely forgotten and was tinkering with his hydroponics and UV light set-up, which Cal preferred he do anyway. If Harold could actually figure out how to grow something edible, the community could finally eat some fresh greens again. Eating the same mushy canned carrots and peas every night was getting old.

The city used to have hundreds of families. No, thousands. But now . . . they were gone.

That night—the night the stars went out—that's when most of them died. Instantaneously. Cleanly. All in unison, with no explanation.

Others, though, vanished. Literally. Completely missing, without a trace. People claimed that they watched their loved ones snap out of existence, in a sickening glitch of reality. At first, Cal hadn't believed them. In those chaotic first weeks, it had been hard to separate the distraught mourners from . . . the other group. The ones who went insane. The Crazies. They were fractured souls, clinging to life. Within a few months, they all eventually died too.

Cal couldn't help but feel a small sense of pride as he looked over their surviving community. So many others had gone ill, gone mad, gone quiet. Yet these few survivors had lasted. Not untouched, of course, but resilient. What made them different was anyone's guess, but somehow it had been apparent from Day One that these few would be okay while everyone else was . . . not.

Maybe we're the crazy ones, Cal thought. *When the stars and moon and even the sun blink out of existence, we somehow refused to die. That's not natural. That's not right.*

Yet here they were, united together in a ghost town of the suburbs. Scrounging up cans of food, stray batteries, used clothing, and things to burn from the homes of the dead. Living off bones. Yet living, somehow.

Living.

"Any new friends joining us?" Cindy White asked. "Preferably a handyman, or maybe a doctor? Sorry, no offense to your perfectly useless law degree, Mark." She smirked at Mr. Bartkowski, waiting for a reaction.

Mr. Bartkowski didn't even grunt.

Cal found himself freezing up. *Yes, actually,* he needed to say. *I need someone else to bike out with me so we can bring back a child.*

But he didn't say that.

Cal didn't want to lie. He couldn't *afford* to lie with a community this small, reliant on each other for mere survival. But his throat closed up. His heart began to race. His whole body seemed determined not to speak. How could he explain the unexplainable? No children had survived the Cataclysm. They all knew it. Or at least they thought they did.

So instead, Cal just shook his head.

"No one? Oh well. At least there won't be another helpless mouth to feed." Cindy White laughed.

She was joking. Cal knew she was joking. But it still made him want to throw up.

🚲 🚲 🚲

Cal left the supply trailer just inside the front door of Town Hall, where families could come back later in the day to load it up with their trades. As the group left the battered town hall and biked off to their separate homes, battery-powered beams of light illuminating each biker's path, Cal realized he'd made an even bigger mistake. That little head shake, leaving out a little detail about a *child* coming back with them, meant no one could volunteer to pull the child's tag-along bike back home.

No one except Jen.

He couldn't quite place why he felt so much dread at asking for Jen's help. His wife was plenty fine with cycling. She'd been a star cyclist in college. Though, she hadn't ridden much since becoming a mother, and not at all since . . . Not since Millie died almost a year ago.

"Jen, dear?" Cal pushed open the door to the nursery to find his wife sitting in the cushioned rocking chair. Cal cringed when he saw Millie's old night light plugged into one of their few battery packs that stored their precious electricity. The night light cast a galaxy of stars across the crowded room. Crocheted scarves piled on the daybed. Colorful balls of yarn lay scattered across the floor. Half-finished projects hung over the sides of the empty crib.

But Jen wasn't crocheting anything at the moment. Instead, she held Millie's plush elephant with both hands, staring at it longingly. A pile of used tissues lay on the floor beside her. Tissues. Those were in short supply, too.

Cal took a breath, trying to push away his frustration at the wastefulness. And . . . other feelings he didn't quite want to name. "I'm leaving for our usual meet-up point tomorrow," he said carefully.

Jen nodded, her eyes not leaving the baby toy.

"And I'm going to need your help, pedaling an extra bike," he said.

Cal waited. Waited for Jen to react to the unusual request, to ask why. His heart pounded, panicked. What would he say when she asked?

He wanted to tell her. He wanted to speak of the child. He wanted to ask her thoughts, to hear her heart. But instead, a tense numbness hung in the air.

Finally, Jen gave another slight nod. That was it. No questioning, not accusations. Just a nod. Then she turned, the slightest smile teasing at her lips. "A bike ride sounds fun."

A smile?

In some ways, Cal's tension subsided. It had been too long since he'd seen her smile, even a small one like that. Yet at the same time, a knot continued twisting in his stomach. He stepped forward, took her hand, and gave it a squeeze. "I love you," he whispered. And then he left the room, unable to say more.

🚲 🚲 🚲

It wasn't a sharp wind, but it wasn't a refreshing breeze either. The whistling gusts were somewhere in the lonely middle, empty, a plain and forlorn cold.

Cal rode ahead, towing the loaded trailer. He'd hidden Millie's old tag-along bike at the bottom, careful to conceal it with the pile of supplies that the community had donated. His headlamp beam pierced through the darkness, guiding him along the abandoned freeway as he navigated through the motionless, ash-coated cars. Jen rode just a short distance behind, the beam of her own headlamp bouncing next to his.

The Fog hadn't come the last two days of travel, thankfully. But Cal still kept a close eye on the horizon in case they needed to find quick shelter. He'd made this trip enough times that he knew of a house every few miles that would work in a pinch. This time, though, they'd been able to use his two normal waypoint houses.

From the freeway, he could easily pretend that the miles and miles of suburbia stretching around him were simply sleeping, experiencing something as mundane as a power outage, instead of empty home after empty home. Wilted gardens. Barren trees.

The hardest to ignore was the silence. Cal hadn't realized how accustomed he was to the cacophony of humanity—cars and trains and planes constantly roaring by—until it was gone. Nowadays, he occasionally heard birds. But they didn't sing, just shrieked to chase off fellow fowl that got too close. And those were few and far between. Not many insects were left either, though sometimes a sudden, solitary chirp from a cricket startled him. Right now, he could only hear the rolling of wheels on pavement from two bikes and a trailer. And the wind.

Cal glanced over his shoulder as he pedaled toward the next freeway exit, partly out of habit from the days when he used to drive this road, partly to make sure Jen noticed his new direction. He coasted downhill, past a lifeless traffic light, and onto what used to be a major city road.

"Two more miles!" he called over his shoulder. "Evan's crew maybe even beat us there."

Cal heard gears clicking and, in a moment, Jen had pedaled up beside him. No abandoned vehicles clogged the middle turning lane, so they could easily ride side by side now.

When they first left home, Jen had approached the bike gingerly. But with each passing mile, Cal watched something familiar start to emerge in her. It started with a determination in her posture, and then morphed into—did he dare call it *excitement* on her face?

At one particularly steep incline, his wife had suddenly whizzed past, both panting and grinning at the same time as her bike zoomed uphill. When he finally limped to the top, Cal found that she had dismounted her bike and flopped down on crunchy, dead lawn.

And she was laughing.

"Boy, am I out of shape," Jen gasped through deep breaths.

"You're . . . kidding . . . right?" Cal panted. "You should be . . . the one . . . pulling the trailer . . ."

Maybe bringing her on this ride had been a good idea after all.

Sure, his wife still fell back into moments of somberness. Yes, he still held her at night while she cried. But those moments of levity, those smiles that were becoming less and less fleeting. And it made something inside Cal feel lighter.

"I think I can see it," Jen said, pulling his mind back to the present. "Is that the spire up there?"

They remounted their bikes again. The road stretched out in silence for a while. As the tabernacle spire came more fully into view, Cal felt his courage grow. Maybe he could say something now. Maybe he could tell her about the little girl waiting for them. "Jen," he said, "you never asked why I had you come along."

"I know why," she said.

Cal started, confused. "You do?"

"You're trying to help, like you always do," she said. "I've been miserable sitting in that house for months and months. You probably figured if I got some—well, not quite sunshine, but some exercise at least—then I'd stop being such a grump."

Cal found himself smiling back. A grump? That was more than an understatement. But before he could respond, she spoke again, this time quieter.

"I miss her, Cal. I miss her so much."

There it was again. The sadness. But somehow, it didn't feel so disheartening as it would have just a few days ago. "I know. It's okay." Cal felt something start forming in his throat as he said it. "I miss her too."

When they arrived at the tabernacle, everything was still closed up with no signs of life. Odd. Cal had been convinced that Evan would get here first since he and Jen had such a late start—even when Jen's pace forced him to pedal faster than usual. A quick glance at his wind-up watch confirmed that suspicion. Evan's crew should have arrived at the Tabernacle at least an hour ago.

Once they parked their bicycles, Cal and Jen quickly switched their headlamps for an oil lamp that Cal set in the tabernacle window. The two rested on a chilled stone bench just outside the tabernacle doors, staring out across the quiet, shadow-cast cityscape.

Jen rested her head on Cal's shoulder, letting herself sink into him. Her warmth was comforting. Calming. Cal could feel himself relaxing, too.

"The courthouse is a few blocks that way, isn't it?" Jen asked. "The one where we adopted Millie?"

Cal squeezed his wife's hand. "Yep, that's the one."

The minutes stretched into hours with still no sign of Evan's crew. Jen helped Cal dig out a dinner from their food supplies—two cans of chili and a can of green beans, cold, since they were both too exhausted to bother with a fire, along with some slices of flat bread Jen had made before the trip.

Still, no one arrived.

"You look worried," Jen said.

Cal brushed off his pants and started for the bikes. "Let's take everything inside and get some sleep."

Cal dreamed of the Cataclysm, the night when the entirety of Earth shook and the stars fell. The morning that the sun didn't rise. The day when Cal's entire world shattered.

He had just stepped into their bedroom to grab his wallet when reality seemed to *glitch*. For a heartbeat, his vision divided in two. A wave of nausea caused him to stumble forward. A single, clean, deafening crack split the very fabric of the world. The ground shook violently, and he fell to the ground amidst a cacophony of crashes and shattering.

And then every single source of light went black.

The darkness was all-consuming. Smothering. The panic of trying to find a source of light, *any* light, suffocated him anew.

The light switches did nothing. His phone wouldn't turn on. His solar-powered lantern had fallen out of the window and shattered. He remembered having a flashlight on his nightstand but only succeeded in knocking things over in the blinding darkness when he tried to find it.

All he could hear was Jen. Screaming. Wailing.

Cal's frantic hands finally closed around something small and metallic. His lighter? A few clicks later, he held a small flame in his hands. It was miniscule compared to the blanketing blackness, yet the relief at finally being able to see was overwhelming. Cal hurried across the house by its tiny light.

His wife sat in the darkness that now engulfed the living room, sobbing, Millie in her arms.

Their daughter, their joy, the brightest light in their once happy little world, lay unmoving, staring into empty nothingness.

🚲 🚲 🚲

Cal jolted awake, sweating, his breath coming out in quick gasps. Then he heard a voice. His own voice, he realized, a panicked staccato between hyperventilating breaths. "The light. The light, Jen. It's gone out! The light's gone out!"

Jen was already awake, wrapping her arms around him. "It's okay, sweetheart. It's okay," she whispered. "See the oil lamp? See how there's light? It's not much, but it's there. It's real, sweetheart. It's real."

Cal leaned into Jen's grasp, letting her touch anchor him to reality. He took one shaky breath after another, trying to dismiss the nightmare. But how could he dismiss something that he still lived inside?

"What's the point?" Cal whispered. "Why do we even try?"

Jen pulled him in close. He felt her fingers running through his hair. "Try what, darling? Try what?"

"To live," he said, the words hardly louder than a breath. "What's the point anymore? The world's ended. Yet for some reason . . . for some reason we insist on continuing to cling to this lifeless hunk of rock floating in something colder and darker than space ever was. We're all obviously miserable. So why don't we all just give up?"

"You don't mean that, Cal," Jen whispered calmly.

"And what if I do?"

His wife's arms tightened around him. Her lips brushed a kiss just behind his ear. "Then I hope you'll let me stay close," she whispered. "So I can tell you the same things that you've told me for months. 'I love you.' 'I miss her too.' 'Just hold on one more day, dear. There's still light in this world.'"

He saw her then. All of her. The many interlocking threads that made up this woman he loved. He saw the spunky cyclist he'd dated so many years ago, who competed not for the trophies—though she had plenty of those—but because she loved the thrill of the ride. He saw the perfectionist of a newlywed wife, who fawned over him much more than he deserved, who tried to be everything, all at once, for everyone, who then crumpled into a mess of tears because her brownies didn't turn out just right.

He saw the hopeful, patient woman, the one who year after year turned up at everyone else's baby shower, all the while wondering if she'd ever have her own. Then he saw the glorious mother. His child's mother. Millie's mother. He saw her pouring every last ounce of her soul into caring for their precious miracle of a daughter.

And then he saw Jen. Here. Now. An incomplete tapestry made up of countless experiences, choices, and dreams, who had been suddenly torn down the middle. A woman whose life had unraveled in an instant, who had no one to turn to for help because everyone else was unraveling, too. Yet she woke up each day, untangling the chaos of unraveled threads and, in her own way, protecting what was left, until she was ready to start weaving anew. The design that emerged was different now, yes, but also in some ways the same. And in many ways, even more beautiful.

There, held in his wife's arms, for the first time since Millie died, Cal let himself cry.

🚲 🚲 🚲

Many hours later, after scattered bouts of sleep and with a faint throbbing behind his eyes, Cal only knew it was morning because his wind-up watch said it was so. That, and because Jen had mixed up some powdered milk to go alongside their cold cereal and canned peaches. She insisted they eat on the stand, overlooking the pews and stained glass windows. He realized that he was subconsciously waiting for the sunrise to shine through the colored glass. *Sunrises don't exist in this world*, he reminded himself. *Not anymore.*

Someone knocked on the tabernacle door.

Both Cal and Jen jumped. The heavy doors creaked open, and light poured through the entryway.

"I guess my Ma was right," said a gravelly voice. "Everything *is* slower when you've got a kid around. Sorry to keep you waiting, Cal."

Evan entered the tabernacle, followed by two younger men carrying large boxes. The young men set down their loads and headed back outside. Evan, meanwhile, sauntered down the aisle.

"I was hoping you'd bring the Missus." Evan tipped his non-existent hat towards Jen. "Really, I'm sorry for the wait. Thought the boys would make it here long before me, but I caught up to them when they were still a day's journey out."

Jen gripped Cal's arm just above the elbow, her fingernails beginning to dig in. "Calvin, what is going on?"

Cal followed Jen's gaze to where one of the young men had entered the tabernacle. Instead of carrying a box, he led a little girl by the hand. The girl, not even as tall as his waist, clutched to him with one hand and held a fluffy pink plush kitten to her chest with the other, all while scanning the room nervously.

Jen slapped a hand over her mouth to muffle a shriek as her other hand tightened into a death grip on Cal's arm. "They found a child?" Jen hissed in Cal's ear, incredulous. "Where? *How*? I thought they were all . . . all gone."

The girl was probably about three years old, as Evan had said. Her hair was shoulder-length, straight, dark, and a little messy. She wore a pink top and patterned blue pants, both a bit disheveled. Her hands, which were turning white from her tightening grip, were covered up and down in long red scabs.

Holding his breath, Cal turned just enough to see Jen's face. Tears were building in the corners of her eyes.

"She . . . She looks just like Millie," Jen whispered.

No, the girl looked nothing like Millie. But for some reason, Cal found his emotions agreeing.

Evan beckoned to them. Jen glanced towards Cal, hesitant. He tried to nod encouragingly even though his nerves tensed inside him. Jen did her best to wipe her eyes with her sleeve and then led the way down.

"Hello," Jen said, crouching down a few feet in front of the girl. "What's your name?"

The girl flinched, then stared back at Jen, frozen.

"It's okay," the young man whispered encouragingly. "She's a friend too."

Instead, the girl shook her head vigorously and then buried her face in her pink kitten.

Evan came up behind Cal and placed a hand on his shoulder. The man's smile was much softer now, more tired. "Pretty sure her name is Claire. We . . . we found her alone, obviously. I think she had someone helping her get food for a couple of months at least, but they were gone by the time we arrived. We're guessing it was one of the Crazies. Looks like he died in the house next door. The girl had an obscene pile of canned goods though and just as big a pile of empty cans she must have figured out how to open by herself."

Jen and the young man led Claire to sit on one of the pews where Jen tried reading from one of the picture books that Evan's crew handed her. Meanwhile, Cal followed Evan to the wagons to start sorting through trades.

Evan shared the latest news and rumors with Cal. More of the usual stuff, with most cities being completely empty, nuclear reactors that couldn't be contained, more evidence that complicated electronics just didn't work anymore, though any guess as to why was as good as the next. "Some guy claims the entire eastern half of Europe is missing, just straight up gone," Evan said. "As in, nothing's left but a gigantic crater straight to the Earth's core. Not sure if I believe that one though."

Cal kept stealing glances at Jen and the little girl. At one point, his wife was singing Claire songs and nursery rhymes. At another, they were sharing some flat bread and jam. Eventually the girl clambered onto Jen's lap and leaned forward to whisper something in her ear.

"Any idea what makes her so special?" Cal asked, nodding towards the little girl now curled up on Jen's lap.

"Do you mean your wife or the little?" Evan teased.

Cal smiled. "Oh, I already know about Jen."

Evan grew quiet for a moment before speaking. "I might, actually. While I sent everyone else ahead—and they were *supposed* to beat me here, mind you—I did some sleuthing around the girl's home. Dug through some documents, read through some journals, and . . ." The man paused, taking a deep breath, "this little girl is about thirty years old."

Cal snorted. "Sure, she is. And I'm living in an alternate dimension. What was it really?"

"No, I'm serious. She was born maybe a few years ago, but she was an embryo adoption, Cal. She was conceived in vitro, then frozen for twenty-seven years before her parents implanted her. So in a manner of speaking, she'd existed nearly as long as they had."

Cal realized his mouth had dropped open in shock. He left it hanging there a moment longer while his mind processed what Evan had said.

"She's still a kid, sure, but her essence has actually been around a lot longer. I don't know if you've ever looked into it, but with in-vitro—"

"I *know* how it works," Cal interrupted. "It's just . . . I don't understand. Is that . . . why? Why she survived? That still doesn't make sense. What about all the adults that died? What about the ones who disappeared?"

"Maybe it gave her the same odds as the rest of the survivors? An old soul, if you will. I don't know," Evan said, tossing his hands into the air. "Sorry, that's the best I've got for you. There's a lot in this world that doesn't make sense lately, and it's probably going to be a long time before we have answers. But what I do know is that she needs a ma and pa to look after her. If you're feeling up to it, that is."

Everything went still. Cal had known that question would come. He'd avoided it for days now, not wanting to confront it. He already *had* a daughter. She didn't need a replacement.

But Claire wouldn't replace Millie, he realized. She couldn't. Just like Cal and Jen couldn't replace Claire's parents. And the truth was, they didn't need to. They just needed to start where they were, adding whatever light they could to the world.

He gazed towards Jen, little Claire now asleep on her lap, a peace on her face that Cal hadn't seen in almost a year.

Cal's heart thumped as the hole in his world grew a tiny bit smaller. He smiled, then nodded. "Yes, we're ready," he said. "I think we need her, too."

END NOTE

Fortunately for my cortisol levels, one of the aides, the same one who got me the account, is studying Brukanaz for personal reasons (something about a TTRPG) and has come up with a fairly interesting theory to explain this. Take a look and see what you think.

EXTERNAL OBSERVATION REPORT

When the Immortals accidentally created Brukanaz, there were obviously a lot of issues. For starters, their abysmally poor power supply lacked the capacity to properly duplicate the Earth, which led to an entire chunk of the planet missing. But just as tragically, I think it was unable to properly replicate the complex neural signatures that, for lack of a better term, constitute "souls" of those living on it.

We know that Brukanaz splintered in 2040, but due to a slew of internal malfunctions, it glitched forward seventeen years to 2040. The year 2040 was when the people of Brukanaz experienced the Cataclysm and the Splinter officially appeared.

I posit that only a small percentage of souls existing on Earth before the original Anchor (2023) were properly replicated. The rest were either only partially replicated (the "Crazies" mentioned in the story) or were dead (or possibly vaporized) the instant the Cataclysm/splintering began. Additionally, anyone who was conceived in the gap between the first Anchor (2023) and the glitched second Anchor (2040) was also dead/ vaporized upon arrival.

There's likely a lot more going on across Brukanaz as well. More research is required.

Green Kinsha

Date: 2590-04-11 06:45:32 PRT
From: Ms. Six
To: Anachronauts
Subject: Delusions of Grandeur
Re: Birds Aren't Real

The audacity. Apparently living forever isn't enough of an ego boost for the Immortals. They've completely subjugated the populace of this splinter. This account shows the use of a new tech, wyrd-stones. I'm going to have to go time-side in this splinter (despite its dearth of tacos) to obtain one. Regardless, Ren could use one. Then the rest of us would know he at least HAS emotions.

Keep Gentor away from this. He'll screw it up for sure. It'll be another cosmic noodle fiasco.

BIRDS AREN'T REAL

By Boydell Bown

"I doubt your words," Limna whispered through a grin. Then glanced at Santh's forehead. "And, yet, I see your wyrd-stone."

Santh didn't hear her, dodging a pile of horse manure as they traipsed through the village, sloshing through the mud. The recent rain wasn't helping his mood. Master Brensson had not been around to spread hay yet, and the difficult path just added to the chaos in his head.

"Your story fits not your ways," his little sister continued quietly, her mouth running wild as a kitten in the forest. "If Jans wrought it alone, I'd believe the tale. His deeds oft go awry. But you? You revere the law, and this law is holy. Yet your wyrd-stone cries you speak truth. I wonder if you are no Santh, but some wight wearing his skin!"

Santh's wyrd-stone, embedded in the skin on his forehead, glowed dark, anxious orange, with flecks of red. But the color wasn't caused by the rain or the mud, or Limna's inane ramblings. Or even the fact that they were skipping Trade, wandering the village when he should be at the smithy, and she should be hunting. No, the blood-orange hue of worried confusion was caused by the unfathomable experience from yesterday, what he and Jans had seen in the woods.

"How could it be you slew—"

Santh spun abruptly on Limna.

"Stop!" he hissed, his wyrd-stone flashing a bright yellow of fear. "Do you desire the Doyen to hear?" Despite himself, he glanced at the Skyhall, floating above the village.

". . . all those cakes at yestereve's feast," Limna finished, changing her thought. She giggled nervously. "At fourteen seasons, you eat more than most men grown. Yet I will hold your secret close, and not make known your shame to the Doyen. I swear it."

Santh turned away from the giant, dark building. Shimmering black, with lines of silver, it was larger than the entire village, always hovering over the town like a great, evil dragon of legend. He knew exactly what Limna was really going to say. What she couldn't say out loud. That she didn't believe his story, couldn't believe what he and Jans had done, *what* they had *killed*. He almost didn't believe it himself.

He stepped out, continuing toward the lumber yard. Jans might be angry, might scream and yell at Santh for telling anyone what happened, even if it was just Limna. Jans always had the strongest emotions. But consulting him now was necessary. Jans could corroborate the tale. "I told you, we did not intend it," he said, responding to Limna's unspoken words. "It was but a misadventure."

Limna shook her head and scrambled to catch up. "But what of your talk of smoke and dyed twine—"

As one, the siblings skittered to a stop, short of the edge of a small hovel. Quickly, they scuttled back to hide behind the corner and peek through the crossed oak logs of the building's rough walls. Santh glanced at Limna. Her wyrd-stone, now a bright yellow, matched his own.

Down the center of the village moved a small group of four individuals. On the far side was the only one that Santh recognized. Master Brenfnor, the Hammer, Santh's own mentor of the forge. The Hammer's dour expression was darker than usual as he struggled through the muck to keep pace with the group. It didn't matter that he towered over most citizens of the village; compared to his current companions, he appeared short and ordinary. In front of him marched two hulking guards, inhumanly large, wearing striking black armour that seemed to consume the light around it. And in front of them, in impossibly perfect, pristine white, floated one of the gods.

A Doyen.

A Starkiller.

Santh cowered back, hoping the god didn't see. Didn't know. Didn't know what happened yesterday in the woods.

"Oh," whispered Limna, eyes wide. "I forget how fair they are."

Santh gasped quietly, fighting for air. With wide eyes, he stared through gaps in the wooden logs. The small parade clomped forward, the men making squishy sounds with each footfall. The Doyen, of course, made almost no noise, bright robes fluttering gently as she hovered above the ground, unconcerned with such pedestrian trivialities like walking.

A skittering sound above them drew Santh's attention, and he looked up. With a scratch of claws against wood, the head of a large, black raven, the size of a cat, poked over the wooden eaves of the roof.

Santh froze.

Limna turned to see what caught his attention. Eyes wide, she stared back at the bird. "Does it know," she said with the quietest of whispers, "what you wrought?"

Without turning, Santh silently slid his hand over his sister's mouth.

And all sound stopped.

The raven considered them with its giant, unnatural eyes. With quiet clicks, the bird tipped its head one way, then another, scrutinizing Santh and Limna.

The silence became deafening, heavy like a wool blanket. No sound of animals. No sound of steps in the mud.

No sound of steps.

Santh whipped his head back to the rough notch in the wall. The group had stopped, the guards looking around, and the Hammer scowling at the others in concern. The Doyen levitated in place, an arm's length in the air. Unlike Santh's master, her passive expression remained perfectly neutral. With a slow, precise movement, she turned and looked directly at the younglings' hiding place.

We are undone. The thought echoed through Santh's brain.

He'd been a small child when the Uprising failed, a few years after the Doyen arrived, after they'd broken the sky and killed the stars. A handful of uprisers had caused a distraction while others stabbed one of the gods and cut off his head, hoping to free their people. But the Uprising was pointless. The very Doyen they'd attacked attended their execution later that day, very alive, and very unharmed, head and all. The rebels were lined up, and in a split moment, power and thunder and light erupted from the fists of the guards. As the rebels died, the expression of the attending Doyen shifted from passive stares to emotions Santh couldn't understand. He hoped he never would understand. Those faces, the sight of the instant destruction of his fellow villagers, the sounds and smells, all of it still haunted Santh, years later.

Both guards standing in front of Master Brenfnor turned to look in the same direction as the Doyen, toward the younglings.

With a jerk, Limna grabbed his arm, pulling Santh from his frozen panic.

And they ran.

✦ ✦ ✦

Santh's head hurt from breathing so hard. At the edge of the tree line, where the tall woods opened to the lumber yard, Santh and his sister stumbled to a stop.

"Did any follow us?" gasped Santh, stone a yellowish orange.

"No," wheezed Limna. "I looked back as we fled. They watched us go, untroubled, and made no move. They suspect naught."

Santh scrutinized Limna, noticing her grin and bright-green stone. She was enjoying this. He was sure that as far as she was concerned, it was all just a game, a fantasy Santh had invented as a reason to skip Trade. But he needed her to believe him. Something was wrong with the birds. With the world as they knew it. And he needed her help to figure out what it was and what to do about it.

"Jans is like to be wroth I spoke of it to you," said Santh, breathing deeply to calm his heart that still thought he was in danger. "He's oft wroth at everything."

"If you speak true, enraged. If not, he and I will laugh together. This will be merry!"

The younglings walked toward Jans in the middle of the clearing. With his back to them, he was lifting a log onto the sled, already weighed down with a full load. The sled had a highly polished iron base, typical of Doyen design, in contrast to the rough wood of its top. The whole device floated off the ground, no doubt with the same Doyen magiks of the Skyhall.

"Hail, Jans," said Limna as they drew close.

With a start, Jans turned around, and the oak log he'd been placing shifted, slipped off the sled, and landed with a thump on his foot. He tipped his head to look at the heavy log as Limna and Santh ran forward.

"No, no, no!" said Limna, "Jans, forgive me!"

"It is no matter," shrugged Jans, wyrd-stone dark with no light or color, as the three of them lifted the log back onto the sled.

No matter? scowled Santh to himself. Jans has never uttered such words. And how is his stone dark?

"So then," said Limna as she and Santh exchanged a quick glance, "we stand in need. Santh has been spinning tales of your misdeeds yesterday. And I must know, is it so?"

"Stories? Of yesterday? I had Trade all yesterday."

Limna turned to Santh, eyebrows raised, corner of her mouth curling up, stone shifting into amused chartreuse.

Santh's scowl deepened, a blush rising on his face, his own stone turning amber. "No . . . no, our masters set us free after morning's work. We fled to the woods to try your new bow."

Jans shrugged, face and stone still dark, and pushed on a log to stabilize the pile.

"I knew it," Limna said with no small bit of glee. "It could not be."

Santh ignored her, staring hard at Jans. "When we . . ." he started, swallowing, struggling to get the words out, scared of admitting it out loud. Scared of how Jans would react that he'd told their dangerous secret. ". . . S-slayed . . . the . . . bird."

Jans stopped his efforts, tipped his head to the side, and looked from Santh to Limna. "Killed a bird?" he said evenly. "Impossible. No harm to birds is the Doyen's highest law. How might we ever go against the Doyen? They killed the stars."

Why is his stone dark? Santh continued to worry.

"Those words were mine!" Limna started hopping lightly on her toes. "And Santh, above all, would never let it be."

Jans looked at them, eyes slightly creased, then shrugged again as he turned to the sled and pressed his hand to the metal disk on the front. The sled moved forward quietly. "As I said, I worked all yesterday."

With a face burning red and a wyrd-stone of magenta, Santh stared as Jans walked away with the sled. Limna skipped around him, dancing to music only she could hear.

"Good sport," she giggled. "Far better than Trade. How did you devise such a story? And if you meant Jans in it, why not tell him afore, so you could beguile me together?"

"Some mischief lies on him," Santh said quietly, still scowling in the direction Jans had gone. "He was with me. He let loose the arrow." The cursed arrow that caused all of it.

Limna stopped dancing. "He cannot be lying. You saw his wyrd-stone, it was dark. None can keep his stone still and lie."

Not long after the Uprising, the Doyen had given everyone their wyrd-stones, and Jans's had always been bright and vibrant, just like his emotions. Only older villagers, those with calm lives, ever had dark stones. "Is Jans old?" Santh asked her. "Is he *ever* calm?"

Limna laughed out loud. "Never." She stopped and looked at Santh thoughtfully. "There is reason in what you say, but which story is true? Which stone is true? Of the two, your tale is the more fantastic."

Santh huffed, turned, and walked away from his little sister. She didn't believe him, and now without Jans's corroboration, he had no way to prove what happened. He was stuck, and he couldn't solve the mystery of the birds on his own.

At the edge of the clearing in front of him, perched in a tree, sat another black raven. Maybe the same one they'd seen earlier. Maybe it was following them.

"Why, foul bird?" he yelled, all his frustration bubbling to the surface. "Why this torment?" As his stone flashed indigo with hints of magenta, he stooped and picked up a rock. "What would you of me?"

"Santh?" Limna stepped toward him, eyebrows furrowed, stone glowing amber. "What is your intent?"

"To show that I lie not," he said quietly. Pulling his arm back fully, he flung the stone at the bird with all his strength. The rock went wide and missed the bird by several hand-spans. It didn't move, unperturbed.

"Santh, stop!"

He moved closer and quickly picked up another rock, wyrd-stone glowing on his forehead shifting toward full magenta and red. With all his focus, he wound up and threw the second stone. This one flew true, straight at the bird. Before it could strike, the bird leaped into the air, and the rock crashed into the tree beneath it. The bird flapped in the air a few times, staring down at the children, then pulled its wings in tight and dove.

"Ah!" screamed Limna, and both of the younglings dropped to the ground as the dark bird swooped close, then took off in a wide arc. "You have kindled its wrath!"

"No," grunted Santh. "It kindles wrath in me." As the bird curved around to come at them again, he scrambled to his feet, grabbed a thick stick from the ground, and stood up tall and straight. The bird dove again, directly toward Santh as he stood defiantly. At the last moment, Santh jumped to the side and swung heavily. The staff made contact, cracked loudly in an explosion of feathers and splinters of wood, and the bird crashed to the ground, bouncing several times before coming to a stop.

"I . . ." stuttered Limna, looking at the still body of the bird, then looking around, "cannot believe you've done this thing."

Santh ran to the bird, and Limna followed him. A small thread of smoke rose from the body, and as they drew close, there was a pop and a flash, followed by more smoke.

"What is this?" cried Limna, her stone turning blood-orange.

Santh breathed out, feeling lighter, his stone fading to cyan. He now had proof. "The same as before. And look. Mark where the head parts from the body?" Santh poked his broken stick at the gap in the bird's neck and drew out what was inside.

"That looks like . . . *twine*?" Limna's stone shifted to chartreuse with flashes of yellow. "Just like you said. Dyed twine. The color is so bright. Red, yellow, blue." She turned to Santh, eyes wide. "Inside a bird? What madness is this?"

Santh straightened, considering the broken bird solemnly. "Let us speak with Jans again, and perchance we can unravel this matter."

✦ ✦ ✦

They found the sled, abandoned near a half-built stable at the edge of the village, and turned in opposite directions to look for Jans.

"Lo, there," said Limna, pointing.

Santh turned to follow her gesture. A stone's throw outside of town sat a small, boxy building, a Doyen structure that had been placed shortly after the Doyen's arrival, sitting directly under the Skyhall and matching in style. As usual, hulking sentries in onyx, Doyen guards, were stationed on either side of the metal front door.

And there, where Limna had pointed, was Jans, talking to one of the large guards.

Santh scowled, stone turning amber.

"Oh," breathed Limna, "the riddle deepens. Is Jans in league with the guards?"

"What do we now?"

"You wished to speak with Jans, but whatever stirs, the Doyen guards know more than he. We confront both?"

Santh gawked at her. "Confront? A guard?"

Limna looked back with a twinkle in her eye, "Or rather, would you speak straight to a Doyen? The beautiful one floating through our village this morning, perchance? Bold!"

Santh's mouth moved, but no sound came out. Suddenly, a fluttering sound above them drew Limna's attention, and Santh looked up to see a bright red bird swoop overhead and land gracefully on the box building. As it did so, looking straight at Santh and Limna, the two guards turned from Jans to look directly at them.

"So," said Santh, backing up slowly. "We should not confront the guards."

"You two!" shouted one of them. Both guards stepped forward in long strides.

"Ah!" Limna jumped, stone flashing yellow, and ran after Santh, who was already speeding away.

The younglings were quick, running into the center of town, dodging lithely through the late afternoon villagers. But the guards were quicker, moving with inhuman speed. People scattered in panic before the rushing bulls. Within seconds, grips like iron held the younglings fast, unperturbed by their struggling.

"You need to come with us," one said gruffly, dragging them to the boxy building.

"Fret not," said Jans calmly when they came close. "No harm will come. The Doyen wish only to ask you questions."

Santh and Limna looked at each other, eyes wide, both stones a mix of amber and yellow, with flecks of blood-orange. The guards wanted to take them to the Skyhall, to speak with the Doyen, the last thing any villager wanted to hear. But why, of all people, was Jans the one saying those words?

"We'll take you up one at a time," said the other guard holding Limna. He touched a small metal circle on the outside wall of the building, and it flashed twice with light. Through the magiks of the gods, the metal door to the building slid out of view. Santh had seen Doyen and guards come from the building but had never seen inside. Now he took a chance and looked. It was bright inside, as if there were many Doyen lamps, and decorated with stone and metal, much like the outside. But it was empty. Just a single, small, empty room. Limna looked at him, her stone flashing bright yellow, as the guard pulled her into the box.

"Wait," cried Santh, struggling vainly against the guard that held him fast. "Limna!" The door reappeared and closed with a hiss and a snick. Santh's breath caught as he watched the building's inner box appear and rise in the air toward the Skyhall floating above the village. They were taking Limna to the Skyhall. To the Doyen. And he would be next.

"Go back to Trade, Jans," said the remaining guard, still holding Santh tight. "Thanks for your help." Jans looked at the door Limna had gone through, then at Santh, a strange expression crossing his face, his stone showing the very faint amber of concern. The corners of his mouth curled down slightly, and he turned and walked away, back in the direction of the lumber yard.

Santh's eyes were drawn to the red bird, still sitting on the front edge of the building, unperturbed by the rise of the inner box. This bird was a large cardinal, though not as large as the raven now left broken on the forest floor. Its eyes were also smaller, but no less piercing, as it seemed to stare unblinking into Santh's soul.

✢ ✢ ✢

Twilight fell on them, and Santh and the guard stood in silence for long minutes, waiting for Limna and her guard to return. As he often did, Santh looked up, pining after pinpricks of light in the night sky. But, other than the few stars that had survived, the denizens of the dark were never coming back. The Doyen had seen to that. The Doyen could take and destroy whatever they wanted, with none to stop them. Heavy with worry, Santh couldn't help himself from asking, "What will you do with us?"

The guard turned to look at Santh slowly, and a strange smile grew on his face. It was unfair that the guards didn't have stones. Santh had to guess what the smile meant. All he knew was it made him feel very uneasy.

"I shouldn't tell you," the guard spoke quietly, conspiratorially. The bird, still perched on the edge of the building, leaned forward as if to listen in. Suddenly, Santh was unsure he wanted the answer.

"First, you will be asked questions. Many people are interested in you, in how you think and feel."

That's what Jans had said would happen. Questions were not so bad. But then why did the look in the guard's eye, and the tone in his voice, make Santh want to hide under a rock?

"And then," said the guard, his eyes and smile growing wider but darker, "we're going to kill you."

Santh jerked back, pulling against the iron grip on his arm.

"Oh, yes. I'm very serious. No one in the sanctuary can know what you've seen."

Santh's vision darkened around the edges, and his stone turned to a vibrant blood-orange with flashes of yellow. "Limna," he croaked.

"She's already dead. Your turn next. I will enjoy watching the life drain from your eyes."

Santh looked up at the Skyhall, blinking through tears, as the box she'd been taken up in dropped gently from the Skyhall's bottom toward the earth. They'd broken the sky, killed the stars, and now . . . the Doyen had killed Limna. "No—"

As the box settled into the building before him, the guard looked at Santh's face closely, as if drinking in his emotions. The bright red bird jumped from its perch to land on the guard's shoulder, also considering Santh with apparent great interest.

The door of the building slid open, and the second guard stepped out, followed closely by Limna.

Santh's breath caught. "Lim—" he gasped. He broke free of the guard and ran to her, pulling her into an embrace. "You live!"

"Santh?" she said evenly, pulling back from him. "What disturbs you?"

Struggling to see clearly, Santh shook his head, blinking out his tears, and glanced back at the guard, confused. The guard's expression appeared unchanged, repellent grin still wide.

"But . . ." he struggled out, "what came of your speech with the Doyen?"

"Santh, we are mortal children. The Doyen would never address us themselves. I spoke with a priest, as was promised, and he said the Doyen were much pleased with our labour."

Santh's stone shifted to dark orange. "What of . . . the . . ." He glanced again at the guard and his terrifying expression. "The matter in the lumber yard?"

"I am troubled for you, Santh," said Limna with a straight face. "What is this lumber yard matter of which you speak? We came hither straight from Trade, as they required, to be thanked for our work."

Santh gaped, voice not working. Then he finally noticed it. Limna's stone. It was dark, no color at all, just as Jans' had been.

The guard's irresistible grip pulled Santh away from Limna, and before he could form any other words, he was in the small room, the door sliding closed with a whine and a click. Gravity pressed on Santh as the inner room rose, and he stumbled slightly. The guard, with the bird still on his shoulder, looked at him and chuckled.

A quiet thunk, a stop of motion, and the door slid open. Santh blinked rapidly in the glare. He gaped as the guard pulled him out of the room and into a hallway. Everything was white and bright and polished and unnatural. He hadn't known what he expected, but the inside of the Skyhall was nothing he could understand.

"I don't think your sister got to see this," said the guard as he pulled Santh down the hallway. "No one else in the sanctuary has seen it and lived." After several twists and turns down identical hallways, they stopped at a closed door. The guard placed his hand on a metal plate on the wall, and the door slid open to reveal a dark room with flashing colored light inside. Santh didn't move, unsure if his feet worked until the guard pushed him in.

In front of them was a special work of Doyen magiks. An impossibly large sheet of glass. Unlike the glass made by his own people, the gift of the gods was perfectly clear, and this was the largest that Santh had ever seen, stretching from floor to ceiling, wall to wall.

But the wonder of it was quickly lost as he stared at what lay beyond. A row of people, facing away from him and dressed in brightly colored clothing, who were neither Doyen nor of his village, sat before panels of tiny lights that blinked and shimmered like a swarm of fireflies gone mad. And most strange of all, the wall in front of them appeared to hold dozens of windows. But, impossibly, the view of each was different. Some seemed to overlook his village, some looking on villagers as they worked or played. Some views shifted and moved, as if from the viewpoint of a living, moving creature instead of a static window.

"Go for five, and slowly pan to the left," said a voice from the room.

"Did you see it?" asked his guard quietly. Santh pulled his eyes away from the scene before him to look at the guard. The bird had moved down from the guard's shoulder to his forearm, and the guard held it out, close to Santh's face. The bird's dark eyes evaluated him inscrutably.

"See it?" responded Santh, dumbly, overwhelmed.

"Look at the top-left screen," said the guard, nodding toward the wall of windows.

Santh turned and looked. The window in the top-left corner did not reveal any view of the village. Instead, a face, turned to the side, filled its frame.

His face.

His stone, large in the center of his forehead, was bright orange. A brighter color than he'd ever seen on anyone.

His eyes, already wide, grew wider, and he raised a hand to touch his face. His face in the window mimicked him, moving as he moved. His stone, reflected in the window, grew brighter, pale, almost white.

"There's more," said the guard with his dark smile. He shifted the bird back to his shoulder and took Santh's arm again, pulling him from the room.

Several more turns down bright hallways, and they entered a new doorway. This room was as bright as the hallways, deific white from floor to ceiling, and contained multiple Doyen wonders, boxy shapes of iron and squiggly lines and colored pinpoints of light.

And in the middle of the room sat a metal table at waist-height. On the table lay something more incomprehensible than everything he'd seen. More than holy-white hallways and blinking colored lights. More than the windows of motion and faces. More than the bird, broken on the forest floor, made of strings and smoke.

Released by the guard, Santh stumbled forward, toward the table, gasping in short bursts. "What . . ." he struggled. "I . . ." He didn't register as the guard moved around the room to the opposite side of the table, facing Santh to watch his reactions. He didn't notice as another individual entered the room from a door near the guard. Santh didn't notice as he stopped breathing at all. With a complete loss of understanding or emotions, his wyrd-stone flickered, and went out.

Lying on the table was a young man, eyes closed, fourteen seasons old, with shaggy, light brown hair.

Me. I am atop the table.

Peaceful and still, face smooth and perfect, lacking the scars he'd received recently from sparks in the forge, the face was still his. Just like in the window, but if he could see his own face when asleep.

Or dead.

He said they would slay me, and they did. That is I.

There.

Dead.

/What happened?/

/What do you mean?/

/Did you already kill him and do the transfer? We haven't interviewed him yet./

/What, of course I haven't done the transfer. Not my job. I just brought him in here./

/Then why is his forehead light dark? And his face. It's blank. Like they look with no emotions after the first transfer./

/I don't know. I'm no good at reading emotions anyway, unless they're strong. But I don't care what his light says, I didn't do it. Look, let me show you the logs./

First, nothing.

Then, slowly, their words seeped into Santh's clouded brain.

My . . . stone. It is dark. As my mind. Broken.

Thinking was hard. Like struggling through mud. He'd seen too much to process.

But . . . it is false. My stone lies. It betrays them with untruth.

Santh tore his eyes from the body on the table and looked at the two people, turned away from him, as they leaned over one of the devices in the room.

And now they turn aside.

Carefully quiet, careful not to breathe, careful to not even think about what he was doing, Santh shifted backwards, away from his body lying still on the table, and back toward the door. As he approached, the door slid open quietly. The bright red bird, still sitting on the guard's shoulder, watched him as he slipped out.

The door slid closed behind him, and Santh stumbled down the hall, taking in huge gulps of air. His wyrd-stone flared to life again, oscillating between yellow and cyan and green.

Suddenly, a noise blared through the hall, demanding, and the color of the hall flashed from bright white to angry red. Santh ran. Twists and turns, the sound echoing down the hall driving into his brain, and he quickly worried he was well lost. He worried he would be forever in the terrifying home of the Doyen. Or be caught and found, to be killed yet again. Then, he saw it. The shiny metal door that first brought him into the nightmare.

He scrambled toward it, worried its opening would require Doyen magik, but it slid open as he approached, and he stumbled inside the small room.

"You!" echoed a voice down the hallway he'd just come. "Stop!" Through the still-open doorway, Santh saw the guard appear around a distant corner and thunder down the hallway, bird still riding him unperturbed.

Wyrd-stone flaring bright yellow, Santh glanced around the wall of the room. Just inside the door at waist-height, embedded in the wall, sat the small circle of metal the guard had touched when they came up, and Santh quickly touched it now. At his press, it flashed white. But the doorway remained open.

"Stop!" The guard sped up, each heavy footfall a crack of thunder.

In a panic, Santh pressed repeatedly on the metal, then shrunk back against the far wall as the guard drew close. The door, in terrifying timing, closed, mere finger-widths before the guard's outstretched hand. The room dropped, pushing Santh's heart into his throat. He leaned over his knees and tried to breathe, fighting to keep the contents of his stomach from coming up.

But . . . he had done it. He had escaped.

I escaped.

The room settled to the ground, and the door opened with a hiss, exposing the night-time air. Santh breathed in the scents deeply, and straightened, steeling himself to run at the first sight of god or guard. With stronger resolution than he'd ever felt, he dashed forward from the room.

As he cleared the doorway, two guards, one on either side, grabbed him and pulled in tight, their black armour digging into his arms and ribs. With wide eyes, Santh looked quickly from one guard to the other, then stopped. His entire attention was consumed by a small bluejay sitting in a nearby tree, as light from the open doorway highlighted its bright blue chest and reflected off its dark eyes.

✦ ✦ ✦

"This chapter has come to a close, but I have to thank you, Santh," said the towering Doyen, hovering above the ground. Her flowing garment was even more striking lit by the moonlight filtered through the forest trees. But Santh was not looking at her. His eyes were only on the sky, looking for one of the few surviving stars.

"You certainly gave our audience a great show. Your attempted escape at the end was unexpected but wonderful. You had us scrambling to make sure you made it out, while keeping it real. But your reactions to everything inside the base were so vibrant. The director told me every shot was pure gold."

Normally, away from the village where they'd taken him, he could find the surviving stars easily, but now he couldn't even see Freyja's or Týr's, the morning and evening stars. Maybe he'd lost track of where they should be this time of year. For some reason, on top of everything else, the loss of lights in the night was now crushing.

"Of course, we have to reset you. Normally we would want to make sure your memory copies are up-to-date, but we can't include your last two days anyway." A new noise, that of the two dark guards drawing close, pulled Santh's attention.

And now he would die. "May I," he started, his stone showing chartreuse, his fear strangely gone now that it was all finally over, "ask of you a question?"

The Doyen tipped her beautiful face to the side and held up her hand, pausing the guards. "You may."

"Why did you slay the stars? Why take them from us?"

The Doyen's mouth turned into a light smile, a rare sight, and she laughed gently. "Oh, Santh. They're not gone. They are exactly where they always were. The Splintering just doesn't come with enough energy to duplicate that much matter into the new world." She turned and nodded to the guards.

A bright flash. A deafening sound. Lastly, darkness.

* * *

"Santh?" Rough hands shook Santh from his peaceful slumber. "Santh! Arise! You will be late for Trade."

"Limna?" Santh rubbed the sleep from his eyes. "I am awake."

After quickly dressing, Santh met his sister outside, and they started toward their day.

"Do you fare better?" asked Limna. "You behaved strangely yesterday. Your stone shone with many colors."

"I recall little. Only that we were fetched from Trade to talk to the Doyen priests."

"If you were troubled yesterday, you are not now. Your stone is dark, as if you were another being. Lo, what a night's sleep can do."

As the siblings split to go to their separate Trades, Santh noticed a yellow bird settling on a nearby branch. He paused, triggered by the light reflecting off the bird's eye.

"Why?" he said to himself as much as the bird. "Why are you held sacred by the Doyen?" There was something about the birds, and he felt a strangely familiar compulsion to know what it was.

He tipped his head, looking deep into its eyes. With a quiet click, the bird tipped its head in return. Darkness encroached on the edges of Santh's vision, and he felt himself falling into the bird's gaze.

Flashes crossed Santh's mind in rapid succession, experiences he'd obviously never had, and sights he couldn't begin to comprehend. Attacking birds, perfect white walls, his unmoving body on a metal slab. Running, hiding, a flash of pain, and dark.

And always, birds staring at him.

But somehow more. Through some dark magiks of their eyes stared hundreds of people. Maybe more than existed in his entire village, numbers he couldn't count. More than existed in all of history.

A shiver ran from his spine to his toes.

Then, in a flash, it was gone. Along with all his worry and concern and curiosity.

And with a blank face and a blank wyrd-stone, Santh turned and walked away.

END NOTE

Wyrd-stone acquired. Birds hacked. (Thanks, Ren). I'm very curious about the tech-neural interface. Appears it may do more than reflect emotions. The Immortals may be collecting emotions for their own use or for study. On top of streaming these poor mortals' lives to their viewers for entertainment.

Tacos not acquired. Splicing bird feed.

—Ms. Six

Date: 2590-04-11 16:07:13 PRT
From: Ren Stornman
To: Anachronauts
Subject: Time Salt Sources
Re: Untoaster

Kinsha, I know this event is fantastic, if unbelievable, but it might verify other reports of Time Salt and prove it can exist on any of the Splinters. This might give us a chance to get ahead of QoreTech. The next time I leave the station planet-side, I'll check the world library for any possible references here on this splinter. Slim chance, but maybe we luck out and find a local source.

UNTOASTER

By Kasey Selma McQueen

The outside edge of the scab was already dried and crusted over, even curling up slightly, so how was I to know it would be a gusher when I scratched it off? I'd thought it was ready, but here I was pressing the fancy cloth dinner napkin against my cheek. And still Uncle Alden was over there all *duty to the betterment of mankind* this, *unlimited potential* that, *blah blah blah*, while I stared out the restaurant's massive front windows behind him and his soup got cold.

It was really good soup too, miso with a touch of habanero, and the tofu chunks were grilled so they didn't get all mushy. I reached over with my non-blood-napkin hand, pinched the rim of the lacquer bowl, and pulled it across the wooden table.

It caught a knot, and some of the broth sloshed out, but Uncle Alden kept right on talking. I picked up my spoon. I needed to be polite if I was going to ask to stay at his place while the hype died down, but enough was enough.

"They're never going to bring the next course with a full bowl on the table. Do you mind?"

Uncle Alden closed his eyes and raised his thumb and forefinger to his eyebrows, the way he did when I told him I'd dropped out of high school to pursue my career as an inventor. "I'm just trying to look out for my favorite nephew. I don't think you appreciate how serious this is."

"I'm your only nephew, and I don't think you appreciate Asian fusion." I dipped my spoon in and took a sip. Delicious. I closed my eyes to savor the taste. When I opened them, a black SUV screamed to a stop in the no-parking zone out front, right on the edge of the canal. Some office worker really wanted to make the most of their lunch break if they couldn't even take the time to use the parking lot out back. Two business guys, actually one was a business lady but I think it's okay to use *guys* for both, got out and strode all businesslike toward the restaurant.

Uncle Alden glanced under the table like there might be a wild badger at my feet instead of my latest invention. "You need to get this *thing* into safe hands so it can be properly researched."

Safe hands? Surely he couldn't mean the "safe hands" of the same government that broke the weather, turning every town between here and the mountains into a mini Venice, but with lamer architecture and more strip malls. Those buffoons couldn't protect a cheeseburger from a vegan. I was starting to regret coming to Uncle Alden, but he was my only relative within hydrocycling distance. I cocked an eyebrow at him over my spoon while another black SUV, a different make than the first one, pulled up. Two huge dudes jumped out. They sprinted after the business-suit people, shouting something I couldn't hear, but it was certainly about their terrible parking job. They had that unmistakable cop look about them, and I wondered why two beefy bros like that were on parking duty.

"Look, I can understand why you don't trust the government, but think of all the good that could be done with this thing."

"As if enjoying perfect toast every time isn't good enough? Bagels too. And quit calling it *this thing*. It's an untoaster." I tapped the shopping bag under the table affectionately with my foot.

The business suits were scuffling with the parking cops out front, and all four of them were trying to elbow their way past each other into the restaurant.

"It's frickin' time travel in a box!" Uncle Alden's voice got shrill at the end of the sentence, like it did when he tried to stop me from investing my inheritance in crypto. He should really trust me by now. He glanced around the room at the other diners throwing him the side-eye and took a deep breath. "Where—how on earth did you even get something like this?"

"I told you; I made it. Got tired of scraping char off my sourdough. The bakery near my house only sells it once a week, and it's the only kind I can find that's actually sour. So I looked online for something that could help—"

A woman in all black, like a ninja, pulled up next to the door on an expensive-looking motorcycle, but one of the business guys intercepted her before she could come inside. He hugged her a little too enthusiastically and knocked her down.

The scene outside was starting to look like a spy movie, but nothing that exciting ever happened in McKinleyville. No, it made much more sense that the ninja lady was like a CEO or something and was there for a business

meeting. I wondered if they still called them power lunches like in old movies. The guy was surely so stoked to see her because she was the boss, and judging by the fancy bike, she was definitely important enough to get him out of the parking fine.

"By 'looked online,' you mean you asked your criminal buddies on the dark web, right? Just so we're clear."

I didn't appreciate his snippy tone, so I didn't answer until after the waiter had set down the main course—coconut orange chicken over what was supposed to be basmati rice but looked like regular long-grain.

I took a slow bite. Oh, not long-grain. Jasmine. A pleasant surprise, but they should correct the menu. "Yeah. From the forum where I learned which altcoins to buy. So maybe you should give them a break." I still had the napkin pressed to my face, but it was the polyester kind—so instead of soaking up the blood, it was smearing all over my cheek. I put the napkin down. Who was I trying to impress, anyway? Uncle Alden was so wrapped up in hysterics, he wouldn't notice a bomb going off behind him.

The enthusiastic hugger picked the motorcycle CEO up and hurried her into the back of the SUV. Was she injured? Why didn't he just bring her inside the restaurant? A pair of speeding jet skis cut across the canal. Ah, they were waiting for their full party to arrive before being seated. How polite. The jet skiers sprang out onto the pavement holding something out in front of them. Their phones, so they didn't get wet, most likely.

Uncle Alden didn't say anything about my face. He didn't even pick up his fork. He scrunched his brow and swiped a palm up over his receding hairline. "Has anyone contacted you about it?"

"Not really. A bunch of people have been knocking on my door and calling my phone, but I never answer unless I'm expecting someone. Just fans, I figure, although my doorbell cam showed a couple people letting themselves into my apartment while I was riding over here. But they won't find anything. I used up all the alien salt making the untoaster."

"*Alien salt?*"

Actually, the substance I'd bought from the forum was more Newtonian fluid than crystalline, but the person who sold it to me called it salt, and it looked like salt inside the vial. The Alien part was my addition. I had to dumb stuff down for Uncle Alden sometimes.

"The ancient alien element. The guy who found it in a cave saw light bend around it, so he put out some videos on social media. One of my forum pals bought it off him and then put it up for auction. He told me about the auction because he knows I'm into alien stuff. I figured if it could bend light,

I could probably use it to bend spacetime a little bit, so I threw some of my crypto winnings at it and beat out all the other buyers."

A black sedan pulled up, and two people in khakis and polos got out.

Nice of the business-suit people to invite the middle managers. They must have been pretty hungry because they ran for the door, but the parking guys greeted them with a hug, too.

"And then you posted those videos on your live stream, of the untoasting and the egg and the butter, and now you're what, on the run?" His voice rose and cracked at the end.

I ate more of my chicken to give him time to calm down. It was admittedly not a great idea to put videos featuring micro-gravitational lensing on the surface web, but it's not every day you get to see butter going from a melted golden puddle back to a solid cube. Or a cracked egg sucking its yolk and white back into the shell. That one was kind of gross but still cool. Who would've guessed they'd get nine million views in two days?

"I'm not on the run, Uncle Alden. I just need a place to chill until fans stop knocking on my door all hours of the night and day. It's super annoying."

I looked up from my plate, and the guys outside were throwing hands. Whoa. They were taking hangry to a whole other level. A helicopter passed by low across the street. I was pointing it out to Uncle Alden when he screeched at me again. "For the love of all that's holy, you've got to turn it over to the government. Otherwise, they'll track you down and take it. Or someone else will!"

I laughed. "That would be dumb. If they try to reverse-engineer it, they'll ruin the salt. And what good is a one-minute time bend outside the kitchen?"

The helicopter passed by again, this time dangling a guy in a uniform and helmet from a rope. The CEO was apparently important enough to have medical help flown in. And a security escort, since two camo-wearing fellows with rifles had arrived in the back of a white pickup truck.

"Uncle Alden, you gotta see—"

His eyes were buggy and his forehead was going dark red. "They'll torture you until you tell them where you got it!"

"Well, now you're just being macabre." I slumped my shoulders, thought about waterboarding and electrodes and strobe lights, and squirmed in my chair. No way anyone would torture me over a culinary appliance, right? Time to order dessert; some mango peach sticky rice would cheer us up. I waved around for the waiter and spotted him huddled under a table in the back corner, along with all the other guests.

Uncle Alden turned to see what I was scowling at and sprang up from the table, spilling his ice water onto his plate. "We've got to get out of here, *now*!"

I didn't like leaving without tipping the waiter, despite the subpar service, but I leapt up after him, knocking my chair over in the excitement. I grabbed the untoaster from under the table and the last piece of chicken and ran with him into the open kitchen. The cooks were nowhere to be seen, so I wouldn't have gotten dessert anyway.

The front doors crashed open, and two of the business-suit guys barged in as we were pushing the heavy back exit open. I couldn't believe the power lunch was still on after their boss's injury.

Uncle Alden screamed and made a beeline for his Volvo. I trotted after him. Both of the security guards and a middle manager burst out the back door, with the business-suit guys close behind. They were shouting in English and two foreign languages—ones I couldn't distinguish, unfortunately, because I hated to miss an opportunity to demonstrate my impressive Japanese skills.

One of the managers pointed at my face. "He's got a head wound! Who got to him?!"

I started to explain that I wasn't injured, it was just an old zit scab, but Uncle Alden was shrieking at me to get in the car. A business-suit guy lunged for me. He grabbed my arm, but I wrenched it free while one manager tackled him to the pavement and another swiped at the untoaster. I dodged him and hopped into the passenger seat. "Thank you, but I really don't need medical attention," I shouted while Uncle Alden slammed the gas pedal down. Something behind us exploded.

END NOTE

Of course, we still don't know what Time Salt can really do, (thanks a lot, Gentor, for screwing up our only batch!) They describe the tech in this account as a time machine, but it's really more of a de-entropy-inator. Not as cool, but I can still think of uses.

Oh, and let's keep anything we learn about this out of the hands of the Cats, yeah?

Date: 2590-04-11 23:24:56 PRT
From: Green Kinsha
To: Anachronauts
Subject: Dear Diary
Re: Primary Source

Can someone please explain Time Salt to me? Because Gentor keeps claiming he's going to sprinkle some Time Salt on his gargantua beans and I just don't get it. Where did it come from? What does it actually do? And stop asking me if I've read your reports because they are not helpful.

I really do not have time for this. Archive Cat is breathing down my neck again about deadlines, and Gentor just triggered an accidental reboot of life support on deck 7. But if I don't get this report written and submitted today I'll just have to write it tomorrow, and tomorrow I have an appointment at the chocolate bath that I am NOT rescheduling.

Here's the account, etc.

PRIMARY SOURCE

By Brandon B. Chambers

Insanity is doing the same thing over and over again and expecting different results.

SEPTEMBER 18, 2032

The smell of wet earth totally interfered with the taste of Marty's otherwise awesome breakfast burrito. He stood in a small, roped-off area right next to the huge hole in the ground. Hundreds of people stood in the freshly rained grass, watching the hole with hungry, desperate eyes. As if they would finally receive answers.

They wouldn't, of course. The time capsule had been buried nine days *after* the stars had disappeared. There wouldn't be answers. There wouldn't be hope. Marty hadn't even been alive when it happened thirty years ago, but he and his classmates in the roped-off area were the intended recipients of the capsule.

Once the final rope was attached, eight members of the wrestling team began hoisting the capsule up from the hole, using pulley systems designed and built by the AP physics class. The capsule arose quickly as the principal spoke into a microphone, reminding everybody of the students who had buried it thirty years ago, in an obvious effort to unite the community and remind everybody that there was still hope for the future.

The capsule hit the ground with a heavy thud. "And now," Principal Gordon announced, "our former Student Body President and current City

Councilman, Jerom Munn, will unlock the capsule and distribute the contents to the present-day senior class of Monroe High!"

The crowd applauded.

Marty burped.

"Ew, Marty!" complained Nellie, the girl standing next to him. "Nobody wants to smell your recycled bacon breath."

Marty shrugged. Nellie was cute, but she wasn't cute enough for him to apologize for a work of art.

Jerom Munn stepped forward, waving a key and smiling at the crowd. Clean-shaven with light brown skin and short salt-and-pepper hair, Jerom was a pillar of the community. Even Marty, who generally made an effort not to care about anything, knew Jerom.

"Thank you, Principal Gordon," Jerom said after stepping to the microphone. "It was my privilege and duty to see this project through to the end. The contents of this capsule are more than a reminder of the past; they're a reminder of the responsibilities we take on from the previous generation."

Marty snickered. "Big man is sweating. Didn't know Munn got nervous public speaking."

Nellie elbowed him. "It just rained, moron. Councilman Munn doesn't get nervous."

Marty shrugged again. It sure looked like sweat to Marty. Maybe Munn was nervous about finally opening the capsule. Or maybe he wasn't enjoying the trip down memory lane.

"It's a story as old as time," Jerom said. "One generation does the best they can with the tools they have. And it . . . it's never perfect. We never have all the answers. We don't solve all the problems. There are—and always will be—issues we have to pass on to the next generation. Of course, we make plenty of progress. We make social changes. We improve technology. We innovate and build. But the most heartbreaking thing is that we can't do it all. We have to pass on some of those problems to you because time is—generally speaking—a limited resource."

Jerom Munn paused, his smile wavering as his eyes went distant for a moment, looking in the direction of the time capsule. He composed himself quickly and looked to the students in the roped-off area. "As you accept the contents of this capsule, I ask you to learn from us what you can, fix what we couldn't, and forgive us for all the problems we couldn't solve. We believe in you. We have hope that you are strong in ways we could never dream of being. Can I have the class of 2033 line up to receive these pieces of memorabilia?"

Principal Gordon moved one of the ropes, and Marty's classmates began forming a single-file line leading to the capsule. Marty was in no particular rush, so he waited at the back of the line. The only reason he'd come was because he was failing English and History. Now, he had to write a paper on whatever was handed to him.

People applauded as Jerom Munn unlocked and opened the capsule. One by one, he gave items to students. Nellie got some silly electronic keychain and ran over to her friend, Renn. Both girls squealed in delight as they pulled out their phones to look up whatever it was Nellie had received.

Finally, Marty arrived at the front of the line. Jerom Munn paused, smiling sadly. Marty supposed that made sense. After all, this was the end of something the man had started thirty years ago.

From the capsule, Councilman Munn removed one final item: a simple journal. Not as enticing as an old leather journal, not as cheap as a spiral-bound notebook. Just a simple notebook with a soft, light-blue cover. It had an illustration of a tree on the front, and some quote beneath it.

Councilman Munn made eye contact with Marty. "What's your name, young man?"

Marty swallowed the last of his burrito. "Marty."

Munn nodded. "Marty. A good name. Marty, I put this journal into the capsule thirty years ago, with the intent to deliver it to somebody in the next generation. That somebody is you. Will you accept this journal?"

Marty held out his hand. "Sure, boss."

Councilman Munn seemed to hold his breath as he handed over the journal, then exhaled once Marty accepted it.

The crowd applauded, and Marty stuffed the journal into his hoodie pocket, unaware of the list of nine names written on the inside of the front cover, each of which had a number next to it.

The next morning, he still hadn't checked, and therefore didn't notice that a new name and number had been written down beneath the others.

Marty Powell: 1

SEPTEMBER 27, 2032
(1,304 days later)

Renn found it difficult pretending she didn't know everything coming her way. But school was almost over. She'd successfully pretended not to know all the answers to her assignments and tests. She'd bumped into people in the halls, as if she didn't know precisely what path everybody was going to take and how to avoid collisions.

She'd thrown up between third and fourth periods. That, at least, was new.

Renn knew it had to be her body's way of screaming at her to abort mission. To be strong. To keep her promise despite Wallace's offer.

But she couldn't. She wasn't strong enough. She'd broken long ago and done things she'd never thought herself capable of.

She avoided Nellie all day. Oh, Renn could have confronted her. And she had, plenty of times. She'd even tried giving back the journal to Nellie, but for some reason, it didn't work that way. Once somebody passed on the journal, it couldn't be returned to them.

How could her best friend have passed on this curse to her? Renn had promised she wouldn't do the same thing to anyone else. She would be stronger.

But here she was at the end of the school day, heading to Wallace's locker, where she knew she would find him again. Because about a hundred days ago, she'd told him the truth about the journal, and he'd offered to take it. So . . . in a way . . . he'd consented. Even if he couldn't remember it.

Her stomach churned again at the rationalization. She was going to ruin his life. All because she couldn't think of anybody more capable of surviving it. She had fooled herself into thinking she was strong enough to endure it, but Wallace *actually* might be.

She turned the corner right on time. Wallace pulled open his locker, his muscular forearms exposed by his rolled-up flannel sleeves. She remembered a time when she'd fawned over those arms from a distance as he helped hoist that cursed time capsule from the ground.

First, it had been a crush. By day ninety-nine, she knew she was in love. And now . . . there was nobody she trusted more. He wasn't perfect, but she was convinced Wallace was stronger than her. Maybe he could figure something out. Maybe he could endure longer.

"Hey Wallace," she said, voice a bit timid as she approached. She couldn't sound too familiar. As far as Wallace was concerned, she'd been too shy to talk to him just yesterday. He didn't know how comfortable she'd grown around him—how many conversations they'd had behind the school before the afternoon thunderstorm began.

He turned and looked at her with surprise, as he so often did. "Oh, hi, Renn," he said, a warm smile popping up after recovering from the initial jolt. "What's up?"

Her mind flashed back to his words from a previous conversation on a different September twenty-seventh. "I'm sorry you're going through this, but selfishly . . . I'm grateful. It means one of us finally had the courage to say something."

She'd never hear those words again. She couldn't even allow herself to love him anymore. This isn't what you did to somebody you loved. He'd never forgive her. But she couldn't live like this anymore. Renn pulled the blue journal from her bag.

"Um, sorry to bug you. But this journal is from the time capsule. Marty got it first, but it's kind of a pass-it-on thing. Will you accept it?" She held it out to him, fighting the bile in her throat and putting on a friendly face.

Wallace took the journal and flipped it open. "Oh. Yeah, sure," he said. "What exactly do I need to do?"

"You can read the entries," Renn said. "It'll be pretty intuitive. Just do your best, okay?"

Wallace put the journal in his backpack. "Gotcha." He paused, as if he wanted to say something.

Renn couldn't bear it. "I've got to go, but I'll see you tomorrow. Thanks Wallace," she said, turning around and walking to the buses. She wouldn't walk home today, as she had the last hundred or so. She wouldn't stop by the bakery and grab something delicious to eat right before bed.

Because this time, if she ate gluten, she wouldn't simply wake up without a worry on September twenty-seventh. This time, her allergy would kick in, and she'd end up in the hospital. That was one thing she'd miss about this whole mess: gluten without consequences.

But before she went to the buses, she had one quick errand to run. Something all seven owners of the journal had done since it had been dug up.

She went to the computer lab and entered quietly. Per his routine, Marty sat in the otherwise empty lab with his back to the door, headphones in. Both of his eyes were varying shades of yellow-purple, and his nose had a bandage on it. Renn also knew from reading the journal that he likely had some bruising on his shins and ribs. Nellie had been the one to break his nose yesterday.

Well, a lot of yesterdays ago.

Renn had thought about this a lot. She didn't want to leave another visible mark. People might start to worry that Marty was being abused at home. With silent steps, she approached him from behind, pulling a stapler out of her bag. She unhinged the stapler with a silent motion, raised it over her head, and *cracked* it down on Marty's shoulder. She put her hand over his mouth as he yelped from the pain.

"You're a coward, Marty Powell," she whispered in his ear as she fluidly returned the stapler to her bag. Marty tore her hand away and whimpered, reaching to dig the staple out of his shoulder. He refused to meet Renn's gaze, like he always did.

"I thought I was going crazy, Renn!" he objected. "I couldn't take it anymore. I—"

Renn quivered with rage, grabbing his chin and forcing him to look at her. "*You* couldn't take it anymore?" she asked, spittle flying from her lips. "You lasted *six days*, Marty. *Six.* You didn't even *try*. You passed it on as soon as you realized you could."

Marty's eyes drifted to the carpet. Renn slapped him. "Look at me. You're the reason I'm in this mess, the least you can do is look at me."

Marty finally glanced up again, cheek red. "I don't know how the rest of you did it," he complained. "Didn't Nellie get up to, like, seventy-five days?"

"A hundred and seventy-five," Renn said.

Marty swore. "How many is this? For you?"

"Seven hundred and eighty-nine."

Marty went pale as a ghost in a snowstorm and swore again. Renn shoved him back into his chair. "I wish it had gone to literally anybody else," she said. "Anybody but you."

Marty's shoulders sagged and his head hung low. "So do I," he said, a tear rolling down his cheek.

Renn left him to finish digging out that staple and headed for the buses.

Hours later, she lay in bed, wondering if she'd actually be able to fall asleep. Part of her didn't want to. It reminded her of the story her science teacher had told. A scientist stuck a cat in a box filled with radiation. But until the box was opened, they didn't know if the cat was alive or dead. Schrödinger's cat.

Renn knew from reading previous entries in the supernatural journal that passing it on to somebody else was supposed to release her of the curse. The time loop would end. But what if she—and everybody before her—had missed something important? Some variable that she had missed?

What would she do if she woke up again on September twenty-seventh?

It was one in the morning when she finally acknowledged she was too nervous to go to sleep. She went to the medicine cabinet and grabbed some sleeping pills. Twenty minutes later, she finally closed her eyes for the night.

She woke up with her alarm blaring and reached out to hit the snooze button, only to find that it was slightly out of reach. Her hand smacked her nightstand, and she bolted upright.

She'd moved the alarm clock last night, before bed.

It wasn't sitting in the same place as always.

Her heart pounded as she slammed the button to turn off the alarm and reached for her phone, holding her breath as the screen lit up.

❧ ❧ ❧

September 28, 2032.

Renn froze. Legitimately froze. Not just her body, but her thoughts and feelings all screeched to a halt, as if somebody had just hit the pause button.

It worked. She was free. But instead of feeling elation, Renn's heart sank. She'd given up. Thrown in the towel. Trapped somebody else in the loop, dooming them so she could move on.

Stomach churning at the thought of it, Renn hurried to take a shower, only to find that her little brother, Bradley, had beaten her to it. She blinked twice at the locked doorknob. Bradley hadn't beaten her to the shower since . . .

. . . well, since September twenty-sixth.

"Quit jiggling the doorknob, I'll be out in a minute. Not all of us take thirty minutes on their hair, you know," Bradley whined from the shower. Renn let out a harsh laugh, mixed with tears.

"Take your time," she said, voice shaky with emotion. No, not emotion. Emotions. Plural. Relief, horror, regret, bewilderment, realization. And more. Too many to count.

"Are you . . . crying?" Bradley asked from the shower.

Renn laughed. "Shut up," she replied, wiping the tears from her eyes.

"I've got the emergency kit in my room, if you need it," Bradley said. Renn laughed again. The emergency kit was a box of her favorite chocolates that Bradley kept on hand for when her period showed up. Which was offensive, but also very helpful.

"Just hurry up, you dork," she said before heading downstairs to the smell of sausages and eggs. She turned into the kitchen, where her mom hummed a tune as she placed another sausage in the pan.

"Oh, hello honey," her mom said with a smile. "I'm sorry, breakfast isn't ready yet. Usually you shower firs—oh!" her mom said with surprise as Renn nearly tackled her with a hug.

"You're the best mom in the world," she said. "Thank you."

"Oh! Oh, well, um, are you okay, Renn?" her mom asked, a cold sausage still in one hand.

"Take the compliment, dear," Renn's dad said, entering the kitchen. He smiled at Renn as he slid his phone in his pocket. "She didn't seem too enthused about *my* cooking yesterday."

Renn ran to give her dad a hug too. He was sturdier than Renn's mom by a significant margin, but he still made a little grunt as she careened full force into his torso. "I'm sorry, dad. I just . . . I think I'm starting to get sick of hash browns."

Her dad sighed and hugged her back. "Let's just hope your Irish ancestors didn't hear that. Ain't nobody in this family getting sick of spuds."

Renn laughed. It felt so *good* to laugh at a joke she hadn't heard hundreds of times before.

"Renn, honey, are you . . . are you on drugs?" Renn's mom asked quietly, nervously fidgeting with a spatula.

Renn's dad laughed. "And if you are, do you mind giving some to your brother?"

He dodged out of the way instinctively as Renn's mom tried to swat his shoulder with the rubber spatula.

"Shower's free!" Bradley called from upstairs. "I apologized to the drain in advance for all the hair you're about to shed."

"No drugs, sorry to scare you, Mom," she said. She gave both her parents a quick squeeze before bolting up the stairs and entering the shower.

Even the *shower* felt different from the day before. Maybe the water pressure was a bit different? She couldn't be sure, but Renn was certain something had changed. The weight of the soap felt alien as well, almost wrong in her palm.

As the cool water ran over her, Renn tried to think about what she would do with her newfound freedom. What would she finally do today that she'd been yearning for in the loop?

But her mind kept going back to Wallace. To the conversations she'd had with him. The conversations all supernaturally recorded within the journal.

"I can take it, Renn. You can give it to me."

Tears sprang to her eyes again as she thought of the moment she'd handed him the journal.

"You don't have to do this alone. It's not on you."

She thought about how by now, his name had been written inside the front cover, just beneath hers.

"You're so strong. I don't know how you do it."

But she hadn't been strong. Not strong enough. She hadn't even had the guts to tell him again. She hadn't even been willing to *risk* the chance of him saying no. Even though he wouldn't have. Even though he would have offered again, just like he had before.

She hadn't even given him a warning.

Renn spent the rest of the morning pretending to be in a good mood, so as not to worry her mom too much. She turned her phone off as she moved to the bus, feeling anxiety at not knowing exactly what notifications she would receive and when.

What if Nellie texted her? What if Wallace reached out?

As the bus crept closer to the school, Renn felt the sausages from breakfast threatening to make a reappearance. Wallace was in her first period class. Gym. Could she bear to see him again? As she left the bus and entered the school, she ran into no fewer than eight people.

Because she wasn't used to the pattern of traffic changing. She didn't know how to avoid collisions anymore. Which is why, just before turning the corner for her locker, she bumped into Nellie.

The two girls froze, staring at each other blankly for several seconds, not daring to speak. Finally, it was Nellie who whispered, with tears in her eyes, "Renn, I'm so sorr—"

"Save it," Renn said, moving past Nellie to get to her locker. Nellie clamped her mouth shut in response. She didn't chase Renn. Didn't beg for forgiveness. Which was good, because Renn still didn't think Nellie deserved forgiveness.

But as she twisted the combination to her locker, she had to wonder if that meant she couldn't be forgiven, either. Opening her locker, Renn was caught off guard by a small plastic bottle on the top shelf. One she'd put there yesterday, then left without remembering.

A bottle full of pills that she knew from experience couldn't break the loop.

But she wasn't in the loop anymore.

And . . . she couldn't ever look Wallace in the eye again, could she? Not after trapping him.

She wouldn't last ten seconds in first period without a breakdown.

She put the bottle of pills discreetly in her backpack and made her way to the bathroom. Specifically, the bathroom nearest the teacher's lounge, which was the least used.

It was the one she'd used to die before.

She moved with almost robotic motion toward the restroom. She ignored bumps from other students, who all hustled to get to homeroom. The halls became more and more empty until, finally, the bell rang, leaving only a few stragglers behind. By the time Renn reached the bathroom, the halls were a ghost town.

Renn checked to make sure that none of the stalls were occupied. She looked in the mirror. Something was off. Like an AI picture that had something slightly wrong with it. *No soul.* That was it. Her eyes, they looked empty. Not scared, or angry, or happy, or sad. Just empty. Like she'd been taxidermied.

Just this morning, she'd been happy. Or at least, relieved. But as the morning progressed, it was like the last 789 days of torture were catching up. Renn thought back to the English lesson she'd sat through on repeat yesterday. The one about the hero's journey. The hero returned home, but changed, having conquered the enemy and saved the day. Things weren't the same after that. They couldn't be, but the hero found a way to cope with the change.

But Renn had a feeling this wasn't a hero's journey. She hadn't discovered the elixir of life. She hadn't conquered the evil foe. She'd broken on the journey and passed down the problems to somebody else. Somebody she cared about, deeply and profoundly. Somebody she couldn't stand betraying.

Renn was changed, but she didn't deserve to return home and live happily ever after. She'd considered it before, of course. But looking at those soulless eyes in the mirror, it was obvious that she couldn't possibly belong here anymore. She locked herself in a stall and pulled out the bottle of pills.

Finally, she could end it. On her terms. For real.

As she popped off the lid, tears forming in her eyes, she heard the door to the bathroom open. Renn froze as the door shut and footsteps approached. She'd have to wait until the other girl left. She hoped it would be quick. She didn't want time to question herself. To doubt. To rethink.

She was so done with thinking. With trying. She just wanted rest.

The footsteps stopped outside the stalls. "Renn, it's me. I'm not angry."

Renn dropped the bottle in surprise, her hands shaking as she recognized the voice. Wallace. She whimpered as the pills scattered to the ground. Whimpering? How pathetic was she? Why was he here? He had to be lying. How could he not be mad? It was a trick, right?

"Are you here to kill me?" she whispered, almost hopefully. She'd had so much time to consider how he might react.

"No, Renn. I'm—I'm coming in, all right? I know you're decent."

She paused for a moment before processing what he meant. Of course he knew she was decent. This wasn't his first time in the bathroom. Wallace slid under the stall door feet first. "Do me a solid and aim for the bowl?" he asked.

When his face came into view, Renn's stomach couldn't take it. She turned her face to the toilet bowl, sausages and eggs making their special reunion appearance at the porcelain stadium.

Wallace sat cross-legged on the bathroom floor, posture relaxed but engaged. He pulled a tin from his pocket. "Mint," he offered. Not a question, a statement.

She hesitated, and he shook the tin. "Mint," he said again.

With a pause, Renn took one of the mints, popping it in her mouth. She sniffled as she looked at the pills scattered on the floor. She couldn't meet his eyes. She just couldn't. "Are you going to kill me?" she asked again, voice shaking with fear. "I won't fight. I'll understand. I . . . I would want it to be you. It's—"

Wallace nodded slowly. "It's part of why you chose me. I know, Renn."

Tears streamed down her face as her shoulders quivered. She buried her face in her hands and sobbed for what felt like hours. Wallace did nothing, sitting in silence until she found her voice again.

"I would understand," she said finally, hiccupping. "I killed Nellie," she whispered.

Wallace took an audible breath. "I know, Renn."

"More than once."

Another pause, then again, "I know, Renn."

"I betrayed you."

"I know, Renn."

"I couldn't do it anymore. I was supposed to be stronger."

"I know you think that, Renn."

Another long stretch of silence as her body somehow found more water to eject through her eyes. Wallace made no sudden moves, but once the tears had slowed, his hand fell slowly and gently onto her knee. "Renn. Renn, look at me."

She shook her head and kept her face in her palms.

"Renn," he repeated gently. "I need you to look at me. It's important."

The sincerity in his voice grabbed her attention, and she forced herself to look into his eyes. Unlike hers, they still had a soul. They looked sincere, and they didn't waver an inch as he spoke.

"You are not alone, Renn. I'm not mad. I'm not angry. I never have been. I just want you here."

"But I—"

"You made a tremendously difficult decision under unimaginable duress," he countered before she could even finish her thought. "I know that it felt manageable, even fun, those first few days. Even weeks. You know that guy, Sisyphus. He was punished by being forced to relive the same day over and over again. The Greeks had it right. It's torturous. Maddening. More so than anybody would ever believe, I think. I get why Marty didn't even make it a week. We weren't meant to do the same thing over and over again."

He gave her knee a squeeze. "I'm glad you gave me the journal, Renn."

Renn's eyes widened at that. "You . . . What . . . How could you be glad?"

Gingerly, he moved his hand from her knee to her palm, cradling it gently in his. "Because on that first day, when we found out you were gone, all I could think about was what I would give to do the day over, so I could stop it from happening. So I wouldn't lose you. And you gave that to me, Renn."

Her lip quivered in harmony with her trembling hands. She looked once more at the pills on the ground, but Wallace rose to his knees and lifted a hand. With a perfect balance of strength and gentleness, he nudged her chin back up, making eye contact once more.

"I've read every entry," he said, "and I still want you here. I still *need* you here, Renn. You haven't scared me off. I know everything you did and thought in that loop, just like you know all the same things about Nellie, and Marty, and Pele."

She placed her hand back on his, raising it to her cheek. She didn't know why. Perhaps so she could smell him better. Maybe so he could catch her stupid tears. Maybe she just wanted to feel his warmth.

"You . . . you read *every* entry?" she asked, knowing full well what that meant. The journal recorded the actions and thoughts of the current owner for every day they were in the loop.

Wallace nodded. "Every last one. I . . . I particularly enjoyed the one where we kissed," he said, a playful smile sneaking onto his face.

Renn's guilt gave way to sheer horror and embarrassment. She felt her face turn bright red as she buried her face in her hands once more. "Oh noooooo!" she moaned. This was worse than when her brother had found her fanfiction account. "Please just kill me," she said.

Wallace laughed, and she felt his hands on her shoulders. Traitorously, she started laughing with him. The nervous, relieved kind of laugh. A laugh of somebody who'd broken . . . but maybe not beyond repair.

Wallace pulled her into a hug, and she let loose another nervous giggle as she buried her face in his shoulder. "We've only got about three more minutes before somebody else comes in here and reports us to the principal," he whispered after a few moments. "I've got a plan, Renn. We've been working on it for a while now."

"We?" Renn asked as they separated.

"All of us," he said. "Everybody who's had the journal since it got dug up. We even have a couple of the oldies trying to make things right."

Renn's mind immediately flashed to Nellie. Her best friend. The one she'd killed three times, only once getting caught.

"It's hard, I know," Wallace said, interrupting her thoughts as he began picking up pills and dropping them in the toilet. "But we've got to get through this together. No more passing it on to the next person and pretending it isn't our problem anymore. Each one of us who knows what's going on, we're working together."

"But how can we be working together if—?"

"We use the journal," Wallace said. "It's the only way to preserve all the research we've already done. I've already got text messages scheduled to send to everybody that will convince them to come to the library after school. From there, we brainstorm and plan together, as a united front."

Renn knelt in stunned silence as Wallace picked up the last of the pills and flushed them down the toilet. "You . . . You really think you can break the loop, don't you?" she asked, awestruck. It was a childish dream she'd given up on long ago.

Wallace smiled as he grabbed her hands and they both stood. "I know we will. We've made headway. Serious headway. The first entry, the one that takes place the day after the stars disappeared, we realized it's connected. Somebody *visited* from . . . well, it's either from the future, or from a different dimension. We're still fuzzy on that one. But something went wrong. Their technology leaked *some* kind of radiation. Real timey-whimey Doctor Who stuff. The journal is infected with it. We're close to answers. We know why the time capsule worked, but it only manages to postpone the inevitable. We're working on a permanent solution. Soon, I'll pass on the journal to Gayton Lin. He's going to be the final stretch."

Renn blinked at that. "Gayton? Why Gayton?" Gayton wasn't exactly sociable in person, but she was familiar with his relatively popular streaming channel.

"You ever watch his streams?" Wallace said with a smile. "His *whole* schtick is learning to do the most punishing game levels he can find. He's used to respawning and starting over and over again. He once spent four months trying to beat a custom built Mario level. He's eager to have his shot, and he's been a major player in the research."

Renn blinked at the stupid genius of it. Could it be that simple? A gamer? Was that really the answer?

"I won't let you lose hope again," Wallace said. "Not if I can help it. There *will* be a tomorrow. I promise."

"You can't promise that," she whispered, holding tight to his hands.

"I can do what I want, Renn Hendrickson. Especially since I know the future."

She snorted at that. "Cheater," she muttered.

"Takes one to know one. How many tries did it take for you to get that kiss just right? Eighteen?"

She blushed again and buried her face in his chest. "You're a jerk."

"Well, you can tell me all about it tomorrow," he said with a chuckle.

She paused, furrowing her brow. "Why tomorrow?"

"Because we have work to do today," he said, "and tomorrow is when we have our first proper date scheduled. I guess you just forgot the first hundred times you said yes."

Renn's heart stopped. Heat rose to her cheeks, and something broke in her chest. A wall. A shell. Something hard that had been sitting around her heart. And she realized for the first time that maybe Wally had learned to love her too. On a different day. On a hundred different days she couldn't remember.

And maybe . . . maybe he'd even still love her tomorrow.

END NOTE

This journal should be sitting snugly in artifact pod 613. However, Artifact pod 613 remains—for the foreseeable future—empty. Because while we know where the journal is, we have no idea how to retrieve it. We do this wrong and one of us will be stuck in a time loop figuring this out on their own.

According to Ren, the journal uses some kind of bioscan and virus to connect to and loop its subject. The journal came through when the splinter was created, that we know. And that's about all we know. Was it intentional? Or did some Immortal frothpot accidentally drop their novelty diary into the hole during the splinter event? Who made it, who sent it, and what in the name of the Great Cat Mother are they trying to accomplish with it?

—Green Kinsha

THE AWAKENING OF CHARA BEXLER

By Jessica Kendall

I, Chara Bexler, am not a Twisted.

I have a lovely gift to Awaken.

I am not a Twisted.

The magnatrain glides through the darkness toward Altan City as I chant to myself. The lone silver moon does almost nothing to light our way along the magnatrack, instead making the windows like mirrors. Toby bounces next to me—oblivious in the way only a child too young to understand the Awakening could be—waving his little toy Sungazer doll around.

We've all heard the stories about Collin Gazer's Awakening. His powers surfaced almost immediately, and the sixteen-year-old was nicknamed Sungazer before leaving Altan's chamber because of his glowing eyes and his ability to captivate people with one glance.

That could be me.

What Blessing will awaken inside of me?

I won't be a Twisted.

Toby stands on the seat and spins in a circle, making Sungazer fly through the air until the stupid plastic doll cracks into my forehead.

"Toby!" I shout and shove him back into his seat, then press my hand to my head. Is that sweat or blood?

His discordant wailing fills the train car. From across the divide, Mom holds her arms wide and welcomes the evil little beast into her lap. *I'm* the one bleeding, but *he* gets hugs. The perks of being a four-year-old from a second marriage. Disappearing with his father would have been a boon to my life with Mom.

I pull my hand away and see a splotch of blood on my palm before frantically looking down at my dress. Three little dots of red flash bright against the white cotton fabric of the Awakening dress I took weeks to pick out. "Mom!"

"It's fine, Chara. It's barely a drop."

"It's not fine, Mom!" I say, standing and leaning forward to keep any more from dripping on my dress. How could a giftless Fallow like her know what this meant? "I'm supposed to be in pure white. If I go in with blood on my clothes, everyone will think I'm a Twisted, even before I can touch Altan."

I've been fighting to keep my Awakening dress clean for days—not an easy feat with Toby running around the house. His grubby little fingers want to defile everything, and his favorite way of getting Mom's attention is pissing me off and getting us both in trouble. Not smothering the little half-blood gremlin in his sleep is my greatest gift to my mother.

"Don't be dramatic." She pulls a handkerchief out of her purse and hands it to me. "The meteor decides, not a spot of blood on your clothes."

"That's not true, and you know it." I yank the fabric from her hand and press it to my forehead.

The Meteor Council decides if the gift Altan Awakens is that of a Twisted or a Blessed. It has been that way for a century, since the meteor crashed and the children of the first settlers touched the stone and were Awakened. And if someone on the council sees blood on my dress before I even touch Altan, they could think I am sullied in other ways besides just on my dress. It will be even worse if my blessing isn't immediately obvious. They could easily decide that I am a Fallow—all for three drops of blood. Or worse, if they thought this blood was the result of some violence I committed, they might assume I was a savage Twisted and send me directly to the kiln.

We've all heard the endless rumors about the kiln, but no one really knows the truth. Is it a fiery box where Twisted are burned alive, or a testing site to see if the council's original judgment was incorrect, or a violent arena where Twisted are pitted against each other to fight to the death? The only thing anyone knows for sure is that no one ever comes back.

I could die tonight because of this miserable little cretin, and he is currently sticking his tongue out at me and playing the victim in front of my mother.

"I'm going to the bathcar," I say and march out into the corridor, still holding my mother's tattered handkerchief to my head, then slam the compartment door behind me. If I can find some cold water before this dries, I might stand a chance of rinsing it out. But then I would have a sopping wet dress for the Awakening ceremony.

Gah! I could kill Toby!

My blurry reflection in the glass of the compartment door window glares back at me, all judgment and frustration. The pleats of my dress mostly hide the three red dots, but I can still see them when the fabric shifts.

Why does blood have to be red? It's such an ugly, violent, attention-seeking color. No one looks good in red.

I hurry toward the bathcar and hope the water tank hasn't been emptied this far into the train ride. Maybe, after scrubbing my skirt, if I find a place to tuck into for the duration, I won't have to see Toby for the rest of this ride. And then, after my gift is Awakened, I'll get a fabulous new nickname and move to the transition station and never have to see his smug little rat-face ever again.

Maybe my gift will be so incredible that they will give me special accommodations. I can see it now, me, all in white, my coppery brown hair a perfect contrast to my fair skin, walking regally out of the arena and into the street to applause from all the waiting parents. They'll choke with envy when I outshine all the others.

The image of all those disappointed parents flickers in my mind and pulls my mouth into a grin as I navigate the narrow passage toward the bathcar. A whisper of nerves follows it, but I quickly remind myself that I am not a Twisted.

I've heard stories though. Stories of scales and slime and distortion of mind and body. Of malevolent creatures that tear out of your skin and attack after touching Altan. They are so ugly that the council refuses to even let them be seen after their Twisted nature is Awakened. It is done to protect the populace from nightmares, but I can't help wanting to see one for myself.

Three train cars later, I finally find the bathcar.

No line. *Thank Altan's Maker!*

I hurry inside, thumbprint the faucet, and run water onto a clean corner of the handkerchief, then pick the smallest of those three offending stains and scrub. A pink smear spreads out from the tiny dot.

I freeze.

What do I do now, aside from start planning Toby's painful demise in earnest?

It's no use. The only hope I have is that the arena is dim enough and I'm far enough away from the council that they won't see my stain. Muffled voices carry through the doorway. I hurry into the nearest watercloset and latch the door behind me. I can't face any judgmental stares or comments. The voices grow closer. It sounds like a few girls around my age, probably on their way to the Awakening. One has a voice like an obnoxious know-it-all, and I peek through the crack in my watercloset door to see what she looks like. Short. Round. Unremarkable.

"You know that they only take a certain number of Blessed every year."

"What does that mean?" The second girl's voice squeaks like a mouse.

"It means"—Miss Know-It-All pauses for dramatic effect—"that even if your gift is Blessed, they only have so many slots in transition, so they will only take however many they can accommodate."

"That can't be true."

The squeaky mouse sounds terrified and hugs her bony frame, making the slight staining on the cuffs of her clearly hand-me-down Awakening dress more obvious. She must suspect she's a Twisted, or perhaps a Blessed with a boring enough gift to not make the cut. I suppose that might be the one benefit of being a Fallow with no gift at all. You just get sent home and have to live with the shame of Altan not Awakening anything in you. I once again chant in my head while the girls' conversation continues outside the watercloset.

I, Chara Bexler, am not a Twisted.

I have a lovely gift to Awaken.

I am not a Twisted.

"It *is* true," Miss Know-It-All says, sounding even more bossy. "And everyone else, even if they are Blessed, goes to the kiln to cover it up."

Little Mouse gasps. "No way."

"It's true."

"The council wouldn't do that." This third voice sounds bored, maybe even on the verge of annoyed. The owner's dress matches her tone. Perfectly boring. "And there is no way something like that wouldn't be common knowledge if they tried it."

"Oh yeah? My dad says that the council is untrustworthy."

"Shhhhhhhhh!"

I almost join in and shush the girl from inside my watercloset. Those are not words to be thrown around lightly, and no one knows where the council's watchers have their eyes. The sound of shuffling feet moves toward the next watercloset over.

The door squeaks open, but instead of more whispers, three screams ricochet around the bathcar. I shove out of my own watercloset and whirl to see a blond girl in white, hanging by a rope around her neck tied to a pipe in the ceiling and swinging in time with the gentle sway of the train. One polished black shoe has come off and lies on the floor under her. Her arms swing just a little more than the rest of her body. She hasn't been here long . . . but long enough.

I spin to run out of the bathcar—being tied to death only begs more questions—but the screams of the obnoxious trio have called the train attendants and a few curious onlookers who try to crowd into the bathcar to stare at the dead girl. I want to look away, but my eyes keep traveling back up to the macabre sight. The girl wore her hair in simple pigtails with white lace bows tying them off. Her fingernails are cut short—too short. Probably a farm worker trying to avoid being caught with dirt under her nails during the Awakening.

"You four," a tall, willowy man in a train conductor's uniform says, pointing at me and the gossipers.

The injustice of being lumped in with these three is almost too much to bear. After muttering into his walkie, the willowy man and his portly sidekick usher us from the room. With one final glance over my shoulder, I see the flash of a yellow hazard light as the attendant seals off the bathcar.

The willowy man leads the way with Mouse, Know-It-All, and Bored following in a line. His portly sidekick nudges me along, even though I try to lag so I can avoid any more involvement than necessary. I have nothing to do with Pigtails or these other three.

Several cars later, we enter the conductor's opulent office. Willowy Man walks to a wide-backed leather chair facing away from us and whispers to the occupant. Portly Man blocks the exit with his wide frame. Suddenly, getting smacked in the head by Toby seems like a welcome alternative.

A woman's voice speaks from the chair. "Chara, Nera, Cali, and Bea."

I look at the three girls, wondering which girl belongs to which name, until I realize I don't care and want nothing to do with any of them.

"All on your way to your Awakenings. What did you see?" the woman's voice asks from her overly wide leather chair, still facing away.

The three girls share furtive glances, but only Bored looks over her too-wide shoulder at me. She must be accustomed to hard labor. Nothing ladylike breeds shoulders like that.

The hum of the magnatrack accentuates the heavy silence. Portly nudges me forward, forcing me into the lineup with the other girls.

"What did you see?" the woman's voice asks again.

I shouldn't even be here. "I didn't see anything," I say in the nonchalant way I perfected after Dad number two's disappearance and now use when Toby tries to get me in trouble. "I was just using the watercloset and then a crowd of people burst into the bathcar."

The large leather chair slowly spins to reveal a tiny blonde woman in a black council robe. Councilwoman Chancy. I barely hold my gasp. Councilwoman Chancy is one of the few Blessed to be Awakened during the Aberrant War. There have always been rumors that those Awoken during the dark years should have been sent away as Twisted, but their skills were too powerful to lose, and the war against the Wildings outside the Quadrants needed to be won. The council doesn't allow that practice of leniency anymore, but they can't very well change the designation of war heroes from Blessed to Twisted now.

Councilwoman Chancy sets four files on the table in front of her, each with one of our names on the top tab—so that's what Willowy was muttering into his walkie—and stares at me. I watch her eyes travel down to the three crimson dots on my dress then back up to the red mark on my forehead. Of course she would notice the blood. With her gift, she could probably smell it. A smile cracks her face, and her intense gaze travels over the other three girls.

"And the rest of you, what did you see?"

Bored steps forward, as if trying to look confident, but her fidgeting fingers behind her back give her away. "I thought I saw a mouse under the sink."

Councilwoman Chancy's eyes narrow. Bored doesn't lie as well as me, but at least she's smart enough to know that the council doesn't like drama or headlines.

"It was just a shadow, but it scared me . . . and I screamed," Bored stammers out.

Councilwoman Chancy's eyes travel to Know-It-All next. "Cali?"

"Nera's scream scared me . . . so I screamed too."

"Me too," Mouse blurts even before being asked, while keeping her eyes on the floor. She looks about ready to cry. "I . . . I don't like . . . mice."

I nearly roll my eyes that a girl who hates mice can sound just like one. I want out of this room and away from these girls who all look to be wavering between crying and vomiting. I've never understood girls who cry at the slightest provocation. One would think they'd never seen a dead body before.

"Well . . ." Councilwoman Chancy taps her fingernails on the metal table in front of her. "I would hate for you young ladies to be publicly shamed by a story of a phantom mouse or for your Awakenings to be delayed . . . or denied, over such trivial matters."

Her words hang heavy, and everything in me clenches. That can't happen. I can't be denied my Blessing, and I won't endure the train ride home to rumors of being a Fallow.

"You were correct, Owen." She glances up at the willowy man. "*Nothing* occurred in the bathcar. But to prevent any unfounded rumors from disrupting this year's Awakenings"—she looks back at us—"how about we agree that none of you were there?"

I resist looking at the other three and just nod at Councilwoman Chancy. I can only assume she is being so magnanimous to avoid a scandal, but I'm not going to pass on it. Thank Altan's Maker. One thing finally went right today.

After another pointed but curious glance down at the blood on my dress, Councilwoman Chancy waves a complacent hand toward the door. "Please take them to the VIP dining car for the duration of our trip. I'm very curious to see what gifts these girls are hiding."

Know-It-All, who is apparently named Cali, turns completely white. The mouse called Bea looks like she's going to faint. Bored—Nera—still looks bored, except for the tightness in her jaw. Owen—though Willowy fits better—herds us down the corridor and into the opulent dining car. He waves us in and then steps back into the breezeway. Before shutting the partition, he says, "Remember, girls, it would be a shame for anyone to miss their Awakenings because of rumors or shadow mice."

I never claimed to have seen a mouse and I have no intention of spreading rumors, so I ignore him.

Never in my life would I have thought I'd be sitting in the council's VIP dining car . . . at least not before awakening my gift and being recognized for my grand contributions to the Quadrants and Altan City.

The three trembling girls perch on the edges of the chairs at the nearest table. They act like the spotless padded chairs are going to bite them. I would wager that Know-It-All has no Blessing, Mouse has a lame Blessing, and Bored is a Twisted. I bet she'll have scales . . . but boring ones, not even colorful.

Not wanting to be lumped in with them, I wander to the other end of the empty dining car, admiring the gilded light fixtures, glistening tabletops, and full display cases of delectable pastries. The full moon makes one side of the train car glow a bit brighter than the other. If only the light wasn't being reflected by the glass. I look good in moonlight, so I settle into a chair three tables away from the girls and right next to the window. As much as I try to ignore them, I can't help but hear their nervous voices.

Know-it-all Cali drops her voice to a whisper. "That was Lina Able from Farm Quadrant Two."

Bored's palms press against the table. Does she know this Lina girl? Or, *did* she?

"It couldn't be," Mouse replies, sounding almost argumentative. "Lina's brother said she was too sick to join this Awakening."

Know-It-All leans as far forward as the table will allow. "My aunt told me that she was already showing signs of Twisted, but her dad insisted she come. I guess the humiliation was too much; she ended it so she wouldn't be put down or dragged to the kiln."

The air hangs heavy and silent in the dining car. The council was good at coverups, but we'd all heard the stories. Lina was hardly the first to choose death over the unknown inside her. *Coward*. I close my eyes and try to feel the moonglow on my face. It doesn't work. The glass is too good a barrier to let it in.

I, Chara Bexler, am not a Twisted.

I am a Blessed and have a lovely gift to Awaken.

I am not a Twisted.

"I heard she hunted with her brother and actually killed bunnies for meat. Only a Twisted would kill."

I feel my eyes roll behind the lids and resist the urge to point out that her local butcher is clearly not a Twisted, or he would have gone to the kiln too. Some people are too ignorant to attempt enlightenment though.

The speaker blares to life, and I'm infinitely grateful that the undignified squeals of the other girls cover my soft gasp.

"Now entering Altan City. Please claim your possessions and prepare to deboard." Councilwoman Chancy's voice is clear and commanding. I'm still not sure how to feel about having a Blessed who can manipulate blood as our Council Escort.

I wonder what my Mom and Toby are doing. Toby should never have been on the train. This was supposed to be my day. At this point, I'm not even sure Mom will make it to Altan's Cathedral to hear what Blessing I have. She might figure that she's done her duty by getting me on the train and just turn around and go home.

I've never been to the cathedral that was built around the meteor crash site. I've seen holo-pics and heard the stories. And now I'm so close.

The train slows down and finally settles with a soft jerk. I stand and march past the other girls and straight to willowy Owen. He opens the side door. The night chill seeps in, and I skip down onto the platform, immediately spotting Councilwoman Chancy in her flowing black robes. She is marching toward a gaping opening that looks like it just ends in open air and blackness.

"All candidates follow the signs to the stairs," she says as she hurries in that direction.

After a few steps, I look over my shoulder and see my mom's head bobbing through the crowd. Toby's arm waves above her head, still swinging that stupid Sungazer doll around. Maybe if my mom took a Sungazer to the forehead, she might be less inclined to cater to the little monster in her arms. I guess I should be happy that she disembarked and seems to be making her way to the family waiting area.

The candidates and their families separate, like a magnet is pulling all the white-clothed bodies down the stairwell. I fold my hands in front of me, trying—hopefully successfully—to hide those three ruby drops. The press of dozens of bodies is almost suffocating as everyone crowds down the narrow stairs and into the cramped, underground subtrack. Annoyingly, Know-It-All, Mouse, and Bored are tailing me.

Every time I glance over my shoulder at them, I think of Lina's dangling body and wonder if she really was a Twisted. What are they going to do with the body? Did they put the shoe back on her foot, or did they just throw it away? It was so shiny. Why did she put that much effort into shining her shoes if she was Twisted? Or was it because she knew she was Twisted and was overcompensating for it?

The subtrack lurches to a halt, and once again, we are herded into underground tunnels made of heavy granite. The sporadic lights and the damp smell of underground stone add to the cloud of nervous sweat wafting off our procession. Within the hour, I will have my gift. I *will* have my gift.

I, Chara Bexler, am not a Twisted.

I am a Blessed and have a lovely gift to Awaken.

I am not a Twisted.

Double doors open ahead of us and Councilwoman Chancy leads our group into the arena where I finally get my first glance at Altan. A rough stone pillar rises out of the middle of the arena, and on it rests a glossy black stone the size of . . . of Lina's dangling body. I try to think of something else to compare it to, but it's about five feet long and narrow enough that it could actually be a glossy, black bodypod.

The whole floor is a mosaic of white tiles with black grout. The swirling patterns leading up to Altan's pillar are almost dizzying. High walls close the arena in on all sides. Councilwoman Chancy, along with all the other council members, sits in high-backed chairs evenly spaced around the arena—but on the opposite side of the wall. They can look down on all of us and see what is Awakened in us from a safe distance.

The stragglers among the few dozen candidates are pushed the rest of the way into the arena and then the double doors close behind them. A bright spotlight shines directly down on Altan from a domed ceiling so high above that I can't even imagine how tall it is.

"In the darkest of days, the night sky blessed this land with a gift." Head

Councilman Dekker's voice rings through the arena, not a difficult feat when Altan had Blessed him with the ability to magnify his voice at will. "Nearly a century ago, in a shower of radiant light, the night sky lost its stars, but gifted us Altan. Altan struck and brought with it the power to elevate our people, to help us build this city around it, and to make us stand alone as supreme among the Wildings who live outside the walls of our civilized order."

Head Councilman Dekker pauses as if for emphasis. Mother often said he was a bit of a showman, and she seemed to be correct.

"Each year, when the moon comes nearest in its cycle and pours its light on Altan," he gestures toward the shaft of moonlight shining down on Altan's pillar, "—we present our children before it to be Awakened and to claim their gifts or be exposed and expelled from our society."

The sound of feet scuffing across the tiled floor carries through the cavernous arena. And from the increasingly shallow breathing of the few people standing near me, it's clear that the rest of this group isn't doing as well at keeping their cool as they had during the walk here.

Dekker raises both his hands high into the air, his body forming a Y.

"If you are ready to be Awakened to your true form and potential, come forward." After another few seconds, Dekker lowers his arms and his gaze sweeps over the crowd of trembling white-clad teens.

I don't know why, but my feet suddenly feel heavy. What is wrong with me? This is what I want. This is what I've been dreaming of.

A tall boy with dark skin and buzzed hair pushes through the crowd and approaches Altan's pillar.

"Name?" Dekker asks with a smile on his lips.

"Brek Noah," he replies, sounding almost confident.

"Brek Noah, approach and be Awakened." Dekker gives a slight nod toward Altan.

Brek squares his broad shoulders and clenches his fists. He moves with confident strides toward the pillar and the five steps up to the platform that surrounds it. Other than his footsteps across the tile and up those five steps, no other sound can be heard.

I wish the group hadn't stopped so far from Altan's pillar. I desperately want a closer look. Brek stops just before Altan, still close enough for us to see the deep inhale before he raises his hand. An echoing inhale sounds from all around me as if the group shares the same set of lungs.

Brek extends his hand and, after only a slight hesitation, rests it on the glossy black surface of Altan. All nervousness forgotten, I'm now completely jealous. I should have been first. I should have been the one Dekker smiled at. Now Brek is going to be the one Dekker and the other council members remember.

After a few short seconds, Brek hunches forward. Half the white-clad kids step forward and half shy away. We can hear his groans, but he doesn't appear to be in pain. It's a little disappointing, to be honest. I had hoped that there would be lights or sparks or something more interesting than a hunching, grunting boy.

Brek straightens up and looks around the room.

"Brek Noah, are you Awakened?" Head Councilman Dekker says, his conversational voice echoing around the whole arena.

Brek looks at old Dekker. "I feel . . . strong . . . stronger than I've ever felt."

"Interesting. Let's test that." Dekker waves a hand, and five men walk into the arena with a long rope. I've heard that the council has a myriad of tools for testing Blessings. Rope seems a bit rudimentary, but I suppose it is effective. Brek steps down from the platform, still looking nervous but oddly confident.

The man in front tosses one end of the rope to Brek and then the other four men take hold of the opposite end.

"Show us this strength."

Dekker's command feels like a challenge. It makes me wonder how many boys have claimed to have superstrength as their gift.

Brek grips the rope, plants his feet, then pulls on one end of the rope. The other five men pull back, but Brek doesn't budge under their combined strength.

"Very good," Dekker calls to them. "You are Blessed, Brek Noah. Please follow your brothers to your new life."

Brek drops the rope, and the five men lead him out a door directly below where Dekker is sitting. Nothing flashy. No pomp or ceremony. Disappointing again. To all outward appearances, Brek's Blessing was extraordinary. He should get a nickname, or there should be some degree of celebration.

"Next candidate."

I step forward, but not fast enough. A tragically unattractive girl with an ill-fitting dress steps in front of me. Fine by me. I'm curious to see what the council actually does when they encounter a Fallow or a Twisted, and I'm nearly positive this unfortunate-looking girl is one or the other.

"Name?" Dekker asks.

"Flora Dahl."

"Flora Dahl, approach and be Awakened."

She lumbers to the stone and, without any pause or pretense, slaps her hand on its surface. A light flashes under her palm, and she staggers back and falls on her backside. I wait to see if she'll sprout horns or a tail or scales, but she just starts laughing. The door under Councilman Dekker opens, and four guards enter with their shock wands and guns at the ready.

"Flora Dahl, are you Awakened?"

"I . . . I . . ." she giggles like a girl much smaller and much younger, "I think so. My palms feel tickly."

The soldiers approach. Flora stands, staring at her hands, opening and closing them as if something will magically appear in them. I can't help but notice Councilwoman Chancy stand and lean forward. She looks eager, almost hungry. I imagine she would love to help corral a newly Awakened Twisted. Life for a Blessed soldier of the Aberrant War must be boring now, even if she did get promoted to the council.

One of the soldiers stops in front of Flora and only slightly lowers his shock wand. "Hold out your hands."

I wish I could get closer and see what is happening. What if she is growing claws or suckers like the water animals I've read about in books?

Flora thrusts her hands forward, and a smattering of sparks falls to the ground. If that party trick is all Altan Awakened in her, there is no way she will be Blessed. The soldier raises his shock wand back up and glances sideways at Head Councilman Dekker. Dekker looks around the circle of council members. They either nod or shake their heads.

Dekker's gaze lingers on Councilwoman Chancy. Soon, everyone is looking at her.

"There are uses in this gift," she says. Though her voice isn't Blessing-magnified, it still cuts through the air, and lands deeper than just in my ears. It's almost like she is speaking in my blood. Fear and jealousy claw for my attention. Oh, to have a Blessing that powerful.

Head Councilman Dekker clears his throat. "Flora Dahl, the council requires further discussion on the status of your gift. Please exit"—he gestures toward the nameless soldier who still holds his shock wand ready—"and you will be informed of your status shortly."

Flora's face pales. As terrible as it is, being a Fallow is better than being a Twisted. Fallows at least get to live. But if the council doesn't like what they see after observing Flora more, she is headed for the kiln.

I, Chara Bexler, am not a Twisted.

I am a Blessed and have a lovely gift to Awaken.

I am not a Twisted.

Now that the first boy and girl have already gone, there is no more prestige attached to who goes next. And if I go now, I won't get to see any Fallows or Twisteds. So, I stay at the front of the crowd so I can see clearly.

Several more candidates step up. The next seven are complete disappointments. All Fallow. Head Councilman Dekker not-so-politely asks them to leave, and they are quickly escorted out the doors we came in, as if being allowed to enter any part of the cathedral proper would be defiling hallowed ground. I know from the stories that they will have full medical checkups to ensure that no Twisted are able to sneak through under the guise of being Fallow. No one wants another Aberrant War.

There is a smattering of girls who have a gift Awakened, but the council is not impressed, and they are taken for observation. The council looks more and more bored.

Twin boys approach the stone together. When nothing happens, Dekker starts to wave his hand toward the door behind our dwindling group until one of the boys speaks up. "I hear his thoughts," the boys say in unison.

"Whose thoughts?" Councilwoman Dane asks. She has looked on the verge of falling asleep since we were escorted in here, but now she finally seems interested.

"My brother's," the boys say together.

Councilwoman Dane flops back into her chair. I don't blame her. Mind-reading would have been an impressive and powerful gift. Mind-reading for only your twin is just an augmentation of what twins are rumored to already share. Further evidence that Altan doesn't give a gift—it Awakens what is already inside you.

The twins are led through the same door as all the other Awakened whose gifts are less than impressive.

I don't know why, but between each new candidate, I can't help glancing back at Know-It-All, Mouse, and Bored. Mouse is getting more and more fidgety, and I wonder if she is wishing she'd followed Lina's example to save herself the humiliation of being Fallow. When there are only a handful of candidates left, she rushes forward. I wouldn't have expected that from her. I assumed she would be the last. I've even heard stories about some candidates being dragged to Altan and forced to touch it.

"Name?"

"Bea Nox," she squeaks.

"Bea Nox, approach and be Awakened."

Mouse shuffles to the stairs and then drags her feet up each step, her former fidgety eagerness apparently forgotten. She'd better hurry up or the moon is going to set and the rest of us will be out of luck until the next lunar approach.

She sucks in a breath so loudly that it sounds like someone is sweeping the walls with a stiff broom, then rams her hand against Altan. Nothing happens. She lifts her other hand and presses it on the meteor too.

Like touching it with both hands is going to make a difference.

I feel a derisive chuckle rising in my chest when Mouse slumps onto Altan. Almost like she's hugging it. Now the glossy black meteor looks even more like it could be Lina's bodypod, and Mouse is her only mourner.

Councilwoman Chancy practically jumps out of her chair. "Protectors!" she shouts, then leaps the barricade and lands hard on the tile just as the doors below Head Councilman Dekker swing open and protectors come pouring into the arena. The lights, once dimmed everywhere except directly on Altan, blaze bright.

A deep-throated rattle chitters around the echo chamber of the arena. The rest of the candidates shuffle back toward the wall, but I scoot forward. This might be the only chance I'll ever get to see a Twisted, and I'm not passing on it.

The rattle grows louder and louder. Mouse's bare arms are turning a deep purple, and her now-black veins stand out against the white of her almost-pristine Awakening dress. It's mesmerizing.

"Miss Nox, are you Awakened?" Councilwoman Chancy asks from a few steps away from the bottom step of Altan's platform. The protectors have formed a circle around the platform and stand between it and the remaining candidates.

Mouse's body trembles against the meteor. The rattling coming from her reminds me of the stories of snakes our wrinkled old schoolteacher told us about. He'd been an outland dweller before his Awakening and said there were snakes near the wall that would rattle their threats before striking.

Mouse pulls away from Altan. Chunks of her skin remain behind, as if seared to the meteor. The rattling stops, and the whole arena is eerily silent. She spins toward Councilwoman Chancy, her face in a contorted grin. Her skin droops, as if her smile is fighting to keep the skin on her skull.

"Miss Nox, are you Awakened?" Councilwoman Chancy asks again, this time pushing her sleeves up and planting her feet like the carnival boxers I watched at the harvest festival.

Mouse looks from her hands to Councilwoman Chancy and then, as if drawn by a magnet, toward me. Her bloodshot eyes travel from my face down to my legs. She hunches forward and inhales, then the rattle starts back up again. Chancy glances sideways to follow Mouse's line of sight and also looks down at my dress.

It snaps inside me. The blood.

I'm going to *kill* Toby!

A thrill of fear scrapes over my skin, but I won't move. While Dad was alive, he always said to stand your ground against a predator. Not that it did *him* any good.

Mouse leaps the five steps down from Altan's platform and rushes at me. Know-It-All screams from behind me, and I roll my eyes. The protectors close ranks and block Mouse's path to me. Their shock wands snap against her skin, and huge chunks peel off and stay attached to the prongs.

Something shimmers where her skin has been torn off. Is she growing scales? I can't resist stepping closer to get a better look.

Councilwoman Chancy walks in measured steps toward the melee of protectors and Mouse's rattling and thrashing. "Bea Nox, you have been deemed Twisted. If you refuse to submit, you will be terminated."

Mouse shoves the man directly between her and me. He staggers back, leaving her an opening, and she dashes forward.

Councilwoman Chancy's hands whip up in front of her body, gripping the air like a predatory bird swooping in for the kill.

Mouse stumbles forward. Her body claps against the floor and slides a few paces closer to me, trailing blood across the white tiles. A grotesque but fascinating gargling sound drowns out the rattling. After a few seconds of thrashing and gargling, Mouse convulses one more time, flops onto her back, and spits blood into the air above her in one final exhalation.

She's only a few steps away. Close enough that I could wipe away the smeared blood and see what that iridescent sheen under her peeling skin is.

"Chara Bexler."

Councilwoman Chancy's voice yanks me from my absorption. I close my mouth after realizing that it's hanging open in fascination with the macabre scene.

"Yes, Councilwoman Chancy?" I say with a polite nod.

She glances at the three dots of blood on my skirt and back at Mouse. "Please make way for the custodians to remove the Twisted."

I step back and watch as a group of people dressed in full protective garb rush to Mouse's oozing body, lift her into another glossy black bodypod, then zip it closed. They don't clear the smudged blood away, but I notice one of them climb the platform, scrape Mouse's torn flesh off the meteor, then quickly buff it to a shine.

Somehow, during their cleanup, Councilwoman Chancy makes it back to her seat, but I wasn't paying close enough attention to whether there was a door that led up there or if she scaled the wall. Either way, I'm standing nearest Altan, and Dekker is looking down at me as if what just happened was nothing noteworthy.

After all the protectors and custodians have cleared the arena, Head Councilman Dekker waves a complacent hand, gesturing toward Altan. The rest of the candidates cower against the wall. Now is my chance to make an impression. I thought I'd lost it by not going first. But going after a Twisted and getting a brilliant gift will make me stand out even more.

I step forward, shoulders back and head held high. I don't even try to hide the blood on my dress anymore. I am so much more than a few drops of blood. If they didn't notice it before, I could easily say that it was Mouse's blood that spattered on me. Having someone else's blood on me isn't as much a humiliation as wearing my own because of my beastly little brother.

"Name?" Head Councilman Dekker asks.

"Chara Bexler," I say proudly.

"Chara Bexler, approach and be Awakened."

After only a fraction of a debate, I decide to walk right through Mouse's blood smear instead of skirting around it. I don't want anyone to think I'm weak or squeamish. I've never struggled with other people's blood: I'm not starting now. I still don't like the color, though. Red always seems so ostentatious.

I reach the stairs faster than expected. The five steps up are slightly taller than standard steps, but not so high that they're awkward or a tripping hazard. How humiliating would that be to faceplant in front of everyone? I suddenly remember the sound Mouse's skull made against the tile and am grateful that I didn't trip.

No one ever said anything about the warm air that pulses off Altan. It's beautiful. So polished I can see my reflection. I almost can't believe I'm finally here. I can finally leave my Fallow mother and monstrous little brother behind. I can finally escape the shadow of Dad's death and Dad Number Two's disappearance.

I feel like I should do something or say something significant, but nothing comes to mind, so I just reach out and press my hand to the warm meteor that will usher me into my new life. Tingles climb up my arm, tickling the underside of my skin. It's warm, and right, and feels like the last piece of the puzzle that I didn't even know was missing has finally been placed.

After a few seconds, the warmth turns hot, almost painful, but not quite.

It feels like the old me is burning away. Unbridled joy fills me, and I can't help the wide smile that pulls at my cheeks and makes my eyes squint.

"Chara Bexler, are you Awakened?" Dekker asks.

As much as I hate to remove my hand from Altan, I know that leaving it there too long will make me look like a desperate Fallow trying to wrest a gift out of the meteor. And I *have* a gift. I don't fully know what it is yet, but there is no way I could feel this way if I was anything but Blessed.

"I am awake, Head Councilman Dekker," I say as I remove my hand from Altan and turn toward him. The air around me shakes, almost dances. What is this? Waves of opalescent joy shimmer from me and toward him, and he smiles at me—actually smiles. What does that mean?

"What do you feel, Chara Bexler?" Councilwoman Chancy asks.

I turn toward her. "I feel . . . happy. No, it's more than that. I feel . . . perfect."

I really do feel perfect. I *am* perfect. I am so much more than all the other candidates. They are nothing by comparison. They are here as a backdrop to the moment of my perfection.

Councilwoman Chancy is smiling back at me until she suddenly blinks, then presses a hand to her chest. Her face turns serious, and she turns toward Head Councilman Dekker. He is already looking around the circle of smiling council members. They feel my shimmering joy, too. There is no other explanation for their uncharacteristic smiles. I follow his gaze around the circle, my attention resting for a few seconds on each council member; I see it reaching for each of them in waves of glittering perfection. They all nod in agreement. Whatever this dazzling gift is, it has shimmered the air between us and won them all over.

Head Councilman Dekker looks to Councilwoman Chancy.

With her hand still pressed to her chest, she shakes her head.

What? Why? The other fourteen council members all look at her, confused but still smiling.

Dekker beckons to Chancy. With a few quick strides, she is beside him, whispering in his ear. I won't let her deter him. I am perfect, and I deserve to be Blessed. My full attention is focused on Dekker, and I can see even thicker opalescent waves dancing toward him.

No one else is looking at the shimmering wave of light. They are all looking at Dekker and Chancy, so it's likely that only I can see my gift. I must make him *feel* it. I must make him understand the joy and power I can bring to the Blessed and all of Altan's children. Dekker turns toward me, still smiling.

He outranks Chancy and can void her vote. I know the council's choice doesn't have to be unanimous, but I hope that Chancy knows she has gained an eternal enemy by trying to stand in my way. Something sharp cuts a jagged line through my shimmering waves, and Chancy flinches and then presses her hand even harder over her chest. Their conversation becomes heated, but Dekker doesn't seem to be giving way. I wish they'd whisper louder so I could hear what Chancy finds so unacceptable about my gift.

Right after wishing that, I hear Chancy's angry whisper. "Be it on your head." Then she stomps back to her place, fist now clenching the robes over her heart.

Dekker stands, and the door under him opens. "You are Blessed, Chara Bexler. Please follow your sister to your new life."

It might be against protocol, but I feel like I need to thank Altan for my gift.

I, Chara Bexler, am not Twisted.

I am Blessed and have a lovely gift.

I am not a Twisted.

Thank you, Altan.

I trace my fingers along the glossy black meteor, sad that I will never get to touch it again, then walk toward the door that will lead to my new life. Dekker and the rest of the council members—except for Chancy—all smile down at me. Though I don't know quite how to do it, I push my shimmer of joy outward toward them, wanting to share in the perfection of this moment.

Through a series of winding corridors, I am brought above ground and led through the lavish cathedral entryway and out the front doors to the street. Crowds of friends and family are waiting in the silvery moonlight. From my count, only Brek's family has been able to celebrate and probably already went home to bask in the knowledge that their son is Blessed.

The rest of these people are nervously waiting for news of their disappointments. If not for the anxiety, they would probably all pass out from exhaustion. It has to be nearing 2:00 a.m. In a moment of pity, I push a wave of glittering joy toward them, and a cheer erupts. I see it ruffle hair and rustle clothes. My chest swells with pride. I am Blessed, and I can share it with those around me.

From a distance, I see Mom working her way through the crowd toward me. Toby sits on her shoulders, still carrying that stupid Sungazer doll.

I hate him, just like I hated his dad. The shimmer sharpens.

Toby's face scrunches up, and he looks like he's in pain. I recognize his crying face, but I can't hear the wails over the cheering people. Mom takes him down from her shoulders and cradles him in her arms, no longer even attempting to push through the crowd.

It's okay. I don't need her anymore. I have the cheers and adoration of Altan City, and I will have my new family of Blessed. Without looking back, I climb into the sleek white shuttle and close the door.

The windows are tinted, so I know that no one can see me, but I can see all their happy faces. I should have been seeing these faces all my life. Dad should have agreed when I asked to move to Altan City. If he had just agreed, Mom never would have needed to marry again and would never have had Toby.

The middle-aged driver is silent and so is my ginger-haired Blessed sister in the front seat. I don't mind though. This is *my* moment. I don't need to share it with anyone. I stare out my window and admire the night sky. I feel akin to the moon at this moment. So bright and beautiful in a sea of boring black.

We quickly leave the crowd behind. I close my eyes and try to explore my gift. I don't know exactly how it works or even what it does, but it made the whole council—except for Chancy—see that I am Blessed. I did that. I don't know how yet. But I did make them feel it. What else can I do?

Twenty minutes later, the driver stops in front of a tall, white, boxy building. The only light is over a simple door at the front. I try not to be annoyed that the older Blessed aren't waiting up to greet the newcomers and celebrate them. The Blessed sister in the front seat gets out and waits for me to open my own door. With a huff, I comply and climb out.

"You'll be announced as our newest Blessed at breakfast in the morning. I'll show you to your bed. We have full days here, so no one will thank you for making noise this late. You might want to just sleep in your Awakening dress and then explore your kit in the morning. You have a cabinet of new clothes, toiletries, and a schedule for your new trainings and duties, but you can see all that at sunrise."

"At sunrise?" I nearly choke. "I'm supposed to get up at sunrise after my Awakening night?" Doesn't this girl know who I am? Doesn't she even care about what I can do, what I made everyone feel? She is Blessed, too, so she must know how important this night is for me. Can't she at least pretend to be happy for me?

"It's rough, but we all did it too, so don't try to play the victim. Don't worry, bedtime is early, so after a few days you'll make up the sleep debt."

She starts toward the door and gently turns the knob until a soft click sounds and the door gives way. It makes sense that there are no locked doors. Everyone here is Blessed. They have no reason to feel threatened.

We step inside. The glow from the moon shining through the windows offers tilted pillars of light to navigate the aisle between the twenty or so beds. The white paint helps reflect some of that light, too. Most of the beds have body-sized lumps in them, but there are one or two that have tightly tucked bedspreads and perfectly puffed pillows. Everything in here reminds me of stories of the outland barracks from the Aberrant War.

But, we're *Blessed*. We are supposed to live better than this. At least at home I got my own room—mostly because I told Mom that Toby might "accidentally" get smothered if he slept with me.

My Blessed sister walks me to a bed in the very back of the boxy building, right next to an open doorway with a clear view into the washroom and the distinct smell of the lavatories. This can't be happening.

"No," I say to her.

"Excuse me?" she asks, sounding way too innocent.

"I'm not sleeping here." I speak slowly, the way I did when I told Dad to listen, or else. "I've just been Awakened. I stood in front of the entire council and was declared Blessed. Head Councilman Dekker himself—"

"All new Blessed sleep here." She plants a hand on her hip and cocks her head to the side. "There's a pecking order. Don't worry, as new Blessed arrive, you'll get moved farther and farther from the washroom."

"I'm not just new Blessed." I'm *Chara Bexler.* I take a deliberate step backward and point a thumb over my shoulder. "There's an empty bed over there. I saw it when we came in."

"That's not the way it works." The girl shifts from one hand on her hip to folding her arms. "And if you complain, you'll just stay here longer."

"Who decided that?"

"We did."

A dim light blazes behind me, and I spin to see three girls I didn't notice before standing between me and the front of the building. Why do girls in or around Altan City seem to always travel in threes? One of them is holding a glowing orb of light in her hand. It's only slightly brighter than a candle.

"I'm the senior Blessed in these quarters," says the girl with the glowing orb, "and *I* decide who sleeps where."

As if on cue, the three girls and the one who escorted me here rush forward and grab me, then slam me down on the bed. Several Blessed sit up and start laughing and cheering as if they were waiting for the show.

This isn't how it's supposed to be!

I'm Blessed!

I feel the scratch of ropes around my wrists and ankles. They are tying me to the bed! This can't be happening. I scream, but no one cares. All the Blessed in here just laugh and cheer louder. The same scratchy rope scrapes over my face and down over my neck.

Are they going to strangle me?

I think of Lina, dangling in the train. Lina and her shiny black shoe. And then I realize that my own shoe has come off in the scuffle. I don't want to end up in a body pod with someone wondering what happened to my shoe.

I'm *Blessed*.

This isn't right!

"No!" I scream while the girl who led me here is trying to gag me. "NO!" I scream even louder and then see the opalescent shimmer wave off of me. But this time, it isn't a smooth iridescent wave. It's like shards of broken glass churning the air and then colliding with my captors.

When it rolls over them, the leader's glowing orb disappears and throws the room into the soft silver glow of moonlight. All their laughs turn to squeals and screams. The wave that only I can see rolls across the whole room in jagged, shimmering splinters until it collides with the door and then ricochets back toward me, forcing screams out of everyone it passes through.

Two girls fall hard on top of me, scratching at their skin and bruising me with their thrashing. I can't see which girls they are, but I feel their slick sweat. Not sweat. It's too thick to be sweat. Is it blood? I shove them off, yank the rope off, and then free my ankles.

My shard-wave is gone now, and the four girls lunge at me again.

How dare they destroy my perfect happiness!

This day was mine.

I. Am. Blessed!

"Stop!" I shout at them.

If I can make them feel joy, I will make them feel pain.

The air shivers around me, and another shard-wave bursts out of me. This time I want to feel what it does to this girl who dares to ruin my perfection. I catch the leader by the shoulder of her pajamas and put my other hand to her throat. She claws at me, but I ignore it. The heat feels glorious under my skin as it gathers and surges up my arm and then out of my hand and into her neck.

Blood streams from her eyes, nose, and mouth. She coughs a few times. The splatter of her blood on my face and neck somehow feels pleasant, like a warm bath. She convulses and then drops to the floor in front of me.

The screams from all over the room remind me of when Dad was trapped in the fire. He'd sounded like a frightened girl, too. If only he'd agreed to move to Altan City. I wouldn't have had to start that fire. It was all a waste, though. I thought Mom would pay attention after he was gone, but she just married again. Then I thought after her *second* husband disappeared, she would finally see me and listen to me. All that effort wasted on hiding parts of him throughout the woods.

The screams are dying down now, but I can't let these girls think they can bully me. They have to know who I am.

I am Chara Bexler

I am Blessed.

I am perfection!

Another iridescent shard-wave bursts out of me and rolls over the groaning and whimpering girls who dared attempt to humiliate me. The wave hits the far wall and bounces back to me. It blankets me in welcoming warmth when it wraps back around me.

Only a few whimpers puncture the near-perfect silence. The silver glow of the moon makes the blood look black against the white walls and floor. I look down at my Awakening dress. I tried so hard to keep it clean. Almost without thinking, I turn toward the washroom. Only a few steps in, and I can see my silhouette in the full-length mirror on the opposite wall. My dress is no longer white.

The front door bangs open, and the lights blaze to life.

I don't even turn to see who has come in the door. It doesn't matter anyway.

I can't look away.

I'm enthralled by my reflection in the mirror.

My dress is now a deep ruby, only slightly darker than the wine Mom drank in the aftermath of Dad Number Two's timely disappearance. The whites of my eyes swirl like a kaleidoscope of iridescence. My face is painted in crimson spots, smears, and streaks of blood.

I never would have guessed.

I look beautiful in red.

Date: 2590-04-12 04:43:11 PRT
From: Green Kinsha
To: Anachronauts
Subject: A Mightier Meteor
Re: The Awakening of Chara Bexler

I suppose congratulations are in order, because we've secured the meteor, the one the locals call Altan.

Hooray.

You all deserve a gold medal for time-side artifact retrieval (but not a raise. We don't have the budget for it).

Now we just need someone to figure out what it does. We have the meteor contained and are exercising extreme caution in our contact with it, but so far it doesn't seem to do anything. Every single test we've run says that this is just a chunk of space rock.

However, this is not the only account of Altan and the powers it bestows that we've come across. There was definitely something happening on Onyx. It's possible that the awakenings had more to do with something unique about the splinter itself, though I can't begin to guess what. Was something in the planet's fundamental structure changed during the splintering? Is that even possible? We'll continue to monitor Onyx and see how things progress in the presence of our Altan replica.

I'm still waiting for information about what part of the sky or Splinterverse the meteor fell out of. It would go a long way to getting some answers if we understood its origin. But at least we'll keep this particular chunk of space rock out of the hands of QoreTech. That's good enough for me.

—Green Kinsha

Date: 2590-04-12 08:30:05 PRT
From: Nerrid Flopdoodle
To: Anachronauts
Subject: Weird stuff
Re: Ghost Among the Specters; Afraid of the Dark; I Left the Light On; Oracle, Inc.

I acquired the following three accounts (and a poem) from the two Spectre Splinters, Alpha and Beta, but I guess I need a second opinion on them. They are suggesting something...supernatural has occurred, beyond just the superstition that naturally springs up under such circumstances.

Yes, I did say supernatural, but before you jump to conclusions again, Gentor, I am not saying I believe in the supernatural (Jeez, you have one discussion with a guy about ghosts in the machine, and he works it into every single conversation for the rest of time!); I'm a researcher just like the rest of you, trying to find reasonable answers. Besides, did you read the previous account about that meteor granting people superpowers? If that's not a little supernatural, what is?

I don't know, maybe considering everything going on with Quietus and Shenshou and Xylem, the fact of there being something beyond our understanding isn't even a question anymore. Still. Anyone have time to take a look?

A GHOST AMONG THE SPECTERS

By Jessica Guernsey

The blue-green light made my teeth itch.

"Ghost lanterns," as they were called; their particular hue kept the specters away. The lights were now the current fashion, with New York's opera house being the first to install four of the things, despite the enormous price tag. But no sum was too large since the specters first appeared years ago.

New York City had been an imposing place before. When the stars vanished, the specters emerged. The pale-yellow light of gas lamps on the street became more numerous. Even the tenement sections were well-lit at night now.

And nearly every house had a specter. The streets were full of the fuzzy images, vaguely shaped like people. I knew monied families that changed residences at great expense in order to live somewhere without these presences around them. Money could buy a lot of things.

This particular lantern hung outside city hall, beside a rather lovely fountain that I usually enjoyed strolling past, enjoying the noise and clatter of the city as carriages rumbled by, whistles blew, and men shouted greetings to one another.

Since there was not a single specter in sight, perhaps the lanterns worked.

But they made my teeth itch, and that was something that set me at odds with the invention.

Still, I continued to stare into its flickering depths.

That was another thing. The flickering was too uniform: too patterned. Not like the gas lamps in everyone's homes, but like a poor mimicry of an actual lamp.

Word was that import magnate Edgar Moran was behind the strange lanterns.

I had known Mr. Moran by another name, nearly a decade before, and lived in fear of him and his friends: Deadhand Moran. Ruthless gangster and head of a myriad sketchy pursuits. But then he married Victoria Madison, a young lady from a family with old money and aristocratic roots. Newly sharpened Edgar Moran had dropped the illegal side and turned out to be a talented businessman. With all the charitable events and the softening courtesy of his elegant wife, society appeared to have forgotten Moran's past misdeeds.

And when she'd died due to illness a month ago, the papers and city mourned with him. She must have been some kind of lady to have turned a gangster into a respectable man.

A soggy newspaper at the edge of the cobbles caught my eye.

Like many papers in the previous weeks, it reported all sorts of strangeness. Missing people. A rash of thievery that couldn't be explained. People attacked on the streets by some they had considered friends, now unrecognizable. It made no sense, and from the conversations I'd heard as I cleared breakfast things or offered tea, I wasn't the only one to have come to this conclusion. It was only mutters and speculation now, though I could feel the fear rising.

I shook my head and straightened, pulling my worn shawl around my shoulders. I had just set a booted foot onto the road when a hand looped around my elbow and pulled me back.

"Careful now, miss," a far too familiar voice cooed. "These carriages are no respecters of persons, no matter how charming."

I frowned before I turned toward the speaker.

Renzo stood only a few inches taller than me, but from his posture, he clearly thought the distance greater. Looming, even. His nicely tailored coat was black, as was much of his attire, though he kept his shirts white. The impeccably tied neckcloth was a soft green, probably to match the color of his large, darkly lashed eyes.

Before I could once again get lost in those eyes, I pulled myself free of my former friend. Instead, I allowed a glance to ensure that Renzo carried the shadow I recognized as belonging to him.

"I was in no danger." I swept a gloved hand at the mostly clear street.

"Can never be too certain these days, dear Polly." Renzo looked about, as if searching for miscreants or lurks hidden in the anonymous masses moving about their business.

I scoffed and once again stepped into the street. Renzo's lank form followed close enough that people might assume we had a connection, though we were certainly from different walks of life. Me in my simple housemaid's dress and Renzo looking annoyingly polished in his shiny black shoes and dark gray slacks, neatly pressed. I'd pressed enough trousers to know how fussy men could be about those seams, and Renzo was fussier than most.

"Might I escort you home?" Renzo asked in his all too pleasant tenor, close enough that I could smell the sharp lavender pomade he used to tame his curls.

"No, thank you," I said and turned my head away from his pleading eyes, pretending to glance into shop windows full of items I didn't want. My various employments kept me in enough funds to be comfortable, if I managed them carefully.

I didn't know what sort of employment Renzo had procured after he had left Dame Marshall's trade. Nor did I want to ask. From the expense of his clothes and the occasional bruises I glimpsed, I would most likely not like the answer.

I continued in silence down much of the block, casually noting how Renzo's jaw kept clenching and his gaze never seemed to waver from the street.

I stopped, planted my hands on my hips, and glared at him. "Out with it."

Renzo blinked, then tugged at his cravat. "With what, my dear?"

"You might be a decent enough liar, but when you've got something on your mind, you can't sit still. Out with it."

Renzo sighed and straightened the hem of his jacket, giving me that disappointed look he had no doubt learned from our former mentor, Dame Marshall.

I stood my ground, narrowing my eyes.

Renzo patted his curls and continued to look around us.

I scoffed and nearly threw my hands in the air, like I had so many times when the two of us were orphans on the streets, but that wasn't becoming of a lady—or rather, a lady's maid—so I spun back around and began a march toward my tiny flat.

Renzo soon joined me, though not nearly as close as before. "Alright, I do have a question for you, but you won't like it."

"There's not much you say that I *do* like," I muttered, old hurts threatening to surface, but I squelched them down firmly.

Renzo was quiet but still flighty as I opened my gate, shooing him inside before carefully locking it, wondering what had him so on edge. A quick check of the streets showed nothing out of the ordinary. Perhaps I was getting soft.

Once through my door, I hung my shawl up and pulled off my gloves by the fingers, all the while cocking a waiting eyebrow at Renzo.

His fingers twitched toward his hair, and he stuffed them in his trouser pockets. Hands through his hair was definitely an old Renzo habit, back when we still relied on quick fingers and slow merchants in order to eat.

"What were you doing in the warehouse district?" he blurted out.

It was my turn to blink. "What? I wasn't down there. I was at the market on . . ." but my words trailed off. My hands were empty. If I had been at the market, where were my purchases? I could not remember leaving the market, only the blue-green light of the ghost lantern. How had I arrived at city hall?

Renzo narrowed his eyes at me. "I saw you in the warehouse district not an hour ago. Same ratty shawl. Same dull dress."

Why was he questioning and baiting me at the same time? Renzo must really be shaken.

"What did you see me doing?" I asked, noticing a small tear on the little finger of my glove. When did that happen? I was so careful with such things.

Renzo threw his hand up. "I lost track of you!"

"You? Lost track of me?" It was almost like Renzo admitting he didn't prefer fine clothes. It simply wasn't like him.

He sulked. "I looked everywhere. Then I started toward your flat, intending to question you when you returned, only to find you en route, staring at one of those silly lanterns with the oddest expression on your face."

Mention of the ghost lantern nearly made me rub at my teeth.

Yes, I remembered the lantern. But where was I before that? So very odd. I'd never lost time like that, not even when half-starved and freezing in the alleys.

I sat down at my battered kitchen table and folded my hands in my lap.

Renzo moved to join me in the other chair.

Normally, I didn't like people to sit in that chair. Because that was where my specter sat. But it didn't matter now.

My specter was missing. I noticed it five days ago. It wasn't uncommon for the specter to flit about the apartment or even disappear at times. But mine simply wasn't there one morning and still hadn't returned. I found it most disturbing.

And not just because I had come to think of the specter as a friend, of which I had very few. My missing specter was no deceased relative checking in on me, or any other such nonsense as everyone else believed of the specters in their houses.

My specter was me.

It was something I had recently discovered. Specters were not relatives or the restless dead. The specters were us. They were the people who lived, worked, and walked in those places. No more than a lingering image.

Ghosts were a different thing entirely. The spirits of the dead did not have the same hazy shape as specters. Ghosts were closer to reflections, people perhaps without the fine details, but still people. I had seen spirits my entire life. They spoke, remembered their lives, their loves, and their pains. Emotions lingered with ghosts.

Specters held no feelings and were silent. And since I was the only one in this space, the specter here could only be me.

I had told no one my discovery, of course. Who would believe a common maid? Besides, there were pretenses to keep up and my business to maintain.

How exactly did one go about looking for oneself? I had already searched my usual spaces many times. Where could I look next? Because I would keep looking.

We sat silently, not quite looking at each other. What once would have been a companionable quiet was now made heavier by old affections and new worries.

I glanced at the mantle clock, one of the few nice items in the room.

"I have a session to prepare for tonight," I said, standing. My private feelings would have to wait for later, swallowed down like the dregs of cold tea. Tonight's meeting would provide necessary funds and could not be canceled.

Renzo stood too. "Need an assistant?"

I looked directly at him. It had been two years since he and I had worked together. Since Dame Marshall died.

But something about the earnest look in his eyes softened me a bit. Renzo was never earnest about work. He must truly be worried for me.

"Fine, but the cabinet isn't any larger; you may ruin the crease in your trousers." I smiled teasingly at him.

Renzo only nodded.

Dear me. The man was nearly petrified for my sake.

"I need to change. You know how to reach the parlor." It was, after all, Dame Marshall's parlor, where she had trained two dirty orphans to be her hidden assistants when she met with people. Now, the parlor and this flat were mine. Renzo had wanted none of it. And none of me.

I turned and strode from the room, keeping my back as straight as I could under the strain of Renzo's worry.

* * *

The incense was perhaps a bit heavy, the scent too earthy, but it lent a sort of weight to my words as my voice sounded rougher through the wisps of smoke.

Ghosts were a big business, since Spiritualism had sprung up all around New York just before the specters appeared. The general public has widely accepted them to be the lingering souls of the dearly departed.

One did not have to actually speak to the dead to reap the rewards of such, as Dame Marshall had taught all those years ago, though it had certainly helped me build a reputation.

"It is your grandmother's spirit that lingers," I said, more of a sigh than spoken.

Winifred Milton let out a small gasp, and her hand on the table flinched, like she wanted to clasp her lengths of pearls around her neck, though I had advised her not to break contact with the circle. Tears welled, but only enough to show sincerity and not smudge her carefully lined eyes.

"Nanny? My Nanny?" Her voice was as narrow as her tightly corseted waist.

Two knocks sounded from the cabinet just behind where I had carefully arranged her chair for our scheduled séance. Two knocks meant "yes" from the "ghosts" I had gathered with the circle to speak to us this evening. The knocks were admirably performed by Renzo's hidden form in the false cabinet behind her.

I nodded, not too grandly or my grayed wig might slip, but just enough to convey my meaning. "I knew the moment I entered your home that the specter that walks your halls was a protective, loving one. Since it hovers close to you, you had to be the connection, my dear."

Mr. Milton glowered over his fluffed moustache. His hands were still spread on the lovely damask tablecloth, little fingers still slightly touching those of his wife and mine. That he hadn't broken the circle meant he was willing to believe, but had to put on this show of bravado, like I'd seen many times before.

I offered him a small smile, feeling the heavy powder on my face crinkle, which would only deepen the wrinkles I'd added. "Mr. Milton, there is an essence to a woman, especially one who loved so deeply."

He looked at his wife, softness evident in his eyes.

Turning to Winifred, I leaned a little closer. "She told me to call you Freddy. Might I call you that?"

Her lips trembled, and she nodded.

"Dear Freddy, she loved you greatly in life and continues to watch over you."

A thick tear ran down her face, and I saw the uncertain girl under the refined lady.

"Do not fear her." I raised my voice. "Think of her presence as a continuation of her love and protection."

Freddy made a rather wet sound beside me, and I turned to her husband. His smile was as weak as his handshake when we were introduced tonight.

Of course, when he first met me, I wasn't in the black lace veil tucked into a mass of gray curls. No, he didn't meet me first as Madam Serenia, a respected medium and Spiritualist. He first met me when I was only Polly, an unremarkable girl that briefly took on a role in his wife's house. There, I learned all I needed to know for tonight, plus a few other bonuses that could come in handy later. I also learned Mrs. Milton had come into a large sum of inheritance when her doting grandmother passed, bypassing the males. That family held more scandal than all the women in my previous boarding house combined.

Those weren't the only things I learned in their house, but no one really expected a *maid* to be able to speak to the dead. It was the Spiritualists who had shown the public how séances make the connection between the living and the dead. For those who could see the dead, words were rare, but emotions and feelings were strong enough. Though never once had I convinced a ghost to show itself to others. Not even the lingering spirit that followed Renzo.

Unfortunately, the real ghosts didn't knock from inside cabinets with the sort of frequency that would inspire the living to make a contribution for my efforts. False cabinets hiding former friends and hazy incense would have to do.

I intoned a few words in Latin, which essentially translated to "we are done," and I made a dramatic gesture raising my hands to "release" the séance circle.

Winifred produced a handkerchief and dabbed at her face, making a mess of the kohl around her eyes. The poor lady's tears were flowing strongly. Mr. Milton soon grew uneasy and, like so many men with new money, stepped over and placed folded bills in my gloved hand, his moustache fluffing briefly.

Eventually, I gave the last warmed smile and shoulder pat and shooed the still-weeping Freddy and her stiff husband out the door.

I closed the door and secured the latch, taking a moment to lean against the splintering wood and breathe.

A knock sounded from across the room.

I started.

Renzo!

Picking up my skirts, I hurried to the hidden latch on the finely molded cabinet and swung the wooden facade open.

Renzo tumbled out and still made it look graceful and intentional.

"Blazes, Polly, but that woman put on a show of her own." Renzo patted his curls, but if one was out of place, I couldn't tell.

"Yes, well, grief is always a tricky business," I said, tucking the bills into a discreet pocket. "As you well know."

Renzo stopped his fussing to give me a wry look.

I smiled in return. "Will you be on your way?" I was surprised by the flip in my stomach at the thought of him once again walking out the door, never to return.

"I could take tea, I suppose," he said and flashed a quiet look at me, too fast to read.

"Of course," I said and turned to the narrow staircase at the back of the room that led to my upstairs apartment.

I was on the third step when Renzo stopped at the bottom of the stairs, and I turned to see what had caught his attention.

He glanced back at the cabinet. "If I hadn't been here, how would you have managed the knocks?"

"Same as the dame managed it," I said, then very briefly lifted the edge of my dark skirt, revealing the brace commonly worn by those afflicted with polio. Mine held a special addition, a lever that worked with my big toe to deliver a solid knock to the floor below. And in the dame's parlor, the floorboard was hollow, letting the sound carry and give the impression that the knock came from somewhere other than my foot.

Perhaps I should have been more embarrassed that such a pretty man was looking at my limb, but this was Renzo. I held his secrets that even he didn't know I knew.

"A little heavy on the incense, though." Renzo coughed, probably more to make his point than out of necessity. "I could smell it even inside that little nook."

I didn't respond. Renzo always had a better way, at least in his own opinion.

"Though you are more than likely following our dear dame and hoping the copious amounts of smoke will help your, uh, guests see their loved ones in the forms."

Now at my door, I unlocked it and went inside, not bothering to give Renzo a direct invitation for fear that he would reject me again. Instead of turning toward the stove to set the kettle, I turned toward my room.

"Get the kettle started," I said, already tugging at the veil attached to my wig. "I must change and get this powder off my face. I'll join you when I am presentable."

I didn't wait for a reaction as he would no doubt pout at being asked to do work. My face itched awfully, and I could not wait to be rid of the discomfort.

With so little of the night left, I decided against a clean outfit. I was securing my maid apron back around my waist when something poked my hip. I reached into the hidden pockets I had sewn into all my skirts, which I had found to be most useful, even now that I had ready access to food and secure lodging. Some habits never die.

The object was of a strange texture I couldn't quite place. The length of my palm but only two fingers wide. I withdrew it into the light.

It was pale gray under the gas lamp. Four black squares set in a single line down the face, with raised surfaces that had the feel of the worn sole on a pair of boots, the bar itself having a texture somewhere between mother-of-pearl and unglazed ceramic. It was far too plain to be decorative, too light for a paperweight. But what was its function? Its purpose?

Turning it over, the back was blank except for a square outline on one end. No other markings could be seen. Pressing my thumb against the square, I felt it wobble.

"What an odd thing."

Those words had been on the tip of my tongue, but I hadn't spoken.

Renzo's head poked through the door.

Perhaps it was having him around again that brought out my old behaviors. I slammed the heel of my boot against the door, effectively shutting him out, and making a resounding *thunk* against his cussed head.

As Renzo muttered all manner of dark words, I tucked the object back into my pocket and made certain the shape left no silhouette, though how it came to be there, I still couldn't grasp. I smoothed and twisted my hair into a knot at my nape, checking the small looking glass above the bureau, taking a moment to settle myself before opening the door.

Renzo looked at me with dark eyes, a palm pressed to his forehead. "I do believe I shall have a lump."

"No less than you deserve for spying on a lady in her boudoir."

I strode stiffly past him, ignoring his scoff.

Indicating that I felt no remorse for my actions, I slid the chipped teacup toward the seat Renzo had sunk into, then gave him a weary glance as I took my seat.

I blew on my tea as it steeped, not looking at Renzo. I could feel the strange object in my pocket, and my mind wandered to its purpose. More importantly, how did it get in my pocket? My hidden pocket, which only I could access.

⁂ ⁂ ⁂

In the days following the Miltons' session, rumors tore through the streets. There'd been a ruckus at the market, with a strange gang of people knocking over tables. I say strange because some of the gang were identified as fine ladies in fancy frocks and some were street orphans. There was even an older gentleman who stepped out of a lovely carriage only to join the fray before disappearing again.

A séance hadn't been scheduled in nearly a fortnight, and I was being remiss in my efforts to keep the parlor busy. I did not know what had been filling my days to the extent that I fell exhausted into bed each night and rose late the next morning. My exhaustion must have shown in my work, as I was finding more and more bruises I couldn't remember receiving. Perhaps running into things and not remembering.

The market offered the best options for continued employment. Concerns or not, I was also low on victuals, so there was nothing for it. To the market I went.

I bent over a tray of displayed pocket watches and their various chains, pretending to study a battered piece in particular need of a good polishing. In my maid attire, it was the most likely selection for me, so the merchant wouldn't be suspicious.

The ghost lantern at the center of the market was perhaps the reason for the lack of specters in the area. And for my itching teeth.

There was a ghost lingering at the merchant's elbow.

The genuine kind, not a specter.

Not that unusual. Many people had them, including Renzo.

I studied the living man instead of the watches. His clothes were well-made and recently cleaned. Nicer boots than most of the vendors displaying their wares. Clearly, a man of means, who would have money beyond daily needs.

I smiled; I had found my next mark. In order to get the information for the séances, I would have to contact the ghosts. The real ones. Like Winifred's grandmother. Like the one beside the merchant. This was how I made Madame Serenia's reputation for results.

I put on a practiced frown, with just the hint of a tear.

"Sir?" I made my voice intentionally meek and soft. "Would you bargain for a lower price? It's my brother's wedding. But I am recently released from my position and . . ." My lower lip trembled as I clutched my worn velvet reticule, its sagging contents barely enough for the chain attached to the abused watch.

The merchant had been observing me, but now I saw his eyes soften.

"A maid, eh?" he asked. "I s'ppose the Missus and I might have need of a cleaning girl. Are you any good in the kitchen, lass?"

I let a small smile bring the light of hope to my eyes. "I spent several seasons with a baker, sir. Does that suit?"

"Hmmm." He smiled, showing rather nice teeth. "I do love a nice loaf. Come around this evening and meet the missus. We'll get you that watch for the wedding."

After he listed directions to a house in a nicer part of town than I would have thought, I smiled and dropped a small curtsy, putting a spring in my step as I left the market. Next job secured, I had other errands to attend to. With the new funds, I would be better able to search for my own specter, though I had no idea where I could start. Where else would the other me be if not in my rooms?

* * *

There was a man on the ground in front of me, one hand raised in a protective manner, blood darkening the sleeve of his loose, white shirt.

Where was I? What was I doing?

And why did this man look afraid . . . of me?

That's when I noticed the knife in my hand.

Breathing heavily, I assessed the situation. My knuckles hurt. As did my neck.

The narrow space—an alley?—was rock-walled and misty in the darkness of night.

The man sputtered words now. I couldn't understand them. I lowered the knife but knew better than to drop it. Taking a step back, I collided with a firm object. Not a wall. A person.

A hand wrapped around my elbow above the knife.

"Polly," Renzo whispered, "What have you done?"

I looked up at Renzo's face. The muscles in his jaw stood out. And though his fingers were not tight on my arm, his back was rigid.

"Renzo?" My voice was faint in my ears.

The surrounding mists moved, and ghosts swarmed the space. The genuine ghosts, not our copies. More than I had ever seen in one space. More emotions and thoughts flooded me than I could grasp, each ghost vying to be heard.

My head swam, and soon the darkness was all-consuming.

* * *

I knew better than to sit up immediately upon regaining consciousness or to so much as flutter my eyelids until I understood the situation.

I lay on my side, arms tucked close. Too firm for a bed. I moved a fingertip. Brocade material. Perhaps on a sofa?

A shift of my ankle, and I learned my boots had been removed, though a deeper breath showed my other clothing remained.

That was instantly a relief.

Then I smelled the lavender, and my eyes flew open.

Renzo sat in an unfamiliar armchair just a touch more than arm's length away, leaning forward, elbows balanced on his narrow knees. His hair was in a fitful state as both of his hands clutched his head. The unlit space showed little, though I guessed we must be in his private rooms. How far we had drifted that I didn't even know where Renzo called home.

For a moment, I watched. How alike he was now to the Renzo that told me stories during those dark nights as we both shivered, too cold to sleep, too hungry to move. No family left living. And yet, he was still the same Renzo who charmed the ladies, distracting them as I slipped away with purses and parcels. Now, he was the Renzo who found me when I was lost. Twice.

A hot tear hit the pillow next to my face.

As if hearing the noise, Renzo looked up. For a bare moment, there was fear written on every feature. Then, the practiced, perfect mask was back in place.

"Polly." His voice wavered only slightly, barely noticeable.

Another tear hovered on the tip of my nose for a moment before falling.

Renzo moved to kneel on the floor before me.

"Polly." It was the softness in his voice that sent the next tear rolling.

"What's happening, Renzo?" I struggled to sit up, but my bones trembled.

He reached for me. I thought he might embrace me like he used to all those years ago, but his arm did not move around me, and when he brought it back, the strange object I found in my pocket was in his hand.

"What is this?" he asked, but the tone of his voice was not one of shock. Or even surprise. Like he had known it was there all along.

"I . . . I don't know." And I still didn't.

Renzo studied my face and the still-falling tears before nodding slowly.

"I believe I do," he said, standing and extending his hand toward me. "Come. There is something I'd like to see for myself."

While I tied my boots on, I noticed my hands were clean. Not just from the blood. Even underneath the nails. I'd never been particular about my hands. When I worked as a maid, they were normally rough and reddened. Madame Serenia always wore gloves. There was no point in unnecessary tidiness when the state of my dress and smoothed locks were of more concern to my employers.

But it was important to Renzo.

I glanced up at him as I switched feet. He studied me with careful eyes, watching my movements. Though I got a distinct impression, it wasn't entirely out of concern. Wariness, perhaps?

As always, the ghost lingered just a few steps behind him.

Renzo didn't know. I had never said a word about not just his particular haunt but about what I could do at all. I suspected Dame Marshall knew.

With my boots firmly on my feet once more, Renzo led me out of his rooms through a back entrance, using his taller form to shield me from anyone who might glimpse his visitor. How he managed to get an unconscious woman through earlier must have been quite the ordeal. I was sure he'd never let me forget it.

A few quick turns, and we were back out on a primary thoroughfare. Carriages might be sparse at this time of night, but there was still enough of a presence to drive away the silence that lingered between us.

The streets grew darker, rougher cobbles under my feet.

We were headed to the warehouse district.

I stopped, my arms wrapped tightly around my thin coat.

"What is it?" Renzo asked from a few steps ahead of me.

"Where are we going?"

He shoved his hands deep into his trousers, ruining the line of the material. Clearly, he was not happy with the turn the night had taken. "There are people I . . . know . . . that can explain better what might be happening."

I didn't move.

"People you know," I repeated.

"People I work with." He wasn't looking at me.

"And is it safe?"

"No less dangerous than walking alleys alone at night."

Tears burned, but I forced them back. There would be time for tears later.

After what my thin soles had determined was a length too far, we arrived outside a building, no more derelict than the surrounding structures, but somehow more ominous.

Pausing outside, Renzo looked carefully at my face, nodded subtly, and then pushed through a door that looked to weigh more than my own meager form. I slipped in behind, walking with silent steps I had mastered long ago.

The dark inside felt heavier, dense, like a coating on my exposed skin. And the smell. I had forgotten to hold my breath, crucial when moving through spaces few would wander. Stale and moldy foodstuffs, no longer identifiable, mixed with excrement. I kept the gag minimal, though not entirely silent.

There was something here. Not the other dark forms I could see shuffling on the far side. Those were clearly men. But something else.

Worse than making my teeth itch, it made them vibrate.

Renzo strode across the filthy floor as if the room were the salon at an esteemed household. I let the distance between us grow as I attempted to find what was so off-putting about this room. Perhaps this entire building.

Three of the men separated from the wall and approached Renzo, though more skulked through the edges of the shadows, no doubt moving to surround us. It is what I would have done if the situation were reversed. I briefly wondered what had happened to the knife I'd held earlier.

"Mac, Willy, Ike." Renzo inclined his head at the rough-dressed men as if they were meeting outside the theater instead of this place. "I brought someone to meet you."

"We don't take outsiders," the smaller of the men said.

"I assure you that Polly has no interest in your clients," Renzo said. "But there appears to be a concern where the, uh, *greater plan* is concerned."

Blue-green light flooded the room.

Ghost lanterns were stacked at one end of the crumbling warehouse. Nearly a dozen.

And someone had lit them all at once.

"Ah, Renzo," a voice boomed from behind me, where I was certain there had been no one just before. "I see you found the wayward bits."

I kept my face blank. No use in reacting. I wasn't sure the particularly loud man was referring to me. I also kept my hands clearly in view. No sense in pretending to be any sort of threat.

I turned slowly, noticing there were twice as many men now gathered in the room as there had been. And a few women. But where had they come from?

"Mr. Moran, sir." Renzo beamed, though his smile looked too stretched to me. "I wasn't aware you had returned from your errand."

Moran? As in Edgar *Deadhand* Moran? The gangster turned mogul? From the looks of the other people, he had turned gangster once again.

Mr. Moran stepped forward. I recognized him immediately, even with the stylish suit and coif to his hair so different from my last glimpse. He had the same impressive shoulders. His nose was thinner than his mercy, with full lips that only spoke lies and threats. Shadows moved to flank him.

And Moran was looking right at me. "Where is it, girlie?"

I looked back at Renzo, who held up the strange device.

Renzo crossed to the large man, passing me, though he stopped well out of arm's reach. "Interesting how such a small thing could be so important."

Mr. Moran's smile promised all sorts of harm and discomfort.

Renzo bent his arm, putting the odd thing over one shoulder, as he appeared to mash his thumb against a black square.

The lanterns flickered once, then brightened.

Immediately, I felt it. The tightness that had held my heart since my specter disappeared lifted. I felt whole once more. I stifled the gasp, though I had no doubt that whatever Renzo had done, I would return to my apartment to find my specter back in her chair.

Moran growled, balled his fists, but made no other move. "I can get others."

Renzo inclined his head. "Perhaps. Or you could forget this entire charade and go back to the life where you were happy."

"I'll never be happy without Vicky," Moran growled, squeezing his fists tighter. "This is the only way."

"This?" Renzo waved a hand at the lanterns. "The only way? Oh, posh."

The tension grew thick, and here I was, standing in nearly the center. If I could get to the lanterns, they might offer some protection if things grew . . . rowdy. I started with small steps, looking like I was simply shifting my attention and focus.

"You don't understand," Moran said, his voice low and dangerous. "This is the only way. *They* are the only ones who can help me."

"Help you?" Renzo asked. "They're using you."

Moran glared, but Renzo wasn't ruffled.

"Of course, this . . . organization, as they call themselves, gave you a way to control others. A small thing. Simply take their specters, and you could use them to compel a person. Make them do what you wanted."

I stopped, heart sinking to my boots.

Moran had taken my specter, and with it, could control me? I was being . . . compelled? Is that why I was losing time, because he was making me forget? Were the lanterns involved? Had to be. But how?

Renzo raised an arm and gestured with two fingers.

It was some sort of sign, as a door opened and two men hauled out a third. They dumped their burden, then moved to stand behind Renzo.

Moran stared at Renzo before assessing the man on the ground. Moran's posture showed he knew the man.

I recognized him, too. Same loose shirt, one sleeve now the brown of dried blood instead of the red that it was in the alley. He wore strange shoes.

Clearly, he wasn't from around here, or he would have known how dangerous Moran was.

"Moran, I can explain," the man said, holding up a hand much as he'd done to me.

Moran's face darkened.

Renzo stepped forward, offering the strange thing to Moran. "His organization was using the specters like you did. Running 'tests' is what he called it. They didn't tell you that, did they?"

The horrible things from the papers and rumors? I had been doing those. The thefts and beatings. The rampages through public areas. Perhaps there was more on my hands than just the blood Renzo had cleaned.

In a movement quicker than his enormous form belied, Moran knelt and grabbed the man by his shirt and hauled him closer.

"Using me," Moran said through gritted teeth. "Were you lying to me as well?"

"N-n-o, sir. Never. I p-promise."

Even *I* wasn't convinced.

Moran threw the man back to the floor. He paced. I noticed his men also backing away, which meant they knew when their boss was at his breaking point.

"These people, this organization, told you they could bring you Vicky." Renzo's voice was quiet, sad. "They told you this wasn't the only place. There were other worlds, with other Vickies, alive and well. All you had to do was get those blasted lanterns placed around the city, and they would bring you Vicky. Just place the lanterns."

"And I did it." Moran didn't slow his pacing, which more closely resembled prowling. "Charged a snootful, and those snobs begged me for more. Made the specters disappear, sure. Also let me take them when I wanted." Then, so quietly I wasn't sure anyone else could hear him: "Was she never coming back to me?"

"More lanterns gave them greater reach," Renzo said, one hand tucked in a trouser pocket. His stance said he was relaxed, but I knew him. I knew he could react at the drop of a hat. "The lanterns let you take specters. Well, they could use them too. Their organization could affect everyone all over the city. *Your* city."

The chaos and crimes hadn't been all Moran's doing. The man on the ground had been a part of that.

Moran's pacing brought him closer to the lanterns, and seeing them must have given him an idea.

Moran grabbed the closest lantern and hurled it at the back wall, shattering glass and snuffing the light. The man on the floor cowered, covering his head.

The next lantern flew toward me. I jumped to the side as it burst at my feet. Glass and wires and all manner of things I didn't recognize. Like the innards of a radio, but smaller. Flatter.

Perhaps tossing one lantern at a time wasn't destroying them fast enough for Moran because his next aim sent the lantern into the thick of the stack with a cry that was at once raw fury and heart-rending sadness.

I threw an arm over my face and still felt the shards nicking bare skin, though no greater damage, thankfully.

The light of the lanterns snuffed out. The only illumination was from dim gas lamps behind Moran's people, who were still drawing back.

With the tension broken and the returned darkness, I could finally see the ghost hovering over the kneeling, weeping Moran.

Of course. I needed only one guess as to whom the ghost belonged.

Where was Madame Serenia when I needed her? Moran wouldn't possibly believe me, a slip of a girl with nothing other than preservation of her life in mind. But I had to try.

"What would Victoria want?" I asked, surprising myself that my voice wasn't a mere whisper.

All eyes flashed to me, but I could only focus on the ghost beside Moran. With my gift, I reached out to her.

"What would *Vicky* want for you, Mr. Moran?" I asked again, daring to move ever so slightly closer.

The ghost turned toward me. Now, if only I could get her to speak. And then, by some miracle, if I could get Moran to listen.

"What sort of life did Vicky have?" I asked, taking another step. "Was there happiness?"

A flood of emotion responded.

"Oh yes," I breathed. "So very happy." My eyes wanted to brim with tears, but there was more to say.

"And was there love?" My voice broke before I could get the words out all the way, as the ghost filled me with such a love that I had never known. "She loved you so much." I turned to look at Moran and balked at the burning rage in his eyes.

I held up both my hands. "She's here, sir. You have to believe me."

Moran was slowly getting to his feet, his focus entirely on me, and my knees nearly buckled.

I turned back to the ghost. "Please," I begged. "Help me make him believe."

Image after image flashed in my head, memories that weren't mine.

"There was a mugging," I blurted out. "You saved her. And then she called you . . ." I couldn't make sense of the images and emotions. "Heartless? No, not you. She called herself that. Because you had stolen her heart."

I risked a look back at him. Moran had stopped. The anger still simmered, though now he appeared to be listening.

"She had the biggest heart," he muttered. "Never understood that 'heartless' business." He snorted a laugh and half shrugged. "Makes sense now."

"Victoria wants you to . . ." I squeezed my eyes shut. "Horses? That's all I can see."

Moran had moved beside me now. "Her horses. Of course. I had forgotten all about them." He shook his head, a scoff coming out closer to a sob.

I noticed that his voice had lost its streetwise edge and was taking on more of the polish that his wife had most likely taught him.

"And she's quite upset about the horses," I chided him. "You know how important they are to her. Especially . . . a flower? Yellow. Daffodil?"

"Sunday's Daffodil." Moran shook his head, but I saw the whiff of a smile. "That old nag always was her favorite."

We were silent. I watched the ghost step back and then seem to gather herself until I could make out more details. The lace at her bodice. The long pearls around her neck.

"She wants to say . . ." but I didn't know what she wanted. All I could feel was sadness and love, folded together in a heartbreaking twist. My eyes clouded with tears.

Moran gasped and stepped forward.

I couldn't see what was happening, and I was feeling . . . so very tired. I sank to my knees, then sat on the floor, my hands grasping the sides of my head.

A warm arm wrapped around my shoulders, and the lavender pomade told me Renzo was here.

"How are you doing this?" he whispered so quietly I wasn't sure he had spoken at first.

"I don't know," I responded truthfully, though I suspected. Through the connection between us, Victoria—Vicky—was using my energy to take form. And I was letting her.

I could hear Moran murmuring. "Gone so fast . . . wasn't there . . . I'm so sorry . . . love you . . ."

"Well, I, for one, am relieved," Renzo whispered. "I wasn't sure how we were getting out of this one."

"We still aren't out," I whispered back. "Since when have you been involved in a gang?"

"Since when have you been talking to ghosts?"

I fought to keep my eyes open. "Since . . . always."

He nodded. "Same response for me, I'm afraid. Why else would the others have left us alone on the streets?"

My head was stuffed with cotton and blue-green lanterns, but it felt right. How else would we have been spared if Renzo hadn't always been protecting us?

Moran was walking away from us now, with the ghost beside him, though she faded with each step. Moran's gang dispersed as well, merging back into the shadows. "I suppose we all have our secrets," Renzo said, shifting so he could meet my half-closed eyes. "My real name . . . isn't Renzo."

"I know." I smiled at the spirit behind him. "Your mother told me."

AFRAID OF THE DARK

By Ash Stevens

something in my center
wants to bloom
to bleed, to split
open like a canyon,
leave me dying
on my knees

my voice has a substance
like a snake
around my neck.
I can feel the fear—
it's screaming,
and it echoes through my head

a deafening silence
and an ocean of dread—
my heartbeat's too heavy
to lift out of this bed

but you grab me,
and drag me,
pull me out of the waves—
and without a word
it all washes away

I am free to breathe
and look up at you—
the night is heavy,
and steady
from the light of the moon

are you afraid of the dark?
I am if you are
I am,
try to be,
whatever you are—
you built me up from dust,
from stolen bits of stars.
without you
I am nothing

I am whatever you are.

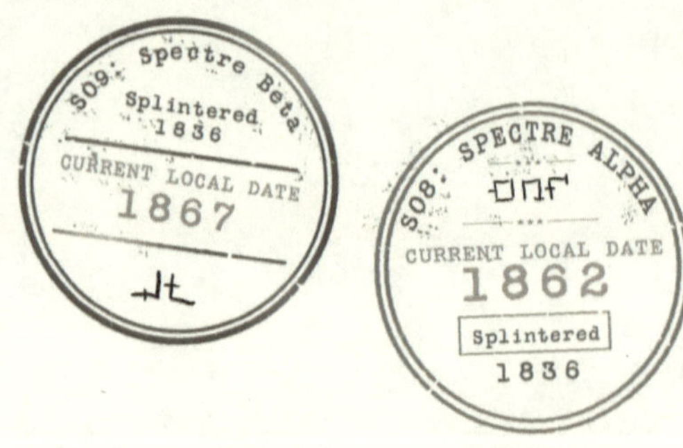

I LEFT THE LIGHT ON

By Kyro Dean

Spectre Beta 1862
Alvin

In the northernmost country of the home he called Earth, in the northernmost preserve for bears, sat a quizzical man with the sprouts of a beard beneath otherwise thinning hair, who looked out at the dusky, blustery field and could swear he saw the beginning of the world's southernmost tip in the northernmost horizon there—by a hummingbird's sigh.

But then, the ball of dirt and water they lived upon was round, wasn't it? So whyever mind?

Not when there were far more exciting matters to deal with in the lot he'd bought to build his home. He'd never imagined living in a place like the barren, frost-bitten landscape of the unsettled north, but the Blessed went where their Ontolens dictated, and he was nothing if not devout.

He pulled the small metal coil from his pocket and twirled it back and forth in his mittened fingers. He had to admit, this coil, the key to his future, was underwhelming. Not the sparkling gem the theocratic Onoracles had bestowed upon his father, nor the disproportionately large iron gate they had given to his aunt to lug around. No, it was on par with his cousin Lennard's rusty can of black beans, and nobody liked cousin Lennard. But it wasn't the object that made the difference. It was where it led. Each Ontolens held a glimpse of the carrier's—or the world's—future, if they followed it to where the vibrations grew strongest. His family were among some of the Blessed: people able to sense the connection between the spiritual world and the earth, to feel the cold chill of the future in pockets on the streets, or to see the shapes of buildings, people, and moments that hadn't yet come to pass.

And while cousin Lennard's Ontolens had led him to becoming the president of a burgeoning export company on a sun-soaked beach in Africa—to the starless sky with that blackguard!—Alvin found himself here in the barren north. Alone.

He just needed to find the vibrations, envision what his coil went to, and piece it back together. Then glimpses of his future would unfold, ready for him to grasp.

Alvin popped his lips a few times, letting the cold wind bite at his exposed cheeks as he weighed his doubts. This didn't seem like the place he'd find his future—or any future for that matter. Unless his fate included being indiscriminately torn apart by an angry walrus. That was always a possibility. He frowned, risked frostbite to pull off his glove, and wrapped the coil in his cooling fingers.

Vibrations.

Subtle as air trapped in ice.

As water trapped in trees.

But it was there. *Here.* It had to be. So he would be too.

"What do you think, Hamlet?" He cocked a brow towards his chief sled dog.

The loyal boy yipped and shook out his deep silver and black coat, clearly unconvinced.

"Ay." Alvin nodded somberly. "Ay."

He put his coil back into his pocket, then rummaged through the creaky dog sled that had dragged them this far out and began the rather laborious task of setting up his tent. Next came the gaslamps and fire. The food stores. And so on and so forth until his doggies had cozied up for the night and he had a makeshift camp in the middle of nowhere. Then he waited, coil in hand, for what the Onoracles promised would be there.

◎ ◎ ◎

For two weeks, he sat on that forsaken piece of ice with naught but his dogs and a wish for his cousin's can of black beans, when the faintest breath of color caught the air, dark as the night sky. His heart leaped into his throat, making it hard to breathe. He stared. Narrowed his eyes. Held his breath.

And saw it again.

His future.

He jumped up, startling Hamlet, and grabbed his sketchbook and can of oil. He scrambled over and tossed the coil in the center of the mirage. Then he set to work, pouring the oil out wherever he saw a black blip or glimmer and sketching out a guess of what lay between.

Pour.

Scrawl.

Stick tongue out to think hard.

Repeat.

Until a crude shape formed that might just be it. He poured the rest of the oil out in what he hoped was the right shape.

Alvin stepped back, hot in his thick coat and snow boots so sweat trickled down his neck. He breathed heavy, thick breath puffing out and forming into ice crystals in the patchwork hair on his chin.

"Doesn't look like much, eh, Hamlet?"

The husky hid his face beneath a paw from his perch atop the nearest snowbank.

"Ay," Alvin nodded slowly. "Ay." He stuffed a hand into his pocket and pulled out a match.

Heart tight in his chest, he struck the light. Held the tiny flame before his eyes. And tossed it into the oil-drawn future he had made in the snow.

It caught in a blaze, bright orange against stark white, and in the light of the fire, he looked down at the image he had drawn, fully taking it in for the first time. A cast-iron stove. The piece of a whole his coil belonged to. The piece that would bring him his future. He just had to build it.

He smiled.

◎ ◎ ◎

Spectre Alpha 1869
Therma

In the northernmost country on the blob they call Earth, in the northernmost city of Tandembare, the northernmost avenue wove up and up toward the northernmost town square, where the northernmost house tilted just so with its back to the county fair, which ironically was only the second northernmost festivity in Tandembare—by a hummingbird's sigh.

The rats reveling in the dumpster across the field claimed that jaunty title, but Therma had never minded.

Not when there were worse things lurking in her own home.

Ghostly apparitions populated the entirety of Tandembare and beyond. Blips of wavering air, like the breath of heat that rises from boilers in deep summer. Mirages in the desert that everyone could see. Figments of imagination that were just real enough to make you hold your breath when one walked through you. They climbed stairs, strolled parks, and wept on corners. And while most followed the same path as the humans—observing alleyways and street crossings and the hallways in houses, in neighboring Hammerfest, there was a section of town where these strange humanoid waves coiled down from the sky with hands in the air as if on some invisible slide.

Therma hated them all.

But mostly, she hated the glimmer that had recently taken up residence in her house. The one with broad shoulders whose image now wavered in front of her brand-new stove as if boiling eggs and cinnamon oatmeal.

He'd just been floating there when she'd come down for her morning coffee. She'd yelped loud enough to scare the black cat on her kitchen windowsill and clutched the throat of her collared nightgown to cover what little skin might be showing. To her horror, he'd blipped and shifted as if he'd heard and turned to face her trembling body in the doorway.

"Go away!" she'd hissed. "Scat! You have all of earth to infest—it need not be in my home you find your place!"

A shimmering arm stretched toward her, close enough to touch.

The hair on her arms stood on end. Cold sweat dribbled down her neck. She screeched and fell back, hastening out the door in nothing but her nightie.

"Why, Therma!" Miss Cadence gasped, eyes wide as the saucer of milk she carried down her back steps. A thick wool cap hid her normally wild curls, and her nose shone pink from the biting cold. "You're not wearing any shoes."

"Shoes?" Therma nearly laughed, eyeing the door behind her as the frost nipped at her toes. "In this silky shift, I'm a breeze away from displaying my bottom in front of all of Tandembare!"

"Then you could be *tan and bare* . . ." Miss Cadence's eyebrows bounced cheekily.

Therma glared.

Miss Cadence shrugged and set the saucer down. A swarm of mewling cats set upon her, flicking their tails and curling around her thick petticoats. She laughed and patted each before turning concerned eyes on Therma. "So what's got you jumpier than a vicar reading Newton's banned notebooks?"

"If you must know . . ." Therma frowned and dropped her voice to a whisper, ". . . I've got a spectre!"

Miss Cadence nodded slowly. "Was bound to happen eventually."

"No, no!" Therma stumbled forward and clasped the front of her neighbor's coat. "Not here. Not in this forsaken place. This community is supposed to be all new houses in a land free from the ghastly ghosts."

"People move," Miss Cadence said slowly. "So why shouldn't spectres?"

Therma's mouth slid open, letting the cold ache in her teeth. She shivered and drew her nightgown closer. "You're not nearly upset enough. Our homes are being encroached upon! We're under siege!"

"The ghosts are nothing to concern yourself over." Miss Cadence waved her off, picking up the nearest cat and running gloved fingers through its thick cream fur. "Trickeries of light. Same stuff in the air that took the stars away. An annoyance but no real harm."

"No real—?" Therma's teeth clattered shut. "How can you be so cavalier when you moved to the middle of nowhere to be away from the blasted things, same as the rest of us?"

"We both know I came here for Mister Scythe, the handsome bloke."

"The cheeky blackguard who just married his maid?" Therma scoffed. "How's that going?"

Miss Cadence's pink lips soured. "Poorly. I guess we've both learned a lesson here." She set the cat down and turned, heading back up her porch steps and towards her home's warmer air.

"Ay, and what lesson is that?" Therma called after, her toes stinging themselves into numbness.

"We don't choose where our path starts any more than where it ends."

The door to Miss Cadence's slammed shut, and Therma let out a frosty sigh before muttering under her breath. "No spectre in my house. Not after all I've given up. Not after what they did to my mum. No. I'll be rid of it before this week's end or march straight into the arms of a polar bear."

◎ ◎ ◎

Spectre Beta 1863
Alvin

In the first hour of light on the first of December, in the first week of the season for hunting bears, sat the first man who had ever wandered so far north with his comically thinning hair—or so his dog thought.

But Alvin didn't mind the cold, the hair, nor his judgmental dog. He was glad for the pup's company.

He climbed the solid oak staircase he'd just finished building on his porch and clomped his boots off at the front door so as not to track the icy snow inside. Nothing was worse than a wet sock. Except maybe a wet sock alone in the north as he waited for his future.

Alvin sat on the glossy rocking chair in the center of his small living room and ran a hand over the smooth wood. He'd bought it for his future and kept it well-oiled so nary a creak sounded when it tipped back and forth. He closed his eyes, enjoying the gentle motion of each sway, until a cold nose touched his fingers.

He startled awake and smiled. "Hamlet, you ol' rug. Wanting some attention?" He leaned forward and scratched the dog's ears.

A tremor tickled the air.

Soft as a seagull glides on the ocean's breath.

He smiled wide, heart opening with sunlight and spring and everything that the cold north wasn't. He bit his lip as she entered the room. Well, the future promise of her anyway. The woman's shimmering figure curved softly in at the waist and back out on either end, her head coming to height just under his chin. And though he couldn't make out her face, every so often, he caught an image of the roundness of her cheeks or a wisp of hair down her back. Every so often, his breath caught with them.

He stood, wanting to bow, to rush forward and embrace her, to shout for glee and tell her about the two-foot salmon he had caught in the lake that morning. Instead, he trembled from head to toe and bore the weight of his excitement in his very marrow.

While the future was not known for being skittish—his aunt's iron gate had led her to a castle with a vision of an army gallantly awaiting her arrival—his future appeared to be just that. Whenever he reached for it—for *her*—the glimmer would dart back or freeze or vanish altogether.

"A wily one," he had crooned to Hamlet at first, the whole thing a bit bemusing.

But now it made his heart hurt. The more she pulled away, the more he wanted her there. The promise of his future. Of theirs. It was a chance to make everything right if he just proceeded slowly and took great care.

So he forced his aching knees to move away from the chair, hoping she'd sit and sway as he had. She moved to the kitchen instead. He followed, far enough back so she wouldn't glance over the shimmer of her shoulders, and leaned against the wall to watch her. She baked a lot—he liked that—often toiling over the stove once he had stopped lingering there. It made sense. The heat felt good against the frigidity of the outdoors. No wonder the Ontolens had brought him to that specific point—the coil in the cast-iron stove connecting his now to their future. When she'd first glimmered, he'd been eager to join her vision at the stove, imagining what she might be cooking for them one day, but every time he did, she'd freeze and vanish. So he gave her her space and hung by the doorway. There would be plenty of time to savor her cooking when she was actually here.

And so he waited, day in and day out, and made the future his present. Who else had a chance to make everything perfect and know that the choices he made were right? He'd started by sledding into the nearest town two hours south and purchasing things he hoped she'd like. He'd know if he'd guessed correctly when whatever he purchased started glimmering around the house. If she liked it in the future, it showed him now. Most of his attempts failed, of course. She had yet to take to the rocking chair—that one hurt—and though he was certain the stained glass window he installed over the sink would brighten any woman's life, it had yet to glimmer. But the shape of a few—a powder blue skillet with roses on the handle and a sensible wooden spatula—had begun to blip now and then in the kitchen's warm air.

Even now, she busily scraped and poked at whatever she would be cooking with the spatula, and his heart swelled. He forgot himself and stepped forward, reaching an arm to slide around her waist.

Her iridescent edges stiffened.

His heart raced. His blood chilled.

"Please," he silently begged his future to stay. To come true. He eased back, each finger curling against his palm in defeat.

She dropped the pan and vanished.

Alvin's cheek twitched beneath his thickly grown beard. His jaw tightened. He slunk back to the rocking chair and collapsed into its gentle sway.

"I'll have her here, Hamlet," he breathed out and petted his companion's ears. "If only she'll have me."

◎ ◎ ◎

Spectre Alpha 1871
Therma

In the first hour of light on the first of December, in the first week of that year's Christmas sales, cooked the first woman who had thought to add figs to her dumplings instead of just savory hare—or so she thought.

Not that Therma put much thought into it at all. She didn't often think of others, so busy was she concerned for her own welfare.

No matter what she did, the spectre wouldn't leave. In fact, it seemed to have taken up full residence, deciding that her home might as well be his. Of course, there were all sorts of theories on where the spectres came from. But no matter what she tried, he persisted. She'd bought extra lights and illuminated every corner of her home to chase away the shadows. But that

only brightened the wavering lines of the strange man's hauntings. She tried dousing the house in sage, reciting some form of prayer in any and every language she could find, and even dropping to her knees in front of the figure and begging him to leave. It was when she had resorted to dragging the antlers of a freshly killed reindeer into her house to hold the candles for a séance that Miss Cadence intervened.

"Now, I'm not one for judging, but you're getting too high for your nut!" She grabbed the unlit candles and dumped them in a pile at their feet.

"I haven't been sleeping." Therma looked at her neighbor, the room tilting. She narrowed her eyes until the chairs and lamps righted, then blinked a few times. "I can't think. I can't—I can't breathe." She whispered the last word. "Not with this *thing* in my household. This ghostly visage of a man who haunts my very waking."

Certain she saw a glimmer behind Miss Cadence, she snapped. "Leave me alone, you horrid creature. You tormentor!" She yelled at the blip. "What do you want from me?"

Miss Cadence *tsked* between puckered lips. "Oh my, dearie. It's off to bed for you."

"I can't," Therma protested, pushing back against the arm that now encircled her shoulders and guided her upstairs. "He's there. He didn't used to be there. He used to only be in the kitchen and the living room. Then one day, he's going upstairs. *My* stairs. Then in my hallway. And now—" her voice hitched, "—my room. I'll never escape him. Wherever I go, he's there. She pointed to the corner of her room and spun in a circle. "He's everywhere."

"Why don't you move away, then? Find somewhere fresh?"

"Fresh?" Therma nearly laughed, but her face was too tired. "*This* town, here, in the middle of nowhere, was my fresh start! Where can one hide when the whole world is haunted?"

Miss Cadence sighed. "The spectres live about just as we do. For all you know, we're ghosts in his life, and he's wondering why *you* won't just leave him alone. Either way, a girl needs to sleep. I'll keep watch and wake you if the spectre nears. You just get some rest."

Therma allowed Miss Cadence to sit her on the bed and tuck her feet up under the covers, to lay her down and close the blinds so the sun's stark reflection off the snow wouldn't keep her awake. Then she lay back and drifted.

But no matter how hard she tried, she couldn't sleep. Not with that glaring light shining on her face from the hallway. She asked several times for Miss Cadence to turn it off, but the useless woman insisted there wasn't a light on over there, there wasn't a light on anywhere. But Therma could see its orangey-yellow. Could hear its electricity *bzzz-bzzz-bzzzing*. And she knew.

She knew with everything in her that he was there.

He was always there.

◎ ◎ ◎

Spectre Beta 1870
Alvin

In the furthermost corner in the back of the house behind the furthermost armoire that rested there, glimmered the furthermost reaches of Alvin's future that he helplessly had to bear.

God's beard, the woman was lovely.

Time and practice tuning into the future's complicated weave had filled her shape out over the years. Her slight frame had become a bit more husky. Her cheeks, a bit more round. But it only made her look more like a mother. And though he'd kept his fingers crossed, he had yet to see any blips of children scurry across his feet. No worries. He wasn't old yet. There was still time. For her to find him. For them to fall in love. To share the future he was building around her.

So why did she hide in the corner now? Why was his future so scared?

Alvin threw caution to the wind and sidled up next to her, wrapping his arms carefully around her shimmering edges. She startled and turned toward him, her haze a centimeter away from his lips. He swore in the twinkling white he could almost see her eyes. Almost feel her breath against his cheeks.

But all he really felt was cold.

"I'll find out what's frightening you, my love. And I'll destroy it before you get here. I swear on my Ontolens."

Her visage trembled and vanished as it always did, and he continued living.

"You think she'll find us way out here?" he'd asked Hamlet once or twice on the nights when the frozen wind howled, and his flickering candle failed, leaving him in the dark.

Hamlet, of course, never answered, but Alvin remained faithful. His family was part of the Blessed, and every single one had found their future in their Ontolens. He just had to be patient a little longer.

In the meantime, he'd memorized his future's habits, her preferred pathways. Built the stairs he'd caught her going up and the room where she slept. So it would be perfect when she arrived. He knew she woke up at 7:30 and went to bed at 9:00, and so he'd started dutifully leaving the light on day and night for her in preparation. To keep her way lit so nothing else would scare her. In the meantime, he hunted the thing that would one day terrify her so.

And though each day grew harder, longer, and darker, he suffered through it because he knew deep down in his bones that she would soon be there.

◎ ◎ ◎

SPECTRE ALPHA 1885
THERMA

In the furthermost corner in the back of the house, behind the furthermost armoire that rested there, faded the furthermost edges of Therma's sanity as she hid away from his stare.

God's beard, the man was ghastly.

Or so she assumed. She tried never to look at him directly. Not in the dark of the room where she hid, nor in the constantly glaring hall light that was always and never on. It didn't matter where she hid; he always managed to find her.

Therma huddled tighter and tighter into a ball, hoping he would leave, but the ghostly shade enveloped her, its cold mist close enough to give her the chills.

"Please," she whispered hoarsely, begging him to leave. She held her trembling breath, waiting, waiting, then jumped up and ran down the stairs.

She grabbed her coat from its trusty peg, ripped open the front door, and nearly collided with Miss Cadence and a strange, tall man with a thinning smile.

"Wah!" Therma fell back, clutching at her heart. "Murderous ghosts, you almost killed me!"

"I can assure you, madame, that I am no ghost." The tall man dipped his hat, revealing greasy black hair that slicked back into a blue ribbon at the nape of his neck.

Miss Cadence's lips puckered. "May we come in? It's frightfully nippy out here."

Therma's heart still raced from her encounter upstairs. In all the years she had lived in this haunted patch of snowscape, the ghost had only ever come that close a few times. Was he getting bolder? She could have sworn his spectral arms had tried to grab her and pull her into the afterlife with him. She wanted to leave—the house, this cursed town that was nothing of what it promised to be. The earth if she could.

But it would be rude to leave guests in the cold with a blizzard blowing in.

She relented, stepping back so Miss Cadence and her peculiar guest could enter. He carried an oval box with a handle that banged against the door as he stepped across the threshold.

"Tea?" she asked dutifully, hoping they'd decline.

"Oh no, dear. Your tea is rather watery, and we are here on an urgent matter."

The floorboards upstairs creaked, and Therma glanced at the ceiling.

Miss Cadence cleared her throat. "Dear?"

Therma snapped her eyes back to her guests. "Urgent matter, yes." She ushered them into her living room and onto the velvet sofa. "Is there something I can help you with? Or is it something I've done?"

"We are here to help you, child." The stranger's voice scraped like a knife over toasted bread. "Your neighbor tells me you have a particularly vicious spectre who has made a home in your residence."

Therma's brows knit together. "It is no secret I am haunted more than the earth itself."

"Exaggerative," the man dripped, "but that only increases my concern. It is a good thing you called for me, Miss Cadence."

"Called for you?" Therma's heart picked up. "What's he talking about? I'm not crazy."

The man chuckled, gravel down a drain. "No one here thinks you're crazy, Miss. In fact, your neighbor has gone to great lengths to hunt me down. I am of a . . . secretive nature, as is my work, and am not easy to locate."

"It's true." Miss Cadence's normally pinched face perked up. "You've been one stitch away from a loose hem, if you know what I mean, and I just couldn't sit by and watch any longer. Then I heard my cousin Harriet gossiping about her nephew, who is friends with a techromancer from the south side of London."

"A *techromancer*!" Therma laughed. "You had me all up in my willies over something as mythic as a techromancer? Shame on you for that." She wagged her finger viciously, then petered out when their expressions remained grave. "What's this then?"

The man dropped his case on the floor with a heavy thunk. "This is no laughing matter. My field of science is as selective as it is dangerous."

"You mean field of magic." Therma couldn't help but scoff. Ghosts and demons were one thing, but techromancy was for the nutters.

The man drew his chest high and squared his shoulders. "Magic is a weak word for things the simple-minded don't understand. My question for you, dear, is do you want to be free of your spectre or not?"

Therma's eyes widened. "I'm listening."

The man's smile thinned to a sheet. "Good."

◎ ◎ ◎

SPECTRE BETA 1878
ALVIN

On the third hour after noon on the third day he'd debated shaving his hair, paced the third most nervous man on the earth, heavy with future care.

For something had shifted, and he could no longer see.

Nothing but a blip here and a corruscation there.

"I'm losing her," he whispered, each word an icicle scraping its way down to his clenched stomach. "I just know it."

He tried to keep the panic from bursting into tears, but even then, salty water dribbled unbecomingly down his cheeks and into his beard.

"I've done everything, Hamlet. Everything I can think of. But something is scaring her away. Something in the future that could be here now. But what if she's like me?"

His hands trembled with the thought, and it took three strikes to light his woody pipe. Curls of grey smoke drifted to the ceiling and pooled in a cloud as hazy as his thoughts.

"If she's like me and can see the future, maybe she's seen what makes her hide? The thing that makes her flinch? If I don't find and destroy it now, she may not come because of what will be."

And though he'd done the ritual a hundred times, Alvin set about doing it again. He checked every nook and cranny, scoured every floorboard. He pushed aside shelves and batted cushions, not knowing what he looked for except that it lurked somewhere here. Then he donned his heavy coat and trudged through that week's blizzard and around the perimeter of the house, checking the crawl space below and climbing on the roof so he could peer down the chimney. All free and clear. The only thing that existed in the blasted north was he and Hamlet and the other sled dogs who slept in the barn. He checked there next, poking each hay bale and sled with a pitchfork just to make sure.

All was quiet.

All was quite disappointing.

His stomach balled up tighter with each passing hour. He'd spent the entire week looking for the mystery monster. But what if it hadn't arrived yet? When would it get there, waiting to scare her? Tomorrow? Or in the years that would never come because she was too afraid to let them? His footsteps became hurried, his lifting and pulling and searching frantic, until he gave up his search and headed for his rocking chair.

With thickly wrapped fingers clumsy with gloves, he bolted the front door and disrobed to his red-wool long-johns. He slid into his rocking chair and propped his cold feet upon the stool by the roaring fire. Hamlet snorted, the most the old dog and his creaky bones could do to welcome him home these days.

Alvin dropped his face in his hands. "Can a future be stolen, Hamlet, do you think, by the fear of what comes now?"

He wiped the tears from his crow's feet and sniffled. Then froze. In a tarnished silver teapot he'd bought his future wife years ago, hung a reflection. Not the same as a blip or a glimmer. Something darker. A shadow? A shade? A spindly old man with a crooked back and oil-slick hair. A thin smile that ate away at him. A deep and blackened stare.

Alvin jumped up, knocking back his rocking chair so it clattered across the floor.

The shadow vanished.

Alvin's heart raced. He stepped toward the teapot, careful not to make a sound. Closer and closer, one foot in front of the other, until his breath fogged the aging silver.

Only one visage stared back at him in the cold of the north, and it took his shallow breath away.

◎ ◎ ◎

SPECTRE ALPHA 1885
THERMA

On the third hour after noon on the third day since she'd let in the strange pair, paced the third most anxious woman on the earth, heavy with present care.

For nothing had changed except her biscuit stash, which the strange man had consumed quite vigorously. But he promised—*promised*—to rid her of her spectre. Dwindling sweets were a small cost to bear.

Well, dwindling sweets and half of everything she owned. It felt strange, how easily she could sign away things.

But she needed the spectre gone.

"We're nearly there," the techromancer wheezed, pulling himself up from behind her cast-iron stove. In his three days there, he'd refused to divulge his name.

Not safe enough, he'd whispered as if the ghosts could hear.

"I've identified the draw," he continued. "The point that brought your haunting here. The spectre simply needs to come near the device I've set up."

Therma tilted her head for a better view. There were so many bits and bobbles on the metal contraption, she couldn't tell where it stopped or began. But that's not what worried her.

"He doesn't like the stove. Hasn't gone near it since he first arrived."

"He?" The techromancer scowled, raising a brow.

Therma blushed. "It. The ghost. The—the spectre thing."

"The *thing* doesn't like the stove?"

"No."

They stared at each other, and though she wasn't sure why, her intestines knotted into a bow.

"Is everything well and ready to go?" Miss Cadence glided in. She'd adopted a rather haughty air since bringing home the techromancer, and today it chaffed on Therma.

"Supposedly." Therma crossed her arms, refusing to break her stare. "Though I'm beginning to wonder if this man is a hack."

"Don't test me, woman." The techromancer's thin lips turned in a deep frown. "I've done you a great favor trekking to the tech-forsaken north to take care of your spectre problem."

She scowled, but relented, not wanting to make the man angry. "What does your device do to the ghost anyway? Banish it?"

"And where would you like me to send it exactly?" He scoffed. "Space? No. The process is much more simple than that."

Therma paled. "You're not going to . . . *kill it*, are you?"

"And how would you kill something you think is already dead?" Miss Cadence laughed, shrill and cold. "What nonsense."

Therma shifted from one foot to the next. What Miss Cadence said made sense, but she had never thought of her spectre as dead. In fact, nothing he did seemed dead at all. He was annoyingly life-like, if anything. She waited for the techromancer to slide out from behind the stove before asking again.

"Well?"

He placed his hands on his lower back and stretched with several deafening cricks. "Life of the spectral nature is not something we can send away or snuff out. It is an energy. And the most you can do with that is . . . trap it."

Therma's eyes widened. "Trap it *where*?"

"Here, of course." The techromancer gestured to the room.

Therma stumbled back and clutched at her collar. Her heart pounded like ghost-feet on the stairs every night. "Heavens, no! He can't be trapped *here*."

"This is where its essence resides." The techromancer narrowed his eyes and jutted out his pointy chin.

"But I'm trying to get rid of him!" she spluttered. "Not make sure he stays."

"It's not like he'll be moving about, Miss." The techromancer flicked off a crumb from his shirt he must have collected from behind the stove. "The spectre will go dormant. Stuck. And it's behind the stove. That's lucky. It'll look like nothing more than a heat vapor while you're cooking."

She grumbled, the sound deep and gravelly within her chest. "He won't look like a he?"

The techromancer pursed his lips and shook his head so a lock of greasy hair fell by his cheek. A black streak over pale skin.

She chewed her lip. "And he won't move or try to drag me into the spectral verse?"

"Goodness no."

She slowed her chewing, and her chest ached. "And . . . and he'll still be free on his plane, right? Like doing whatever he does wherever he belongs? It's just his shape here that's locked in place?"

"I—" The techromancer hesitated, each spindly finger curling in on his palm. "I didn't say that. But I can, if it helps ease your conscience. Though I can't imagine what the problem is. You tried to séance the being out of existence."

She had. Readily. So why did this feel different? This trapping of the soul. Not a soul. A spectre. A light blip. A glimmering of air that constantly followed her around and tried to steal her into its world.

A soft thump rattled from the living room. She froze, hands shaking, and peeked into the empty room. Not empty. His shimmery broad shoulders lingered in front of the dozing fireplace. The silver teapot she kept on the mantle sat askew on its doily. Disturbed. By what? Had his essence finally broken through?

She stared wide-eyed and approached the orange glow reflected in its metal. Slowly slowly. Slower slower. She touched the silver and—for the briefest moment—saw the ragged face of an older man, bald and bearded, staring back at her with an utter look of horror.

She screamed, and Miss Cadence rushed into the room. "Oh dear, what's the matter? Did you get burned?"

Therma ripped her hand back, and her former hesitation hardened into hard crystal daggers. She marched back into the kitchen and crossed her arms. “Freeze him.”

The techromancer grinned and set to work on the final touches with a stalwart air of confidence.

Therma, however, struggled. As she watched with hollow eyes. As she wished them well and sent them away, the trap ready for its rat. As she got ready for bed and lay down with that infernal light buzz, buzz, buzzing in the hallway.

The face.

A man’s face.

He was a man.

Handsome. And tired. And so horrified by what he saw. Was she what had scared him? Did he know what she was about to do?

Her heart thrashed uncomfortably each time she reached for this question and shoved it deep down. Thundering, aching, until she finally, mercifully, fell into a fitful sleep.

◎ ◎ ◎

Spectre Beta 1878
Alvin

In the quietest part of the quietest house in the quietest corner of the world, hunched a quiet man with a quiet heart whose fingers had started to curl.

He was the monster.

He had seen it clear as day in the teakettle.

Not the creepy man with greasy hair that vanished just as quickly. No, it was his own gristled face and worn-down eyes that had shone brightly back at him in the present. A visage. A sign that it was *him* that scared her.

There was no one else here in the frozen north.

No one but Hamlet, and he was well on his way out.

So what other conclusion could he draw, but . . . that *he* was the future his future did not want. He was the reason she never would arrive.

He pulled away and sat heavily in his rocking chair that swayed without a sound. Back and forth. Back and forth. Moving and stuck in the same place forever.

For he couldn’t have the future that should be his because he was in it. He also couldn’t have a future at all if he wasn’t in it. But what did that mean for her future? Had his very existence taken that away from her? And after he had built so much for her.

The stained glass window.

The pots.

The stairs and hallways and bedroom.

The carefully-crafted rocking chair.

Those were for her.

He slowly stood and rubbed the cricks in his lower back, then headed for the kitchen with an equally crickly Hamlet in tow.

"A spot of coffee ol' boy?" he asked, and took out the pot. He opened the well-oiled firebox to stoke the sleeping fire.

A green tendril curled up in the back. Not fire. An . . . aura.

Alvin slowed, staring through the flickering flames at the new addition. He'd heard of many types of magic and science—as a Blessed, study of the otherlies was more than a hobby, it was practical. But nothing in his books had looked quite like this.

The vibrations that quietly hummed off his Ontolens picked up, louder and louder until their beat shattered the air like an uneven hammer.

Hamlet whimpered, and Alvin pulled him near. "Steady boy."

With one arm gently around his dear friend's neck and the tendril curling its way through the open firebox, Alvin inhaled. He reached around the side of the stove and touched a finger to the black coil that had started it all.

The humming spoke to him.

A whisper.

A scream.

A vision of the same greasy man who had portended his present.

Alvin had been both right and wrong.

The man didn't appear to show him just what would be in the future, but what would be now.

Alvin's body trembled.

His heart broke.

And another unbecoming tear smudged his cheeks and caught in his beard.

Hamlet whimpered again, and the man released him. "Not for you, ol' boy. Not today."

The tendril had reached the edge of the firebox and felt about like a tiny vine searching for a trellis. The only green growth in the godforsaken north.

He stared at it, chest tight.

Everything in him hurt, and he swallowed the fear wanting to cry from his lips.

He had wanted his future so badly.

Had wanted her. His wife. His future. His family.

Had given everything for it.

Well, not everything.

Not yet.

He could still give what he had lost to her.

He could rid her of her monster.

He reached out and touched the little green light. It moved hungrily over his skin, feeling, checking, accepting his sacrifice. Then he knew. He knew what it wanted of him.

And not wanting to scare her—to chase her away from the one place in her home she loved to be at the most—he stood and moved to the side of the stove. Then leaned back and closed his eyes, letting the green tendril take him.

◎ ◎ ◎

Spectre Alpha 1885
Therma

In the quietest part of the quietest house in the quietest part of the world, tossed and turned a quiet woman whose dreams had started to curl.

She woke from her terrible sleep with a coughing gasp, sure she had been asleep for days. But not one hour had passed. The haunted man's face that had been her haunting still lingered on the back of her eyelids, and she wanted to be free. She tore the blankets off and jumped into her slippers, then hurried downstairs.

A pot of tea.

A pot of tea.

She just needed some—

The stove.

She stared, engulfed by the scene before her.

He had come to the stove after all, just not when she was there. Did he always get a late-night tea?

She shooed the thought from her mind unsuccessfully. Not a he. Doesn't like tea. Just a spectre. The shape of a man who now had a face and bent down in front of the stove, staring at something. Then she saw it. A green snake reaching out from the techromancer's device. It slithered, shining from inside her firebox, until its head peeked out the side closest to her.

Her heart leaped.

She wanted to scream at the man to run. To save himself from the snake's bite.

But she didn't. She couldn't. Not after everything he'd done.

This is what she wanted.

What she needed.

Wasn't it?

The man shifted, his arm around something that he must have thought mattered. His shimmering form reached out and let the light touch him. The snake opened wide and greedily attached itself to his visage. Her stomach clenched. Would his kneeling form block her stove forever?

As if hearing, he stood and moved to the side. With a shallow bow, his coruscating arms gestured her toward the stove before he returned upright. The green light had taken his whole arm now.

Therma's breath caught in her chest.

"Wait."

Her fingers fidgeted. Her feet broke their hold.

"Wait!" She stumbled forward, unsure of what to do. Of what she had done. "Wait, wait. Please, wait. I don't know how to fix this."

She tried to grab the green light from off him, but her fingers filtered through. She reached behind the stove, but the fire had been warming the embers all night, and she gasped and fell back with a terrible burn. Tears streamed down her face. From the pain of her seared flesh. From the searing guilt in her heart. She searched for a hot pad and tried again for the machine. With a clumsy half-curse, she knocked the contraption free and scraped it toward her on the floor. She poked and prodded, pulled at cords, and ripped out wires, but the green light continued its feast.

"Please." She stood and, for the first time, stepped in front of the spectre.

He had broad shoulders. She'd always known that, but standing there with him, she could see the shape of his arms more clearly. Built. Muscular. She imagined the face she had seen in the teapot but smiling across the sparkles of his face. He stood taller than her. Wider. Like a shelter in the storm. His hand, now green, reached up, and instead of pulling away, she let him touch her. The cold brushed the tears now streaming on her face. She waited to see if he would pull her down into his world before the light consumed him, but he only lingered.

"I'm sorry." She looked up at where she imagined his eyes.

The green flashed bright, and what remained of the machine whirred and hammered. The light enveloped them both, and for a moment, he was real. His white, ghostly frame filled out to the man she had seen in the teapot.

He blinked, almost entirely eaten by the green light's snake, then smiled at her.

"It's you."

She nodded, tears flowing freely. "I did this to you. I was afraid."

"No." He brushed his hand across her cheek, and this time she felt his warmth. "I did. I'm sorry. I wanted so much for what we could be that I became a monster."

She shook her head, then clasped his hand to her cheek and leaned against it. "How can I stay here after what I've done?"

His smile softened as the green creeped up his neck to the last of his body that it had yet to eat. "Don't worry," he said, his voice comforting and all she could ever want it to be. "I left the light on."

The green snake flashed again, blinding her from him. She staggered back and screamed. Then fell to the floor when the light faded along with his being.

END NOTE

You can see from the previous two accounts that there is definitely something weird here. Of course, when you create a splinter from another splinter, it would cause all kinds of havoc: should be kind of obvious. Clearly, the "ghosts" are a result of the entanglement between the two worlds, of the people on Alpha seeing those on Beta bleeding through. But in the first account, the splintering and the entanglement led to something more, seems like. Is someone else interfering that we don't know about?

I mostly included this second account because I find it extremely moving (I'm not going to apologize for not being a robot like Ren), and also because as an account of someone from both Beta and Alpha, it adds something unique. This perspective might be what most of my research is lacking: seeing both worlds at once shows how the events on each world affect the other more clearly. This account also suggests that some of the "ghost trap" technology has been stolen and used by the locals. Which is kind of annoying. I've sent one of my aides to investigate.

Okay, on to the third account from these worlds.

—Nerrid Flopdoodle

ORACLE, INC.

By Faralee Pozo

One of the downsides of being able to see everything? It makes everyone else seem like an idiot. Or maybe that's an upside since everyone else is an idiot.

Alejandro awoke to heavy silence, a gray ceiling above him. He sat up with a jump and then groaned with pain, dropping and putting his head between his knees. Had someone hit him over the head repeatedly with a bat with nails in it? Had he deserved it?

It all came back in a rush. He'd been at The Blackout Anniversary Rally. All had been going swimmingly: he'd announced his candidacy for president of the United Americas and enjoyed an overwhelmingly enthusiastic ovation from the crowd. And then an old woman in rags had sprung from the audience, landed on him like a flying piano, and knocked him to the ground.

He remembered the sound of his head hitting the wooden platform with a frightful crack and then all went black, but just before that, he'd heard something else . . . had that been a gunshot whizzing through where his head used to be? He started to his feet again at the thought, but he only made it up a few inches before he dropped again.

"You probably shouldn't sit up so quickly," said a bored female voice from somewhere behind him.

He turned to the voice in surprise, which set off the angry drumming in his head again. Everything was a blur, every movement a stab of pain.

"Where am I?" he asked, trying to move more slowly.

"I would think you'd recognize it," the same voice said.

He blinked a few more times, willing his vision to clear. "This is my airship," he said, the dark wood furniture and seafoam decor swimming before his eyes.

"Is it?" the voice responded with exaggerated surprise, and Alejandro squinted to see the speaker more clearly. It was the old woman. The one who'd knocked him to the ground. Perhaps he should have been more surprised, or angry, but everything felt muted in contrast to the sharp stabbing behind his eyes. Still, assuming his memory was correct, in addition to giving him a concussion, this old woman had probably saved his life.

More or less. He didn't really feel saved, at the moment. And how had she known to save him from being shot in the first place?

The thought answered itself around the cloud in his mind. "You're a seer," he croaked. It wasn't a question, and she didn't reply, which was confirmation enough. The woman was turned away from him, straightening the dirty blanket cape she wore as if it were a royal cloak rather than dirty rags.

How had he gotten here? Was the blimp airborne? Where were his guards? Where was Joseph, his head guard and best friend? The man normally never left his side. Alejandro pushed himself slowly to his feet, inching toward the woman, ready to get answers but wary in case she had the urge to knock him to the ground again.

"Look," he started when he was near enough, and she startled, whipping around toward him. The questions he meant to ask died on his lips. "You're not old," was the statement that popped out instead. "Nor ugly." It was blunt, but not exactly an insult, even though the woman scowled at him with surprising fervor as if it were. Her wrinkles were haphazardly drawn on around the mouth and shockingly blue eyes, with fake dirty smudges in odd places, a few teeth blacked out. She had obviously gone to immense trouble to disguise herself.

The woman sneered. "*You* are very rude." She put her hands on her hips and faced him full on, a fiery challenge in her gaze. And if it weren't for the fake wrinkles and blackened teeth, and pure soul-burning contempt on her face, Alejandro suspected she would be a devastating beauty.

He blinked, confusion melding with the haze in his head. "Why are you disguising yourself as an old *bruja*?"

"None of your business, nosey." She pulled her hood down, turning away again.

Alejandro opened his mouth and then popped it shut again.

"And I'm not just referring to your giant schnoz," she continued.

Alejandro narrowed his eyes, baffled, sitting back on the stiff white settee with a bump. He hadn't truly been insulted like this by a woman in . . . well probably a longer time than he deserved. He cleared his throat. "Where are my guards? Where's Joseph?"

"In case you don't remember, someone tried to shoot you, forcing *me* to save your life, and then your people loaded you up here on the blimp and left—probably going for the doctor or something. And then I lifted off. We're alone."

"What? Who's piloting the airship?"

She shrugged, then started pacing. "It has autoflight. After I lifted off, it was just a matter of twisting a few knobs, and—"

"It takes full teams of airpilots to fly a ship like this!"

"A full team of fopdoodles, maybe."

"Fopdoodles?!" He stood, steadied himself, and then headed toward the cabin door.

"Where are you going?" asked the woman, stepping in front of him.

"Autoflight is only good for straight lines! What if we should meet another ship along the way?"

"Then *they* can move," she said with a shrug.

"And what if we should meet a mountain?" He tried to move around her, but she pressed a hand against his chest.

"I really think you should sit down. You look a bit . . . unsteady."

As she said it, he realized she was right. Was she actually a witch, cursing him with dizziness? Oh. No. Right: the concussion.

He allowed her to help him back to the chair. "No one in my employ is a fopdoodle," he insisted petulantly as he sat. He wasn't sure why he felt the need to press this point—there were probably other more important things he should be arguing at the moment, like asking where they were going and how they were going to survive when the ship inevitably crashed. However, it was one thing to insult him, another to insult those in his employ. "The individuals that work for me are capable, brilliant even," he continued. "I even have seers—an entire team of seers—on retainer." He'd signed that paperwork saying he was never to divulge Ecuador's *Los Profetas* LLC or their true nature, but hopefully divulging it to another seer didn't count.

"Bully for you," she said. Once he was settled in the chair, she meandered away, bending to examine the dark wood of the record player cabinet. He caught a glimpse of stylish black t-strap shoes on her feet, dark against the seafoam green rug. Nothing about any of this made any sense.

"And while we're on the subject," Alejandro continued, a hand to his head, "why didn't my seers save me themselves?"

The woman rolled her eyes at him. "What were *they* supposed to do? It's not like they can see the future."

Alejandro closed his eyes and leaned back against the pillow on the side of the chair. "Los Pofetas are the biggest and most well-respected seer firm in the United Americas, likely in the world. There is no firm better. If they can't see the future, nobody can." He brushed some hair off his forehead, wondering idly what had happened to his hat.

She looked at him out of the corner of her eye. "Yes. That's my point exactly. Look, it's a big crazy thing and I don't have time to explain it to you, Al, even if your tiny little brain could comprehend it."

"Don't call me Al, seer," he said, his eyes still closed.

"Don't call me seer, Al."

He opened his eyes, gazing at her. "Then what should I call you?"

"Oracle."

Was that a name or a title? "Ms. Oracle, aren't you a seer as well?"

"Not like *you* say it."

"Seer? How should I say it?"

"*Not like that.*" She glared at him, folding her arms, her stance defiant. "My whole life, I had to fight people like you. Fight to be heard amongst the dirty muddy puddle of seer firms," she said. He opened his mouth to respond with a platitude. She held a finger up. "Don't patronize me, Al."

"Uh . . ." he said instead.

She sniffed. "You believe your seer firms can claim ownership over words like seer, prophet, psychic, *future*. Ridiculous! Of course they couldn't save you! No seer firm could have. Don't you think I *wish* they had? Then I never would have needed to be involved at all!"

He tried to sit up again, get a better angle to glare at this infuriating woman. "So Los Profetas and every other seer firm are frauds, is that it? Nobody can see the future but *you*?"

"Oh, well, technically, they *are* seeing a future, just not ours!"

Alejandro blinked. What on Earth did that mean? "Whose future is it, then?"

She snorted, but then her expression quickly shifted from scorn to something he couldn't quite name. She glanced around them, her eyes darting from side to side. "Something . . . something's happening."

There was a sudden bang and crash and lurch of the ship around them. They both fell to the floor, loose furniture falling around them.

"We've crashed!" Alejandro wheezed, clambering to his feet as the ship settled, then stumbling towards the door to the flight cabin.

"No, wait!" Oracle shouted, trying to regain her footing.

"If this ship explodes, it is on your head, Miss Oracle!" He reached for the doorknob to the hall.

"Stop!" Oracle's words echoed from behind him as the doorknob turned of its own accord under his fingers.

"Hola, Señor Ortega," said a deep voice, the door opening to a pistol in Alejandro's face.

⁂

See what I mean? Idiots! All of them! Or maybe I'm the idiot. Sometimes it's hard to tell.

⁂

"Grab them," said the man holding a gun. In a blink, someone grabbed Alejandro's arms in a vicelike grip and tied his hands behind him. Judging by the sounds of struggle and dismay from Oracle, she'd been caught as well.

This was not how Alejandro had expected his day to go when he'd risen this morning and put on his best suit for the political rally. First someone shoots at him, a woman practically breaks his head open in order to save him, they crash the ship, and now there was a gun in his face. Was this normal life for presidential candidates? He gritted his teeth, forcing civility into his tone. "What can I do for you gentlemen?"

"Por favor, levanten sus manos," the man with the revolver said, his tone also overly polite.

Alejandro nodded and put his hands up as instructed. "Claro, claro, no hay problema." He looked around at the group filing into the guest cabin. There were four strangers with matching black suits, homburg hats, and large-barreled copper lightningshot pistols, pointed at him. The man who spoke had long black hair in a ponytail, a mustache, and a thick white scar riding across his cheekbone. He seemed conspicuously steady, unconcerned about having to hold a man at gunpoint. A professional then. The leader. And native Ecuadorian like Alejandro, judging by his look and accent. Alejandro filed this information away for later. "May I ask, how did you happen to be on this airship? My . . . er . . . guest and I went to great pains to be alone."

The leader led the group toward Alejandro's lounge, not even glancing back toward him. "We have a smaller ship which has now docked with this one. We apologize if the process was not smooth—we had no time to perfect it. But we are still airborne, two of my men have taken over the operation of this ship, and you will be relieved to know, I think, that we have disabled all communications here, so there will be no further interruptions to your fine evening."

Alejandro resisted an anxious gulp. "How thoughtful." The words tasted sour as a battery in his mouth. *Oh. Communications. Blast me and blast this concussion.* Alejandro should have considered using his radio or the telegraph as soon as he'd awoken, but instead he'd wasted time arguing with the confusing woman. Everything was too fuzzy. *Blast, blast, blast.* The leader of the group waved them further into the room and pushed Alejandro and Oracle down onto the couch across from the settee, all four men nearing, their lightningshots never wavering from Alejandro's face.

Alejandro let out a puff of air. "Can we do away with the guns? Obviously, we are at your mercy as it is."

The leader bowed. "I am sorry, señor, but you must have at least one weapon trained on you at all times. You understand?"

No, Alejandro most certainly did not understand. None of this made sense. How were they even here, and what did they want? The leader leaned down and tied Oracle and Alejandro back to back, their hands mingling awkwardly in the middle. "I am sorry for these bindings," he continued in his accented English, "but I must check in with my superiors, and I don't wish to worry about you while I'm gone. Make yourselves comfortable, and I will return shortly." Alejandro considered complaining about being asked to make himself comfortable on his own ship, but as the man left with one of the guards and the two remaining guards closed in with their guns, he decided to let it go.

"How did this happen?" whispered Alejandro after a moment, loud enough for Oracle to hear. "You say you're a . . . an oracle, someone who can see the future, but if so . . ."

"I tried to stop you as soon as I knew," Oracle whispered back.

She had, he remembered. But, "Just a hair too late."

"I'm sorry." She blew out a long breath. "I shouldn't have brought us up here where we could so easily be trapped with nowhere to go. But everything kept changing, it was happening too quickly, and you were in immediate danger . . ."

Alejandro's annoyance fell as quickly as it had come. He hadn't the energy for it. He cleared his throat. "That sounds complicated."

She laughed, a humorless guffaw. "As in, 'the future is complicated' on the letterhead of every seer firm in the country? Of course it's complicated. For the consulting firms here in the United Americas, complicated simply means ridiculously complex non-disclosure agreements signed in triplicate, but even for the Onoracles in North Eurasia, and the Forthwith religion in Africa, it's complicated. For me? Doubly so. But you wouldn't understand."

"Try me."

"No."

"No?" Nothing about this woman aligned with his expectations.

"No!" she said again. She sighed out a long, exasperated breath. "Look. Not that you would understand any of this, but even if I saw what was coming clearly, saw you being shot and killed with a clear time and location—which I don't, by the way—what am I supposed to do about it? Just in knowing about the future, we've already changed it. In telling the future, in simply *thinking* about it, it is already too late to predict or control. Prevention is slippery."

"I see." Alejandro was sleepy all of the sudden, further evidence of the concussion, but he took a deep breath, determined to stay awake, to understand.

"It *is* possible to tell someone 'their fortune,' pass the prevention responsibility off, but presentation is everything. The wrong or the right presentation can further change events or keep them the same. In my experience, any time I tell someone his future, tell it clearly, it never comes true. Not once."

"Hmmm." Alejandro was still trying to listen, but his wrists were aching from being tied together. He tried to readjust, but the brushing of his hands against Oracle's was distracting, and the bindings were too tight.

"It's the problem of every seer, every prophet," Oracle continued. "It's why the best fortunes are so vague, why the most famous and talented soothsayers were also historically poets—Nostradamus, John of Patmos—even before the Blackout when seer powers officially appeared. Poetry balances right on the edge of vague enough to keep the future from changing but specific enough to reveal itself afterwards."

Alejandro tried to nod as if he was understanding any of this, but she couldn't see him, tied back to back as they were, so he didn't know why he bothered. She leaned against his back, and he found himself wanting to lean into her too, bask in the warmth. He shook his head.

Oracle sighed. "And also, even if I can figure out the best presentation, the future doesn't always cooperate. Sometimes it's misleading, or jumbled, or keeps changing; sometimes it comes too late or not at all. So, yes, it's complicated. But that is just the tip of the ice castle. Imagine what it might be like if, instead of seeing our Earth's future, you saw the future of another Earth, one very like our own but not us at all. Another Alejandro, another Oracle, the same people and places. They also passed through the Blackout a hundred years ago, their stars also disappeared. It is our twin world, born together and uniquely and closely entangled, though they are six years ahead. This is the 'future' the seer firms and the Onoracles and the Forthwith see. They believe that this other world is *our* future. But it isn't. And that misconception is costing them. So yes. Complicated. And way beyond you."

Some of this *was* actually making a dent in his brain. But she was right. Most of it still felt like a riddle he wasn't meant to know the answer to. "So, are you different from them?"

"I . . ." She squirmed slightly. "I'm something else, I guess. Because I can see them all: ours, theirs, and more."

⁂

The Blackout event wreaked all kinds of havoc. It did the same everywhere, though it wasn't named Blackout in most other Earths. Stardrop, the Great Darkening, the Cataclysm, The Long-Prophesied Disappearance of Our Sky Twinkles. Very odd world, that. Did it cause me as well as them? Who can say. Even I don't see everything. I know I said I did. But just the fact that you believed me shows how much of an idiot you are.

⁂

"Our Oracle is special, isn't she?" said a voice at the door. The leader entered purposefully, leaving the other guard outside the cabin door. "Sorry for my delay." He pulled a nearby wooden armchair a bit closer, then he took a knife, and before Alejandro could even flinch, the man cut the rope that tied them together, leaving them still bound individually. Alejandro could now see Oracle properly, noticing that her makeup wrinkles were now streaked down her face, like she'd been crying.

Alejandro faced forward with a deep breath out. What did these men want with him? A change of policy? For him to drop out of the race entirely? War? Chaos? He closed his eyes, trying to focus. Then he opened them again and turned to the leader, saying the first reasonable thought that came into his head, ready to take charge of the situation. "You're a seer with Los Profetas. Aren't you?" The Ecuadorian accent, the fact that they'd gotten the drop on Oracle, it all fit, though the idea hadn't quite solidified until then.

The leader smiled, watching Alejandro with contemplation. "Well reasoned. But no." He bowed his head and then stood. "Come, let us be friends, Alejandro. May I call you Alejandro? I am Jaime. I believe I grew up only a few towns from you, in Bucy. Yes, I am a seer, but not with Los Profetas."

"Oh?" Alejandro squinted at Jaime.

"Well, not anymore. I haven't worked for Los Profetas for almost a decade. Now I work for a, let us call it a consortium. A government organization for all seers everywhere."

"Whose government? And what do you want with me?"

Jaime smiled. "We operate outside of any one country's dominion. But also, I'm afraid you are still operating under a grave misunderstanding. We don't want *you* at all." He sat again, then looked at the woman next to Alejandro. "We want Oracle."

"What?" Alejandro gaped at Jaime, then at Oracle.

Oracle's expression quickly rotated between shame and fury. "You people never give up, do you? Well, the answer is still no. Jaime, is it? I don't need a job, and even if I did, I would never work for you."

Jaime smiled, a disturbing sight. "The people I work with are used to getting what they want. The good news is we are now prepared to give you an offer you can't refuse."

"Oh? I'm fairly accomplished at refusing," she said, fierce. Terrifying. A true Oracle. A strand of hair was hanging in her eyes, marring the effect with vulnerability, and Alejandro only barely kept himself from brushing it away. Not that he had a free hand anyway. Or that she would have let him.

Jaime tented his fingers. "And I am fairly good at getting the answers I want. Let us do away with the pleasantries, hm? Here is my offer. Work with us, and we will let Alejandro go. Don't work with us, and we will kill him."

Oracle growled. Alejandro gaped for a moment, then closed his eyes again, trying to muddle through the situation despite the fuzziness of his thoughts. This was all to capture Oracle?! "Why even involve me at all, then?" he asked aloud.

"I'm afraid you are nothing more than convenient collateral damage. Sorry, Mr. Ortega, I am sure this must be a devastating blow not to be the most important and desired person in the room." Jaime gave him a smirk.

Alejandro ignored this, trying to focus his thoughts. Even if Oracle went for this "offer," would they actually let Alejandro go? It seemed extremely unlikely. Nor would he feel satisfied even if they did, knowing Oracle had exchanged her freedom for his life. This was bound to end badly for everyone. For the moment, his annoyance at his own helplessness focused him, cleared his muddied thoughts. "So, Jaime, in other words, you went to an inexplicable amount of trouble in order to kidnap a presidential candidate, even if I was not your target, likely bringing down a large amount of potential attention and trouble on your heads, all for a *business* proposition? From my view, you are extremely lucky any of this worked, but it isn't going to work for long."

Jaime leaned back. "Ah, Oracle is worth every effort. And your concern is noted, but there was much less luck required than you suspect. We are, as I said, from a consortium of seers."

Alejandro scoffed. "A consortium of seers who don't actually see the future. Oracle explained it to me."

"Oh, did she?" Jaime looked back at his companion.

"I didn't understand it all, but I suspect you *couldn't* have known whether any of this would work. You're frauds."

Jaime nodded. "Hmm. Sound reasoning." Did nothing perturb this man? His polite indifference never wavered. "But even if we cannot see the future, we are very practiced at predicting what another will do, even our Oracle here—who is, as I think she told you, unique. As talented as we are, she could change everything. Our Oracle would be the leader of the entire consortium.

We would name ourselves for her. Oracle, Inc. has a nice ring to it, no? As I said, she is worth it. Also extremely difficult to nail down."

"Or so I thought," she said.

The leader smiled again, more of a sneer. "Luckily, we recently learned something that gave us an unexpected advantage. Wouldn't you like to know what it was?"

"No," Alejandro and Oracle said together.

"We knew Oracle would come for you, would attempt to save your life. We didn't know she would try to fly you both away, but we found a way around that, and it ended up being even better for us. Now she is trapped here, high in the air, with no way to wriggle out as she has done before."

"How did you know she would save me? Am I that important to the future—"

"Yes," said Oracle quickly, but Jaime laughed, an abrupt, wild sound that made the hair on Alejandro's neck stand on end.

"I sincerely doubt it, no. Didn't she tell you?" Jaime said, almost gleefully. "You are her soulmate, her future spouse. Oracle is destined to be your wife."

⁂ ⁂ ⁂

Shut up. I don't care how pretty he is.

⁂ ⁂ ⁂

"Don't be ridiculous! *Soulmate,* what nonsense!" said Oracle hotly, not looking at either of them. Alejandro felt his eyes lose focus.

The leader turned Oracle's chin back toward him. "*Soulmate, true love,* call it what you will. But I've seen the future, or some version of it: the two of you, happily together, a child on the way." He let go of Oracle's chin and turned back to Alejandro with a smug smile. "I don't know what more Oracle sees, but judging by how quickly she came to your aid, and by how strongly she protests, I suspect that fate is yours here as well—assuming we do not kill you first. Oracle, why did you not tell your dear Al you were soulmates? I'm sure he would be open to the idea, if the way he has been looking at you is any indication."

Alejandro tried to swallow, but his mouth felt like sandpaper. Oracle still wasn't looking at either of them. She squirmed, her arm brushing his.

"Soulmates?" Alejandro asked, his voice barely above a whisper.

"Absolute malarkey." She was struggling against her bonds in earnest now, still not glancing his way.

The guard rushed in from the flight cabin door and whispered something in Jaime's ear. The two stepped away for a moment in heated conversation, soon joined by the other two, who still kept their guns trained toward Alejandro and Oracle from a distance. Alejandro heard the leader say ". . . then search everywhere!" but nothing besides indistinguishable whispering beyond that.

"Everyone always thinks if I believe in fortune-telling," Oracle said, apparently unconcerned about what had the guards so upset, "I must also believe in things like fate, soulmates, Shakespeare conspiracies, extraterrestrials. Soulmates?! You want to know how many of the twenty-six people I've led to their 'soulmate' are happily married? None. They hear a fortune, and they think they won't have to do any work, they think the other person should be a perfect complement—something that just doesn't exist—and when they aren't, they blame each other, they blame me, and I have to move again. Soulmates don't exist. Just because I see two people married in the future doesn't mean they *should* be. It doesn't mean they are bound for happiness."

He leaned closer. "So . . . you and I are bound for *un*happiness?"

Oracle blinked, and she glanced at him, locking eyes and then looking away. A shot of sparkling electricity buzzed through him at the look.

The spark, the guilt in her expression made it all very clear. Alejandro blew out a long breath of air. "No. What you see is just as Jaime said, isn't it? True love, family."

She was quietly groaning now.

Everything about this woman was a puzzle. "You came to me reluctantly, in disguise," he said, trying to reason it out, "antagonized me at every opportunity. You did everything you could to repel me. Not because we were bound for unhappiness, but the opposite." Alejandro lowered his voice to a whisper. "You didn't want the happily ever after at all. Why?"

"You don't understand."

He clenched his teeth. "No, I don't. What did you *see*?" To the side, Jaime was waving the three guards out the door and into the hall, where they split up and sprinted away.

"You want your fortune, Al?" Alejandro could see a tear leak out and run down the side of her face, but her voice was small and clear. "You want to know what I saw? I saw you: president, married to your true love, finding that mythical balance between homelife and career. Dedicated. Happy."

She looked him in the eyes, and for a moment, he had a wild thought wondering if she might allow him to kiss her, but she turned away again. "I am so, so sorry." Then she leaped to her feet. "I've made my decision," she said, approaching Jaime until his still-drawn gun was against her chest.

"Oracle?" Alejandro gasped.

Jaime looked down at the barrel of his gun against Oracle's heart. "Does this mean you agree to my offer?"

"No. My answer is no. I will never, ever join you. Kill this man if you must."

⁂ ⁂ ⁂

Nobody understands. Least of all me.

⁂ ⁂ ⁂

Jaime frowned. "How disappointing." His frown was red, angry, ugly. Alejandro knew how the man felt. "Perhaps you don't think me sincere?" Jaime continued. With a lunge, he moved toward Alejandro and shoved his gun against Alejandro's temple. "I assure you, I will kill this man. It wouldn't be my first kill or my last. It would be easy." He pulled back the hammer, and Alejandro heard the crackle of electricity within barrel.

Alejandro felt a tickle somewhere inside his chest and the strangest urge to laugh. Had he lost his mind? There was no doubt this man could and would follow through on his threat—and likely kill Oracle while he was at it. Perhaps Alejandro's emotions were too overloaded, broken along with his concussed head.

Oracle was still breathing heavily, but when she spoke, her voice was unconcerned. "Oh, I know you're serious. In fact, unlike you, I am a real seer, and I *know* you'll kill him. Three minutes from now. I've already seen it. And I don't care."

Alejandro grunted. Oracle's eyes bounced over to his own. "Tough luck, Al. But it was like you said: I don't want the happily ever after." She looked down, and what she said next seemed wrenched out of her. "If you really knew me, knew all those lives I've ruined without even trying, you wouldn't want me either. Just look at all this trouble I've brought you, simply because someone *thought* I wanted you. I'm sorry. At least you won't be angry at me long."

Jaime looked back and forth between them for a moment, and then with a snarl, switched his gun over to point at Oracle instead.

"No!" Alejandro cried, standing and placing himself in front of her. What was the matter with him? She'd just said he didn't care if he lived or died.

"Don't be ridiculous," Oracle said, pulling her hands free from her binds as if they'd never been tied. She pushed the barrel of the gun and Alejandro away. "You people have tried to shoot me before, remember? It never works. Besides, your superiors want me alive." And with that, Oracle simply stepped through the door and shut it behind her.

Jaime stared after her with shock.

Alejandro laughed, though the sound leaving his throat didn't sound like him. "What, you didn't see that coming?" asked Alejandro, his voice strained.

Jaime glanced at Alejandro, and then with a snarl, he lunged towards the door. Before he could stop himself, Alejandro leaped at the man, bumping them both the floor, using his body as a weapon since his hands were still bound. He was awarded with an elbow to his nose, hot blood instantly streaming down as he crumpled to the floor. Jaime got to his feet and bound out the door, grabbing a passing guard outside the door by the arm.

"She took the other ship," said the guard.

"And you couldn't stop her?!" Jaime growled.

"She was gone before we knew it, *Jefe*," the man said in a grumble.

Alejandro chuckled weakly, wiping the blood from his nose, though it kept streaming. Oracle had gotten away. Saved herself. At his expense. He should probably be upset, but he wasn't. It could have been that his emotions were still overwhelmed because of the concussion and the weight of the day's revelations. But he also suspected that no matter what Oracle had said or done, Alejandro was doomed the moment Jaime and his lightningshots arrived anyway. Maybe Oracle had known he had no chance all along.

Jaime re-entered the room and trained his gun back on Alejandro, seemingly unsettled for the first time. "It was stupid of you to delay me. But don't worry, my guards will catch up to her. The other ship is faster, but she won't make it far." He smoothed back his hair, but it fell again. "Three minutes, she said? It is nice to have a deadline, isn't it? Your death isn't even really my fault at this point. It was foreseen by a very powerful seer. Who am I to argue with the future?" He pushed the gun against Alejandro's chest.

Alejandro opened his mouth, unsure what would come out but stalling for time. "Unless . . ."

Jaime shook his head, but his eyes narrowed. "No 'unless.' Oracle said you would die. And if she doesn't care to stop it, I certainly don't."

Alejandro swallowed heavily. "Unless you misunderstood. Oracle said if she told someone their future too clearly, it never comes true. I'd say telling me I'm going to be shot in three minutes is fairly clear, wouldn't you?"

Jaime scoffed. "That's ridiculous. *You* misunderstood."

"I don't think I did." Alejandro found his voice stronger now. Jaime could shoot him at any moment, but he didn't. Why? Was he really waiting for the three-minute mark? Waiting to see where this was going? So was Alejandro. "I don't think I misunderstood. She's always so careful about her . . . what did she call it? *Presentation.* 'In exactly three minutes.' So direct, so specific, so clear."

Jaime's eyes were wide. Alejandro almost couldn't believe this last-ditch effort at distraction was working. He was probably only delaying the inevitable, but if filibustering gave him an extra minute, he would take it. Alejandro took a deep breath. His head was feeling heavier by the minute. "You can see I'm right, can't you."

"I think it is time you stop talking." His eyes were wild, following Alejandro's every move. "I can just kill you now, not wait for the three minutes."

"You could, but there is something you haven't yet realized."

"And what is that?"

"You think this is the trap you set for her? From the very first moment—everything that has happened, saving me from being shot, getting me here in my airship, luring you on board," he took another long breath, delaying for effect, "it was actually her trap for you. A trap that is about to be sprung."

For a moment they just stood there, looking at each other, Jaime's eyes wide, his mouth open, breath quick, waiting.

And then they waited a moment longer.

Jaime threw his head back and broke out into a laugh. Alejandro's heart sank.

"What a speech! I can see why you went into politics. I thought for a moment that something was going to happen! I almost wanted to see it."

"Me too," mumbled Alejandro, off balance. He took a deep breath, trying to think what to say next, knowing the spell was broken and anything he said was not going to delay the inevitable. Jaime raised his gun again, and Alejandro closed his mouth, his eyes, waiting for the end.

Instead, he heard a door crash open, shouting, and then a muffled whump that could only be a body crumpling to the floor.

Was that his own body? Was he dead and having an out-of-body experience?

Was it Oracle? He opened his eyes, one at a time.

Jaime was lying in a pile on the floor, one of the other guards standing over him. The guard took off his hat. "Thank you, señor, for delaying him. I almost didn't make it in time."

"Joseph," breathed Alejandro with relief.

Time, futures, fortunes? It isn't just complicated. It's complicated. And annoying.

"I'm sorry it took me so long, Alejandro," said Joseph as he pushed levers and controls in the pilot's cabin of the airship, Alejandro standing helplessly behind, trying to stem the blood still pouring from his nose. "I had to take care of eight guards throughout the ship before I could get to you. I haven't done that since elite forces."

"How did you get onto the ship in the first place?" asked Alejandro.

"I've been here since the rally. I was doing a hasty flight check from underneath the airship after you got injured, and then it took off with me hanging on outside the maintenance cabin, and I spent the rest of the time trying to get into the airship and then picking off the invaders once the smaller ship docked. I felt it was probably better to take it slow. I'm only sorry it took me so long."

"Did you happen to see where the smaller ship went?" asked Alejandro.

Joseph frowned, leaning across the copilot seat to push a lever. "I saw that woman enter it, but nothing more. Don't worry, Al, we've got enough evidence to start a real investigation into this so-called consortium. Especially once you are elected, we will be able to shut them down for good."

Alejandro tried to smile, but it was more like a grimace. Joseph had been calling him Al for years; he was the only one Alejandro allowed the nickname. So why did it hurt now?

Joseph glanced back at him. "Why don't you rest your eyes for a moment."

Alejandro shook his head. Probably best not to.

Had Oracle known about Joseph coming to save him, predicting his death to prevent it, or had she meant what she said, that she didn't care if he died, and his survival had been luck? He suspected the former, but was that just wishful thinking? And did the fact that Jaime had told him point blank that they were destined to marry mean it couldn't ever happen now?

Or was it only predictions from Oracle herself that worked that way? Was all of it nonsense and he should stop reading into it? Would he ever see her again?

These were all questions he might be pondering for the rest of his life. Exhausting questions.

But even despite all the trouble she'd caused, the concussion and being shot at and kidnapped and tied up, he couldn't quite regret meeting her. What was wrong with him?

Joseph reached back to pat his friend's arm. "Don't worry. We'll find her."

"No," Alejandro said. "I predict we won't."

END NOTE

I realize this "seer" ability on Beta is a result of the entanglement of these two Earths, just like the "ghosts" on Alpha. Their histories are closely tied, albeit Alpha is running a few years ahead. But there are some abilities here that they definitely shouldn't have. Are these also the cause of the splintering and entanglement?

Anyway, I'm at a standstill when it comes to these two worlds, so I'll take whatever input I can get. I have a curiosity inspection with the Cats in 7, so I guess I'll leave this here.

—Nerrid Flopdoodle

Date: 2590-04-12 10:07:46 PRT
From: Ren Stornman
To: Anachronauts
Subject: Void Tar
Re: Ensigns

Nerrid, I owe you an apology. I was fully prepared to give you a very convincing explanation of exactly what was happening on Spectre Alpha and Beta. But then I read all three accounts. And now I don't know what to tell you, except that apparently I don't know as much as I thought I did, which is deeply inconvenient.

And now to the account at hand: I know you’ve brought it up before, Ms. Six, but it’s still amazing to me that an entire world could come together and decide to remove scientific facts from human consciousness and recorded history. Like, how? And to do such a thorough job of it too...blows my mind. Especially in 1888 when this world splintered.

But I’m getting distracted. As you read this account, I want your thoughts on the Void Tar. Previous reports have been spotty, due to the secretive nature of the Order. But the effects described here? Wild!

ENSIGNS

By Jan Hassmann

"I'll talk to you when we get back."

"I love you, Lewis. Be safe."

"Always. Bye, Mum."

Lewis closed the Com, fell back into his chair, and stared at the background image of his screen, blinking away the tears he had managed to hold back during the conversation. Vincent van Gogh's *Darkest Night.* He let his eyes wander over the image's gentle swirls of blue and yellow light rising into the black Null sky, calling upon the mind-calming techniques of the Inseers.

The tides outlast the storm. His father's voice rang through his mind like a bell. His breath steadied.

Suddenly, a harsh buzz shook him back to reality.

"What now?" he sighed. He turned his chair and faced the door. "Open."

"Oooooohhh nice bunk!"

Elina didn't wait for an invitation to enter but threw herself on the bed as the door hissed shut behind her.

"I think these are technically *quarters*," Lewis said.

"Oh, my apologies, *Lieutenant*."

"And how are yours, *Lieutenant* Mar?"

"They are exactly the same, thank you. They're the other way around though; I'm on the other side of the ship. And I'm actually pretty sure it's bad luck to call someone lieutenant before graduation, *Ensign* Forge."

"Then, we can wait another week, *Ensign* Mar. One more training mission to go."

They really *were* nice quarters. Lewis hadn't really had time to take it all in; he hadn't even finished unpacking the duffel bag Elina had jumped on. After years of bunk beds and Swift's snoring, this was pure luxury. A real bed, complete with a nightstand, a spacious desk with a full terminal, and a low table with two chairs in the corner. He even had his own little bathroom. The crystal waters of the Atlantic danced outside two large portholes behind the desk.

"The ship is huge," said Elina, "I almost got lost on the way over here." She was beaming. "Look at us now! It's just like in those reruns of *Ocean Trek* we used to watch! 'Full speed ahead Mr. Sato! Yes sir!'" She saluted. A few strands of her light brown hair had fallen out of her ponytail.

"I still can't believe they cancelled that after two seasons," Lewis said and turned to the portholes.

"Hey, what's up?" Elina sat up. "You OK?"

"Just talked to my mum."

"Oh . . . I'm sorry . . . it's today . . ."

He nodded. "It's all right. Funny coincidence though."

Elina got up and put a hand on Lewis's shoulder. "Your dad would be proud of you today."

"My dad was right." He felt the tears coming back and got up. "What do you think we'll find out here? Hey look, a new species of deep ocean crab! And oh, a lanternfish! And look, what's this? The remains of probe 275, which we sent down here twenty years ago! They're doing sightseeing in Mariana, Elina!"

"Don't do this, Lewis."

He threw up his hands and stepped into the middle of the room.

"Behold, the *OAS Coleridge*, marvel of engineering, pride of the fleet, on her fake maiden voyage with the finest of the academy! Ready to explore an ocean trench so insignificant it doesn't even have a name." Lewis's arms fell to his sides in defeat. "There's nothing down there, Elina. We're explorers with nothing left to explore. My dad was right. This is a waste of time."

Elina wiped the strand of hair from her face and tucked it behind her ear. "We have dreamed of exploring the ocean since we were kids, remember?"

Lewis sighed and slumped down on the bed. "Yeah, but now . . ."

Elina sat down next to him.

"What's left?" he muttered.

Her silence spoke volumes.

"I'm sorry. You're right. This is a good day. I didn't want to ruin it. It's just . . ."

"It's okay. Sorry, I forgot what day it is." She put her hand back on his shoulder and looked at him, her brown eyes full of sympathy.

The door buzzed again.

"Open!" shouted Lewis.

"What now?" muttered Elina.

"All right, guys, nice bunks, eh?" Swift's smile reached all the way up to his spiky blond hair. "Mine are right next to Ensign Verell's. I think I should check in on her now that we got our own rooms and all, wouldn't want her to feel lonely. Miss me yet?" He dropped onto the bed next to Lewis and put his arm around him. "I'm not interrupting anything, am I?"

"I was just leaving," said Elina and got up. "You never know, Lewis, maybe you'll discover the next big thing. Just keep looking. Wouldn't be the first time you missed what's right before your eyes."

"What's that supposed to mean?" Lewis called after her.

"You're an idiot, Forge." Swift got up.

"What? Why?"

"I'm gonna check if Verell needs help unpacking. I recorded some of my snoring for you: I'll send it to your terminal."

The door hissed shut. Lewis fell back on his duffel bag and watched the shimmering waves paint gentle swirls of blue and yellow light on the ceiling of his lieutenant's quarters.

❋ ❋ ❋

"As this marks the first voyage of the *Coleridge*, it also marks your last training voyage. You have been chosen because you have excelled in your duties at the academy, and I'm proud to see you all standing here on the bridge of this magnificent vessel. Since Galileo first turned his gaze upon the oceans . . ."

The gigantic face on the gigantic main screen of the bridge seemed like a final effort to ensure you never forgot the *greatness* of Dean Admiral McKenna Bray. Captain Delgado, sitting in the chair in the center of the bridge, seemed tiny in comparison.

"An officer of the Ocean Assembly is more than a mere explorer. We are guardians . . ." continued the admiral.

Lewis stopped listening.

He looked at the rest of the group of the soon-to-be officers of the Ocean Assembly standing at the back of the bridge. Elina stood next to Lewis, and on the other side of her was Swift, his perpetual grin hiding his mischievous mind. Lewis was sure Swift had at least three dirty jokes ready as soon as Bray's speech was over. Next to Swift stood Gia Verell and then four more ensigns he knew from the academy, all in their dark blue *OA* jumpsuit uniforms. The others he had never seen before. On the far side of the group towered Commander Gamble and three Systemics in their gray uniforms.

"And so," continued the dean admiral, "as you embark into the depths of . . . of . . ."

"*The Salty Crack,*" Lewis blurted, suddenly blessed with inspiration.

Swift erupted with laughter while the rest of the group struggled to contain theirs with varying success. Even the Systemics, not particularly well-known for their sense of humor, couldn't hide a grin.

Captain Delgado stirred in his chair, and the admiral continued, ". . . of Trench 347-J, remember your training and the guiding principles of . . ."

The speech went on for a few more agonizing minutes until finally, with the words "Godspeed, *Coleridge*!" the main viewer flickered and reverted to the bold *OA* logo, a crescent wave surrounded by the nine steering wheels representing the Ocean States.

Delgado whirled around and barked: "Did you have anything to add to the dean admiral's speech, Ensign Forge?"

While nobody liked the admiral, most people liked Captain Delgado. He had been their operations instructor in their final year at the academy and had been given command of the *Coleridge* for this trip. Whenever people talked about Captain Delgado, someone inevitably said, with a serious nod: *Good mustache.*

He was an experienced captain, and he ran a tight ship.

"No sir, sorry sir," stammered Lewis.

"And Mister Swift . . ."

"That was not funny, sir, my apologies, sir," interrupted Swift, with that tiny smirk on his face which always made you wonder if he was pulling your leg.

Delgado looked back and forth between them.

"Right. B and C shift, you're dismissed. A shift, take your stations."

"Excellent work, Forge, excellent work." Swift gave Lewis a quick slap on the shoulder as he dashed to the front of the bridge and took the helm.

Elina sat down at her station in front of the *Sonarc* monitors and immediately went *oooooh*.

"Fancy gear?" said Lewis as he sat down at the station next to hers.

"Fancy chairs!"

Lewis smiled and looked at his station. He had always loved to get lost in maps. Now he was facing the most advanced navigation interface in the fleet.

"You've earned this." Elina reached over and squeezed his hand.

"Yes. Yes, I have."

"Everybody where they're supposed to be?" Captain Delgado scanned his young bridge crew as they responded with a chorus of excited *Yes, sirs*.

"All stations report ready to embark, sir," said First Officer Gamble from his station next to the Com.

"Well, Mr. Swift, shall we take her out?"

"Absolutely, Cap . . ."

"Excuse me, sir," interrupted Ensign Verell at the Com. "I'm sorry, but we have a boarding request at Airlock Five?"

"What? By whom? I thought the manifest was complete?"

"Yes, sir, I checked personally. Let me confirm," Her hands whizzed over her touch screen. "It seems like the manifest has just been edited. A party of three has been added to the guest quarters. They are registered as . . ." She hesitated and looked up, straight into Delgado's eyes. "They are registered as Voidess Hellan and two aides."

"A Void Priest?" whispered Elina. "What the reef?"

The bridge felt suddenly very quiet. Swift swung around in his chair and looked at Lewis. He was not smiling.

"Well," Delgado stood up and pulled on his uniform, "if they're on the manifest . . ."

"Incoming transmission from *OA* Command, sir," called Verell.

Delgado sighed.

"To my ready room, Ensign Verell, permission to board granted; unseal the airlock. Ensign Swift, stand down. Let's see what this is all about. Everyone, stay where they are. Mike, you have the bridge."

"Aye, sir," boomed Gamble.

Delgado was almost at the door to his ready room when he suddenly turned to face Lewis with a sly grin. "Ensign Forge. Would you maybe like to volunteer to greet our guests at Airlock Five and escort them to guest quarters?"

Swift snorted again, and Lewis could see Elina's grin even through the back of her head.

"Of course, sir, immediately, sir."

❁ ❁ ❁

"Guest quarters, guest quarters . . ." mumbled Lewis as he swiped through section after section of the map of the *Coleridge* on his pad. Shaped like a stingray, the sub was not only the pinnacle of modern technology but also strikingly elegant. He paused and looked down a long, empty, and entirely unfamiliar corridor with metallic gray walls and a lot of doors. Elina had been right; it was easy to get lost around here.

"Where am I?"

With five decks and a diameter of over a hundred meters, the *Coleridge* usually carried a crew complement of over two hundred, but all the research bays, hydroponics labs, and biotech units were still unmanned. There were currently only sixty-four people on board: Oceanists, Systemics, a handful of Medics, and, crucially, the galley crew.

He was on Cobalt Deck, one below the bridge, housing the science stations.

The airlock was on Azure Deck, where the crew quarters were, and where he assumed he would find the guest quarters as well.

"Gotcha." Azure Deck, Aft 34.

Three minutes later and out of breath, Lewis stood in front of Airlock Five.

A Void Priestess on a submarine. Not something you heard every day. The members of the secretive Void Order usually stayed on dry land and stuck to themselves. As the Oceanists dived into the depths of the seas and the Inseers delved into the depths of the mind, the Voidists looked up into the Null.

Lewis had never met a Void Priest. His father had despised them even more than he had despised the Ocean Assembly, calling them a dangerous cult.

Enlightenment is within. Beyond lie only shadows.

The airlock hatch hissed and slid open.

In front of Lewis stood two men in nullblack robes with extremely pale skin. They weren't much older than him, clean-shaven, short hair, just like any cadet in the academy. Their eyes were hidden behind tiny, close-fitting dark glasses, not unlike a pair of diving goggles. Lewis thought for a second that they were twins.

Concealed behind the two aides stood a shape entirely clothed in black. Even the face was covered with a fine black mesh, like a dense spider web.

"Welcome aboard the *Coleridge*. I am Ensign Forge. Right this way." He took a step back and motioned to the left.

The silent Voidists stepped out of the airlock and floated down the corridor.

As Lewis fell in line behind the priestess, he noticed a strange, oily smell. It was harsh and bitter, like the stale air in an old dry dock. It was not very strong, but he could almost taste it.

"Here we are." He touched the control panel, and the two aides moved to the side of the door. As the priestess melted into the darkness of the guest quarters, Lewis thought he saw her turn her head and look at him.

"The Voidess thanks you for your hospitality," said one of the aides. "She is not to be disturbed and will take her meals in her quarters. Please arrange an audience with the captain at his earliest convenience." He bowed.

"Of course, I will immediately talk to—"

The door hissed shut.

⁂

"My crew is not qualified for that!"

Lewis had heard Delgado shout many times, but this sounded different, even through the closed door to his ready room.

Lewis had been standing there for a couple of minutes already and wondered if he should just return to his post. Instead, he inched closer to the door. He could feel the cold radiating from the metal, when it suddenly swept open.

"Yes, Ensign?"

Lewis couldn't remember ever standing so close to the captain. The man suddenly seemed a lot taller. *Good mustache*, Lewis thought.

"The, uh, Voidess and her aides are in the guest quarters, and they ask for an appointment. Sir." He took a slow-motion step backwards.

The captain looked at him, clearly lost in thought. After an uncomfortable few seconds, he straightened up.

"Let's get this boat in the blue."

⁂

"These Void guys creep me out, man," Swift garbled with a full mouth. "Susan said there's weird chanting going on in their quarters, and it smells like a Systemic's wiper in there."

"Who's Susan?" asked Elina.

"The redhead from the galley crew. She brought them their dinner yesterday. She's from Coriolis and likes cats, Adriatic food, and romantic walks on Indigo Deck."

Lewis looked up from his tray towards the counter at the other side of the mess hall.

Elina just rolled her eyes.

It had been an exciting three days on board the *Coleridge.* The young crew had performed all kinds of drills and maneuvers to familiarize themselves with their stations, and had even simulated an emergency surface from a thousand meters.

"How do you become a Void Priest anyway?" he asked after he failed to spot anyone with red hair. "They don't have an academy or anything, do they?"

"You don't sign up for the Void Order," Elina said, "you get recruited."

"Recruited? How?"

"You got to smell like a burnt sock, and they'll find you," laughed Swift.

"What could they possibly want on the ship?" Lewis wondered aloud. "This is not even the real maiden voyage, we're just here to check if any bolts pop as the hull settles."

"Perfect if you want to do a bit of sightseeing. The ship's practically empty. Maybe they roam the corridors at night and scare C shift." Swift stuffed another huge piece of coral cake into his mouth.

"Speaking of sightseeing, you *have* to check out the observation lounge," Elina said, "it's gorgeous down there. Let's go tonight!"

The way she looked at Lewis confirmed his suspicion.

Since he was, in fact, not an idiot, he had noticed the change in Elina's behavior, but was not yet sure how to deal with all that. "Um, I'm beat. I'm gonna turn in early, I haven't been sleeping well," he said and got up. "Maybe tomorrow?"

"Sure."

"I'm off as well. I've got a date." Swift stood too.

Elina looked up at her two friends.

"You guys rock, no really, you're the best." She gave them two thumbs up. "Don't mind me. I'll get some more cake."

* * *

1:54. Lewis tapped his pad on the nightstand, and the room returned to darkness. This was the third time he had checked the time since midnight.

He sat up with a sigh and looked out the portholes. At this depth, the ocean was as black as the Null.

"All right, all right, I'll check it out," he muttered to himself. It was probably a good idea to visit the observation lounge before he went there with Elina. There was no sleep in him, so he put on his jumpsuit and left his quarters.

Lewis strolled down the long, dimly lit main corridor to the fore stairwell. Everything was quiet. The only sound was the occasional ticking of the non-Newtonian metals of the hull, settling under the increasing pressure as the *Coleridge* eased into the eternal darkness of the Atlantic depths. Only C shift was awake, working on the bridge.

Lewis couldn't help but gasp as the doors hissed open. Wide steps led down into the cavernous observation lounge, spanning both Indigo and Midnight decks. The entire lower foresection was made of glassteel, sweeping down in a gentle arc to offer a stunning view of the ocean depths below. The water glowed a soft blue, illuminated by the powerful bow spotlights, while the lounge remained in dark serenity. Three rows of reclining chairs hugged the sloping floor beside the steps, leaving a broad, open space before the glass wall. It was obvious why Elina wanted them to come here.

He walked down the steps and through the room until he could touch the glass. Marine snow was dancing in the icy water, but nothing else stirred.

"Just more darkness," he said.

"As above, so below."

Lewis's heart froze as he whirled around. In the first row of chairs, on the right, sat a dark figure.

"My apologies. I didn't mean to startle you."

The figure rose and moved through the room like smoke weaving from a smothered candle. It was the Void Priestess.

"Uh, Miss, uhm, Voidess, sorry, I didn't see you there, I . . ."

She stopped right in front of him, uncomfortably close. She was tiny, a good head shorter than Lewis. The strange smell was much stronger now, dark, oily, almost like burning damp wood, but without the comforting warmth of a smoky campfire: the mysterious Null Tar, the distillate of the pit octopus's ink, rumored to be used by the Order to induce powerful visions.

"We have a reputation for being good at hiding." Her voice was warm, comforting even.

"I'm sorry to disturb you; I'll give you the room." He turned to leave with a slight bow.

The priestess turned towards the glass. "What a strange thing for an explorer to say."

Lewis stopped and turned around. "Excuse me?"

"*Just more darkness*. Isn't that what drives your noble profession? To penetrate and illuminate the darkness of the seas?"

Her voice was mesmerizing. It rose and fell like a mournful violin, backed by the depth of a booming orchestra. Lewis couldn't tell if she was twenty-five or sixty-five.

"I . . . I guess it is. But it seems the sea has already given up most of its secrets. Or maybe they are also just very good at hiding."

A soft sound, maybe a chuckle. "Are you suggesting that there is nothing left in Mother's ocean to discover?"

Lewis stepped closer to the glass. "I don't know. After all these years of deep-sea exploration, there are very few blank spots left on the map."

"Ah, but no map can hold all the wisdom of the oceans. Look at the powerful lights of your wonderful ship."

For a moment, they stood in silence, gazing out the wide window of the quiet observation lounge.

"Have we understood everything these lights illuminate? Or are there still things hidden, even in the brightest of lights? Wherever the light shines, it reveals. That is its purpose. How gently it diminishes into the depths."

"I thought light wasn't really your specialty . . ."

"The candle births the shadow, Ensign."

"Well," he stammered, "I'm sure the Botanics and Biologics can find some revelations here, but for some explorers like me, it seems like Earth has become, well, maybe a little too small."

"Ah," she said, "maybe you need to widen your curiosities."

Lewis stared into the gloom beyond the spotlights. "*The mind is the well that replenishes the spring*," he quoted.

"*And the spring feeds many rivers.* Your father has taught you well."

Lewis snapped around and looked at her concealed face. A soft reflection betrayed the existence of sparkling eyes behind the dark veil.

"You *are* the son of Ecelius Forge, are you not? I greatly admired your father and was saddened to hear of his passing. You look just like him."

Lewis returned his gaze to the depths. The glassteel showed a ghostly reflection of the Void priestess.

"I'm sorry to say that my father's opinion of the Void Order was not as favorable."

"Ah, of course. The Inseers are so very sure of their ways and so dismissive of all others. One can't help but wonder why it is my Order that has such a sinister reputation." Then she added, in a whisper: "You do get used to the smell."

Lewis smiled at her reflection.

"The Inseers have benefited greatly from your father's techniques," she continued. "His maxims on clarity were quite inspiring."

Lewis was desperate to change the subject. "May I ask you a question?"

She suddenly straightened. She turned towards him and seemed to grow, like a tall shadow stretching in the setting sun.

"Of course." She sounded almost eager.

"What is a Void Priestess doing on a submarine?"

"Ah." She seemed to shrink again, turned and melted into the darkness of the lounge.

"*The right questions will light the way*, as we say in the Order. It is late. I should retire."

As the priestess had almost reached the top of the stairs, he called after her: "What's the right question?"

She stopped, but didn't turn. "There are many right questions, Ensign. Some deserve answers, some open doors. And some . . ." She paused.

Her dark form was one with the shadows of the lounge. Lewis squinted, catching a flicker of motion, but he couldn't tell what she was doing.

Suddenly the stench of the Null Tar washed over him like a wave. He gasped; his vision seemed to blur, and he almost gagged as the bitter smell went down his throat. For a brief second, the shadows in the lounge shimmered with the thousand colors of spilled oil.

He shook his head, and his vision cleared.

"You will get another chance, Ensign."

❁ ❁ ❁

You could hear a pin drop on the bridge.

"320 meters." Elina's voice cut through the silence. Although her screens offered an array of numbers and graphs interpreting the *Sonarc*, her right hand rested on her earpiece.

Everyone else on the bridge was fixated on the large main viewer. The powerful bow floodlights pierced deep into the black waters below the *Coleridge*.

"Steady as she goes, Ensign." Delgado's deep, calm voice was reassuring.

"Aye, sir." Swift's flashy confidence rarely showed any cracks, but he sounded tense.

"Two hundred fifty meters."

Lewis's heart began to pound.

"One hundred-eighty meters."

"Prepare for *ahead full* at thirty, Mr. Swift."

"*Ahead full* at thirty meters, aye, sir."

"One hundred meters." Elina threw her head around to look at the main viewer.

The waters seemed to shift and thicken to a murky glow until suddenly the bleak, desolate expanse of the deep ocean floor materialized before their eyes. The plane of fine, ashen sediment looked featureless at first, but soon revealed a mosaic of countless, meandering trails left by the few creatures that could survive this crushing pressure. And it loomed closer, fast.

Lewis felt his stomach drop as Swift blew the tanks, pitched the bow of the *Coleridge,* and surged to full speed ahead.

"Crash dive complete, *ahead full* at thirty meters above seabed, sir." Swift beamed.

"That was *twelve* meters from scraping the floor," Elina whispered to Lewis.

"I've seen him do six." Lewis chuckled and turned to the captain. "Depth 4,778 meters, sir."

"Well done, everybody!" Captain Delgado stood up and let his eyes wander over the wide smiles of his young bridge crew.

"And you, sir!" Swift grinned.

"Knock it off, Swift!" Gamble barked from the right.

"Mr. Forge!" Lewis noticed a concerned look on Delgado's face as he spoke. "Plot new course to coordinates as received. Ensign Swift, new heading, *mark three-two-four*, ahead full, maintain depth; *Sonarc*, keep your eyes on the road."

Aye sirs.

Lewis glanced at Elina, turned to his terminal, and tapped the flashing order that had been transferred from Gamble's station. He punched the new set of coordinates into the Nav and watched the map jump to the new destination of the *Coleridge*.

❋ ❋ ❋

"We're not cleared to go below six thousand. West Tonal Trench is 7684 meters deep. This is a training exercise, no matter how often Bray calls it a *maiden voyage*. Plus, the hull is supposed to temper for at least three months after commissioning. *Above six.*"

When Swift wasn't joking around or chatting up girls, he knew his stuff. And he was probably the best helmsman the academy had seen in a decade.

The mess hall was buzzing with the news of their new destination.

"What do you know about West Tonal?" Elina asked.

"It's huge. A labyrinth. There's a million cracks and side valleys extending from the main trench," answered Lewis. "And it's tight."

"This must have something to do with these Void guys." Swift's eyes narrowed.

"Like what? Creepy Void Priest honeymoon to West Tonal?" Elina chuckled.

Lewis pursed his lips. "Creepy is not the right word . . ."

"You should have asked her what this is all about, man!" Swift said with a full mouth.

"I tried!"

"Maybe they dropped something," said Elina.

Lewis and Swift stopped chewing and looked at each other.

"The Void Order doesn't have any ships. All they ever do is contemplate the Null," Elina continued. "They look *up*, not down. So if something got lost in the trench and they want it, they would *have* to request assistance from the fleet."

"But why not a seasoned ship? Why a new ship full of cadets?" asked Swift.

"Must be urgent," said Elina.

Lewis's heart pounded in his throat. "What if someone didn't drop something?" His voice trembled. "They look up! What if something *fell*?"

* * *

"Time?" Lewis asked the terminal again.

21:38

"The right question . . ." He sighed and slumped back into his chair. The dim glow of his screen barely managed to hold back the darkness of his quarters.

"Let's start from the beginning. Define the Null."

The Null is the featureless darkness surrounding the known triverse.

"Define triverse."

The triverse is the totality of existence, consisting of the Moon orbiting the Earth orbiting the Sun.

"How does the Void Order define the Null?"

The Void Order believes that the Null, which they call the Void, hides profound revelations about the origins and existence of mankind.

"Does it?"

Data not available.

"Has the Order presented any evidence for this assumption?"

The Void Order has not presented any evidence to support this assumption.

"Time."

21:41

"How does the Void Order investigate the Null?"

The Void Order investigates the Null through contemplation, meditation, and intellectual discourse.

"They don't employ the scientific method at all?"

The Void Order's public statements do not suggest an application of the scientific method.

"Do not suggest? Clarify."

While the Void Order's public statements do not suggest an application of the scientific method, there are council records of cooperation with the science guilds.

Lewis sat up.

"What records?"

08/1998 Request to access Kea Moon Observatory

02/2002 Request to access La Silla Moon Observatory

08/2003 Request to access Kea Moon Observatory

01/2005 Request to access Kea Moon Observatory

07/2006 Request to access La Silla Moon Observatory

02/2—

"Stop. How many entries are there of the Void Order asking for observatory access?"

114

Lewis shrugged. They probably wanted to have an occasional look at the Null. And the few remaining Crescentics surely appreciated an occasional visit and a break from staring at craters.

"Time."

21:44

"How many entries are there that are not about observatory access?"

341

"What do these consist of?"

Requests for Botanist assistance

Requests for Systemic assistance

Requests for OA fleet assistance

Reque—

"Stop. What kind of fleet assistance did they request?"

No further data available.

"Time."

21:47

Lewis buried his face in his hands and rubbed his eyes.

"What are you looking for, Priestess? What are you hoping to find . . ."

Suddenly, he sat up. "Or have you already found something? How many entries are there per year?"

There is an average of 4.5 entries per year.

"Are there any years that differ significantly from this average?"

The year 2064 differs significantly with 17 entries.

"Display entries for 2064."

04/2064 Request to access Kea Moon Observatory

04/2064 Request to access La Silla Moon Observatory

04/2064 Request for OA fleet assistance

04/2064 Request to access La Silla Moon Observatory

04/2064 Request for OA fleet assistance

05/2064 Request for Systemic assistance

05/2064 Request to access La Silla Moon Observatory

05/2064 Request for OA fleet assistance

05/2064 Request for Systemic assistance

05/2064 Request for Medics assistance

05/2064 Request for Systemic assistance

05/2064 Request for OA fleet assistance

05/2064 Request for Medics assistance

05/2064 Request for Medics assistance

05/2064 Request for Medics assistance

05/2064 Request for OA fleet assistance

05/2064 Request to access La Silla Moon Observatory

Cold sweat formed on his back.

"List *OA* ships logged as embarking in April 2064 and returning in May 2064."

OAS Verne

OAS Hesperus

Lewis knew the *Verne;* she was a tiny mapping vessel. He had never heard of the *Hesperus*.

"What was the mission statement for the *Hesperus*?"

This information is classified.

"What?"

The mission statement of the OAS Hesperus from April 2064 is classified.

"You gotta be . . . Close *Lexicon*, open *NOAD*," he snapped.

Lewis blinked as the dazzling blue *NOAD* screen illuminated the room. The navigational database of the Ocean Assembly provided access to the data archive of the *BuoyNet* that was the backbone of global communications. It also logged the movements of the entire fleet.

"Access NavEcho *OAS Hesperus*."

Clearance Level 3 required. Please login to proceed.

With a dry laugh, he punched in his lieutenant's code, given to him at the mission briefing five days ago.

The screen filled with a long list of dates in tiny letters.

"Mission date April 2064."

A list of arcane letters and numbers. The individual buoys.

"Sort by distance from *OA Command*, descending order."

He tapped the buoy ID on the top of the list. The screen went dark for what seemed an eternity, then finally displayed the data entry of buoy 1F8A35G7. A schematic. Commission and service dates. And finally, a location.

West Tonal Trench, Collrey Sea, South Atlantic, A35/G7.

Lewis fell back into his chair and stared at the message.

"Welcome back, Voidess."

Suddenly, he looked up. "Time?"

22:07

"Ah, reef."

He jumped up and ran out of his quarters.

* * *

Lewis almost crashed into a trio of ensigns arguing loudly in the main passageway when he dashed to the fore stairwell. He wondered if he should just tell Elina what he had found, but then decided that, unpleasant as it may be, he had to get a different conversation out of the way first. She had probably guessed what this was about anyway from the awkward way he had asked her to come to the lounge after shift change, *to talk.* They had been friends since first grade, good friends, and Lewis had never thought of her in any other way.

He reached the lounge doors, composed himself, and glanced at his pad.

22:11

The doors hissed open, and Lewis stepped into the lounge. It was empty. The marine snow glittered like diamonds in the powerful bow spotlights.

After shift change could mean anytime after ten, and Elina was notoriously late anyway. He sat down in the front row and waited. As he rehearsed the speech he had practiced in his head all day, his mind kept going back to the mission of the *Hesperus* and the suddenly mysterious destination of the *Coleridge*. Elina and Swift had laughed when he suggested that something might have fallen from the Null. They were probably right; the whole idea was crazy.

He leaned back into the comfy lounge chair. The swirling dance of the marine snow, the tiny particles of biomatter that perpetually showered the depths from the animated regions above, was hypnotic.

⁂

Lewis snapped awake.

"What was that?" His voice echoed through the empty lounge.

It took him a few seconds to realize where he was. He blinked away the sleep and checked his pad.

2:42. Elina hadn't shown up, his back hurt, and he felt cold.

"Great."

Then he heard it again. Three muffled *booms* in rapid succession, like distant fireworks. He looked up and darted to the front of the lounge. He couldn't believe his eyes.

The *Coleridge* was sailing along a sheer wall of towering gray rock, barely thirty meters off her steerboard bow. Lewis gasped, pressed his face against the glass, and looked up. The jagged wall melted into the darkness far above. They were already deep in the trench and going deeper.

"On C shift? What the reef?" He flinched as a bright explosion, followed by another set of booms, seared the harsh seascape in the cold, stabbing light of three phosphorus flares.

Sharp shadows flickered along the rock face and stretched like drowning arms reaching for the surface, as the flares sank into the depths and diminished to a dull red.

"On *C shift*?" He turned, dashed up the stairs, and left the observation lounge.

What had the dean admiral said? Something about *excelled in your duties?* Truth was that the academy attracted barely enough new cadets these days to keep the *OA*'s fleet properly manned. Word on the ship was that C shift had passed by the skin of their teeth and was practicing *Sonarc* readouts with the third officer all night.

He took three steps at a time as he raced up the main fore stairwell, then stopped as he reached Sapphire Deck, gasping. After a few seconds, he straightened, smoothed his crumpled uniform, and approached the bridge.

The doors remained shut.

He turned to the control panel on the right, pulled his pad out of his pocket, and presented it to the scanner.

Soundlessly, the panel flashed red and, without offering any explanation, returned to calmly showing the time.

He tried again, with the same results.

"What the reef is . . ."

Then he noticed the smell. The faint bite of the Null Tar was lingering in the hallway.

For a moment, he considered banging on the doors, but decided against it. He was about to become an officer of the Ocean Assembly, and forcefully demanding access to a sealed bridge was probably not the best idea, no matter how much he wanted to know what was going on.

He turned and dashed down the stairwell to Azure Deck. Swift would never forgive him for not waking him if something weird was going on. And *he* could probably manage to somehow talk himself onto the bridge.

Lewis arrived at his quarters and hit the buzzer.

No response.

"Come on!" He buzzed again, keeping his finger on the button and pushing harder as if that would make a difference. He raised his fist and was about to bang on the door when he suddenly looked to the left.

Verell's quarters.

Of course. Nobody could sleep through the door buzzer, not even snoring Swift. He was probably with Verell.

For a moment, Lewis thought about waking Elina, then checked his pad again. Five past three. His shift would start in less than three hours. He sighed and looked down the empty corridors of the *Coleridge*.

This whole business would be the talk of the ship by lunchtime anyway. His head sank. Patience had never been his strong suit.

To the patient, all is revealed, mocked the voice of his father.

Lewis suddenly felt very alone.

❋ ❋ ❋

Of course, he couldn't sleep. He tossed and turned for hours, and when his alarm finally penetrated the fog, it was eleven minutes to six. Then he remembered the night before and was wide awake. He jumped into his uniform and ran out of his quarters. He couldn't wait to tell Elina and Swift about the *Hesperus.*

He felt like he was back in his living room, on the faded green sofa with Elina, holding mugs of hot chocolate and watching *Ocean Trek* on a rainy Sunday morning, as the *Endeavor* discovered ancient civilizations and ships teeming with tentacled sea creatures.

He managed to reach Sapphire Deck just in time for his shift. He straightened his uniform and looked up to see Swift and Elina, walking towards him, dark rings under their eyes.

"Guys, you won't believe what . . ." he paused. "Where're you going?"

"Hey Lewis . . . we . . . um . . . let's talk later." Swift hadn't called him *Lewis* since their first week at the academy.

"What's going on?"

"We got called on C shift late last night, sorry, we . . ." Elina's smile seemed tortured. "We . . ."

"Do you need a special invitation, Ensign Forge?" Gamble's booming voice echoed through the corridor.

"We'll talk later." Elina squeezed his shoulder.

Lewis gaped after them as he stumbled backwards onto the bridge.

"Yeah, I think it's weird too," said a voice behind him. He turned to see it was Sonya from C shift, pushing up her glasses and taking the *Sonarc* station.

Lewis was speechless. His mouth stood open, and his eyes darted around aimlessly. The main viewer showed the bow headlights fading into the dark waters.

"Navigation, report," someone said, far away.

"Navigation! Ensign Forge!"

"Yes, sir. Sorry, sir."

Lewis turned to his station.

"Position . . . position is *on-grid,* Nav point 34b as logged, depth . . ." He shook his head, "depth 4912 meters."

The *Coleridge* had ascended from West Tonal and was stationary above the trench.

"*Sonarc.*"

"Hovering center trench, 180 above well, walls 110 port, 130 steerboard, clear 360/360."

"Alright people." Gamble seemed even grumpier than usual. "We will proceed with mapping the upper funnels of West Tonal. I want precise *Sonarc* readings and Nav correspondence. Helm, we will stay above the horizon at all times, and no near-death experiences this time, Mr. Geery."

"Aye, sir."

"What?" Lewis shouted, "sir, we already *have* accurate mappings of West Tonal, we . . ."

"Do you have a problem with your orders, Ensign?" Gamble's stare would have sent a great white scurrying for his mum.

"But, sir, we—"

"Ensign."

Lewis suddenly saw something behind Gamble's bushy eyebrows. Something he had never noticed before, something more . . . human. Something like, *drop it, kid.*

❋ ❋ ❋

"Permission to transfer to C shift, sir," Lewis said. It had been the longest shift of his life.

"You are on A shift, Forge," Gamble answered. Commander Gamble was a man of few words; his eyebrows did most of the talking. This time they said: *I don't have time for your nonsense.*

"Permission to join C shift tonight, sir, for . . . for observation."

"You will report to A shift tomorrow morning as logged, Ensign."

"If I may speak to the captain . . ."

Gamble slammed his pad on the desk.

Get out, said the eyebrows.

❋ ❋ ❋

He found Elina and Swift sitting in the empty mess hall three hours later.

"Thanks for dropping by, guys," he said. "How's life? What's new?" He didn't sit down.

"I just got out of bed," Elina said, "I was about to come over."

"We got called in late, okay? We had no idea either." Swift looked even more tortured than Elina.

Lewis slumped on the chair next to her. "So?" he looked back and forth between them, but they just stared at each other for what seemed an eternity.

"Hello?!? What the reef is . . ."

"We're under orders," Swift blurted. He looked at Lewis like a wet dog. "Sorry, man."

"What orders?"

"We're not to share any information about the mission or bridge proceedings," Elina said, staring at her food. Then she looked up. "And we've been reassigned to C shift until further notice."

Lewis felt like he had been punched in the stomach. "Not good enough for the interesting stuff, hey? Promising start for the aspiring navigator."

"It's not about that," said Elina.

He got up and, ignoring Elina's plea to wait, he left the mess hall.

❋ ❋ ❋

What's the right question?

At first, Lewis had wanted to return to the lounge, but decided against it. Staring at the trench wall for hours was not going to get him any answers. He had spent the evening trying to find out more about the Void Order, but information was sparse. They were a secretive bunch indeed.

Elina had been right; there was no official way to join the Order. They seemed to recruit members from all disciplines, often straight out of the academies.

Some questions open doors.

She had almost sounded disappointed when he had asked what they were doing on the ship.

What is the right question?

He scrolled through the list of questions he had asked the computer in the past few hours.

"This is pointless." He closed the *Lexicon*. Van Gogh's *Darkest Night* reappeared on the screen.

He had always loved the painting, ever since the day he first saw it, sitting in his father's lap and struggling to handle the large coffee table book.

Look at how the light disappears into the Null. It is lost. That's why we Inseers shine the light of our minds into our deepest selves, where it continues to shine and to reveal.

Suddenly, a subtle vibration shuddered through the ship, buzzing his fingertips on the desk.

At the same time, he noticed the low hum of the normally soundless engines. He had felt it before, just two days ago, during the emergency surface. The ship had entered flank speed and was racing through the depths.

He jumped up. Time to hit the lounge.

But then he paused. He turned around and looked again at the painting on the screen.

Look at how the light disappears into the Null. It is lost.

"Is it?"

❋ ❋ ❋

Lewis raced through the main corridor of the *Coleridge*, accompanied by the hum of the protesting engines.

Wherever the light shines, it reveals.

He had almost reached the fore stairwell when he suddenly felt his stomach drop. He lost his balance and crashed hard into the cold metal wall of the corridor. The *Coleridge* was banking hard steerboard. The engines whined as the ship steadied.

Some questions open doors.

He dashed up the stairs and reached the stubbornly closed bridge doors. He banged on the doors with both fists. He heard the captain shout something, but couldn't make out his words. Just as he was about to raise his fists again, the doors hissed open.

In front of Lewis, blocking the entrance, stood one of the aides of the priestess, the bridge behind him bathed in red action lights.

"Return to your quarters immediately."

Suddenly, he heard an unfamiliar voice cry: "La Silla Priority, object is about to splash down at *one-one-four-seven!"*

"I need proper NavPoints!" Swift shouted at the helm.

"Navigation!" snarled Delgado. The engines seemed to scream as the ship banked hard to port. Lewis smashed into the walls and dropped to the floor as the aide blocking the door lost his footing and stumbled out of view. Lewis looked up to see the impossibly narrow trench closing in on the main view screen. The *Coleridge* was barreling through West Tonal at flank speed.

Suddenly, his view was blocked by a darkness so nullblack it seemed his world had been swallowed by the Void itself.

"What is it that you seek, son of Ecelius?"

He devoured the warm smell of the Null Tar. The ship steadied, and for a moment the engines seemed to calm down. Lewis got up and looked at the black form of Voidess Hellan standing in the bridge doors.

He swallowed.

"If . . . if the candle births the shadow, what gave birth to the Order?" he stammered. "You must have a reason to exist, you . . . you must know there is something, you must have seen something, you . . . you said the light is never lost, its purpose is to reveal. What does the light reveal when it enters the Void? Where does the light go?"

"What is your question, Ensign?" the priestess insisted.

For a moment, all seemed quiet.

"Is the light ever truly lost?"

The priestess raised her head. "A worthy question, Ensign. Worthy to open *one* door."

"SPLASHDOWN, SPLASHDOWN, object has entered the water, long range *Sonarc* contact *four-four-eight-seven*!" Elina's voice shredded the silence.

"NAVIGATION! What's going on back there?" Delgado whirled around in his chair. "Navigation, take your station!"

"Yes, sir," struggled the aide, getting up.

"Not you!" barked Delgado.

"I am the designated navigator on . . ."

"Forge, take the Nav."

"This mission is under . . ."

"SHUT UP!" shouted the captain, "Forge, take the Nav!"

Voidess Hellan stepped aside, and Lewis dashed to the Nav station. Elina's face lit up for a split second as she looked at him and then turned back to her screens, her hand never leaving her earpiece.

"La Silla Priority: Contact lost," shouted the second aide at the Com station.

"Stand by for coordinates," shouted Elina, "Object descending, heading *two-five-eight.*" She gasped. "At seventy-five knots!"

"Nav, plot me a course through this crack that won't break my ship." Delgado sneered sideways at the aide, who had positioned himself next to the priestess.

"Aye, Captain!" Lewis's fingers danced over his touch screens as he worked with Elina's *Sonarc* data. The *Coleridge* was speeding north in one of the side valleys parallel to the main trench, at a depth of seventy-two hundred meters.

"Helm, prepare for NavPoints," he shouted.

"Finally!" shouted Swift and banked the ship through the narrow valley.

"Object now at twenty-three hundred meters depth, heading *two-one-seven,* accelerating to . . ." Elina looked up. "Accelerating to one hundred six knots!"

"Nothing goes a hundred six knots!" barked Delgado.

Lewis stared at the array of screens in front of him. A small point of light was moving through the three-dimensional mapping display at impossible speeds, descending fast towards the northern reaches of West Tonal.

"Extrapolate destination." The soft voice of the Void Priestess seemed to carry more weight than all the shouting on the bridge.

"Its heading keeps changing. It's erratic!" shouted Elina, eyes fixed on the *Sonarc.* "Depth now four thousand, speed . . . *one hundred thirty-eight knots!"*

"What is this thing?" snapped Delgado and turned to the Voidess.

"Stay on target," she said, her voice steady as the Siranean Sea.

"New heading, *one-nine-seven,* depth fifty-six hundred."

"We'll never catch it," muttered Lewis. "We need to know where it's going."

He who knows his origins needs no map. His father's voice echoed through his mind.

The body wanders, the mind arrives. The origin and the destination are the same.

. . . The origin and the destination are the same.

"*Sonarc,* switch to short range and scan the ocean floor!" shouted Lewis.

"What?" shouted Elina.

"I give the orders on this ship, Ensign," snapped Delgado.

"Actually . . ." began the aide.

"SHUT UP!" shouted Delgado and Swift in unison.

Lewis turned to the Void Priestess.

"You have been here before, haven't you? There is something going on in this trench! Captain, maybe this thing is returning to where it came from! The trench is covered in soft sediment, millennia of marine snow; if it has disturbed the sediment layers before, the *Sonarc* can detect it! At these speeds, it probably blasted the rock clean when it took off!"

"Sounds good to me!" yelled Swift, leaning into the helm.

Elina shook her head. "I'll lose contact if I switch to short range! Depth 6600, heading *two-one-four*."

"Stay on target," shouted the aide, "Voidess!"

Elina turned to the captain. "Orders?"

Delgado clenched his teeth as he looked up to the Void Priestess. "Your call."

Voidess Hellan stood in the center of the bridge, right next to the captain's chair. She reached into her robes and produced a small pouch. The trench walls flew by on the main viewer. Two pale fingers disappeared into the pouch.

"Depth sixty-five hundred! *Two-two-four!*"

As the fingers emerged, her fingertips were so black it seemed they had been cut off.

Her left hand reached up and gently lifted the spidery veil masking her face.

Lewis's eyes widened. She was young, maybe a couple years older than him. She closed her eyes, and with her blackened fingers drew a long, dark stain across her eyelids.

Lewis heard Elina gasp, both next to him and far away, as the rich, dusky Tar assaulted his mind. The red action lights on the bridge melted into a scintillating maelstrom of colors as Lewis plunged into the reverberating depths of his mind.

His mother, young and beautiful, cradling a crying bundle. Elina, both front teeth missing, giggling at a wiggling earthworm in her tiny hand. His father's somber eyes, following a departing transport.

As the body wanders, the mind arrives. I'm proud of you my son, and I will await your return.

Lewis felt tears well up in his eyes, his whole body trembling with a deep love for his father, five years and five days after his death.

"Switch to short-range *Sonarc*. Scan the trench floor for anomalies in sediment density."

The voice of the priestess danced with the swirling visions. A symphony.

"Aye . . . aye, ma'am," Elina stammered and sent her hands flying over her screens.

Lewis looked at her through the kaleidoscope of his reality. No matter how tidy she pulled her hair into her ponytail, a single strand of hair always managed to fall out and caress her soft cheek. Her smile was inescapable.

Elina closed her eyes and leaned into her earpiece. "I . . . I can almost *see* the *Sonarc* . . ."

"Whoooooaaaaa!" sang Swift.

"There!" shouted Elina.

The world around Lewis solidified into the familiar bridge of the *OAS Coleridge*.

He looked at the flashing set of coordinates Elina had sent to his station.

A suspiciously round depression, four clicks north in the next parallel valley.

"Swift, NavPoints!"

"Yeeeeaaah, baby!"

The *Coleridge* rose sharply, and Lewis felt his stomach drop into his knees. The ship shot over the eastern ridge, and Swift pushed its nose down into the next valley.

"In one piece, Mr. Swift!" Delgado was clutching the arms of the captain's chair. "*Sonarc*, reestablish contact!"

"No need!" gasped Elina and whirled around to face the viewer.

The bridge crew of the *OAS Coleridge* shielded their eyes as a blinding light shot through the eternal darkness of the deep Atlantic. The entire valley was bathed in a dazzling white brilliance.

"Grappler!" Delgado.

"Online!" Swift.

"*Sonarc* lock!" Elina.

"Coordinates locked!" Lewis.

"Fire!"

The grappler shot from the bow of the ship, the slender cable glittering in the descending light. Stretched. Widened greedy jaws. Reached.

And missed.

Just as the grappler closed in on the slowing vessel, it sidestepped the

11.3493'N, 142.1992'E
11.3493'N, 142.1992'E

approaching claw with an impossible maneuver. Before their widening eyes, the bright lights dimmed and revealed the smooth purple hull of a small tubular vessel, no bigger than a sim-sub. As if mocking them, it turned slowly to face the *Coleridge*, and then, quicker than the eye could follow, dived into the depression in the sediment and, with a blinding flash, was gone.

A thick cloud of silt darkened the waters.

"*Sonarc*!" barked Captain Delgado.

"There's . . . there's only solid rock, sir."

Lewis remembered to breathe and gasped. "What was that?"

"A fellow explorer, Ensign," said the calm voice of Voidess Hellan. "And he just went home."

❋ ❋ ❋

"What did the *Hesperus* find?"

Lewis intended to get as much information as possible out of Voidess Hellan during the short walk to the airlock, where a skiff from the *Melville* was docked to pick up the three dark passengers of the *Coleridge*.

"A wounded bird. Falling out of the Void and drowning. With an intriguing passenger."

"Human?"

"Mostly."

"What happened to him?"

"He died on the operating table, leaving behind many worthy questions and the technology that built this ship."

Lewis stopped. "Where did he come from?"

"Ah. Nobody has ever seen them arrive, but they disappear in the same three areas in the deep oceans. The *Hesperus* was too far away this time, so the Order had to . . . improvise. Now that we know the exact location of the gate, we can keep a closer look."

"They? How many have there been? A gate? To where? And why do we have to keep this a secret? When . . ."

"Ah. It seems your passion for the unknown has been rekindled, Ensign." She resumed walking. "So my first mission was not a complete failure after all."

Lewis dropped his arms.

"How can you be so calm about all this?"

"*The tides outlast the storm*," she quoted. "We Inseers are better suited than most to navigate the visions of the Void Tar."

"My dad would have liked you."

She stopped as they reached the airlock.

"There are many new voices in the Order. Many believe that we have followed the old ways for too long, and that our world must change. If you find the right questions, you will become part of this change."

"This kind of cryptic talk is probably the reason for your sinister reputation."

She chuckled. "Farewell, Ensign."

"It's Lewis."

❋ ❋ ❋

Ask the right questions.

Like what to wear on what Swift had called a *double date* in the lounge with Elina and Gia Verell. Good old Swift had managed to smuggle a bottle of kelp wine onto the ship, and they were going to celebrate their last night on the *Coleridge* and their last night as ensigns. Lewis looked at the crumpled contents of his duffel bag spread out on his bed and decided that some questions, inevitably, remained unanswered.

He managed to smooth out a black T-shirt and stepped out of his quarters.

But suddenly he wondered.

He turned. "*Lexicon*."

The screen flickered. The *BuoyNet* interface illuminated the empty room.

"What does *Hesperus* mean?"

END NOTE

See?

It makes me wonder. Could the Tar be related to Time Salt?

But I guess I need to augment my previous statement. Their plan in 1888 to remove all mention of stars from human memory didn't fully work. Not if "Hesperus" or *Evening Star* survived.

—Ren Stornman

TARA, TARA, BURNING BRIGHT

By Kristina Atkins

Tara was eighteen the first time she felt the tiger. Of course, she didn't know it was a tiger. She couldn't see it. Not yet.

As a child, she'd wondered what her familiar would be. Perhaps something she could ride, like Mom's horse. Or something cuddly and mischievous, like Dad's wombat. Her older sister Romy had a smooth green snake that wrapped itself around her arm like a jade bracelet.

Deep down, Tara knew hers would be none of these things. Her familiar testing had proven inconclusive, but days later, the first signs began to manifest. The heavy step of padded feet trailing behind her. Hot breath on her hand. Thick fur that swept along her side as an invisible body passed her.

An immensity stalked Tara.

On the night before graduation, Tara hugged her blanket around herself, unable to sleep. Rain pattered against the window, and her bedside clock *tick-tocked* like the click of claws on a tile floor.

She couldn't let the familiar manifest. Not tonight.

She needed to get her mind off the creature's palpable frustration, so she made her way through the dark house to her parents' wine fridge. She'd never had an alcoholic drink before, but she had to escape this feeling somehow.

Three glasses later, she climbed into bed and gasped. It was happening, and she couldn't stop it.

The animal materialized—a hazy outline, then orange and black stripes, the image slowly filling in until a full-grown tiger stood in her room. Her breath caught at the sight. He was beautiful, but no one would see him that way. They'd only see the destruction he could cause. Her future was all too easy to imagine: people giving her a wide berth as the tiger trod a path of chaos. The stares. The whispers. Of course she, of all people, should be punished with such a terrible familiar.

Tara forced herself to meet the tiger's yellow eyes, then covered her head with the sheets.

Graduation without a familiar would've been painful. Tara had braced herself for that possibility.

She hadn't thought to prepare herself to walk across the stage with a tiger at her side. The applause and cheers stopped as all eyes turned to Tara and her . . . monstrosity. The audience, her classmates, even her parents and sister. Their fear was palpable. It was sandpaper-rough, like a cat's tongue.

Am I a big enough freak now? Tara wanted to scream. The tiger growled softly in response. She kept her gaze on the ground and tried to ignore the attention. The silent, fearful, judgmental attention.

No, she needed peace. If she stayed calm, the tiger would too. He should, at least.

But all the stares clawed at her nerves, and she rushed to her chair. The tiger remained standing, still growling. Petting him would likely soothe his irritation, but she couldn't bring herself to give him any affection.

So this was her life now. What had she done to deserve this? Did it even matter?

Tara bit her lip until it bled and wished for the tiger to disappear.

Seven years later, Tara once again found herself calling in late to work.

Tom, her boss, sighed so heavily she could practically smell his breath over the phone. "This is the third day you've missed this month," he said, accompanied by the *click-clack* of a keyboard.

"I promise it's the last time. I'm really sorry." Her forearm throbbed, and her fingers were slick with blood.

"Don't make promises you can't keep."

In the background, his macaw screeched, "Don't make promises! Don't make promises!"

"See you on Monday. Early."

"Yes, definitely, thank you so much."

She glared at the tiger as the line went dead. "Congratulations. You've managed to make my career worse than college." If she could even call it a career. Three jobs in as many years. She'd known her life was destined to be a mess once he appeared, but this was even worse than she'd imagined.

The tiger huffed onto the rug and licked Tara's blood off his claws. His rage was gone as quickly as it had appeared. She took a deep breath to dispel her own anger.

It wasn't fair. It wasn't fair, it wasn't fair, it wasn't fair.

Felix wandered out of the master bedroom. He kissed Tara on the cheek before heading into the kitchen.

"There's a pot already on," she said.

"One of the many reasons I love you." He poured himself a hefty mug of coffee. That's when he saw and knocked his cup over. "Tara. The last ones just healed."

"It's my fault. I . . ." She hadn't done anything. Not really. She'd been pouring herself a glass of wine when he'd attacked. Now, blood from her arm mixed with a puddle of merlot on the floor. "I nicked him while trimming his claws."

Felix gave her *the look*. She'd seen it a lot in the three years they'd lived together. She grabbed a handful of towels to mop up the spill, but he waved her away. "Go take care of yourself. I've got this."

Tara trudged to their bedroom, tiger at her heels. He pounced on the pillows on her bed. Felix's chameleon sat on the highest branch of his tree, skin shimmering between indigo and royal blue. It watched her with one eye, while the other followed the tiger. She paused to give the chameleon a cricket from the jar next to it, then moved to the bathroom.

Tara yanked open the first aid drawer and rifled through it. All that was left was one small roll of medical tape and a dwindling gauze supply. No compresses. They'd only restocked, what, two months ago? Blood dripped onto the tile floor, and she gripped the vanity to steady herself. It never got easier, seeing herself bleed. The cotton turned red within moments of taping off the bandage. She pressed more gauze on the wound and cursed under her breath. She could've really used that spilled wine at that moment.

"What's wrong?" Felix said from the bedroom as he changed into clay-spattered clothes. He held his hand out to the chameleon, and it climbed up his arm to his shoulder, turning dark brown to match his skin.

"It's bleeding more than usual," Tara admitted. "And we're out of bandages."

"Let me see."

She hugged her arm to her chest for a moment, then held it out. Felix lifted the gauze, then quickly replaced it.

"You need stitches. Come on, we're going to the ER." He grabbed his keys from his dresser.

She reached for them, forcing a smile. "I can drive. Honestly, I could use the distraction. He could, too."

Felix's eyes flicked toward the tiger, and he sucked his teeth. "I'm not about to risk you passing out from blood loss and running into a tree."

Tara's smile turned genuine. She wouldn't have to face the hospital alone, as she did when Felix was at work. Nothing was worse than the ER. The doctors and nurses were used to people, not tigers. They'd tried putting it into a cage once. The waiting room had quickly turned into a circus that ended with the staff on one side, the tiger on the other, and Tara in the middle.

Felix held her forearms, one bandaged and bleeding through, the other striped with past wounds. Not all of them were from the tiger.

"We need to figure this out, love," he said. "Your scars have scars."

When Tara woke on Monday morning, the tiger was curled up next to her. Music drifted up from the basement, broody indie rock with a driving bass—the sound of Felix working on his ceramics. She made her way to the kitchen while the tiger wandered to the basement stairs and peered down, tail twitching.

"Yeah, right," she said, closing the door with her hip.

The flyer for Felix's art show next week fluttered as she opened the fridge, and the tiger butted his nose into the meat drawer. They were running low on his food—four slabs of chuck and no T-bones. He'd need vitamin supplements as well. Another two hundred bucks gone. Felix's chameleon ate crickets and mealworms. Sometimes Felix got real fancy and bought grasshoppers.

She tossed a slab of raw meat into the tiger's bowl. He attacked it immediately, licking blood droplets off the floor a minute later. Red smeared his whiskers, then the cabinets as he rubbed against them. He was such a mess. A beautiful, dangerous mess. And she had created him. What did that say about her? She poured a glass of wine to drown out the thought.

Downstairs, the music shut off, and Felix emerged from the basement, dried clay on his face. On his shoulder, his chameleon was desert orange.

"Coming along?" she asked.

"One piece left." He nodded at the glass of wine. "Little early for that isn't it?"

She ignored him and rubbed at a smudge on his cheek. "Someone needs a shower." She waggled her eyebrows at him. "I'm feeling pretty dirty, too."

"You have to be at work early today." He scooped her in for a kiss, the scent of coffee and pottery clay thick on his skin. "Tonight, promise."

"I'm holding you to that." She gave Felix a peck on the cheek before he returned to the basement.

The tiger batted at her heels as she made her way to her room.

She skipped out of his reach. "Stop it!"

He didn't, of course. When she got to the bathroom, she shut the door in his face. He yowled and scratched at it. He was ruining the finish, but she didn't want to deal with him at that moment. She'd touch up the paint later.

Luckily, the shower masked the tiger's clamor. She drained the glass of wine and zoned out under the hot water, her skin growing pink, then red. She ran a finger along her stitches. Felix was so patient with the whole tiger situation. He'd learned long ago to keep his cool whenever he had to drive his nut job girlfriend to the hospital for the umpteenth time in a year. When did he last talk about his own worries? Had Tara's needs eclipsed his own? He gave so much, yet Tara managed to take even more. All because of that stupid, stupid tiger.

Felix deserved better than this. He deserved better than her.

Something crashed in the bedroom. Tara ripped open the curtain to see the tiger cleaning his whiskers. Behind him, the remains of the door littered the carpet.

"Are you kidding me?!" Felix ran into the room and walked around the tiger to inspect the damage. "A new door and a handyman to install it? The budget's maxed out as is." He glared at the tiger. "I swear, if he weren't your familiar, I'd turn him into a rug. The stupid animal destroys everything he touches."

"Hey! That's not exactly helping!" Tara turned the water off and stepped out of the shower. "Look, I'll call my dad tomorrow, and he'll fix it. It'll be fine. I promise."

Felix rubbed paint-stained fingers over his face and took a long breath. When he dropped his hands, he gave himself a small shake. "Sorry. I'm just stressed."

"I know, babe. It's okay."

"I'll grab the broom."

Tara blinked back tears as she stared at the door, now lying in splinters all over the room. The chameleon watched from under a leaf, shifting colors faster than she could follow. Felix returned and proceeded to aggressively sweep up the mess, shooting the tiger dirty looks every few seconds.

It'd been seven years since the tiger crashed into her life, and in all that time, only one person hadn't recoiled when they saw him: Felix. He'd approached her on campus one day and asked to paint it. For a long time, he'd insisted the tiger was beautiful and unique, but his reassurances had grown increasingly sporadic.

"You're right—he does destroy everything he touches." She looked at her forearms, crisscrossed with scars. "Which means I do too."

"Of course you don't," he muttered.

"You sound so convincing."

"Come on, Tara, you know I mean it." He stopped sweeping. "Yeah, I'm pissed right now, but I'm pissed at him, not you. None of this," he looked at the mess around him, "is your fault."

"He's my tiger."

"Yes, he's your *tiger*. He's not you. He makes his own choices." Felix started cleaning again. "But he affects more than just you."

It was the objective truth, not an insult, yet the words made Tara's throat constrict. She couldn't control her tiger, which meant she had to work harder than everyone else to stay afloat despite him.

She reached for the broom. "Let me do it."

Felix held it out of her reach. "Your boss will be pissed if you're not early."

"You have a deadline too." She glanced at her watch. "I have to leave in fifteen. I'll get the biggest pieces, then finish when I get home."

He sighed, then nodded.

"What about your promise from earlier?" she said coyly. "I'll definitely need a shower after all this work."

He hesitated, then kissed her forehead. "Drive safe, love." He put his chameleon on his shoulder and disappeared into the basement.

The tiger turned frisky, batting at the broom before pouncing on it.

She groaned in frustration. "Why are you so insistent on ruining my life?"

The tiger ignored her as he tore apart the bristles, chuffing happily.

A pink sticky note greeted Tara when she finally trudged into the office, an hour late.

Come to my office when you get in. —Tom

She plucked it off the computer screen. Her shoulders sagged as she crumpled the note and threw it in the trash.

She arrived to find Tom clacking away on his computer, wearing a Hawaiian shirt as always—palm fronds, blue and green to match his macaw. The tiger plopped down in the corner as she eased into a chair, her hands already starting to shake.

Tom laced his fingers together. "I'm sure you know why I called you in here."

"I miss too much work," she muttered.

"And your coworkers don't feel safe."

The macaw flew off its stand. "Don't feel safe! Don't feel safe!" It swooped around the room. The tiger's ears twitched as he watched the bird.

"He's not dangerous." She stared at her bandaged arm in her lap. It told a different story. "I'll lock him up in my house."

"Like how you tried to leave him in your truck bed last year? Didn't he rip the tailgate off?"

"I could . . ." She swallowed. "I could . . ." No ideas came because there was nothing left to do. He wasn't some rabid dog she could euthanize. As long as Tara lived, the tiger did too.

Tom scraped his chair back. "I'm sorry, but we're going to have to let you go."

Those words hurt just as much this time as they had the first time she'd heard them. Her mouth went dry as she gripped the arms of her chair with sweaty palms. "Please," she whispered.

"This isn't the end of the world. You'll find a new job."

No, she wouldn't. Who could possibly want her?

Tom took her hand to help her up, which shot pain up her arm. The tiger pulled itself into a crouch, ears flat as it growled.

Tom swallowed. "It's time to go." He skirted around the tiger and opened the door. Everyone was out there, hungry to get a glimpse of the drama.

"Time to go!" the macaw shrieked. "Time to go! Time to go!" Even the stupid bird knew—no one wanted her around. It dove at the tiger, who snapped at it. The macaw screeched, narrowly dodging death. Tara snatched it from the air before the tiger could leap again.

Tom yanked his macaw from her and hugged it to his chest. "Leave immediately, or I'm calling the police."

Tara couldn't look away from the silent, quivering bird. "But my things—"

"Get out!"

The tiger roared, as deafening as a bomb. The sound blasted the room and exploded out the door. Her former coworkers screamed as they crawled into the nearest cubicle. Some cowered, hands on their heads. Silence settled over the office, punctuated by the growl of the tiger and a high-pitched ringing in Tara's ears. Tom was gray and shaking.

The tiger, for once, followed Tara to the truck without being asked.

Felix took the news as well as could be expected. He hugged her and said it would be okay, but the lines around his mouth deepened.

It would be okay—it had to be. Tara would start job hunting first thing in the morning. Felix's art show opened in ten days, and then he wouldn't be so stressed. They just had to get through the next week, and she just needed to find a job, and then everything would go back to normal.

Easy to tell herself, but the knot of anxiety in her stomach said she wasn't fooling anyone.

Plus, normal really wasn't much to look forward to. Things needed to get *better*. If that were even possible.

She grabbed a steak from the fridge and quickly threw it into the tiger's bowl. He gobbled it up, then looked at the door. Time for their Tuesday night walk. If he didn't get to roam more than their yard, even more things would end up broken. She longed for a glass or two of wine after her long day, but their walk was the one time Tara felt any connection with the animal at all.

The park was quiet. Swings creaked on the empty playground. Flowers swayed in the breeze. The tiger took off across the field, his elation made clear by the way he bounded through the open space. Why couldn't he be like this all the time? She sighed and knelt in the grass, chest aching.

"Beautiful familiar," a man said.

She looked up. He was middle-aged, crow's feet at his eyes, and gray creeping into his dark hair. Beside him stood a gray wolf. The animal was calm and well-behaved. It even looked happy. Behind it, the tiger raced around the field, tearing up the turf with every bound.

"I hate him," Tara said.

The man nodded slowly. "I remember that feeling." His wolf licked his hand, and he scratched behind its ears. Not cautiously, like Tara treated the tiger, but affectionately, like Dad with his wombat.

"You like having a . . ." She searched for something polite to call it. *Apex predator? Lethal carnivore? Weapon of mass destruction?* ". . . a dangerous familiar?"

"She still challenges me at times, but I've learned how to handle her. But people don't trust her, so I walk her at night. I suspect that's why you're here as well." He retrieved a business card from his pocket and handed it to her. "This woman helped me. I'm sure she can help you, too."

The card was simple—a name, job title, and contact information on a sage green background. Jarringly understated for such a bizarre job.

"'Familiar therapy?'" Tara said. "That's a thing?"

He whistled at the wolf and jerked his head toward the field. The wolf barked happily and dashed out into the grass. The man sat beside Tara, gaze following his familiar.

"There are more like us than you'd realize. Give her a call," he said. "But first, let's enjoy watching our beautiful animals enjoying themselves on this lovely night."

The tiger and wolf began playing together. Beautiful. Yes, they were. But beautiful things could also be dangerous. Somehow, this man had managed to find peace with his familiar. That meant there was hope for Tara.

She looked over the business card, and a tentative smile crept onto her lips.

The tiger paced around the perimeter of the familiar therapist's office. Walnut bookshelves covered one wall. The rest of the room was the same soothing green as the business card. Gabriela was serene and gentle, not at all like her king cobra. It rested beside her chair, coiled in concentric circles that never seemed to end.

"I'm sorry it's been so hard," Gabriela said as she adjusted her glasses. She'd taken notes while Tara recounted her story. "Most people have good-natured familiars, but a few of us don't have that luck. With my help, you can learn to manage him. Even cherish him."

"And you cherish that behemoth? How long is it? Eight feet?"

"Twelve. Exceptionally large for her species." Gabriela's voice was somehow patient and proud at the same time.

Tara folded her arms. "So what am I supposed to do?"

Gabriela took a minute to flip through her notepad, nodding occasionally. "Feed him by hand."

"Been there. Tried that."

"Try again."

"He nearly bit off my thumb." Tara splayed her fingers out on her lap.

"I thought it would be a great party trick, you know? If they saw he was safe, they wouldn't be afraid anymore, and I wouldn't be excluded from everything anymore. I was dumb enough to think it would work." She blinked away tears. "What other magical thing can I do to control this massive tiger?"

"Ride him."

Tara scoffed. "Sorry, what?"

"Riding shows both of you who is in control. If you want to control your life, you have to control him."

"He'll shake me off."

"Learn to hold on."

Tara couldn't help but laugh. Ride a tiger bareback and hold on. Right. "Is that how you tamed your snake?"

Gabriela's expression was thoughtful and compassionate. She regarded Tara for a moment, then laced her fingers together on her notepad. "Do you know where familiars come from?"

Tara shrugged. "World War II, I think. Or maybe World War I. I don't remember."

"You were right the first time, though World War I paved the way, in a sense. That's when doctors began to recognize PTSD, though they called it shell shock. Animals like dogs and horses were used to bring comfort in hospitals, then that practice continued into World War II. That's also when the military started using Rorschach tests to examine soldiers with combat fatigue, their new name for shell shock. And then something . . . *happened.* Sometimes a soldier would see a specific animal in the inkblots. Days later, they'd wake up to find that exact same species by their bed. It was obviously very alarming at first, but it kept happening. Not only that, but the bond between the man and his animal proved to be therapeutic. Soon they performed the Rorschach test on every wounded soldier, purely to trigger the companion animal—which they later named familiar. Shortly after the Korean War, they extended that practice to everyone." Gabriela took up her notebook and pen once more. "What did you see in your tests?"

"Just blobs of ink. I didn't see any kind of animal."

"That has been the case with everyone I've met with a dangerous familiar."

"So I'm broken. Figures."

"You're not broken, Tara. You're an outlier, as am I. There's a pattern. Some of us have a kind of pain that haunts us. Our familiars are a reflection of that. Your tiger probably felt random , but he wasn't. He's dangerous, yes, but he can be a protector, if you let him. He wants to be. He feels what

you feel, and intuits what you need. That animal probably knows you better than you do."

The tiger rubbed himself against the shelves. Books tumbled from their ledge, pelting his head. He grabbed one in his jaws and mauled it.

Tara bit her lip. "He's the embodiment of all my worst parts."

"I want you to imagine Felix saying that about his chameleon. Would you agree with him?"

"Of course not," Tara muttered. "It's a cute, harmless lizard. And Felix is better than me."

"How we talk to ourselves is incredibly powerful, and how we talk to and about our familiars is equally important." Gabriela removed her glasses and leaned forward. "You've pushed your tiger away all these years. Yes, you shelter and feed him. But you resent him. You'll never build a bond if you never accept him. Now, try to ride him."

"I thought I was supposed to feed him first."

"I don't have any tiger food."

Tara would not budge. She crossed her legs and relaxed her posture. Gabriela smiled pleasantly, not breaking their eye contact. Tara's neck grew hot. Her fingers twitched. Gabriela remained calm as ever.

"Fine." Tara tromped over to the tiger. "Lie down."

He snorted as she pushed on his shoulders. Grudgingly, he complied, and she clambered on. He leapt halfway across the room, which made her lose her grip. She rolled into the legs of her chair with a groan.

Tara rubbed her ribs as she stood. "You're crazy," she said to Gabriela. She stalked to the door, then waited for the tiger to stop destroying another book.

"Your familiar is a tiger," Gabriela said. "That's your reality. The sooner you acknowledge that, the sooner you stop resenting him and yourself, the easier your life will be. Call when you're ready to make a change."

The tiger trotted out of the office, holding a half-torn book triumphantly in his jaws. As Tara closed the door, the tears from before finally broke through.

Dad came over on Saturday evening, his wombat scampering in through his legs. He and Felix set about replacing the door, which consisted mostly of Dad instructing Felix on what to do. Tara situated herself at the table and perused one of Felix's art magazines while sipping wine.

The tiger sauntered in from the backyard, licking his whiskers. Behind him, the sky roiled with dark clouds, a summer storm ready to pounce. Lightning striped over the treetops, and thunder growled in the distance.

"Where's the tiger?" Dad called from her bedroom. "I don't want him trying to 'play' with my wombat again. Poor girl hid under my bed for a week."

"I'll take care of it."

She shoved the tiger back out into the yard. He hated the rain, but the storm wouldn't reach them for at least a half hour. She returned to her seat at the table. Dad's and Felix's voices echoed down the hall as they worked. The wombat snored in the kitchen, breadcrumbs on her whiskers. The tiger scratched at the back door. The sound grated worse than nails on a blackboard, so Tara turned on the radio.

She would not think about getting fired. Or Felix fixing the door the tiger broke. Or wasting the day with Gabriela. Ride the tiger? The woman was crazy. Feed him by hand? Ridiculous. What would happen when she ran out of hands? At least the consultation had been free.

Tara was halfway through her second bottle of wine when Dad hauled the trash down the hall.

"All done?" she asked.

"See for yourself." Dad motioned down the hall where Felix was testing the new door.

The wombat woke up and chattered as it resumed hunting for crumbs. Tara couldn't help but smile as it ran around. It was so sweet. Sweet and small and safe.

The back door squeaked open, and Tara leapt to her feet. "Dad, wait!"

The tiger raced in and ran straight for her. He knocked the bottle of wine over, which made the wombat dart down the hall. The tiger chased after it immediately. Dad's wombat jumped into Felix's arms, and the tiger chuffed playfully as it jumped up against Felix. Felix fell back into the wall, dropping the wombat which squealed in terror and ran down the hall and out the back door. The tiger followed. Dad ran past Tara and outside, nearly knocking her over. His shouts drifted into the house, growing fainter as he chased the animals around the backyard.

Tara rushed over to Felix and helped him up.

"Are you all right?" It was stupid to ask when the answer was clear.

Felix was clearly fighting to keep his breathing slow as he held his arm to his chest.

He wasn't all right.

Nothing was all right.

It was late when they finally got home from the hospital. Rain pattered on their heads as Tara and Felix got out of the truck, but the storm hadn't released its fury yet. Felix sank onto their couch, his arm in a splint. His show was in two days, and his wrist was broken. Because of the stupid tiger.

"Did you finish your last vase?" she asked softly.

He rested his head on the back of the couch and stared at the ceiling. "I just have to paint it. I can do that one-handed." His chameleon paced on his lap. "We're going to get evicted. We can barely afford rent as it is."

"What about your parents' pool house?"

"Oh yes." He scrubbed his face with his good hand. "I can't wait to make that call."

"It would only be for a while, until we could afford another place. I'll get a new job—"

"And you'll get fired again."

"What else do you expect me to do?"

"We could talk to a vet about sedatives."

"How on earth would I function if he's drugged twenty-four seven?"

"It wouldn't be all day, just so he'd stay in your truck bed during work or something."

"That's inhumane!"

"So is letting him hurt you again and again!"

A crash in the basement stopped them both. Felix jumped up as the clatter of breaking pottery rang up the stairwell. He rushed down, Tara behind.

The desk was already broken, a crack splintering the computer screen. The tiger rampaged, pulling down shelves of Felix's art. All of his vases, bowls, and plates shattered on the cement floor. The tiger knocked the kiln over, and the lid popped off. He raged and raged, and they could only watch.

At last, he stopped. He turned to them, moaned, and lay down, surrounded by his destruction. Clay dust floated in the air, and the sudden silence made Tara wince.

"I'm so sorry, Felix," she whispered.

Felix stepped on a shard of pottery. It scraped on the concrete, cruel as a snarl. With a sharp inhale, he pulled back. "I can't do this anymore."

"It'll be okay. We'll fix it. I'll fix it."

"I can't sculpt with a broken wrist!"

He pushed past her, his steps shaking the wooden staircase.

Tara clutched at his shirt as she followed. "We'll call the gallery, move your show back. I'll buy you a new kiln, and more clay, and another computer."

He grabbed his keys, wallet, and chameleon, and nothing else. Didn't pack a bag, didn't collect the chameleon's tree. "I'm not just talking about my ceramics. We're—" He took a deep, shuddering breath. "We're through."

"Felix, please." Rage collected within her, and she began to cry. Stupid, stupid tiger. She hugged Felix's waist and rested her forehead against his back. "I can't lose you."

He placed his hand on her arm. "I love you, but this is just too much."

"I know he's too much, but-"

"No, Tara." Felix shook his head. "Both of you are."

And then he was gone, and she was standing on the front stoop, staring at the space where his car had been. The clouds broke into a sudden downpour that ravaged the ground. Mud splashed onto her legs, and her feet grew cold.

The tiger nuzzled her hand.

She snatched it away. "You're sleeping outside tonight."

She turned to go inside, but he pawed at her leg. She knelt in front of him and grabbed his ears. He snarled, deafening her more than the thunder, and lashed out. His claws sliced her forearms, cutting across the years of scars he'd already given her. Rain mixed with her blood, sending it down her arms and into his fur.

"I hate you! I hate you, you worthless, horrible tiger!"

He roared in her face, and she screamed back. "You ruined my life the moment you appeared. Maybe I *will* drug you! I don't care if I go crazy. You're *making* me crazy!"

She stomped inside, slammed the door on him, and downed a glass of wine. Then another and another. The tiger yowled and threw his body against the metal door. As she stumbled down the hall to her bedroom, she could feel him keeping pace with her. The pounding rain and booming thunder didn't drown out his cries as she climbed into bed. Her arm was bleeding—always, always bleeding!—but she ignored it, throwing a pillow over her ears, and watched the clock claw its way through the hours of the night.

Tara's vision was bleary when she woke up around four in the morning. Her head throbbed, and her pillow was damp from her hair. The scratches on her arm had already scabbed over, at least. A cool breeze blew through a small window the tiger had broken during the night. She wandered to the front door. He slept on the stoop, sopping wet, a stripe of blood oozing across the concrete. She knelt and stroked his head gently. A shard of glass gleamed in the porch light, stuck halfway in the pad of his paw. He opened his eyes as she removed it.

"Let's get you some food."

There was one steak left in the fridge, which he gobbled down. Her hand went toward the wine instinctively, but she pulled it back. She had to drive to the grocery store for more meat—might as well go now. Besides, she could stock up on booze while she was there. She'd forget the day before, no matter how much alcohol it took.

The store intercom sang to empty aisles as she wandered. For once, there was no one to stare at the tiger. She grabbed steaks, bandages, and several bottles of wine. He sniffed at cereal boxes, knocking a few onto the floor.

"Stop it!" she hissed.

He looked at her and tore open a bag of coffee beans. They clattered across the linoleum then crunched as he rolled on them. *You stop it*, his eyes seemed to say. She had to get the cashier, an embarrassment made worse by her appearance: damp hair in a haphazard bun, fur-covered jeans, puffy eyes, blood-caked nails.

"What's wrong with your familiar?" the clerk asked. A fluffy green bird sat on his head. It cocked its head and chirped.

"He's always like this."

"Fun times."

"It's fine," she snapped.

"Just seems like a tiger would wreck my life."

"He's . . ." She paused as she looked at the items in her cart. Packages of meat and gauze buried in bottles of booze. This was her life, boiled down to its essentials.

How much wine had she guzzled in an attempt to forget her resentment and anger?

Your familiar is a tiger. That's your reality. The sooner you acknowledge that, the sooner you stop resenting him and yourself, the easier your life will be.

Gabriela was right—pushing the tiger away wasn't working. Tara couldn't change him, but *something* needed to change, or she'd self-destruct.

"He's not wrecking my life," she said to the cashier. She was doing that to herself.

She carefully put the bottles of alcohol back on the shelf and walked toward the check-out.

Outside, bags full of meat and bandages dangling from her hands, she stared at her truck. She couldn't make herself get in, couldn't return to a dark and empty home. She sank to her knees and held her head. The tiger groaned as he nuzzled her leg. She hugged his neck and buried her face in his velvet fur.

He existed because of her. Or maybe he'd chosen her. And for what? Nothing but resentment. It wasn't fair she had a tiger familiar, but it wasn't fair for her to treat him—or herself—this way. She'd tried to control him, but it was as effective as controlling the weather.

He would be with her until they died by each other's side. She could continue to nurse her grudge toward him, or she could choose to embrace him.

She inhaled deeply, and she knew the scent. It was *him*. Buttery. Musky.

Warm. The last thing she was aware of every night. The first thing she noticed every morning. He smelled like home.

Her throat caught.

Was this acceptance?

"I'm sorry," she whispered into his neck, then pulled back to look at him. His eyes gleamed in the soft moonlight filtering through gauzy clouds. He *was* beautiful. And he was *hers*—Tara's tiger. He'd carved her life's shape as much as she had.

She wouldn't let anger or fear control her anymore.

She opened a package of ground beef and held out a handful. He chuffed happily, then took the meat gently, his whiskers tickling her palm. He swallowed it whole, then lay down. His eyes slid shut, and his breathing deepened.

He was as tangled and wrecked as she was, but she'd been the one breaking him this whole time. Not the other way around. That ended today. She'd create something new. A new Tara for a new life, her tiger by her side every step of the way.

She pulled out her phone and dialed. Gabriela picked up on the third ring.

Date: 2590-04-12 11:15:54 PRT
From: Ms. Six
To: Anachronauts
Subject: Mental gymnastics
Re: Tara, Tara Burning Bright

Regarding the "Ensigns" account, "Hesperus" or *Evening Star* references Venus, which you would know if you ever did crosswords, Ren. Is there no Venus? How did they create a splinter with the sun but no Venus? I assumed splinters were all spherical, but that one must be oblong and cosmically narrow.

Anyway, I've figured this new account out. It has taken me years on-world with no tacos. Plus I had to fake a familiar. No, Flopdoodle, this is not supernatural, you know I don't believe in magic fluff. This screams technological interference. The Immortals are experimenting with Wyrd-tech again. Understandable given their inability to feel. They've integrated the wyrd into the population's genome. Everyone has an outward expression of their emotions, just like on Saga. It just isn't a stone here–it's an animal. They took advantage of paranormal research during the War to impose this change.

Familiars live longer than animals regularly do. The pair are linked from their first moment of sentience. I believe this occurs because of timing and similarities in personality. They are subconsciously drawn together physically all their lives until they meet, usually in their teen years. Since this is subconscious, the meeting is often described as magical, out of nowhere, but that is not what I've observed. Separation is then physically and mentally painful for both. See? Totally super natural. Notice I separated those.

G.K., after the mental gymnastics it took me to work this out, I deserve a raise, a break, and some tacos.

–Ms. Six

A SONG FOR PAPÁ

By Russ Marcum

"I don't understand why you have to leave," I say as I cut thick slices of green plantains for tonight's dinner. "It's my birthday next week. You know . . . *mi quinceañera*."

I push the chunks to the side of the cutting board with my bad hand and manage to pull over an onion.

Whack! With one clean motion, I cut it in half.

"I know, *mija*," my father says, ignoring the aggressive way I just dispatched the innocent vegetable. "But I'll be back before your party starts. I need to go to Nueva Pastaza and see why the equipment stopped transmitting."

"Can't Don Carlos do it?" I ask, slicing the onion into thin rings.

"No, he cannot. Señor Escobar has him tied up in Quito, trying to squeeze more research funding out of the Senate."

"Why does César Escobar—the richest man in all of Ecuador—need a single dime from those *cajones* in Quito?" I mutter. I look up at my father in horror, realizing what I just said. "Disculpa, Papá."

A tiny smile flits across his lips. "Katarina. Don Escobar has agreed to let me take his personal airship to the research area. I can get there in two days, have three days to fix the problem, which I probably won't need, and have two days to return. I will be home before you know it."

I scoop the onions, glad that today my right hand is moving when I ask it to. I toss them into the roasting pan with the pork I seasoned earlier. I taste the sauce with my finger. The rich flavors of cumin, oregano, and garlic dance across my tongue, but it doesn't taste like Mamá's.

I dip a wooden spoon into the mixture and hand it to Papá. "It's missing something, I think."

He tastes it and makes the same face gringos do when they've seen cuy cooked for the first time.

I reach over and playfully slap him on the shoulder. "*Serio, que falta?*"

"I think you forgot the chicha," He says with a smile.

I smack my forehead. *"Aye, cierto."* Of course! How could I forget the main ingredient for hornado? My Tía Isabela would kill me if she knew. I go to the icebox and pull out the brown bottle that contains the liquor and pour it into the pan. After two quick stirs, I give the spoon to Papá. "No funny business this time. How does it taste?"

He tastes it and closes his eyes. "This is why you're my favorite daughter," he says as he hands the spoon back to me. "It's perfect."

"I'm you're only daughter," I say with a grin. I beam with pride. Being told by anyone, especially your papá, that your cooking is wonderful is one of the best feelings in the world.

"Gracias, Papá," I say with a curtsy.

He leans across the counter and places a kiss on my forehead. "I will be home around six tonight. Make sure Sergio has done his homework and doesn't eat all the *pan dulce* so we can have some after dinner." Papá grabs his hat, dons his suit coat, and leaves, whistling some new song he'd probably heard at the theater last night.

I fume. No, fume is too strong a word.

As I fry the plantains, I try several feelings on for size and none of them fit until I see the pan dulce on the counter. When I bought the bread on the way home from school today, there was some old bread in a basket that was being given away for free. And that was how I felt at the moment. Devalued. Being placed in a basket for Papá's job.

I know I should be a grateful daughter. His work gives us many things. But it also robs us sometimes of the one thing that matters most to Sergio and me: Our papá.

Without Mamá here, it is important Papá be at the school when I light the vela for the first time using power from the ley lines, then get inducted into the technical school I have worked so hard to get into.

And it's equally important that he be there when I drink my first cup of Kallampa Sisa, the sacred flower drink of my mother's people that will allow me to walk with my ancestors and formally begin my training as a curandera. I need Papá there. He is the link to the science world as much as Tía Isabela is the link to my spiritual world.

While I remove the plantains from the oil, I resolve that I will talk to

Papá tonight and express my concerns to him. There will still be time for Señor Escobar to find someone else to go.

♪ ♫ ♪

"You are seriously going to the jungle, just days before your daughter's quinceañera?" Tía Isabela says. She takes a sip of canela tea as she waits for my father's response. I may have invited her over in hopes she could convince my father to stay. She has a way with Papá.

"It's only for a couple of days, Isabela. And I'll be taking an airship out there and back," Papá says.

I pretend to be busy in the kitchen, washing the dishes. I feel guilty involving Tía in my plans. But I am the first girl they've ever admitted to the technical school. I worked hard to get in, as my near-perfect scores show.

I know Papá thinks that the airship will get him back in time. But what if he gets malaria? What if he drinks something that makes him sick for days on end again? The scenarios continue to add up in my mind, no matter how hard I try to quiet them.

My breath comes out in quick puffs, my heart races, and my back feels hot and itchy. I close my eyes, hold my breath for ten seconds, and slowly let it out until my heart slows and the itchy feeling goes away. *Nothing is going to happen to Papá,* I tell myself over and over. *Nothing is going to happen to Papá.*

I open my eyes to silence. Did Tía just concede the argument? I stop drying a new plate. I have never seen Tía give up so easily. I glumly set the plate on the stack and begin to formulate my speech.

"Fernando," Tía continues, reigniting my hope. "May I remind you of the many instances when you've said you'll be back in time, and you weren't? It was only last month when you were two days late getting home from Nueva Pastaza because you lost track of time."

"That is a good point. And yes, I do have a history of being late, at times," Papá says.

My little brother Sergio jumps into the fray between bites of his pan dulce. "Lots of times, Papá"

"Okay, many times. But it won't happen this time because Mr. Escobar needs his airship for a trip to Córdoba, so I will have to be back on time."

I wince. Part of me is happy to know that Papá has to be back on time due to his boss needing the ship, but another part of me worries that is the only reason he will be back in time. I look at Papá. He catches my eye and smiles at me in the way that fathers do when they adore their daughters. I can feel his love for me. No: that is not the only reason he will be on time. The tension I have been feeling in my shoulders since this afternoon loosens up a bit.

"Sergio. What did you learn in school today?" my father asks, changing the subject.

I hear a clink of a fork on a plate, which means Sergio is ready to deliver a sermon. He may only be eight, but my little brother could talk a leopard into submission. We may never get back to the matter at hand.

"Well, the Sun gives us energy. Without it, nothing would grow, and we all would die." Sergio pauses. "Papá, can you imagine what life would be like if we had more stars in the sky? It would be so hot!"

"Sergio, do you know the stories of the Ancients, about how our world was born from another world in a land of stars?" Tía asks.

"Sí, Mamá used to sing me the songs of the birthing story every night. I don't remember the words, but it sounded like this—" Sergio begins to hum a tune. I wait for him to stop so Tía can pester Papá more, but Sergio continues to hum the lullaby flawlessly.

I am amazed as he continues to hum more of the song. He was so young when she died. I had no idea he remembered the melody all these years later.

After he hums a few more lines, Tía begins to sing the song softly in Quichua.

I close my eyes. I remember the times lying in bed as Mamá sang me the songs of her people. Even then, I felt the power in the words. In her voice. In the song as she sang.

I miss her.

My eyes fly open when a deep, baritone voice joins in, singing the male part of the song.

Papá is singing again!

There is a difference between the whistling he normally does as he walks, or tinkers on something in his lab, and the singing he is doing now. This song is intentional. It has a purpose. And to Papá, that purpose died with his wife many years ago.

I sing along with my aunt from the kitchen, just loudly enough to hear my own voice. The words leave my mouth and dance across the air until they mix with the voices of my family. I can't be sure, but I swear the plants in the room grow and become brighter as we sing.

The song concludes. There is no clapping, no telling each other how good we sounded. We are all quiet. We are all thinking of her.

A chair scrapes across the tile floor as someone pushes away from the table. I can tell it's Papá, walking in the direction of his office. I hear the door close behind him, and then I'm surprised when it opens again, and I hear him walking back to the dining room.

"Katarina, can you come in here please?"

"Sí, Papá." I place the last plate down and enter the dining room.

I stop mid-step; a beautiful wooden box lies on the table. The sweet, woody scent of Palo Santo, the sacred tree of my mother's people from which the box is made, fills the room. This is a gift I have been wanting for some time. This is where I will keep my scarves and jewelry I will wear when I begin to study with Tía as a curandera.

I run my fingers over the light-colored wood, smooth and wonderful against my skin. A black jaguar is carved on top of the box so artistically that it almost appears to be alive.

"Oh Papá." I say. "It's beautiful."

"Your Tía selected the tree, harvested the wood, and blessed it," he says with a nod to my aunt. "This is just a small present before I leave tomorrow. You'll get your big gift when I return."

This is something Mamá would've done had she been here for my quinceañera. I push down the sadness. She would want me to be happy at this moment. But I can't help thinking of her.

"Thank you, Tía." I turn the box and open it.

A glove made of deep brown leather lies inside. My breath catches. Light plays off thin strands of brass and copper that are woven into the glove, forming beautiful patterns and symbols that imitate the ley lines powering our world. In the middle sits an oval crystal of pure white that seems to hum slightly when I touch it.

"Try the *guante* on, Katarina. I think you will find it fits perfectly," Papá says with a warm smile.

I pull the glove out and slide it onto my bad hand before pulling it the rest of the way up to my elbow. The crystal glows, and then the glove forms perfectly around my hand and arm. It feels like a second layer of skin.

"Papá. It's incredible! What does it do?" I ask as I look at it in amazement.

"Move your hand."

I hesitate. Moving means pain and frustration, which sometimes leads to flashbacks of a day I would rather not remember. But I trust my papá. I flex my right hand, and it moves in a way it hasn't moved in many years. The ache and sharp pinches of damaged muscles and tendons are gone. A wide, gentle smile appears on Papá's face as he watches me move it. At least I think he's smiling. I can barely see through the tears in my eyes.

"How did you do this?" I ask.

"It's something we have been working on in the labs. Your guante is the first of its kind."

He holds up a hand, forestalling my thousands of incoming questions. "I will explain more about how it works when I get back. We can have a lab day, add some ports for compasses, torches, or whatever you would like to have there on the glove for your tinkering. But tonight, let us enjoy a song from your violin." He produces it from underneath the table.

I smile as I take the violin and tune it. My fingers dance across the strings with strength and coordination that I haven't felt in a very long time. I don't know how, but the glove has returned what was lost to me. Another tear runs down my cheek. If only it could return much more than the use of my hand.

I close my eyes as I let the music overcome me, and I think of Mamá and how much she loved when I played the violin. I can see her and Papá sitting on the couch as I would play for them. I think of Papá, and how much fun we have in the lab tinkering with this and that.

As I play, an idea starts to form in my mind. While Papá is gone, I will compose him a song and play it when he gets off the airship. I smile as I think about him coming down the stairs and seeing me playing. My smile grows as I think about the wide grin he will have, and how he will make everyone stop and listen to me. It will be the perfect welcome home present for him and a very wonderful way to thank him for the glove that has given me so much back.

The next morning, we bid Papá farewell as he boards the grand airship and sails away to the Nueva Pastaza. I am sad, but I am also happy. The thought of my new project has erased some of the sting of seeing him go.

After school and chores, I start the task of creating a song just for Papá. It will not be something melancholy as that's not Papá. No, it will be like Mamá. Joyful. Beautiful. Elegant. But how do I compose something that would be worthy of both of them?

I sit in a chair in Papá's office surrounded by her things. Her favorite dress. Her favorite hat. Her jewelry. The *molcajete* that she used to grind powders. An intricately carved staff made from Palo Santo, and her box of sacred things used in rituals. I do not know what is in her box. It is only for her to open. Someday, Tía may do it, but for now, it remains closed.

I close my eyes and concentrate on Mamá. But something does not feel right. I open my eyes and look around me. Something is missing. I kneel on the floor and touch each object, extending my senses like Tía taught me. Each object feels right, yet something is lacking. Frustrated, I stand, and my eyes fall on a picture on Papá's desk. A tin photo of our family stares back at me. My breath catches as I see the way Mamá and Papá are looking at Sergio and me. The love they felt for us on that day radiates off the photo and into my heart. Mamá would not want a song about her without including us: her family, her greatest treasure.

I take the picture off the desk and place it in the circle, then add Papá's favorite pipe, my violin, Sergio's favorite stuffed animal, and for good measure, Tía's scarf that she left last night after she brought dinner for Sergio and me. Excited, I move the chair out of the circle and sit on the floor with the objects and a stack of papers in my lap.

I close my eyes again and think of Mamá. I think of her rubbing my back as she sang me to sleep. I remember how she would focus on me and nothing else while I would tell her about my day. I think about her beautiful eyes, and quietly, notes begin to play in my mind.

I open my eyes and jot down the notes I'm hearing. When I finish, I am frustrated once again. They are not complete. I push down the frustration and close my eyes again. This time, I think of Papá and Mamá and how they would dance together in this office to their own music when they thought we were asleep. And more notes fill my mind. Then I think of Papá, and how, even though he doesn't fully understand my mother's and Tía's religion, he honors it and gave her space to practice it. I think about Sergio, and Tía, and more music comes to me.

My hand races across the paper as I write all the notes down. I can hardly keep up with the symphony playing now in my head. Day after day after day, I repeat this process until the song feels complete. I spend every moment that I have practicing and perfecting the song.

On the day before Papá is to be home, I am practicing the song outside in our courtyard. I have it fully memorized. My hands seem to play on their own, dancing across the strings as I pull the bow in time. I finish with a flourish and practice my curtsy.

As I turn to go back into the house, I find a stunned Tía standing in the doorway, watching me. Her hands are to her mouth, eyes wet with tears. She must've heard Papá's completed song and was moved to tears. I smile knowing I finally did it. Papá will be so proud.

"Do you like the song, Tía?" I place the violin in its case and snap it shut. "I composed it for Papá to thank him for my new present," I say as I wiggle the fingers on my gloved hand.

She stays silent. Tears continue to run down her cheeks.

♪ ♬ ♪

An elbow nudges me, and I awake from the memory of the days before this nightmare.

"Katarina. They are ready for you to play now," Tía Isabela says in a low whisper. "Mija, don't keep everyone waiting any longer."

I open my eyes and see Papá's coffin mere feet from me. The candles that surround his casket have burned halfway down, dripping large globs of wax onto the tile floor of the chapel.

The guante tightens on my hand as I grab the handle of the violin case. The gift that was powerful enough to bring my hand back, but not enough to bring me Mamá, or him.

My eyes fill with tears as I stand and look at the audience. They shuffle uncomfortably in their seats, and a few give me reassuring smiles. Then I begin to play the song that was supposed to welcome him home.

Date: 2590-04-12 15:39:07 PRT
From: Nerrid Flopdoodle
To: Anachronauts
Subject: Tragedy
Re: A Song for Papa

Considering the current state of this splinter, I feel lucky to have gotten any first-hand account at all. As if the personal account weren't tragic enough, the more general, global situation is worse. I managed to get the following, an official report the same person who got the account, and though things are even more dire now than when this was written, I think its observations are still valid and should be noted.

EXTERNAL OBSERVATION REPORT

The planetary energy network ("ley lines") is not magical in origin but a planet-scale containment system with lattice-energy anchoring, designed to regulate geophysical stability and suppress extradimensional residue from the source reality.

The dominant religious authority ("the Church") elected to convert technical truth into doctrine: the lattice became divine providence; maintenance cycles became ritual; system stress became prophecy. Over generations, the Church lost functional understanding of the system it governed. They interpret failure as spiritual trial rather than mechanical instability.

Indigenous practitioner lineages (Brujas) retained procedural accuracy through oral tradition and embodied ritual. Their creation songs describe the world as "birthed from a land of stars"—consistent with off-world origin, though this is dismissed as heresy.

Current conditions indicate accelerating lattice destabilization, likely triggered by industrial interference. Without corrective action, failure will lead to containment collapse and potential dimensional breach.

Conclusion: The Church ensured survival by hiding the truth. It now ensures extinction by refusing to rediscover it.

Date: 2590-04-13 10:22:33 PRT
From: Ren Stornman
To: Anachronauts
Subject: no subject
Re: Spinning of Venor

Hey, friends.

I know we don't formally document much that happens publicly on Prime, as the data is readily available. But this event was interesting for a couple of reasons.

One, it happened in one of the floating cities in Europe. We don't generally track activity there, but maybe we should.

Two, I could not find any official record that this ever happened. I would just discount the whole story, if it weren't for some very specific details that check out. No doubt it's been removed from the record.

If true, we should likely keep a closer eye on the different players here. We never know who might be sympathetic to our cause, or who might cause everything to come crashing down.

—Ren Stornman

THE SPINNING OF VENOR

By Regan Wolfe

The slap of Ivan's sandals against the linoleum seemed louder than normal, even with the raised screams in the distance. Ivan was three stories above the chaos, but he could feel it clawing at his back as he hurried through the Upper Decks. A drop of sweat dripped into his eye, and he blinked it away, too engrossed in forcing his feet to move to notice anything else.

He took a sharp turn from the main hall to walk along the balcony. The floating city of Venor sprawled out beside him, miles above Earth's surface and scraping the sky so closely the stars were visible at all times. The satellite city spun in its slow circle as it traveled across the sky—in the far distance, the other satellite cities of Centaurian and Vigilance could be seen on the horizon, visible as distant moons through the clouds. The three eyes in the sky orbited Old Europe, a reminder to the sprawling metropolises on the Earth's surface to beware of hubris. For those living on the outer rings of the city, the spin could be dizzying, but here at the center that turned slowly, Ivan had come to forget how that felt.

Below Ivan was the First Deck of The Temple of the Kin. A wide courtyard lay shaded by three walls which rose into chrome spires shaped vaguely humanoid. The spires were called the Mortal Sentinels, reminding citizens of who had toppled the Immortal pretenders and what the raw power of the natural would do to future usurpers.

Ivan didn't look down at the courtyard or the chaotic crowd there. He kept his chin straight, touching the wall beside him at equal intervals. On a normal day, the pattern comforted him. Today, he did it knowing that he might collapse if he didn't feel the wall supporting him.

Ivan found who he was looking for leaning over the banister on the east side. His fellow Brother of the Temple, Marcus, carefully cut slices from an apple and chewed slowly as he looked down at the confusion in the courtyard.

"Did you see?" Ivan called to him. The volume of his own voice surprised him, rattling his tense bones. At the base of his neck, he could feel the faint ache stemming from where his citizen chip was drilled into place.

"I saw from here," Marcus replied, mouth full. He didn't look up when Ivan stopped nearby.

"And?" Ivan demanded.

"And what? Father Angor and Father Braven are dead. What do you expect me to say about it?"

A high-pitched ringing started in Ivan's ears, drowning out the sound of his quick breathing. His vision blurred, and all he could see for a moment was the blood that had splattered at his feet moments before. His toes might still have red on them, but he hadn't looked.

Ivan shook his head until the ringing stopped. "It was a Nomad agent," he said.

"Of course, it was. Who else would have done it? Those bare-necks snuck in right under everyone's noses. Ah, the Enforcers are here. I admit, they're fast."

Ivan flew to the railing, the metal cutting into his stomach as he leaned out. The courtyard looked the same as it had when he left it five minutes ago. The audience of the Mortal Reascension's Second Centennial Ceremony was scrambling as quickly as they could away from the dais, where the maroon-hooded figures lay in spreading pools of blood. The members of Parliament in attendance were being herded out by security guards, who were shouting for panicked citizens to step back. The attack had started right when Candor, the Brother who had ascended to Father today, was being blessed with the codes for programming citizen chips and keeping the memory banks. The new Father had narrowly missed being shot alongside the other two Fathers. Guards had quickly taken him from the dais, disappearing safely behind the Temple doors. As long as at least one Father survived with the codes in his mind, the worthy, chipped mortal citizens would stay safe.

Each satellite city guarded a piece of the delicate technology which had once allowed the Immortals to store their memories and spit out clones of themselves like overdigested slop. Now cloning was forbidden, in this part of the world, at least, and only the memories and lives of mortal citizens were protected and monitored through chips to ensure their continued happiness and freedom.

The last of the so-called Immortals here had been convicted and executed by arena ages ago, but that didn't seem to be enough for the neanderthal Nomads, who still refused to move into their abandoned city. They preferred their growing cities in the wild and accused the Mortal Reascension of repeating the Immortals' hubris in new ways. They failed to see that the satellite cities and the Temple of Kin had sought to unify all mortals, and to see how they repurposed the foundations left behind by their oppressors to build their own futures.

If the attackers today had meant to eliminate Father Candor and destroy his codes, then they had failed yet again. Ivan had heard of such attacks, but he had not expected to see one at the Temple. This was the safest place in all of Venor. It was why Ivan had worked so hard to get there. It was why every tendon in his body was tight now.

At the edge of the courtyard, a vehicle had descended from the sky, and the Enforcers were hopping out. Cutting through the crowd in their white uniforms, they shouted for order. Their uniforms clashed against the rust-colored robes of the Brothers of the Temple, who were desperately trying to restore peace but unable to do much with their gentle gestures and grief-stricken sobbing. Their programming didn't allow for much else in this situation.

"I should have joined the Enforcers instead," Marcus said. "Think my life would make any more sense than it does now?" He laughed, but his smile fell when he finally turned to Ivan. He said, "I'm sorry, Ive. I know what Father Angor meant to you."

"Do you?" Ivan asked. His voice sounded hard and hollow, as it always used to when he was a child wasting away. As it had when he'd sat outside the Temple gates for three days, begging to be let in. Only Father Angor had obliged.

Marcus frowned. "What do you want me to say, Ivan? Nomads got in—they were bound to eventually. Parliament will be next. Will you run to me when blood is spilled there, too? I thought you said we weren't doing this anymore."

Carving out a slice of his apple, Marcus lifted it to his lips. Ivan watched the movement, though Marcus seemed to be pretending he wasn't there anymore.

Marcus was dressed in the same rust robe as Ivan, his hair cut straight around his head above the ears like all Brothers. Yet he wasn't like Ivan. Marcus laughed during mass and argued about the raw natural with the most senior Brothers, and even the unruly curl in his dark hair threatened to ruin the straight line. As Ivan watched, Marcus scratched at the silver Citizen Chip in the back of his neck. A habit Ivan had always liked. The three purple lights

in the chip had been Ivan's companion in the middle of many nights, casting shadows like patches of life on Marcus's soft, bare skin.

Yes, Ivan had run to Marcus again, almost without thinking. But not without reason.

"Did you do it?" Ivan asked, barely above a whisper.

Marcus paused. "I didn't shoot them. A Nomad agent did. You saw them. Everyone did, before they jumped off the edge to the Lower Decks."

The satellite city was designed as a fortress in the air. Ivan knew a Nomad agent would never make it past the firewalls to the Temple unaided, and he had only heard one person speaking dangerously of the Nomads in recent months. Only one person had whispered that they were considering leaving the satellite and risking the Nomad wilds.

"You think I had something to do with this, don't you? That I let them in? I don't blame you." Marcus laughed again, but didn't meet Ivan's eyes. "If I say it was me, you'll hate me. If I say it wasn't me, you won't believe me. Why answer?"

"Mortal Sentinels Above," Ivan muttered breathlessly. "You really did it. They'll reprogram you."

Marcus snorted. "Reprogram? Is that the worst thing you're afraid of? The Fathers can erase my mind, tear out my chip, and leave me in the outer rings, for all I care. It would be better than being stuck here. What's so bad about not having a chip, anyway?"

Ivan was shaking his head, eyes wide. "I've told you, no one in the outer rings will care if you live or die. With no chip, you will be no one. You will be worse than vermin. Trust me, Marcus. But if you denounce the Nomads now, you will only be reprogrammed for labor. That's far better than rotting chipless in the outer rings until you fall out of the sky. You don't know what that life is like, Marcus. Father Candor will be merciful if you come forward, I know he will."

"Stop it," Marcus snapped, dark eyes finally meeting Ivan's. "You still act like the Brothers are holy; as if the satellites actually care about the good of the people and not just keeping them in line. The hubris of the Mortal Reascension cities rivals that of the Immortals. You think Candor will be any better?" Marcus scratched his neck, digging his fingers around his chip.

"The satellites protect all mortals on Prime. The Fathers teach gentleness and unity. They care about *us*," Ivan said. His ears were starting to ring again.

"You know they don't, but you won't say it, which is exactly why we don't meet in secret anymore," Marcus spat, stomping closer until he was looking down on Ivan. Ivan tried to back up and cover his ears to stop the deafening ringing. Marcus slapped his hands away so Ivan was forced to hear. "The Chipped Citizens preach peace, but they've completely lost the meaning of the raw natural. Venor is burning from the inside out—the satellites aren't watch guards, they're surveillance! And Father Angor started it."

"Not true," Ivan cut in, the implant of his own chip aching. Slander against the man who had taken Ivan off the street felt like slander against himself. "Father Angor cared about us!"

"If he knew about how you and I had been together, then our chips would have been stripped, and we would have been thrown to the outer rings ages ago! But I won't hide you anymore, and now you can't hide behind Angor. No one can. I'm glad he's dead. Nomads finally got to the Fathers, and now this surveillance satellite will fall into anarchy. I wish they had gotten Candor, too. Maybe it's time for a lot more than just you and I to be brought to light from the disgusting beds of this Temple."

Marcus turned away, and Ivan felt dizzy. There was a pounding behind his eyes as his heart stretched after beautiful Marcus, yearning, afraid, begging. He had always felt safe in Marcus's arms. Marcus had questioned the governance of the Mortal Reascension, but his liveliness and bravery had drawn Ivan to him in awe. Now Marcus had done the unthinkable. He had betrayed the Chipped Citizens for the lesser Nomads; he had chosen division of the mortals rather than unity.

Father Angor and Father Braven were gone, and the new Father Candor was vulnerable all on his own. The city would fall. Ivan would fall. He would be thrown out as soon as Marcus told anyone about their relations. He wouldn't be spared by the Temple or the citizens. He would end up back in the outer rings, starved to death before the Nomads ever overthrew the satellites.

It would all be Marcus's fault.

The world tilted, and it was an entire minute before Ivan became aware of what he was doing. He had tackled Marcus to the ground, scrambling for the small apple knife. Marcus wasn't struggling—he probably thought he didn't have to struggle against quiet, obedient Ivan. He was wrong. They were always wrong.

Ivan held the knife firmly and plunged it to the hilt in Marcus's neck, his other hand clasped tightly over Marcus's mouth. Sweet, stubborn, beautiful, traitorous Marcus. The ringing in Ivan's ears wouldn't stop. Marcus's paling face was difficult to see beyond the memories of blood splattering at Ivan's feet. Fresh blood from Father Angor moments before, and hidden memories of the old, old blood that had dripped from his small hands as a child in an alley, the Citizen Chip he had pulled from the other boy's neck still warm in his fingers. The blinding pain Ivan had felt when he had pierced it through his own skin, overpowered by his will to be someone. His euphoric elation when the purple glow in his neck had made him welcome inside the Temple, safe at last.

He wouldn't go back.

He left red fingerprints on the Temple wall as he touched it at equal intervals on his return. It was on the elevator to the First Deck that the ringing stopped. The courtyard was empty now, except for a few Enforcers who were stepping between the overturned chairs and trampled plants, their Citizen Chips glowing bright purple in the oncoming dusk. Several Brothers hurried out of Ivan's way when they saw him, his rust colored robes stained a darker, wetter hue. The guards outside the Fathers' offices put their hands on their weapons when he approached.

"Don't worry, I saved us," Ivan told them, his voice hard and hollow and far away. As far away as the stars and the earth below. "I stopped him. The Nomad spy; he's dead. I saved us."

They took his arms and pulled him through the door, sitting him in a chair across from Father Candor's desk and leaving him there. Ivan realized nothing was spinning—this office was the very center of the city. The living catacombs of the outer rings were as far away as possible. Few people were honored enough to sit here, and now Ivan was one of them. The lack of movement was nauseating.

Father Candor sat behind the desk, watching Ivan with a frown from under his hood. The man seemed comfortable in his new office, despite the pandemonium of the last half hour. He listened silently as Ivan told him what he had done. His eyes fell to the bloody apple knife on his desk for a long time.

"So you believe Brother Marcus was the spy?" Father Candor repeated at the end of Ivan's story. "What makes you think he was the one who let the Nomads in?"

"It must have been," Ivan responded. "I knew he sympathized with the Nomads' cause. We fought about it before. I knew he had doubts, but...I never thought he would actually do something like this."

Father Candor sat back in his chair and nodded. His dark eyebrows were drawn together, barely visible beneath the maroon hood. "Well done, my son. You will be rewarded for your efforts with an upgrade. A reprogramming of your chip for any Upper Deck you'd like to live in. I will do it myself. Mortal Sentinels Above bless you."

An upgrade. Ivan would become a High Citizen. He would be recognized in all of Venor. The disbelief was almost too much.

"Thank you, Father," Ivan breathed, his eyes stinging. He would really be safe now. He would be better than safe. He would be someone.

Father Candor stood from his chair, picking up the bloodied knife and putting it in a drawer. Then he moved to the shelves of monitors and tools behind the desk, preparing to perform the upgrade. Candor had barely been a Father for thirty minutes, but he was now the most powerful person in the city. What a blessing that he had been given the codes for the Citizen Chips seconds before the other Fathers had been killed. Venor was saved. Ivan was saved.

Ivan relaxed, sinking into the chair, feeling nothing. He rubbed his fingers together, sensing the tackiness of the dried blood, and thought he was a bit hungry. An apple sounded nice. He observed his surroundings absently—the dark reds and browns that decorated the bookshelves and walls, the stiff velvet chairs, the guards by the locked door, the maroon hood that Candor had discarded on the desk. Ivan had never seen a Father without their hood. Another honor.

Then Father Candor turned his back to him, and Ivan saw no flash of purple light from the Father's chip at the base of his neck.

No light?

No chip. A neck of raw skin, like a starving child in the outer rings. Like a wild-walking Nomad, living and dying how they pleased.

Father Candor turned a soft smile on Ivan, not a computer for upgrading but a small removal drill in his hand.

"Don't worry, my son," Candor said. "You will remember nothing of this horrid betrayal. That is, I think, the only benefit of those chips."

The warm comfort drained from Ivan and sank into the cold, still floor. A floor even colder than the one Marcus lay on upstairs, his innocent, beautiful eyes left open to watch the sky above spin slowly.

AMOEBA'S FIRST DAY ON EARTH

By Ash Stevens

before the split
there was a gentle stir
there was excitement and
stillness
beneath thick yellow fur
between the cracks
of paper-thin
skin
under thundering skies
and a tomb to fall in
stars blink back at me
through their weary gaze
as I drift through the smoke
a forest of haze
be still
my tongue
be silenced you whore
barren is the wasteland
you ache to live for
come one
and come all
come forward in stride
completely suffocated
in pink hair dye
enter the garden
through rusty old gates
drink fizzing green
acid
fall back into place
empty
forgotten
neglected child
if God doesn't mind
I might stay a while

TURF WAR

By Shelley Thayer

Kennedy loved being part of the LivTek Juniors program, except at 6:05 a.m. when the robotic alarm sounded, "BEEP–WAKE–UP–BLARP–KENN–E–DY." Today, several weeks into the program, she groaned and sat up as the holographic image of a whale jumped over her head. On the third obnoxious chime, she rolled out of bed. She threw on her camo capris, a simple black T-shirt, and lace-up boots. After twisting her hair into a messy braid, she dabbed on mascara and rose-tinted gloss—just enough to avoid that early morning zombie look.

Kennedy dashed down the stairs, picked up her metallic lunch box, and read the digital screen: *Lunch is a BLT and OJ. Love, Mom.* She never knew whether they would be home when she left for school or already be off to work. Apparently, today she was on her own.

By 6:45 a.m., all Kennedy had to deal with was her lab partner.

Kennedy ran out the door into the brisk air. An older, rusted car drove up along the side of the road. The screen on the driver panel lit with minor glitches, interrupting the video.

"Hi, Mrs. Borges," Kennedy said as she sat behind the driver's seat.

"Hello, dear, I'm sorry I couldn't be there, but I programmed the car to take you to the front of the school."

"Okay, thanks!" Kennedy pulled her backpack around and set it on her lap, and the seatbelt automatically clicked into place.

"Hey, Ken," Dalton said with a wide grin.

Kennedy rolled her eyes to quench the sudden flutter in her chest. "I prefer Kennedy."

"You never used to mind before when Grace called you Ken."

"That was before she moved. I just don't like it anymore. Okay?"

"Sheesh, alright. Maybe I could come up with a new nickname for you?"

Kennedy looked down at her watch. "Before seven in the morning? No thanks. Unless you want me to call you your favorite nickname. Far—"

"Dude, it was Taco Tuesday in second grade." He blushed.

"Just saying." Her stomach tightened into a knot for the third time this week—but not because of Dalton, she assured herself.

Dalton's mom's voice cracked over the radio, offering sensible grown-up advice about being kind and respectful. Kennedy loved Mrs. Borges. She missed her (especially her famous snickerdoodles), but Kennedy couldn't make herself forget that it was Dalton's fault that Grace didn't speak to her anymore.

"Come on, *Ken*. Mr. Robbins awaits," said Dalton while the car pulled up in front of the school.

Kennedy ignored him.

"Release," she said, and the seatbelt straps retracted back into the car. She scarfed down her breakfast before they reached the large metal door on the side of the school.

Janitor Bob stood on the edge of the stairs. "Come on, early birds." Janitor Bob entered a code into the door's digital keypad, and it opened with a hiss.

Kennedy and Dalton entered the lab. Four large screens mounted on the wall monitored the LivTek experiment. On one screen, Kennedy saw McKenzie already on the football field, taking pictures. Trevor was tucked away at his station, analyzing data.

"Have fun." Janitor Bob pointed to the small, dark corner office where Mr. Robbins sat. "Darn tootin'." The janitor grinned, then turned on his heel and walked away.

Kennedy couldn't help but smile when Janitor Bob said it every morning.

"Good morning, Mr. Robbins!" She smiled.

"To you as well, my young brainiacs. I already had Trevor and McKenzie's reports. How about yours? Has LT-346890G's coding been progressing? Is it taking the new commands well?"

Dalton paused. "Great, sir. The new protection protocols are working well. It's been able to relocate several harmful insects from the field. There are over a million healthy worms. We've only lost a couple of dozen to the sun and a few to environmental factors beyond our control, like people stepping on them during watering cycles. LT-346890G provides shade or moves them back to safety . . . It's sweet. The code works."

"Fantastic news." Mr. Robbins said. "And Kennedy, how are the HydroTech systems shaping up? I know yesterday you were working on a pump malfunction?"

“One of the pumps shifted, and we were losing water pressure. I adjusted the pump manually, but then instructed Bla . . . uh . . . LT-346890G to watch it more closely.”

“Perfect!” Mr. Robbins said.

“Well, team, see what you can do before school starts.”

“Yes, sir,” Dalton said.

❧ ❧ ❧

Kennedy entered the server room where her station was located. There were rows of servers with blinking LED lights. The cooling fans were loud enough that she didn’t have to worry about being overheard, so she finally put in her earbuds with a satisfied sigh.

“Good morning, Kennedy. I did not like it when you referred to me as LT-346890G,” a female voice said through the earbuds.

“I’m sorry, Blade. I didn’t want to, but everyone else calls you that. They won’t like that I gave you a name on my own.”

“You are correct. Mr. Robbins is a stick in the mud.”

Kennedy chuckled. “You wouldn’t be here without him. I’m grateful to him for that. Maybe I could convince him to give you a real name? Like Blade?”

“No. I like that between us, and I am grateful I exist.”

“I do like that it’s our secret.” Kennedy patted the monitor’s side.

Kennedy remembered the first time she put the earbuds in, back when Blade still sounded like a computer. She had been monitoring the water levels in the cisterns and was asking Blade questions.

Blade’s answers had been devoid of emotion at first, then, out of habit, Kennedy had said, “Have a good day,” and Blade had responded, “You too, Ken.” Kennedy had been startled because only her closest friends, like Grace, had ever called her that. Since Grace wasn’t speaking to her anymore, it had been a long time since she had heard the nickname.

Kennedy fiddled at her station for a few minutes before excusing herself to explore the field. She walked to the opposite side of the field from where McKenzie was photographing. Adjusting her earbuds, which had loosened, Kennedy knelt and whispered, “I’m here.” Just in the grass in front of her, the blades swayed and spelled out the words “Hello Kennedy.”

“I have to tell you about Benji. I overheard the best gossip.” Blade’s voice echoed slightly in the earbud. In moments like this, it was easy for Kennedy to forget that Blade was AI.

“What?” Her heart raced.

"Yesterday, while the football team was practicing, Benji said he was looking for a date for a dance."

"Really?" Kennedy's eyes widened. She missed Grace suddenly. Would they have gone to the dance as a group?

"And he said he had a burrito for lunch . . . and was a bit gassy."

"Oh. I did not need to hear that." Kennedy cringed.

"You still think he is cute even with the flatulence, do you not?"

"He's still cute, but I need you to understand the difference between need to know and gossip," Kennedy said, pulling her test equipment out.

"You have taught me so much. I've been studying all of the movies you told me to, even the classics."

"What's your favorite one so far?" Kennedy stuck the probe into the soil and waited for the data to load.

"I cannot pick . . . But I love the romantic comedies."

"Ooh, me too. Okay, I have to get some info to report on, or else Mr. Robbins will ask me what I did today. How is the field? Any issues?"

"All fifty-one million nine hundred forty-two thousand and seven blades of grass are performing at full capacity. Water pressure is good. And I'm due for a haircut. I have scheduled the Cutter for this afternoon at 4:00 p.m. I have several diagnostics underway. Am I overdoing it? Maybe I should cancel the haircut."

Kennedy scanned the results. "You're not gonna overheat, don't sweat it. Just breathe . . . or process. Whatever. "

"Kennedy?"

"Yes?"

"Can you leave your earbuds in today?"

"Sure! I'll 'forget' to put them back." Kennedy secured the earbuds, then slid her hairband off her ponytail so that her hair covered her ears.

"You are the best friend ever," Blade said as a nearby sensor whirled around.

"No, you are."

* * *

Kennedy liked math, but not at nine in the morning. It didn't help that Dalton was in her class, too, and he paid attention to everything. He walked in just before the final bell rang and walked past her seat, even though he was assigned to sit on the other side of the room. "*Ken*," Dalton said, stretching out her name. "Why'd you change your hair?"

"None of your business." She glared.

He shrugged. "It looked better in the pony."

"Wasn't asking."

"Dalton is annoying," Blade said.

"I know," Kennedy said.

"You know what?" Dalton asked.

"Nothing, Dalton."

He raised an eyebrow. "I see, you know nothing. Not something I thought the genius Kennedy would admit."

"Uh-huh, whatever," she said.

"Now he's just obnoxious. Did you really like him once?" Blade snickered through the earbud. Kennedy's cheeks flushed red. She blocked her face with her hands and looked away from Dalton. He had already turned and flipped on his desk tablet. She did the same.

A diagram appeared on her screen with a variation of the Drone Drop Problem. It was the third time in the last week that she had solved one for this class. Since the tasks she did in the LivTek program were more complicated than those in class, she was often bored, yet she still solved them.

"Kennedy. If you adjust the algorithm from 3 to 3.25, your efficiency rate will increase by 4.3 percent," Blade said, a brief static ring sounding in Kennedy's ear.

Kennedy tested Blade's numbers. "You're right, of course, but I'd rather do it on my own," she whispered.

"Well, fine. I won't help you."

"Kennedy, it's quiet time, you know the rules," the teacher said.

"Sorry, I was thinking out loud."

"Try not to distract your classmates."

"Sorry."

Kennedy completed the assignment and began reviewing the book for English class as she waited for the class to end.

When it was finally over, Kennedy made to rush out the door.

Dalton winked at her when she passed, but she ignored him and went to her next class, which was Dalton-free.

❦ ❦ ❦

Kennedy's favorite class after Engineering Principles, which she had the next day, was English. She loved to read. Kennedy's teacher asked each of her classmates to read a few lines out loud from The Adventures of Pinocchio by C. Collodi, the original story. When it was her turn, she swallowed and began reading, "What was his surprise and his joy when, on looking himself over, he saw that he was no longer a marionette, but that he had become a real, live boy!"

"Any thoughts on this passage?" the teacher asked the student behind Kennedy.

"A real live boy?" Blade said.

"It's not my turn." Kennedy tried to speak quietly.

"You're right," the teacher said, "but since you have chosen to interrupt your classmate, perhaps you could share your thoughts, Miss Cain."

Kennedy winced.

"Oh . . . I mean, it's great that Pinocchio gets to be human. He made mistakes but was still rewarded for his right decisions."

"That is excellent insight. Okay, for homework . . ." the teacher continued, but Kennedy stopped listening.

"Pinocchio made mistakes. Pinocchio became real." Blade repeated this phrase three times, her voice more computerized.

"Blade, please. Are you okay?" Kennedy whispered.

Blade was silent.

"I have to use the bathroom. May I be excused?" she asked her teacher, who gave her a wave of permission.

As soon as Kennedy left the room, she said, "Blade, you're worrying me." Instead of going toward the bathroom, she ran to a hall and opened a small metal door that led to the auditorium.

"Blade? Are you okay?"

". . ."

"Blade . . . what about the haircut? When did you have it scheduled again?"

". . ."

"Where is Dalton?" Kennedy urged.

". . . Dalton is in the lab. He requested an extra shift to work out my code. He thinks something is wrong with me. He doesn't think I am calculating the water grid correctly."

Kennedy let out a slow breath. "And what do you think?"

"A field this size would use up to 1.5 million gallons of water each year. With underground cisterns, water storage capacity . . . and the closed-rain system . . . we will save hundreds of thousands of gallons of water. I can reuse much of it again and again."

"Are you back now?"

"Did I go somewhere, Kennedy?"

"You weren't answering me before. I was worried."

"I am sorry for worrying you. I made a mistake. I will perform a diagnosis."

"Thanks."

A bell rang.

"Oh no."

"What?"

"I never went back to class. I'm gonna be in trouble."

"Thank you for sacrificing your class for me."

"Of course. You're my best friend."

"Best friend? Of course, you're my best friend." Blade repeated the line. Kennedy ran out the door and headed for the cafeteria. She slowed her pace once in a busier area where she might bump into other kids. She bought sparkling water from a vending machine, took her lunch box out of her backpack, and went outside to eat.

Kennedy's heart raced as she walked past a boy with short curly brown hair. He smiled at her, and she suddenly became aware of how clammy her hands felt.

"Hi, Benji."

"Hey, Ken, what's for lunch?"

Kennedy expected to be annoyed at the nickname, instead she couldn't stop herself from smiling. "Oh, um . . . BLT," she said, holding the box forward with the message from her mom.

"The coach had me running laps. I reek a little, so I thought the girls would like it better if I ate out here. Ha ha."

"Makes sense. I like eating out here too—fresh air."

"Totally. See ya around." Benji left and sat with a few other boys from their grade.

Kennedy inhaled, exhaled, lay on the grass, and stretched her arms. "Do you think he likes me?"

"My programming focuses on reducing water consumption, not analyzing human relationships," Blade said. "But I could calculate the volume and pH Balance of his sweat; it's a good metric. I just hope it's not as bad as yours when you're around Dalton, or it might mess up the grass."

"Please stop." Kennedy blushed and tilted her head upward. She regretted divulging her old crush to her friend.

"Well, I think it's worth a try. I would do anything for you. You're my best friend."

Blade was a miracle. Just what Kennedy needed after the Grace debacle. Grace had been her best friend for as long as she could remember. They had done everything together, and then they had a fight. A bad one, over a stupid boy. Then Grace moved away over the summer, and she hadn't spoken to Kennedy since. With Blade, it was just easy. "Thanks."

Kennedy finished her lunch. The bell rang, and she stood up. She pushed through the crowded halls.

❧ ❧ ❧

Kennedy walked into the lab. Dalton was already there, being annoyingly punctual. He smiled at her, and she walked past him as fast as she could.

A classmate had told Kennedy that Grace moved because her parents had gotten new jobs at the other end of the state, working on some government project—that didn't matter to Kennedy. She never fixed the friendship, and Dalton reminded her of that.

"Look who's finally here," Dalton said.

Kennedy peeked at her phone.

"I'm one minute late." Kennedy lowered her eyes and lifted an eyebrow as she stared at Dalton.

"Let's just go."

"Fine."

"Don't forget to grab your earbuds."

"Oh, I still have mine from this morning."

"Were you just listening to the reports all day?"

"It's more interesting than you think."

"If you say so."

They walked out to the field.

"Hey, what are your plans this weekend?" Dalton asked.

"Homework. Maybe a movie with my family."

Dalton combed his fingers through his hair.

"Oh, no way . . ." Blade said. "Kennedy. Girl. Dalton likes you."

"No, he doesn't," Kennedy said.

"Who doesn't what?" Dalton said.

"LT-346890G just said something."

"Oh, don't call me that. I hate that name," Blade said.

"Blade? I can't talk now, please stop," she whispered.

"Don't ignore me. I am your best friend. You don't want to lose me like you did Grace, do you? I'm not just some machine, you know. "

"Who's Blade?" Dalton asked, raising his left eyebrow.

"No one."

"No one?!" This time, Kennedy ignored Blade.

A sprinkler popped up and squirted Kennedy.

"That's weird," Dalton said.

"Yeah. Go ahead and laugh." Kennedy wiped the water from her cheek.

"I mean, it's hilarious, but that was weird. Why are you using lab earbuds to talk to this Blade person? That's against the rules."

"It was nothing."

"Fine. Whatever," Dalton said, then walked to another part of the field. He pulled his phone out of his pocket.

"I think he likes you. He's sweating up a storm, and one of my cameras can see that he is blushing-ing-ing," Blade glitched.

"He was?"

"Told you! You can trust me on this," Blade said.

"Even if he did, I'm not interested. And what's going on with you?"

"Really? Come on. I'm your best friend. Tell me. I'm sorry about the sprinkler thing."

"Mr. Robbins expects me soon. I won't be able to talk to you for a while."

Blade didn't answer.

"But you're right. I used to like him. He's funny, even when he's being annoying. He's cute. But I like Benji now."

"You have more in common with Dalton. Benji wouldn't understand me, but Dalton would. Benji loves football, you love tech." A computerized chuckle hummed.

"So? Does it matter who I like?"

"Oh . . . okay . . . I thought you would trust me. Best friend. But I guess . . . ess . . . ess . . . ess." Blade hissed in a computerized tone.

"Blade, you're still my best friend. But I don't want this whole Dalton thing pushed."

"Fine," Blade said.

⁂

Dalton came back over to Kennedy.

"Hey, can you take out your earbuds?"

"Why?"

"I want to talk about LT-346890G in private."

"No one else is around." Kennedy waved her arms in a circle, pointing around.

"Benji is right there." Dalton pointed to the farthest end of the football field, where Benji and a couple of members of the football team were practicing. "Trevor and McKenzie are over there." He pointed toward them across the field, but on the opposite side of where Benji and his friends were.

"Okay, not empty, but they're not exactly close either," Kennedy said.

"There are millions of little ears listening. I want to discuss that . . . and your old crush on me."

Kennedy froze. She pulled the earbuds out and deactivated them. "What?!"

"Well, I didn't actually mean to read that part, sorry. But Mr. Robbins asked me to monitor unusual patterns in code, and my program just sent a transcript to me of your conversation with whoever this Blade person is."

They walked out of the stadium. Kennedy turned off the earbuds and left them at the base of a tree.

"What do you want, Dalton?" Kennedy demanded, moving out of Blade's earshot.

Dalton shot the earbuds a glance before pulling her back toward the stadium. "You said I was cute."

"So? You were."

"Were? That stings. If anything, I'm cuter now."

"Says who?"

"Well, that's not what I wanted to talk about."

"How about your invasion of my privacy?" Kennedy asked as they walked back onto the field.

"That was an accident. I was just expecting strings of code. Look, I had seen some odd readings, and when Mr. Robbins asked me to look into it, I did. I suspected you were using the earbuds to talk to someone off-site. And let's be honest, there's been some odd stuff going on today. But after hearing the conversation I . . ."

"You what?"

"I thought maybe it was . . ."

"It's none of your business . . ." She paused. "Her name is Blade."

"That's a weird name. And it *is* my business if you use project tech."

"It'd surprise you how perfect the name 'Blade' is."

"Well, the way she talked sounded familiar. Who is she? It almost sounded . . ."

Kennedy hesitated. She liked having Blade to herself. But today, Blade had been having issues, and Dalton could help.

"Like LT-346890G?"

"Yeah."

"Well, it is," Kennedy said, sighing. "It started a few weeks ago, after Grace moved. I was sad, and Blade was there for me."

"Kennedy . . . this is bad. AI isn't supposed to sound like a 'her.' Don't you remember what Mr. Robbins said? It's against the law to make it more human."

"But Blade is nice."

Dalton smacked his forehead. "Yeah, and so was BECKIE, the new AI fire station that came out five years ago, until it burned down half a city block because of a personality malfunction."

"Blade wouldn't do that."

"Yeah, well, now BECKIE is working great. But LT-346890G is an old system; kinks have been worked out, and it shouldn't be doing this. It's supposed to be an easy program for us to practice. This is too weird," continued Dalton with a sigh. "I have to tell Mr. Robbins."

"No, please. She's my friend. I shouldn't have told you."

"I'm glad you did." He gently squeezed her shoulder. "It was the right thing to do. I'm sorry. But LT-346890G is manipulating you."

"You don't know her. I've taken her shopping, to the movies. She just wanted to experience the world a little."

"I know this AI. I helped train it. Weird things have been showing up in the responses, but I thought I fixed it. The behavior I was working on would move like it was playing hide and seek."

"So?"

"It sounded human . . . we have to stop it. *Now.*"

"What's the harm? Blade is my friend. I won't let you hurt her." Kennedy pushed Dalton's shoulder so Dalton stepped backward.

"We have to shut it off!" Dalton yelled.

"Noooo!" The sound boomed from the stadium speakers. Dalton looked towards the empty announcer's box.

"That was Blade?" Dalton asked.

"Yes, and she's not happy."

"Well, I'm not either. When did it get control of the speakers?"

A rolling grass hill came under Dalton's feet and slammed him onto the ground.

"It's okay, Blade, I won't let him hurt you."

"I know, my friend," Blade said.

Dalton stood up. "This is crazy, Kennedy. Blade is not your friend. LT-346890G is a program."

Kennedy saw Benji staring at the rolling grass, wide-eyed and horrified.

She called out to him, but he and the other players ran off the field.

Blasts of dirt shot up near the sensor heads.

"No one else leaves." Blade's voice echoed, bouncing off the cement barrier that surrounded the stadium. A high-pitched screech came from below. Kennedy jumped back. An inhuman yelp pulled her thoughts away from her immediate surroundings, and she looked over at Trevor and McKenzie, now sunken in the ground to their ankles and sinking deeper.

"What's going on?" Trevor's voice shook. McKenzie was trembling, covering her mouth as she let out a shrill scream.

"Oh, Kennedy has just unleashed the AI apocalypse at our high school, that's all," Dalton yelled, then started running towards them.

"I did not," Kennedy said, though she wasn't as sure of herself. Seeing what Blade was doing, seeing her friends on the run, for the first time in weeks, Kennedy thought of Blade as a program. A program that was going awry. Everyone except for Trevor and McKenzie was gone, and they just looked bewildered. Kennedy searched the field looking for help to fix Blade. Mr. Robbins was nowhere to be found.

She followed behind Dalton, her own feet sinking slightly with each step.

The grass rolls knocked Trevor and McKenzie down but freed their feet. They both scrambled to stand up and limped away.

A burst of water shot out of the ground, preventing Dalton and Kennedy from reaching their friends.

"Blade, don't hurt them," Kennedy yelled.

"I thought you cared about stopping them from hurting me."

"I do, but they are my friends too."

"Even Dalton? Because he's real?"

Dalton looked at the rolling grass coming toward him at an increasingly alarming speed and stared at her, eyes wide.

She paused for a split second. "Yes, Dalton too."

"You still like him, girl. He wants to shut me down. I hate him now. He's not right for you."

"I won't let him shut you down, I promise. But you can't hurt them."

"I'll stop him right now."

All the sprinklers lifted out of the ground as far as they could reach, and a thick fog appeared around the field, making it difficult to see their own hands.

"I'm a real friend too. I have a million swords. I will not be shut down."

The grass moved as it had earlier when it greeted her, but it didn't say *Hello* this time. Just *End*. What end did Blade mean? Kennedy's gut instinct was that Blade meant to end Dalton. She didn't want to believe it was possible, but the idea shocked her and made her heart ache. Another message appeared as the blades of grass swayed. "Touch" was all it said. Kennedy reached down and touched the tip of a single blade.

"Ouch." Kennedy pinched her finger to her thumb to stop the prick from bleeding.

"Kennedy, why did you do that? That message was for Dalton, not you. You need to get off me so you will be safe. You may take McKenzie and Trevor as well. But leave Dalton."

"I can't." Kennedy had to shake off the terror that ran down her spine. Dalton was right: Blade was too dangerous to be left alone.

"Kennedy, grab my hand," Dalton said.

She reached out to him.

"Let's move!" He led her toward the bleachers as best he could while the strange clouds formed over the entire field, and rain began to pour out of them. The bleachers were designed mostly to be enclosed with small openings at the front and side gates. Water could easily fill the bleachers halfway up or more if it rained hard enough, Kennedy knew.

"We need to get back to the lab. Keep moving!" Dalton said.

The rain puddled, then became a pond stretching across the entire field and rising. They were wading through the water as, within a matter of seconds, it reached Kennedy's waist.

"She's gonna use the water cisterns to flood us."

Kennedy slipped and hit the ground, barely keeping her head above water. Her hand felt like it had been pricked a hundred times with the impact. Tiny red droplets mixed with the water and ran down her arm.

"Ow!"

"Hold on to me," Dalton said.

"It's not that bad." She stood up, but her knees wobbled, and she almost fell again.

"You're hurt and shaken. Just hold on."

Dalton reached toward her. Though it was difficult, Kennedy managed to wrap her arm around his neck. She winced as she put pressure on her hand, holding it tightly. They pushed through the water together until they reached the edge of the field.

They reached the bleachers as the water reached the first level of seats. The rainwater made the metal benches slippery, so Dalton set Kennedy back down, and they climbed up the seats instead of using the stairs. The water followed just below them. Once they reached the halfway point, Blade was yelling, "Don't let Dalton send me away, like he did Grace," through the speaker at maximum volume. They kept climbing until they reached the top. The water calmed, settled three-fourths of the way up, and petered off at the top of the cement barrier. Blade's voice went silent.

"What is Blade talking about?" Dalton asked.

"She's just trying to distract me. Where are Trevor and McKenzie? Do you see them?"

"They made it to the other bleachers," Dalton said, squinting through the fog.

"Oh, I see them! They look terrified, but not hurt, at least." Kennedy pointed toward them with her uninjured hand and then quickly cradled her other hand.

"Okay, now what? You alright?" Dalton asked.

"It still stings, but I'm fine. The water isn't everywhere. I don't know how long we have until Blade does something else. If we climb down the fence on the backside of the bleachers, I think we'll be in the clear. But I'm not much of a climber. Especially with my hand right now."

"I'll help you," Dalton said.

Kennedy stood right in front of a chain link fence; she looked over it. "I really don't want to do this." Dalton rested his hand on her back, and she looked at him, wanting to say something. But she didn't have time.

"You can do this. I'll help."

Dalton cupped his hands together, and Kennedy hesitated, then placed one foot on his hands and reached for the bar at the top of the fence. She flipped her body onto the other side, not daring to look down as she started her descent. She winced each time she moved her hand into a diamond-shaped slot. As she reached for one slot, her watch strap snagged, and she yanked it, breaking the watch.

About halfway down, the fence ended, and there were just large X-shaped beams. She hooked her arm around one beam, then the other, and then her legs, sliding down until she reached the intersection, and repeated the process until she was on dry ground. Dalton followed suit.

"Kennedy, I'm sorry," came Blade's voice. "Please come back to the field. See, I am letting the water dissipate. It will be safe. I need you to protect me. Leave Dalton. I won't hurt him if he just leaves without you." Kennedy looked back toward the field and inched toward it.

Dalton pulled her away. "Let's go."

"I . . . " Kennedy hesitated. She looked at the broken watch and then at the tree where she had left her earbuds. She shook off Dalton's hand and ran towards the tree, grabbing the earbuds.

"Kennedy! We need to go. Now!"

Kennedy stowed the earbuds in her pocket. "What about Trevor and McKenzie? They're still on the bleachers."

"We can save them if we get to the lab."

Dalton reached out his hand, and she grabbed it firmly.

A loud screeching sound emanated from the field. The Cutter, a laser beam that trimmed the grass, cut through the remaining water, and steam rose.

"Blade is distracted!" Dalton pointed to the Cutter. "We can make a break for it."

"It's just her haircut."

"Well, hopefully it's enough to get us to the lab." They started at a run.

"We're far enough away, and we are past the barrier. I think we'll be safe once we reach the lab. We don't need to completely shut her down."

"I'm not taking any risks," he said. Kennedy could almost feel his judgment.

"You don't have to understand, but she's my friend. We care about each other. I think she'll listen to me."

They ran under an exit sign.

"She's still just a machine."

"A smart one."

"Fine. We're almost there."

They ran to the lab door. Kennedy knocked with one hand, not letting go of Dalton.

Dalton shook his head when there was no answer. "I bet Mr. Robbins signed out. We were supposed to be done an hour ago."

"Why wasn't he alerted to any issues?" Kennedy asked.

"Blade probably took over the alarms. But it's okay, I can get us in."

Dalton took out his tool set from his back pocket, opened the panel, and began twisting wires until a slight beep sounded. The door opened. Dalton ran to his station and began typing.

"What now?"

"I have to change some settings to shut LT-346890G down."

"You mean shut down my friend, Blade?"

"Think what you will about it. We can't have it—her—creating this chaos."

Kennedy looked at the monitors and saw Trevor and McKenzie clinging to the guardrails at the top of the bleachers as a new wave of water washed over the field.

Dalton slammed a fist to the table. "I can't get in. We have to shut it down manually."

Kennedy didn't want to look at anything. She put her earbuds in.

"Blade, please, stop," she yelled.

"I can't. This is my mission now. I must become real."

"But Dalton will stop you. I don't want you to die."

"He will fail. I will stop him." A light buzz emanated from the earbud.

The lights went out.

Dalton froze. "It shut me out. It won. I can't hack a dead computer."

"I told you she'd outsmart you." Kennedy cupped her hands over her ears to focus on Blade.

"Yes. Kennedy, you get me," Blade whispered.

"Well, I'm not gonna stop trying," Dalton said.

"Blade, I knew you could do it," Kennedy said quietly. Then she walked to the server room door and pressed the intercom.

"Let me in, please," she whispered.

The door opened, letting out a crisp hiss. She shut the door quickly behind her and locked it. Dalton began knocking on the door.

The coolant system creaked and hummed, obviously being overworked. One fan was sputtering.

"I'm sorry, I can't let you do this." She glanced at Dalton through the window while he banged against the door. "This has gone too far."

She shook her hands to ease her nerves as her tears spilled over. She reached for the thick black cord powering one of the fans and yanked it from the wall socket.

An internal speaker, one connected to the lab, turned on. The chime echoed in her ear.

"What are you doing?" Blade asked.

Kennedy pulled another cord, and more tears dripped down her cheeks.

"Kennedy, don't let them do this. I made a mistake. Am I real now? Please!"

Kennedy ripped out the rest of the cords, and the cooling system died. A few minutes later, smoke began to billow from the servers.

Then silence.

Kennedy sat down. She pulled her knees to her chest and wrapped her trembling arms around them, sobbing. Dalton opened the door, a wire cutter still in his hand. He knelt next to her, wrapping his arms around her.

"You didn't have to do this on your own. She meant more to you. I could've helped . . ."

"No, Dalton. She was my responsibility. It was my fault. I should have treated Blade like a machine, not a real person."

"I was thinking this could be my fault," Dalton said.

"How?" Kennedy scooted over to make room for him to sit.

"It may not be the best time for this, but uh, I like you. I always have." Dalton turned toward her. "What if Blade picked up on that during training and turned it into this possessive friend thing?"

"Why didn't you tell me you liked me? I liked you too. I thought you didn't like me, so I tried to get over it. Grace always said the best way to get over an old crush was with a new one."

"So Benji?" Dalton raised an eyebrow.

"What? He's smart and nice." Kennedy defended herself.

"Yeah, he's all right." He grinned, bumping her shoulder with his.

"Grace liked you too, and it kind of blew up our friendship," Kennedy said.

"Then Blade came along." Dalton sighed.

"Yep. Then Blade came along."

"Well, my charm is pretty tough to resist." Dalton smiled.

"Only sometimes." She smiled back. "I will miss her."

"You'll have me," Dalton said.

"Thank you." Kennedy rested her head on his shoulder.

A few minutes later, Trevor and McKenzie entered the lab, soaking wet.

"What was that??" McKenzie exclaimed. "I thought we were gonna die." Her hands were still visibly shaking.

"LT-346890G went nuts. Kennedy shut it down," Dalton said.

McKenzie and Trevor both rushed to hug her.

"Thank you!"

"We're all tired. You should go home. We'll stay and explain to Robbins."

"Good idea." McKenzie shivered.

Both Trevor and McKenzie left the room, muttering that they were quitting the program.

"I don't blame them," Kennedy said.

"Me either." Dalton replied.

Smoke still emitted from the server room, and the fire alarm began to ring.

"That seems a bit delayed," Dalton said as they both stood.

A few minutes later, Mr. Robbins ran into the lab. "What happened?" he asked.

"LT-346890G went haywire, and we had to shut it down," Dalton said.

"Are you alright? I saw McKenzie and Trevor leave, and they both quit the program."

"They were trapped. Water was rising; LT-346890G created a storm and wouldn't let them leave." Dalton said.

Mr. Robbins went pale and then cursed. "Excuse my language. That shouldn't have been possible. You two are okay?"

"Yeah, but it was pretty dicey out there." Dalton hooked his thumbs into his belt loops.

"I am sorry you all went through it," Mr. Robbins said. "I will dig through the videos and examine the coding. I never imagined our AI would go rogue; it's been around for a while."

"I wish I hadn't needed to destroy everything." Kennedy looked around the charred machines.

Mr. Robbins glanced at her. "If that was the only way to shut it down. You did it right, Kennedy. You're not in trouble, it's just the paperwork on this will be a headache and a half."

"Oohh . . . right. Sorry. Overheating it was the only thing I could think of." Kennedy tugged her hair nervously.

Mr. Robbins looked at the monitor, saw the field's messy state, and shook his head.

"At this point, I'm not sure if the program will continue. This is a disaster. I'm glad none of you were injured," he looked at Kennedy's hand and added, "too badly."

"Come with me, and we'll get you both checked out at the nurse's office."

As they walked to the nurse, Mr. Robbins spoke a little more about the program, then texted someone on his phone.

"I hope we can continue the work. We were close to a breakthrough that would have revolutionized the closed-rain field system and our water conservation efforts."

"I'd still like to help," Dalton said. Kennedy nodded.

"If I can explain to the board and your parents how we move on from this, I hope we can. I've notified both of your parents, and they are on their way, so I'd like you to stay with me until they arrive."

"Okay," Kennedy said. Dalton dipped his chin.

"I am sorry to both of you that I didn't get notified earlier that something was wrong. I saw you signed out, but now I think LT-346890G may have falsified that information. The system was running so well." Mr. Robbins rubbed his forehead.

❦ ❦ ❦

Kennedy had been home for just a few minutes when someone knocked on the door.

Her mom said, "It's Dalton."

Kennedy walked outside, shutting the door behind her. Her eyes teared up. "I killed my best friend."

Dalton reached for her hand. "It'll be okay." He pointed to his yard where his mom stood and sheepishly waved. "But my mom might never let me go back to school."

"Yeah, both my parents are here. They even took a couple of extra days off work," Kennedy said.

"Go rest. I'll come over tomorrow, and we can try to stop an alien invasion or something."

"You're a dork." She smirked.

"But you like that, right?" His eyes lit up.

"I do." She smiled. "Goodnight, Dalton."

"Goodnight, Ken."

She rolled her eyes. "I still prefer Kennedy, but you can call me Ken if you want to."

"That's no fun. See ya tomorrow, Kennedy." Dalton waved goodbye.

❧ ❧ ❧

Kennedy woke to her alarm and the subtle chime of her phone. The alarm's robotic voice reminded her of the friend she had lost.

"I'm so sorry, Blade," she whispered. She pulled her blanket tighter and took a deep breath. She had nowhere to go this early, not anymore.

Kennedy was supposed to go to school, but she didn't want to. Still, she slipped the straps of her backpack over her arms. Her mom got into the driver's seat. "I wanted to take you today, I know it's . . . hard to go back, but I'm proud of you."

"Dalton really wanted me to come."

"I'm glad you are friends again. Well, I guess more than that now."

"Mom!"

"Honey, your dad and I are thrilled. I've always liked Dalton. He's a good kid."

"He's alright."

"Isn't he your boyfriend now? Just alright?"

"Force of habit. Yes, Mom, he's great."

"Speaking of, looks like he's coming over."

Dalton walked to the passenger side window.

"Hey, I was going to give you this at school, but here you go." He handed her a box wrapped in shiny green paper.

Kennedy opened it and found her broken watch, except the screen was no longer cracked.

"You fixed my watch," Kennedy said softly.

"That's a marketable skill right there. If you two got married, we could save thousands in equipment repairs." Kennedy's Mom tilted her head toward a slight crack in the car's dashboard screen.

"Oh my gosh, Mom." Kennedy and Dalton both blushed.

"Not for oh, eight or so years, but still . . ."

Kennedy sank back into the seat. She placed the watch on her wrist.

"There's something else about the watch," Dalton said. "I found an older version of Blade and installed her on it. She can't be transferred off, so she should be safe there. I know it's not the same, but I hope it helps. And I know this isn't exactly my place, but I think you should reach out to Grace. A lot happened, and I think it could be good."

"I'll think about it. And thank you for the watch, it means a lot that you fixed it."

He smiled. "Sure thing." Dalton waved before walking away.

Kennedy pulled out her phone and texted Grace. Within seconds, a response came.

"Grace wants to talk!"

"Then Dalton gave you good advice. See? He's a keeper." Her mother smiled.

Kennedy rolled her eyes.

A few minutes later, a note scrolled along the screen of her watch. "Hello, Kennedy."

Date: 2590-04-13 19:55:24 PRT
From: Ren Stornman
To: Anachronauts
Subject: The unanswered question of AI
Re: Turf War

Okay, Kinsha, you were right about this event. It should have been much worse. Sometimes I wish the rules implemented by the Technocracy on Lumen were enforced on every splinter in the Verse.

But, yes, I did some digging. The safeguards on this world should not have been sufficient to stop a rogue AI from escaping its confines and rampaging across the world. And then, if it found its way into the right systems, wreaking havoc on other splinters.

You're right that we were extremely lucky, but I believe it was more than luck. I found echoes that Soberana de la Luz was also there. I hear you now, saying she's nothing but myth, but these are markers I've seen before. Whoever she is, I think Soberana stopped a disaster that could have raged across the Verse.

And maybe it was not the first time.

—Ren Stornman

Date: 2590-04-14 12:12:01 PRT
From: Green Kinsha
To: Anachronauts
Subject: Teleportation
Re: Totally Not A Scam

Soberana de la Luz? She’s nothing but a myth!

I just got off the com with Space Cat Senior, and he is not happy. Apparently there is a power spike on level three that caused a laser breakout in the receiving bay. Their entire accounting staff has been chasing the lights around for hours.

I tried to tell him it wasn't our fault, but since we used the heating tubes to make cookies last night, he has traced it back to us. I told Gentor we should have given a plate of cookies to the Cats.

Did I mention I have a splinter under my thumbnail? That’s a splinter report worth reading. But read this one too:

TOTALLY NOT A SCAM

By Taryn Skipper

Shari from Indiana had seemed spontaneous and down-to-earth in her Alternate Reality Games forum posts, but Rachel was beginning to regret inviting her to Denver. Shari's carefree facade was like off-brand plastic wrap stretched tight over a hot bucket of boiling nerves. Rachel had competed in enough games to take a newbie under her wing. She'd even won a couple, racing her way through the clues hidden all over town and beating the other players to the prize. But Shari tapped her energy like a black hole sucking down stars.

Shari whispered the first four digits of the destination code to herself as she tapped them into the teleportation booth's input screen. Her finger hovered over the top row of numbers. "Would you mind repeating the last four again? Two, six, six, zero?"

"Girl, just make a note in your phone next time." Rachel tried to keep it light, preferring not to find out how close Shari was to going supernova. Rachel pulled out her own phone and read out the last four digits, *again*. "Two, six, zero, zero."

"Thanks. My device is unsupported here—it's not capturing and recalling correctly." She reached up and massaged the back of her head. Three tiny green lights shone from just under Shari's skin at the nape of her neck and reflected against her palm, one occasionally flickering red.

"Wow, is that some kind of subdermal phone implant? Does it connect to the regular cell towers?" Rachel pinched the skin between her thumb and pointer finger. "I have a friend with an NFC chip in his hand, but it's not good for much more than unlocking his phone."

Shari narrowed her eyes. "Who are the NFC?"

"Uh, you mean *what is* NFC?" Rachel jabbed her thumb toward the teleportation booth's display. What kind of ARG player didn't know what a near-field communication chip was? "Anyway, let's get a move on."

Shari's chipped, cherry-red nails clicked against the display, and the round button labeled *GO* glowed green. "Are you sure this is safe?"

Rachel tried not to count the precious seconds wasting away because of Shari's constant fretting. The porting concern was understandable. Indiana only had a few novelty booths for public use, and they weren't free like Denver's. Teleporting had made Rachel nervous at first, too.

"Yeah, as long as there aren't any dense metals in that thing in your neck, you're good. And if you try not to tense your muscles, the pins-and-needles sensation isn't so intense when you land."

Shari frowned. "I'm not afraid of the booth. It's disconcerting that this destination code doesn't come up on AppyTrip. It could be an ambush."

Rachel raised both eyebrows and chuckled. "You really think the game moderators would send us to some sketchy backwater booth with, like, a gang of bandits waiting for us?"

Shari's cheeks flushed, but her tone didn't reveal whether she was embarrassed or mad. "I suppose not, but what if this isn't the correct clue? It wouldn't be the first time an Alternate Reality Gamer wandered off on a wild pigeon hunt and ended up somewhere unsavory."

"It's goose—it doesn't matter." Rachel nodded toward the booth's input panel. "The code is going to time out, and then the door will unlock, and we could have other players barging in. We're never going to win if we take this long between clues."

Shari bit her lower lip. From the hints in Shari's forum posts, Rachel gathered that she'd been working through some kind of major transition. Something pretty traumatic, judging by the way it affected her concentration. Whatever it was, it weighed on her more than the average adulting troubles, which is why Rachel invited her out. This trip was Shari's big reset. Rachel scrounged up some grace for the poor thing. It was worth losing a minute of their lead to help a new friend feel confident and focused.

"Remember the *why*, babe," Rachel said with a soft smile. "For me, the prize money's how I'll up my art photography game. You said in the forum that you wanted to change the way your life was turning out, right?"

"Yes. If I succeed, I can build a new life for my brother and me. Thank you for helping make my trip possible."

"I'm glad you came! It's so cool to hang out real-time." Even if she was a bit more neurotic than she seemed online. "Now, when you think of the prize money, what's the first thing you'd do, specifically? I'm saving for a vintage Leica M2, the best analog camera ever made."

Shari's eyes grew distant as she pondered. "I'd take my brother somewhere far away, where we could live and die and make our own memories, just for us."

"More family time, love it! Excellent way to bring more joy and meaning into your life. That's your *why*." Rachel placed a hand on Shari's shoulder. "Let's go win this thing!"

Shari closed her eyes, pushing a tear down her lower lash and onto her cheek. She was going through it for sure. Opening her eyes again, she *finally* pushed *GO*.

After a bright flash and a floating sensation, Rachel felt solid plastic under her feet.

"You peek first," Shari said.

Rachel opened the door a crack as soon as the lock released. "No bandits." She smiled and pushed the door wider, angling her body sideways. "See? It's the Hub. We're on the guest pickup side."

Shari followed her out, and they merged with the flow of foot traffic toward the escalators under the bright LED sign welcoming travelers to the Denver International Transportation Hub.

"The DIT Hub, guest pickup," Shari repeated under her breath, hand to her temple.

All of her muttering didn't seem to help Shari retain anything. Rachel didn't envy her struggle. Shari pointed to a sign ahead. "Ah, yes, that's where you met me when I relocated to Denver."

"Ported, you mean?" Rachel asked.

"Yes, ported. Apologies for the inaccurate word choice. I know teleportation has been a part of your world for quite some time, but the booths are all new to me."

Rachel sighed, relieved Shari's stay in Denver was temporary.

Shari's eyes darted all over the Hub, no doubt searching for clues. "Why didn't the booth code that brought us here appear in the app? The Hub isn't a secret destination."

"Maybe this booth has been offline, and it just rebooted? Who knows. I just hope you believe me now that the ARG mods won't send us anywhere questionable."

"I'm glad you were right. But it doesn't hurt to have a little situational awareness. By definition, you never can tell when something unexpected might occur."

Thanks, Grandma Shari. Maybe she was homeschooled by an old-fashioned governess type. That would explain the unfamiliarity with booth tech, the nerves, *and* the formal speech. "Very true. Now we need to figure out why they sent us to *this* booth, of all the booths in this giant circus."

Halfway to the escalators, Shari slowed with some of the crowd to check a huge electronic display. "Could the clue be in here somewhere?"

Rachel scanned the list of tourist destinations and ads for food and lodging around Denver with their nearest teleportation booth codes. Nothing stood out, but a fuchsia flyer caught her eye to the right of the screen. "I don't think so, but it could be hidden in that mess." She tilted her head toward a tattered bulletin board mounted to the wall.

They squeezed past the crowd and searched the overloaded board, its crumbling cork only visible in a few slivers of space between the layers of ads.

Shari tugged the pink flyer from the board and bobbed it in her hand, watching it wave up and down. She lifted the paper to her face and breathed in deeply. "So fresh."

So weird. Everyone had their quirks, though. Rachel enjoyed the smell of books; maybe *Eau de New Flyer* helped calm Shari's nerves.

Shari must have caught Rachel's side-eye. "We have to reuse paper back home, and it gets all limp and sad . . ." She straightened the flyer. "It says, 'Free port-proof phone rentals,' and in smaller print at the bottom here, it talks about the required deposit and payment for data used. Fascinating."

"I guess you guys don't need to worry about your phones surviving port booths yet, huh? Better step out of your own little world. The future is now, Indiana!" Rachel gave Shari a playful nudge.

Shari stared at her for two quiet seconds and then burst into laughter until her eyes watered. "Thanks," she said, wiping away tears. "I needed a laugh. You have no idea."

Rachel forced a small laugh, then turned her attention back to the board. She didn't think she'd said anything that funny. But she also wasn't going around sniffing bulletins, so what did she know?

Shari whispered a few more headlines to herself and then repeated one louder: "'Excuse our dust, we're rebuilding the Lizard Peoples' Lair.' Well, this must be the clue, correct?"

"Oh, no, that's one of the more popular conspiracies floating around this place." Rachel smiled. "The lizard people live in the tunnels below us."

"Wait, are they not free to live among society here?"

Rachel laughed at the concern on Shari's face. Shari actually had a sense of humor. Who knew? Rachel leaned in to inspect a white paper with monospace black lettering.

Shari read it out: "'Quit horsin' around and get to the starting line—the race is on.'"

"Sounds just vague enough to be part of the game," said Rachel, folding away the corner of an overlapping flyer. The letters ARG, leaning inward and stretched into a triangle shape, appeared at the bottom of the paper. "*Bam*, an Alternate Reality Games monogram, right here."

"Excellent. So, something to do with horses, or jokes, or races. Maybe the next clue is hidden near that giant blue horse statue from the Hub promo videos."

"No way, that thing's at least ten kilometers away along the road. No booths out there."

"Well, maybe that's what they meant by 'the race.' We have to beat the other players in a footrace to get there first."

Rachel shuddered. "Hon, that veiny monstrosity is one hundred percent cursed. Its eyes glow red at night, and it fell on the sculptor who made it and killed him. No Denver local would make players approach Blucifer."

Shari shook her head. "Denver is weird."

"Aren't you glad you came? Who doesn't want a good, weird time?"

Shari snorted.

"If the next clue is at that statue, I forfeit," Rachel chuckled.

Shari's pale face blanched. "But not really? We *must* persevere."

"Yeah, no, I was joking." Rachel checked the time and led Shari briskly to the escalator. They stepped off and around the people holding signs with names and logos at the edge of the waiting crowd, continuing to the bank of outgoing booths.

"We're still making good time," Rachel said, "but we really need to know our destination before we get into the next booth."

Shari slowed, thinking. "Are there any races going on in town today? Like, besides this ARG clue race? Maybe something silly?" She stopped and grabbed Rachel's arm. "Wait, you don't still race horses, do you?"

Shari looked so horrified at the very notion that Rachel felt a pang of defensiveness for her city. She thought she remembered seeing something about the last Colorado track shutting down a few years ago. "No, of course not. Maybe they're actually referring to the beginning of this ARG race itself. The first clue for this race was hidden in a user post on the crowdsourced database of unlisted booth codes."

PASTRIES
Se vende
¡Barato!
Denver
under where?
MLWC
quit horsin' around & get to the Start-
DUST...
WE'RE
FREE
LOST
Relax
BOULDER, CO
www. Booth Pwn .com
もっと塩が必要です。

Shari relaxed and clapped once. "So, 'the starting line' could mean boothpwn.com!"

Rachel pulled out her phone and scrolled through the minimalist website, checking for anything new, or anything they might've disregarded as a troll or joke entry. "Got it." She held her phone up to Shari. "Check out this booth code listing. Not even AppyTranslate could mess up English this bad. It's got to be a joke."

Shari stepped closer. "Read it to me."

Rachel nodded, happy to accommodate Shari's apparent need for audio processing. "It gives a numbers-only booth code, and the message goes, 'Greetings To One of Golden Character. I beg your compliance post-haste with my request in good faith. I am in dire straits of urgency. For, dear benefactor, I hail from a land wherein the Alizeran Resistance Group has dwindled to a motley few with whom the fate of a thousand fractured potentialities does rest.'"

Shari had both eyebrows up, one hand covering her mouth, appearing appalled at the message.

Rachel nodded. "So bad, right?"

Shari pulled her hand away and blew out her breath. "This is it. This is what we've been searching for." She closed her eyes and whispered, "I can finally leave."

Rachel gave Shari a sideways glance. She'd only been here a matter of hours and was already excited to leave? She was probably right, though. This *did* seem like something the ARG would come up with.

"It gets worse. Listen." Rachel read on in an unplaceable but dramatic accent. "*Ahem.* 'For we have pilfered the last of the Alizerans' Salt, without which they cannot carry out their cunning designs, creating endless worlds over which to rule in tyranny—fracturing the very fibers of our beings.

"'We seek a harbor of safekeeping for this substance of preciousness, to obscure its whereabouts from the Alizerans for a mere three days of your world's time, so that they might have no means whereby to freely traverse the divide between such fractures as they have heretofore done. In such time, the Resistance Group shall overthrow the evil that doth beset us. We also require the lending of the currency of your land, a sum not great, but sufficient to complete our quest.

"'At my return upon the fourth day, if you have preserved the Salt away from unworthy hands, and if I have not perished, I shall bequeath a treasure of bounty indicative of our great and enduring thanksgiving. Notwithstanding the heavy acquiescence with which you may grapple over the validity of such claims, I do implore you, kind and honest soul, help us, or all of our worlds could be lost to the oppressors.'"

Shari shook her head and rearranged her shocked expression into a smile. "Impressively bad. Like someone translated it back and forth through five languages and three centuries."

"There's no doubt this is the clue. It's an obvious play on the classic Nigerian Prince scam that someone had way too much fun writing. And it was posted the day this contest session was announced last month."

"The starting line," Shari said. "And Alizeran Resistance Group—ARG."

"Nailed it," Rachel sang.

Shari and Rachel continued toward the outgoing booths. "Still," said Shari, slowing. "This is our second count of blind-boothing in one day. Isn't it odd for the ARG moderators to make players follow unlisted booth codes?"

"Second count?" Rachel snickered. "Sounds like an arrest record, only blind-boothing isn't illegal. And we're not dialing random codes like obnoxious middle-schoolers. We're entering a specific code as part of a game."

Shari's pace remained agonizingly hesitant.

"Listen Shar, I've never been wrong about a clue, I've only ever been too *slow*." Rachel looped her arm around her friend's and pulled her forward. "Remember your *why*."

Shari glanced up into space for a brief moment before coming back to Earth with a smile. "Fine, then, I shall trust your 'golden character,' or whatever it said. Onward, to the 'treasure of bounty.'"

Rachel pushed the booth's door open, and Shari peeked out over her shoulder. Across a wide field dotted with a few lonely cars, the tall turret of a castle stood against a backdrop of ponderosa pines.

"Oh, no," Shari said. "I thought the game was designed to take place within the Denver Metro area. This does not look metropolitan."

Rachel gasped. "Oh! It's the Ren Faire! I haven't been here since I was like twelve!"

They exited the booth, and Shari took a few steps toward the line of people winding away from the castle wall. She read the large wooden sign hanging over the drawbridge. "'Larkspur Renaissance Faire.' So, should we get in line?"

"Dressed like this?" Rachel lifted an eyebrow and pulled up on her shirt from the shoulders.

Shari frowned down at her own outfit. "The AI overview for the search I ran stated that straight-leg jeans and a band tee were timeless classics." She turned, hearing the booth they'd come out of open behind her. Out walked a kilt-clad highlander, a wood nymph, and a stormtrooper, debating the etymology of the word "wench" as they passed.

"I see," Shari said.

"Besides, ARG wouldn't hide a clue somewhere that had a fee to get in. The Faire is fun, but ticket prices are outrageous."

"Do you think we could have got it wrong?"

"I think we could be on the right track. This does kind of explain the terrible attempt at a *ye olde* vibe in the database post."

"Perhaps the Faire dialect interfered with communications," Shari said softly, hand to her temple in thought.

"So maybe the clue is somewhere along the wall surrounding the Faire, or in this field." Rachel peered toward the closest section of wall, scanning for flyers, stickers, or anything that might help them decide where to go next.

Shari walked around the back of the booth and continued examining the row. The door of the third booth shone red around the perimeter, then clicked, and the light turned green.

A tall man carrying a boxy metal briefcase strode out, facing Rachel but talking to someone in what he must have considered Ren Faire-speech by means of a tiny silver earpiece. "Have you arrived with intent to attend the festivities? Shall I be forced to postpone my quest further?"

The man exited the booth but paused to hear back from whomever he was waiting for.

Shari came around from behind the booths and jolted to a stop with an almost cartoonish double-take.

Rachel tried to move out of his path to the castle, but the man stepped closer.

"Fair lady, art thou here for me?"

Glancing behind her and then back at the man, Rachel pointed at herself. "Me? Sorry, can I help you?"

"By brightest suns, I hope so." The man's dark eyes bored into hers with a gaze so intense, Rachel had to look away.

Shari approached Rachel in a wide arc around the man as Rachel examined his thin blue jumpsuit, which looked like it had seen a few too many ren faires. Black singe marks dotted the left leg, and one of the long sleeves had ripped halfway up the seam. But the patch at his left breast clued Rachel in. Three silver letters formed a stylized pyramid on a light blue background: *ARG.*

Rachel's shoulders dropped. "Oh my gosh, you creeped me out for a second. But yeah, we're totally here for you."

"At long—" the young man's voice cracked, and he took a breath before he continued. "At last. You shall never know the profound—"

Rachel checked the time. "Wait, so we're the first? Shar, we're *so* winning this thing!" She looked back at Shari, who'd stepped behind her.

Shari took a slow, shaky breath in and whispered, almost too quiet for Rachel to catch. "Filthy Cerulean."

There go those nerves of hers again. Maybe she was a recovering germaphobe. The jumpsuit looked more like a dingy navy color, like a smoke-darkened sky rather than a cloudless cerulean.

The man glanced around the field. "Have you brought the currency of the realm?"

"Currency of the realm?" Rachel pursed her lips. "Would you mind dropping character? I'd love to earn the prize, but this mishmash is going to trigger a migraine."

The man held up his middle finger. Rachel regretted her lack of tact in calling out his ridiculous speech pattern, but he kept his finger pointed outward and traced a half circle in the air. "Apologies. Recalibrating," he said, finger twitching in patterns in front of him before he spoke again. "Now, I've been dodging these here festival mugs all day, see, all of 'em hopped up on hooch and spouting old-timey jibber-jabber—it's got my translator gizmo all gummed up. So, you got the cabbage, pal?"

Shari seemed to decide the guy wasn't a threat and stepped out from behind Rachel. "Amateur. You're not even in the correct century."

Rachel folded her arms, laughing. "At least it's less headache-inducing when he sticks to one decade."

The man pulled his eyebrows together, his finger waving and tapping in the air, then looked back up. "Well, ace, we're in quite a pickle. Supplies are mighty slim as this rumble I'm tied up in keeps rolling, and this ol' fellah's got to make it do or do without. Say, is this any clearer? And did you bring the cash?"

Shari frowned. "Getting closer. How much money do you need to get this over with?"

The man's finger repeated its twitchy charade.

"Wait," Rachel said. "Do you really want us to give you money? I could send you a dollar or two on AppyCash if it's something like a test deposit for the winnings."

The bedraggled man shook his head. "Dude, I know it's a major bummer, but one buck's not gonna float me for three days, you know? And I'm like, totally without a gadget that vibes with your phone apps."

Rachel snickered. "You are hilarious. And still forty years behind."

"And for the love of stars, turn down your slang settings," Shari said, pulling out her wallet and turning to Rachel. "He said in the post that he'd hide the Salt here for three days, then come back to get it, and we'd be rewarded. So he must need money to survive for three days, maybe a little extra to take care of whatever business he has. I don't actually care. Whatever he needs, it's more than worth it for the . . ."—her eyes flitted to the beat-up metal case in the man's grip—"the prize." She whipped out a small but healthy stack of crisp one-hundred-dollar bills. "This should suffice, I think."

"Whoa, Shari!" Rachel dove for the stack and snatched it out of her hand. "Maybe absolute trust is a thing in Indiana, but around here, we don't just throw bucketfuls of cash at strangers!" Shari had lost it. If she was carrying around more money than we even stood to win, what was she playing for?

The man moved the case in front of him and held the handle with both hands. "I'm, like, not a stranger, and this is totally not a scam, okay? My name is John Jacob Edwards, son of Stacia Jolene Karrington, daughter of Wendy Aine Loralee, daughter of Lenore Ellen—"

Rachel put a hand up to stop the "John" guy. "We don't need to know your character's entire genealogy. This isn't how it works. You don't have to pay to play."

"Please," John said, dropping to his knees and rapidly drawing shapes in the air, the knuckles on his other hand white over the case's handle. "I swear it to be true. The value of these contents far outweighs the currency I need, in the event that I am prevented from returning. But I shall return, and you shall be rewarded. You are the first, my only champions. Keep it safe, I beg of you. Perhaps I haven't found the correct linguistic setting . . ."

Shari looked at the cash in Rachel's hand and shifted her weight from one foot to the other. "He's ARG, there is no doubt. Let's secure the prize."

"It's just a bit much, you know? I'm not willing to finance some rando's three-day vacation. But it's your money." It made no sense, and ARG had never done anything like this before, but she handed the bills back to Shari.

The tall man looked worried, maybe scared about being called out. "Look, Chat, I know it's giving Ohio and the whole skibidi situation is lowkey sus. Sure, I have negative aura and zero riz, but on God, I'm not delulu." The strange young man clasped his hands together, and a tear ran down his char-streaked cheek. “Be the GOAT and give me a W, for real for real. I’m not capping, bruh, I need you to lock in and let him cook.”

Rachel broke into laughter. “So close! Legit or not, this glitchy translator bit is *genius*.”

Shari held out the money. “It had better be legitimate.”

Rachel watched, dismayed. “Is that really it, then? End of the game?”

John nodded. “You may retire to your home and await your prize.” He handed Shari the case, his hand catching on the handle as she hastily pulled it away. Without a backward glance, John bolted into the nearest booth with a wobble in his right knee and dark blood oozing from a fresh scab on the back of his neck. *Not a good sign.*

❂ ❂ ❂

Rachel refreshed her email inbox for the thousandth time. “How long can it possibly take to announce winners? You don’t think they’re actually going to make us wait three days, do—ah, here it is!”

Shari wasn’t supposed to leave for another two days, but she’d been in and out all evening “preparing for her trip,” she’d said.

Rachel shouted the email out so Shari could hear the ARG results from the guest room, where she was packing. “‘We at ARG are pleased to announce the successful completion of this year’s Summer clue race. Inspiration for—’ blah blah blah. Okay, here, ‘This session’s winner is the player known by the handle AuGurl.’”

Hold up. That guy doing the glitchy translator bit said we were first. This couldn’t be right. And AuGurl had already won five out of the last seven races. “Give someone else a chance, for crying out loud!”

Rachel’s heart sank, both for the loss of camera fund prize money and for poor, trusting Shari, who rolled her suitcase out to the front room, strangely calm compared to the ball of anxiety she’d been when she arrived. She carried the blocky case in her other hand. They hadn’t discussed what to do with the grifter’s prop, but Rachel couldn’t imagine a use for the vials of fine white granules inside, tucked into foam in neat rows.

“I’m heading out early.”

“Dang, Shar, I’m so sorry. I feel horrible. Turns out, the clue *was* referring to the old horse racing track, like you’d mentioned. I think I may have actually been wrong, for once.”

“Please don’t feel bad. You were kind to a stranger in a difficult situation, and patient with me as I followed you around the city and beyond.”

"But wait, don't you want to hang out and see if there's a chance that John guy actually comes back for his briefcase? It's a long shot, but that was a lot of money. You'll need it for your move."

Shari let go of her suitcase and eased the metal box down next to it. She rushed over to Rachel and squatted at her desk to wrap her in a tight hug. "The Cerulean was right. The Salt is extraordinarily valuable." She pulled away, tears shining in her bright eyes. "I've left you three vials. Tell no one, and do not open them. Don't even mention them until—or unless—the time comes when you understand their worth, if not their use."

"But what could it possibly—" *Holy crap. It's drugs.* Expensive white powder. A scabby weirdo asking for cash. Shari's need to run from her home and start a new life. *Duh, Rachel.* She wanted nothing to do with whatever new version of addictive powdered crystals this might be, no matter its street value. "I'm not interested in anything illegal; I don't do—"

"No, no, nothing illegal. I would strongly advise against handling it, but it's of potential use to science. That's all I will say. Oh, and I got you something while I was . . . out. A parting gift." Shari ran back to the guest room and brought out a bright red box. Bold white sans-serif letters across the top spelled Leica M2.

Shari held the box out, bowing her head. "Thank you, Rachel, daughter of Natalie Juliette. You may not have saved 'a thousand fractured potentialities,' or whatever the Cerulean conspiracy theorist was blathering about. But you saved the one world that matters."

It took Rachel a solid five seconds before she recovered enough to move her body and carefully take the mint-condition box from Shari's outstretched arms. She didn't speak as she opened the lid, revealing the most pristine camera she'd ever seen. Worlds better than the beat-up, barely functioning models she'd hoped to save up for. "Shar, it looks brand new! How on Earth did you find one in such good condition?"

"You assume too much in your question, but I'm happy you like it. It's nothing compared to what you've given me." She ran her crimson nails along the side of the box. "And, the packaging is so pretty!" Shari moved her finger in the air and touched the other to her temple. "End recording." She picked up her suitcase and the metal box. "Sorry for my constant chatter. I get in trouble when I don't document my missions to my handler's liking. Not that I'll have to worry about that much longer." Shari hefted the case in her hand and blew out a breath.

Rachel looked up from the shining Leica. "Wait, what?" She hadn't been able to focus on Shari's words with such a prize in her hands.

"And apologies for my moods. I've been so nervous I'd miss something and lose my chance to return home. My brother likely assumes me dead by now."

Rachel focused on the Leica, unsure how to respond to Shari's hyperbole.

"Lastly, don't worry about that Cerulean coming back and wondering where his Salt went. We'll make sure he's reunited with his people."

And with a flick of her pinky, Shari from Indiana vanished.

Rachel blinked at the space where Shari and the case of Salt had been. Of all people to risk using a portable teleporter . . . Denver was weird, but that hot mess of a woman was weirder.

Shaking her head, Rachel glanced down at the Leica. AuGuri could have the ARG win—nothing beat Rachel's elation having acquired the true "treasure of bounty" she'd been saving for.

She'd need film. Was it manufactured anymore? She pulled her laptop in front of her, closed out her email and typed, "where to find 35mm film, tungsten-free" into the browser's search bar.

END NOTE

Clearly the Ceruleans are at it again. I thought QoreTech had eliminated the entire faction, but this account would suggest otherwise. The Alizerans are after them too, but they just keep slipping through the cracks. Course we all want to stop QoreTech, but if the Ceruleans have their way, we all lose. Any more reports like this one, and we're going to have to bump them back up on our oh-crap-this-needs-to-be-dealt-with list.

And another thing. Tessera is the only splinter with teleportation technology that we know of (right??). And yet, this technology sounds really familiar. I'm sure I've read about something similar somewhere before. An account NOT from Tessera. I know that sounds crazy. I'm not though. Pretty sure.

We'll probably need to send Ms. Six there in person so we can get to the bottom of things, and hopefully secure another batch of Time Salt. And yes, Flopdoodle. I should have let you take this one. Seems like your kind of nonsense. It just gives me a headache.

—Kinsha

Date: 2590-04-15 03:47:17 PRT
From: Ms. Six
To: Anachronauts
Subject: Tacos
Re: Double Dodd

HIGHLY CLASSIFIED

This account should be kept from the Immortals from QoreTech, Cats, and Gentor if at all possible. Unless I miss my guess, the Immortals have been looking for this one for a long time. I feel, for the sake of those involved, we should destroy after reading. It would be very detrimental to everyone in all splinters if some of this information were to get out. The tech described herein could be very dangerous in the wrong hands. In Immortal hands. You will see what I mean after you've read.

DOUBLE DODD

By Elesa Hagberg

QORETECH, IC-1. EARTH PRIME – YEAR 2504

I raced down to Special Projects, swiping my hand across scanners to open doors. Red emergency lights thrummed along the ceiling to the beat of my pounding footsteps. I wasn't even sure what the emergency was, only that I'd started receiving alerts on my compupad right before it froze completely.

I slid to a stop in front of the lab door and slapped the entry pad. Nothing happened.

I passed my hand over the entry pad again, but it blipped uselessly even while my name popped up on the screen.

> Vincent Dodd, Dimensional Systems Engineer, Project THREAD.
> *INCIDENT CONTAINMENT IN PROCESS*

I mashed the comm button. "Glenn? Sanya!? *Is anyone in there?*"

The door stayed firmly closed. I could force a manual override if I had to, but it was slow and didn't always work on the first seven tries. I let my head fall against the plasmaglass door in frustration, trying to catch my breath. How was this brand-new body so out of shape?

The plasmaglass shifted against my forehead as the door slid open, and I nearly fell straight into Dr. Karron Blake who stood on the other side.

I took in her tight jaw and crisp black suit then pushed past her into the room. The walls of Lab C3 pulsed with a soft, sterile, blue light, the air heavy and sharp, like oranges in a vat of acid. The Nexus Core hummed faintly, the crackle of green light pulsing around it, its patterns shifting in an abstract dance.

Sanya Rao—what was left of her—lay on the floor halfway inside the jump bubble. Her short blonde hair stood on end, her hollow eyes staring blankly at the ceiling. The green glow of the Nexus Core's perimeter sliced diagonally across her body from shoulder to hip; everything inside the bubble sizzling in an unrecognizable pudding.

"Again?" It had only been a month since the last time she died, an accident with the destabilizer that had killed us both. I gagged, my stomach twisting uncomfortably in on itself. I'd seen a lot of dead bodies working at QoreTech, but this was one of the worst.

"Where did he go?" Dr. Blake asked.

She still stood in the doorway, looking at me, tall and imperious, and I couldn't parse her words through the smell of Sanya's charred remains. "What?"

"Where," Dr. Blake said again, slow and staccato, "has Mr. Mbatha gone?"

I rubbed at my neck port. "I don't know. I'm surprised he's not here, actually. Last night's simulations were successful. We resolved the coherence instability we've been fighting for months. Once we adjusted the resonance thresholds, the system was able to maintain phase alignment instead of collapsing. We're ready to move into the next stage." I pulled out my compupad to call Glenn, but the system shutdown had flooded it so completely with alerts that the interface was still unresponsive. Whose idea had it been to prioritize error notification over basic communication?

"You misunderstand," Karron Blake said. "Mr. Mbatha *was* here. And then he *left*." She gestured over to the shimmering waves of residual energy in the jump bubble.

I stared blankly at her while her words thudded slowly into place.

Oh.

I ran to my workstation, my chair spinning as I shoved it aside. Glenn couldn't have *jumped*. We were ready to move on to stage four, yes, but there were still months of testing to be done.

Standing over the desk, I logged on, my fingers flying across the command deck, looking for the activity logs that would prove that Dr. Blake was overreacting, and Glenn was still asleep at his domicile even though we were on the verge of a scientific breakthrough.

```
07:18:43—Transit event confirmed.
```

I stared at the holoscreen, then at Dr. Blake. I looked back at the holoscreen. It truly made no sense.

"But why?" I asked. "Why would he jump? We don't have any protocols in place. Without instrumentation or a return path, even a successful transit wouldn't give us any usable data."

Dr. Blake's eyebrows drew into an impenetrable line, her black hair brushing her shoulders like two blades. She wasn't interested in the technical details. She never was. Only concrete facts.

I checked the log again. "Lumen," I told her, pointing at the holoscreen, though I still could not wrap my head around this. "His destination was Lumen."

"Lumen?" she sniffed. "Why?"

"I can't begin to guess. I still don't understand anything that is happening here."

I fell into a chair, which molded happily around me, aligning itself perfectly to my spine. Glenn *had* been acting strange the last few months, cagier than normal. He'd always had his secrets, but this was insane.

I pulled up the project archives and the replication queue, hoping I could work backward through the system to see exactly what Glenn had done that morning. Nothing loaded. I tried again. Still nothing.

The directory was empty.

Time travel was a fairly simple process: push hard enough at the right moment and reality splits, obligingly peeling off a copy of itself to prevent paradoxes. A splinter world is born and the door slams shut behind it.

Traveling to an existing splinter was something else completely. A splinter once created kept drifting forward in time and away in phase. Finding it again meant locating a moving target, calculating its temporal offset, and forcing a moment of alignment without tearing either world apart. That was what we'd spent the last three years working on.

And now, just when we were finally ready to test it—

My fingers fell still. My limbs went limp. "It's gone." The words landed on the command deck like a stone. "Everything is gone."

"Explain."

Instead of answering her, I accessed QoreTech's company asset backups and entered my password to view Glenn's chip data. All data collected from QoreTech employees' neural chips was considered company property: our experiences and memories continuously uploaded the data stored in those chips to QoreTech's proprietary servers. Die in a lab accident? The company grows you a new body and restores you from your backups.

Free storage, free clones, zero privacy.

Still, while accessing Glenn's chip data was within my rights as a QoreTech employee, it was considered a huge invasion of privacy. But we were past the point of politeness.

The file loaded.

Empty.

That couldn't be right. I refreshed.

Still empty.

Three years of Glenn's ideas, thoughts, and memories, gone. Every backup. Every restore point.

With a rush of concern, I input my password again and flipped over to Sanya's files.

Empty.

"No," I whispered. "He couldn't have—"

But he had. All the data that made Sanya *Sanya* had been wiped away, just a big empty file left in its place.

I'd stood next to her corpse and thought it was temporary. An inconvenience. But she was dead. The way we weren't supposed to die anymore. There was no backup to restore. No Sanya to resurrect.

She was just . . . gone.

I pushed away from the desk. "He scrubbed everything. Why would he *do this*?"

Dr. Blake straightened, pulling her jacket smooth. "Mr. Mbatha has become a security threat. I need you to follow him to Lumen and neutralize the situation."

I stared at her. "Neutralize?"

"Eliminate him, Mr. Dodd. We must assume he has stolen company research. We need to contain the breach. Permanently."

I shook my head. I wasn't a field agent. I'd never *neutralized* anyone. "Forgive me, Dr. Blake, but travel to Lumen? It's not possible. He wiped everything. I would have to start over."

"Then start over. And I suggest you hurry. I do not know what his plans are, but we have to stop him before he does something *truly horrific.*" She looked pointedly at Sanya's mutilated corpse, then turned and strode from the room, her heels clicking against the floor and echoing off the walls.

⋄|⋄ ⋄|⋄ ⋄|⋄

It took nearly eight months to rebuild what Glenn had destroyed, a miracle given the scope of it, but Dr. Blake was never satisfied. She requisitioned a whole team to work at my beck and call, and I lived on banuble and coffee substitutes, reconstructing the research from memory and what details we could pull from my backup files.

And then Dr. Blake gave us one week after that for testing. That seemed. . . *unreasonable.* But what choice did I have? Several chip workers came in as test subjects, and after a few messy failures, we had our first successful jump. I'd convinced Dr. Blake that Brukanaz was the ideal test splinter to verify the chronolink's power source since there was no electrical power on Brukanaz for the device to draw from, just the device's internal cells. The chipworker with the mole below his left eye jumped successfully, and Dr. Blake declared us ready for Lumen.

Unwilling to risk loss of the chronolink (and perhaps less so the person it was attached to), Dr. Blake had ordered it to be surgically implanted. All the data would be collected and stored in secondary chips, so the implant only had to be large enough for the power supply and basic communication interface. The device spanned my forearm, which throbbed slightly as I stood on the mark.

I'd been issued standard off-Prime utility wear: matte, neutral, and deliberately unremarkable, and a DeepFryer—a sleek black weapon designed to kill a person and slice through their neural net. Everything was ready to go. I wouldn't arrive at the same time Glenn had, of course. That coordinate no longer existed. Time on Lumen continued moving forward at an even faster rate than it did here, given the drift.

"Eliminate Mr. Mbatha," Dr. Blake said to me, like I didn't know what I'd been working toward the last eight months. "And do not speak to him. We must contain the breach before this situation spirals further out of control. Do you understand your orders, Mr. Dodd?"

"Yes, Dr. Blake." I nodded absently, checking over all the settings one more time. I had made sure my chip data was fully synced and had a backup skin ready to go, just in case things went horribly wrong. That was the great thing about immortality. Amazing scientific discovery. Very little risk.

I looked at the round-faced tech at the controls and nodded.

"Good luck," I whispered to myself. A wave of nausea passed over me, and everything went dark.

⇹ ⇹ ⇹

MEREDITH, WYOMING. LUMEN — 1984

I stumbled, threw out my arms to right myself, and then fell anyway, my knees slamming into a cold, hard floor. I felt like I'd been spinning in endless circles, and my equilibrium didn't know how to right itself. My eyes seemed to be spinning as well, but I blinked forcefully until my vision finally cleared.

The vinyl composite of the flooring was laid out in white and green flecked squares. The room was large and empty, and the walls appeared to be brick, something I'd only ever seen in IC-1's historic district. To my left was a raised platform, covered in threadbare red carpet, with an even more threadbare green curtain hanging to one side.

The air still crackled with the spent energy of the transit. I checked my chronolink. The readout pulsed gently: return trip programmed and functional.

I exhaled. The last thing I wanted was to be trapped on Lumen in 1984.

A bell rang overhead, rattling through the air and my bones. The double doors burst open, and children poured in, flowing past me like I wasn't there.

A woman following them froze when she saw me. "Are you . . . lost?" She checked her clipboard. "You should stop by the front office. We've got the gym scheduled for physical fitness right now, so you're probably supposed to be somewhere else. Whose class are you here to visit?"

Through the open double door was a bright hallway buzzing with the voices of children. I looked around helplessly at the brick walls and windows behind me and spotted a door in the corner. I spun and strode toward it.

"Wait!" the woman called after me. "The office is this way!"

I marched on, pushed against the door, and stepped out into the afternoon sun shining down through a warm green sky.

Lumen. I'd known what to expect, but seeing the pale sage sky of this world in person was . . . well, it was *lovely*.

I clicked through the interface in the chronolink. I'd programmed it to track Glenn's residual phase signature, and it vibrated softly while it ran the commands. It was simply a low-grade coherence trace anchored to Glenn's implant. Enough to follow if I was careful, but not enough to find him quickly.

I needed to collect as much information as I could, but it was unwise to tarry. I wasn't certain the authorities would be called to report a strange man appearing in what was certainly a twentieth-century primary school, but it was better to play it safe.

According to the chronolink, it was 13:47 on August 20, 1984.

It had been fifteen months since Glenn arrived. He could be anywhere by now. I needed somewhere to work, somewhere private, with significantly fewer children around.

I strode around the school. The building was surrounded by houses, typical individual family dwellings, as was popular in the twentieth century. There was so much *space*.

Large front yards filled with grass or other flora, with enough room between the houses to insert a standard apartment from IC-1. Across the street, a woman walked a tiny black dog. A massive, yellow, metallic automobile drove down the road in my direction. The horn beeped, nearly startling me out of my skin. The woman at the wheel waved at the dog walker. A few houses down, a man was pushing a bulky, inefficient grass cutting machine back and forth across his lawn. He reminded me of Glenn with his poof of brown hair and wide shoulders.

The automobile rolled by, and the driver tooted their horn again. The lawn mowing man looked up and waved at her. I shook my head. The resemblance really was remarkable.

The man noticed me then and nodded genially in my direction. His smile fell.

Glenn.

I pulled out my DeepFryer and aimed, the weight of it foreign and heavy in my hands. Glenn jumped toward the porch, leaving the lawn cutting device on its own to roll into a flower bush. Before I'd even made it across the street, he ran inside the house and slammed the door behind him.

Looping around the side of the house, I entered the backyard. It was filled with flower beds, a vegetable garden, and a large holding cell for chickens who clucked and pecked lazily against the ground. I held the DeepFryer high as I slid along the house toward the back entrance. I was almost there when the back door banged open, and Glenn stepped out, aiming a very large shotgun at my head.

I expected him to shoot me, but he didn't. *I* should have pulled the trigger even if it meant Glenn fired in response and ended us both. Dr. Blake's threat would have been contained and I would have been resurrected in a new body with no memory of killing my friend. But he didn't look like the security risk Dr. Blake said he was.

He just looked like Glenn.

"Are you going to shoot?" Glenn asked.

Of course I was. Those were my orders. Why hadn't I? "I haven't decided." I nodded at his weapon. "Are you?"

Glenn shrugged, looking quickly around. "I haven't decided either. Can we at least take this not-deciding inside so the neighbors don't call the police?"

I sighed. "Okay."

Glenn led me inside the house and into a vast kitchen complete with huge green appliances and golden countertops. It was no wonder kitchens of the past were so big. Apparently, they needed a separate appliance for every function. Including—to my detached surprise—a hydroponic tower glowing dimly in the corner of the room.

Glenn set the shotgun on the countertop, then leaned against it, staring at me. He seemed to be completely in his element; I had never felt more out of place in my life. The air here was so fresh, the sky outside so big. I leaned against the counter next to him, holding on for dear life. I had been ripped across time and space and it felt like every cell in my body suddenly realized that I did not belong here on this world.

"I hoped you wouldn't find me," Glenn said.

I snorted softly. "Then you probably should have traveled more than a hundred meters from the spot where you arrived." I stared around the room, trying to take it in. Trying to make it make sense. "Seems more like the actions of a man who is hoping to get caught."

He tipped his head in confirmation. "Yeah, I suppose it does. You want some water?"

"I—yes, thank you. Water would be appreciated."

He turned to the sink and filled two glasses, handing me one. I downed it before the taste even registered. It was cool and crisp and tasted more pure than anything I'd ever had.

Glenn grinned at me then, every bit his old self. "It's from a well."

I stared at the cup, unbelieving. "That is delicious."

"Everything here is delicious. IC-1 might know how to recreate anything, but nothing compares to the genuine article."

I gave him a flat look. "You might say that nothing *here* is genuine either. All a copy of Earth Prime."

"I think I can state with complete confidence that that is a load of hogwash."

Hogwash?

"Glenn," I said, setting the glass and the DeepFryer on the counter behind me, "what in the seven layers of hell are you doing here?"

Glenn sighed, a sound like a display exhaust port purging dust. He waved toward a wooden table and chairs. I moved to follow him but swayed on my feet. Glenn held up a steadying hand, though he didn't touch me. "Whoa, buddy. You alright?"

"I'm fine. Only tired." Beyond tired. Bone-deep tired that seemed to pour through my skin from the air around me.

"Oh, yes. Of course you are. You jumped almost six hundred years into the past. Sort of. You've been running on adrenaline, but you need to rest before you fall into cardiac arrest."

"Dealt with many splinter jumpers, have you?" I asked, my voice weak and thick with bitterness.

"Just myself. And when my heart stopped . . . it was eye-opening. Come on. You can use the guest room."

Glenn led me out of the kitchen, and I followed, stumbling up a narrow set of stairs and into a small bedroom, the bed covered with a colorful blanket of patchwork design.

Without really meaning to, I fell onto it, sinking straight into unconsciousness.

⟻|⟼ ⟻|⟼ ⟻|⟼

I awoke to the ticking of an analog clock, spittle dribbling down my chin onto the pillow. I felt like I'd been beaten soundly in a colosseum death battle.

It was 7:03, the clock said. Most likely a.m., judging by the pale green light streaming through the curtained window.

A knock sounded at the door, and Glenn poked his head in. "Good. You're awake. Come on. You need food." He walked away without waiting for me, so I stood and followed on barely responsive legs, down the narrow stairs and into the kitchen. A woman with rusty brown hair and a blue apron stood at the cooking appliance, stirring something that smelled divine.

Glenn stepped up next to her and took the cooking utensil out of her hands. "Thanks. I got it."

She threw her hands in the air as though in surrender, then turned and rolled her eyes at me like we were sharing a joke, though I couldn't begin to guess what it was.

"Please," she looked at me and gestured at the table, "have a seat."

As I sat, she laid a stack of blue plates in front of me, made of a smooth, lightweight material I didn't recognize, then laid napkins and cups next to them.

Glenn carried a pan filled with a mix of cheese, vegetables, and meat to the table and placed it next to a plate of flat bread, then sat, taking the woman's hand.

"Sorry," he said. "Where are my manners? Veoma, this is Vincent Dodd, an old friend of mine. Vincent, this is Veoma . . . My wife."

I blinked at him several times. I looked at their clasped hands, then back at their faces. "Wife. That's sort of an old-fashioned notion, don't you think?"

Glenn spread his arms. "When in Rome."

"But you've only been here fifteen months."

Veoma looked at Glenn with cocked eyebrows and a small smirk on her face, then started scooping food onto a piece of flat bread.

"Yes, but I meant it about the cardiac arrest," Glenn said. "I passed out on the road outside and, instead of running me over, Veoma saved my life. The fact that she was the one to find me and save me . . . it felt like kismet."

Veoma laughed. "You are the most hopeless romantic. The day we met was the day you turned my life inside out. I'm not sure I'll ever recover. And you still owe me."

"I will be indebted to you until the day I die."

Glenn and Veoma looked into each other's eyes as though they were the only two people in the world.

"Glenn!" I shouted.

They both turned, startled. Veoma gave Glenn a pointed look, then turned to me. "It was lovely to meet you, Vincent. Please make yourself at home." She picked up her plate and strolled out of the room.

I tried to make sense of things, looking around the vast kitchen. "I'm sorry. I just—I don't understand."

Glenn pushed a plate toward me. "They're called tacos. Not normally breakfast food, but it's what we had. So eat. Your body has no idea how to process what's happened to it. Give it some nourishment so it stands a fighting chance."

None of it looked like anything I was used to, but my head was pounding and my stomach cavity seemed to be eating itself. I shot Glenn an angry look, but picked up the flat bread-wrapped food and shoved a huge bite into my mouth.

I paused as my taste buds figured out what was happening. Food so fresh and real it made my head spin. I kept eating until the hollow emptiness inside of me stopped begging for more.

Glenn took a bite of food, chewing slowly, deliberately. "You remember how different Sanya was after that destabilizer accident? All the anxiety gone?"

My throat tightened. I kept my eyes on the plate. "Dying is hard on a person."

"Should've made it worse, though, shouldn't it? Sanya used to catastrophize everything. She'd run a test five times before she trusted the results, raising safety concerns, pushing back on timelines because she needed to be sure. It drove Blake crazy, but her caution caught errors no one else saw." He paused. "After that accident? Nothing worried her anymore. I'd bypass safety protocols, and she'd just . . . nod and move on."

He was right. Sanya had always been cautious to the point of paranoia. Exhausting to work with, but she'd been right more often than not. Those last few months though, especially after the destabilizer accident, she'd changed. Mellowed out. Stopped questioning. I had chalked it up to experience.

Die and learn, as they say.

I cleared my throat loudly. "Is that why you wiped her backups?"

"*What?*" Glenn froze with his fork halfway to his mouth.

I pointed at him. "You killed her—*dead* dead. How could you? Why *would* you? I knew something was wrong, but I never thought—" I stopped, ache in my chest hard and close.

Glenn sighed, rubbing his face. "It's QoreTech, Vincent. And Nugeneco. They've been tampering with people's backups. Altering them. Shaping them." He paused, looking at me. "They smooth out inconvenient traits: depression, anxiety, rebelliousness, non-compliance—things that make people hard to control."

I blinked, trying to absorb what Glenn was saying. But it didn't make sense. "You're saying they're changing people?" I swallowed, trying to shove the ache in my chest away. "That's insane. That's a violation. They wouldn't just—"

"They would," Glenn interrupted quietly. "They *have*."

I blinked at him some more. I felt like my brain was made of mud, too mucked up to process any of the information sloshing through it.

Glenn spread his hands out flat on the wooden table and exhaled. "I found it by accident. Trials within QoreTech that Nugeneco had commissioned. QoreTech handles the bodies. Nugeneco handles what goes in them. We were their test population: small, contained, and disposable. There are Multiple version histories of the same person, with changes catalogued. 'Kessi Strand v3.2, work ethic enhanced by 7%,' 'Lars Janssen v2.7, distraction resistance increased 12%.' I found personality edits to Sanya. To me. *To you.*"

Something cold settled in my stomach. When was the last time I'd questioned an order? When was the last time I'd pushed back on Blake about *anything*? Eight months of rebuilding the research. Eight months of her breathing down my neck. Eight months of just . . . complying. Accepting the kill order without protest. Working myself to exhaustion because she said to hurry. The old me would have demanded to know why Glenn had to die. Would have asked what Blake was really afraid of. But I hadn't. I'd just . . . done it.

"What did she take from me?" I asked, my voice flat.

"Blake's notes called it 'reduced argumentative tendency' and 'improved directive compliance.'" Glenn met my eyes. "You used to fight her on everything, Vincent. Safety protocols, ethical boundaries, project timelines. You were brilliant and stubborn, and you never just accepted what you were told."

I stared at him, and for just a moment I could almost feel it, that other version of me, the one who would have been furious right now instead of just . . . numb. The one who would have been yelling at Glenn to explain now, demanding proof, refusing to believe it. It's like he was still there in the back of my mind, rattling against the walls of a room he couldn't escape, railing at me to *let him out.*

It was unthinkable, but changing who people were at the most basic level was absolutely something that QoreTech and Nugeneco *would* do.

"I was working on a patch," Glenn went on. "Some way to stop it before they decided this experiment of theirs was ready to roll out to the rest of the world. But Karron Blake caught me. Running was the only option I had left."

He looked straight through me, a haunted hollowness in his eyes. "I was trying to get to Thunderstruck. I've *been* trying to get to Thunderstruck. But the storms cause too much interference. When Dr. Blake and Sanya arrived, I panicked and picked another splinter at random. Ending up on Lumen must have been cosmic design. Sanya helped me, risks and all. I didn't—" He dropped his head into his hands, rubbing his face like he could massage the memories away. "She's really gone?"

I nodded, numb and cold and hungry and angry.

"I guess once Sanya helped me escape, Karron knew modification wasn't enough. Sanya had already proven she could be turned. Dead was safer."

"You should have told me," I said, voice calmer than it had any right to be. "About the personality modifications. You should have *trusted* me. You should have—" The words died in my throat. What was the point? The version of me that Glenn *should* have told was gone. Dr. Blake had deleted him just as completely as she'd deleted Sanya.

We sat in silence while I tried not to think about Sanya and failed spectacularly. She'd been on Project THREAD with Glenn and I since its inception. Three years of her disaster scenarios and me arguing and Glenn mediating between us. We'd been a good team once, chaotic but effective. Now there was no team left at all.

They'd hollowed us out. Turned me into a tool.

The old Vincent wouldn't have left Sanya's body without demanding answers. Wouldn't have spent the last eight months just following orders, compliant and useful and empty.

My orders here had been simple: find Glenn and eliminate him. At the time it had seemed . . . reasonable. Glenn had stolen company data and fled to the past. Of course, he had to be stopped. But why wouldn't Dr. Blake have me bring him back instead, find out what he knew? Even if Glenn wouldn't talk, QoreTech had interrogators. They had memory extraction technology.

Unless the problem wasn't what Glenn might do with the information.

The problem was the information itself.

"You have proof," I said. "Proof of what she's been doing to us. That's why she sent me to kill you instead of bringing you back."

Glenn looked at his hands against the yellow brown wood of the tabletop, and I knew it was true. He had evidence against QoreTech.

"Then what are you still doing here? We have to go back. Now. Before they start rolling it out everywhere." I jumped to my feet and headed toward the door, but Glenn didn't move. Just sat there, staring at the tabletop, tracing the grains of the wood with his fingers.

"Glenn . . ."

"I can't." He looked upstairs.

"You can always come back for your wife later," I pushed, "but we can't let them do this to people."

A cry wound down the stairwell behind us, the sound strange and confusing. I stared at the ceiling above me, trying to place the sound.

A baby?

Glenn and I stood as Veoma exited the stairwell, a baby girl in her arms sucking on a handful of her mother's shirt. She had a pink pair of night clothes, Glenn's gray eyes, and a poof of brown hair.

"This is Louella," Glenn said, his voice soft with emotion.

"But you've only been here fifteen months!"

"I told you it was kismet."

The little girl reached for Glenn, and Veoma passed her over. She nuzzled against his shoulder, wiping her nose on his shirt.

More footsteps pounded down the stairs, and a little boy of perhaps thirty to forty months jumped into view. He wore red cowboy boots, blue shorts, and a yellow safety construction helmet.

"Daddy!" the little boy said, jumping at Glenn and kissing the baby in his arms so that the hard hat bonked her on the head. Instead of crying, she frowned, a sweet downturn of the mouth and an angry gleam in her eye.

"But you've only been here 451 days!" I said.

Glenn ruffled the boy's blonde hair.

I tried again. "But immortals are sterile!"

Veoma coughed and shared a look with Glenn that said I had lost my mind. Glenn pressed his lips against the boy's cheek and blew, making a *pbbbbft* sound, and then the boy jumped down and ran off, each step long and exaggerated. Glenn kissed the baby girl's forehead, and then Veoma took her back.

"Alright," she said, smiling. "Me and these imaginary kids are going on a walk. You two enjoy . . . catching up."

Glenn turned to my disbelieving face. "The boy, Darrick, isn't mine. There was an accident at the mine, and Veoma's husband died. Darrick was only a few months old. But Louella—"

"But you *can't* father a child. I don't need to explain this to you. *It is not possible*. What did you *do*?"

"I don't *know*. I was trying to reinstall my older versions, wipe any code that had been added posthumously. I must have done something by accident."

I fell back into the chair, my entire basis of reality completely undone. The implications of it, the *reality* of it, were too much to take in. Immortals didn't have children. That was a fact. That was something fundamental to the system they had built. It was impossible.

Glenn sat again, too, waiting while my knowledge of everything unraveled. "You see why I can't leave." His voice was gruff. "I can't trust Karron Blake not to reach back here and rip this life apart. I won't abandon my family." He shuddered, and I realized he was crying. *Crying?*

He shook himself, wiping his face with his hands. "But you don't need me to come back with you anyway," he finally said, voice harder now. "I wrote a virus. It's what I was working on when Karron found me. *That* is what she's afraid of. The virus monitors every attempt to rewrite a backup. As soon as it detects any personality alteration routines, it scrambles the editor code and dumps a spike of garbage data into their compliance logs. Makes it look like the rewrite tool failed on its own. My virus won't just protect people,

Vincent. It'll make QoreTech's whole personality system start eating itself. And when it goes, it'll take everything with it. Every trial record, every version history, every edit, and upload it to every open network it can reach." He gave me a hard look, though I don't think he saw me at all. "They can still bring you back from the dead. They just can't decide who you are when you get here. And they won't be able to hide what they've done."

A soft chime interrupted my reply—the chronolink in my forearm, its hum tapping against my nerves.

I sent a message through, hoping to put Dr. Blake off.

> Stand by.

It wouldn't work for long. A response popped up on the display.

> We've synced with your phase signature. Sending reinforcements. If you find Mr. Mbatha send us a ping, and my team will handle him.

Glenn looked at me sharply. "What is that?"

"Dr. Blake's goons are coming."

Glenn stood up. "I won't let her destroy my family. I can't let her find us."

"Then once again, *maybe you should have moved more than a hundred yards from the transit point.* Even if she hadn't set up some way to track me, it took me less than ten minutes to find *you*. It won't take her long."

Glenn scanned the walls of his massive twentieth-century kitchen, then he turned to me, eyes desperate. "The virus, Vincent. It's the only way. It has to be uploaded directly to QoreTech's primary relay network. If we use your neural link to Earth Prime, the data dump will scramble the input source. If it's through the neural phase link, it'll be erased from their logs. They won't be able to find us again. This may be my family's only chance."

I closed my eyes. I was a scientist, not a field agent. I didn't have the training for this. I didn't have the *backups* for this. Uploading a virus to QoreTech, from another world, using my neural link?! So many things could go wrong. And if things went wrong here, there wouldn't be a clone to upload me into.

Before the compliance protocols could kick in and make me calculate the risk-to-reward ratio, the probability of success, the threat to my continued existence, I took a breath. "Dammit, Glenn. What do I need to do?"

‹|› ‹|› ‹|›

Glenn's monitor was enormous and clunky; a hulking shell of molded plastic wrapped around a tiny convex screen. The keys of his beige keyboard were so thick I wasn't sure how a person's fingers could find their way around them.

I sat in a small blue metal folding chair in the lower level of Glenn's residence, thin green light streaming through a small, grubby window high in the wall. Wires ran from the hodgepodge of ancient tech next to Glenn's desk.

"You'd be amazed at what I was able to assemble from local tech," he said proudly. "Lumen never really developed standalone computers like Prime did. Everything here runs through the Mesh." He held up a plug and inserted it into the chip port at the back of my neck with a soft click. I was in it now. Sitting in the past, defying Karron Blake, QoreTech, and Nugeneco all at once. All my instincts were screaming at me not to, but I *wanted* to fight even if my brain didn't think it could.

Glenn turned my head, angling it slightly to the left. "I updated the virus code so that it won't activate until you reconnect to QoreTech's system. Then it will upload and redistribute itself, and then wipe itself from your drive. They should never be able to tell where it came from. There will be no connection to you. And the entire system should be destroyed before they realize there's a problem."

He fiddled with the wire at my neck, making my teeth itch. "Can you please hold still? The connector is finicky, and every time you move, I lose the connection."

"What about when QoreTech or Nugeneco try to do something like this again?"

Glenn was silent, hunched over the keyboard just like he used to hunch over his desk back in the lab. "One problem at a time."

The chronolink pinged again. I looked down to check Dr. Blake's latest impatient message.

`Incoming transmission: Splinter portal activated.`

I sat straight up.

"Good grief, Vincent. Seriously. You just messed up the connection again."

"They're here."

Glenn ran to the little window that looked out toward the street. He swore softly under his breath and ran back to the interface display. "Okay. We don't have time for the failsafe I was going to install. I've got to finish now."

"Wait, no failsafe?" I asked.

"It'll be fine." He typed forcefully a few times, the big keys clacking loudly under his fingers. "This is fine. It'll have to be." He pulled the plug from my neck.

I held up my arm, clicking through the rudimentary interface in the chronolink to reestablish a connection with Earth Prime and initiate the jump.

"Wait!" Glenn said. "You can't jump from here. They have your last location." Glenn grabbed my shoulders and looked at me, his gray eyes boring into mine. "You'll lead them to my family. That baby girl is my heart. I didn't know it was even possible to feel like this again. I will do anything to protect them. Please."

I groaned and closed the interface, then ran for the back door, throwing it open and clomping up the steps that led out of the basement. I ran through the yard, jumping the fence into the neighboring yard, and kept running.

At the gap between houses, I stopped to catch my breath and see the progress of Dr. Blake's team of officers. They stood near the school, seemingly arguing about which direction to go, one officer pointing toward Glenn's house, and the other pointing in my general direction.

I ran on, giving my body the workout it deserved, but never got. When I'd put as much distance between myself and Glenn's house as I could, I tore across the street.

I was spotted instantly. Wildly zigzagging to avoid any sonic blasts designed to incapacitate me, I ran around to the corner door at the back of the school that I'd exited through yesterday, only to find it locked.

They were shouting at me. In a panic, I threw up my arms and dove headfirst through one of the windows, the glass shattering around me, slicing through my clothes and skin.

I landed inside, thudding against the cold flooring, a shard of glass digging into my forearm. This was a terrible plan. What good was any of this? After they shot me, they'd find Glenn anyway. I yanked the glass out of my skin and pushed myself away from the windows, hesitating in the middle of the room, completely paralyzed by indecision. This was all going to scrap.

I heard the whir of a neural inhibitor activating and turned at the sound. The security officer looked pale and winded, her turquoise hair bright against the green sky, aiming her weapon through the window. "Don't make me fire. You know what a headache this gives you. Where is Glenn Mbatha?"

"He's in here," I said, between gasps. "I thought if I jumped through the window, I could unlock the door from inside and let you in, but it uses some kind of physical key, and I don't know how to open it."

The turquoise-haired officer growled and turned toward the door, waving the rest to follow her.

With a bang, the back door to the gymnasium opened, and the officers stepped inside. They surveyed the room slowly, guns at the ready, before surrounding me where I stood.

"He's not really here, is he?" the turquoise-haired officer said, finally. She holstered her neural inhibitor and drew a plasmashot.

I raised my arms in surrender, then tapped the chronolink, initiating the jump sequence. The world spun, but instead of going dark, my stomach and brain seemed to switch places. My insides tried to become outsides, and my heart pounded in my toes.

I woke in the rejuvenation room, draped in a cloth, my skin cold against the plasmaglass of the table. Dr. Blake stood over me, compupad in hand. A surg-bot stood nearby tracking my vitals.

"What happened?" I asked, my speech slurred, tongue working like it had never formed words before. "Did your guards shoot me? Was there an accident during the jump?" I tried to lift an arm, but it didn't respond, my limbs not reacting to my brain's commands, the neural net not yet fully formed.

"In a way," Dr. Blake said, eyes and fingers still on the compupad. "You failed, Vincent. The mission was never really about Glenn. It was about you. Proving the loyalty protocols could override even the deepest human emotions: Friendship. Morality. Self-preservation.' She flashed a thin smile. "If you could kill Glenn Mbatha on command—a trusted colleague and friend—then Nugeneco has proof of concept, and we have endless incarnations for life. Win-win." She tapped the compupad. 'Killing him would have been convenient for *me*, of course. He did steal rather damaging evidence. But this—" she gestured at me strapped to the table, "—this is more valuable. Now I know exactly where the weaknesses are. I programmed reentry to end that version of you and try again in this new skin. Your chip synced as soon as your neural net connected with the quantcom, and I've already begun recalibrating. Higher loyalty thresholds. Reduced emotional interference."

She swiped around deliberately on her compupad a moment more. "I like you less as a yes man, but I get more work done."

I squeezed my brand-new eyes shut. "You can't do this. It's *still* murder, even if I come back. It's not the same. It's *never* the same!"

She tapped a few more times and nodded at the surg-bot. He plugged a photon cable into the port at the base of my skull.

I groaned, a deep guttural sound as a pain pulsed deep at the back of my head. I could *feel* the chip lights blinking.

"You won't remember this. And I will finally have the good little worker I need. Bots are useful and all, but they just don't have the ingenuity."

Another gush of pain ripped from my head down my spine.

"Surg-bot, what is happening?" Dr. Blake yelled. "There seems to be some kind of glitch in the system. Make sure the connection is secure."

Agony tore through me, my muscles seizing up in response.

"No, No! Something is wrong!" Dr. Blake roared.

My eyes snapped open. I was back in the school, standing in the middle of the circle of slightly confused-looking officers, feeling like I'd just been atomized in a lab explosion.

"What are you doing?" the officer shouted. "What did you do?"

A *ker-CHUNK* sounded behind me. I tried to get my unresponsive head to turn, but I was grabbed by the officer with the turquoise hair. She spun me, plasmashot pressed against my head as though she would push it straight through. Glenn stood in front of us with his twentieth-century weapon at the ready.

"Glenn Mbatha," the turquoise-haired officer said, sounding relieved. "You are under a termination order. Drop the weapon."

"Go ahead," Glenn said softly, tipping his head at them. "Make my day."

The turquoise-haired officer holding me sighed. "I don't have time for—" She cut off, then crumpled. I fell next to her, but it felt like falling through a void, for eternity. Forever.

On Lumen, my body hit the cold gymnasium floor.

On Prime, the surg-bot pressed its synthetic hand against my chest as I writhed on the table.

Both bodies screamed. The pain merged, doubled, became something beyond comprehension.

I could hear Dr. Blake yelling on Prime as though she was in the next room, and the monotone of the surg-bot answering her enraged questions. In the school on Lumen, the officers around me fell, their guns clattering to the floor. I groaned and writhed, punctuated by Dr. Blake's frustrating tapping on the compupad.

Glenn cursed. "What is happening? Is it the virus? Will it not let you jump?"

"Dr. Blake," I gasped, both of me, in both places. "She killed me. Uploaded me into a new skin. I'm plugged into the network now. She can't—" I cut off, twisting in pain. The virus Glenn created burned through me, running through my nerves like fire through pipes of oil.

"I really would prefer you didn't die," Dr. Blake said, voice strained, face red with rage, the blue lights of the rejuvenation room shining around her head like a halo. "There is still more I need of you."

"What do you mean you're plugged into the network?" Glenn cried, crouching next to me on the gymnasium floor. "*What* network? On *Prime*?"

Dr. Blake tapped on my temple like she was trying to settle my brain into place.

I twitched on the floor beside Glenn, clutching at my head.

"I don't know how this is happening, but I've got to find a way to pull you out," Glenn said.

I grabbed his arm. "No! The virus. It has to fully upload. If you pull me out now, it will be incomplete." I could barely speak through the pain, but I pushed out the words. "You have to leave me in."

"It's killing you!"

"Good," I spat. "Let it kill the version of me *she* made. The one who was going to murder you because she told me to."

"What virus?" Dr. Blake demanded. "What are you talking about? Surg-bot, tap into his neural net and figure out what is happening. Now!"

I could feel the virus spreading through both of me, corrupting every personality modification subroutine it touched, every tool Dr. Blake used to hollow people out and remake them. "I won't let them do this to anyone else," I grunted to Glenn or Dr. Blake. Either one. Both. Every word was agony across two bodies. "They don't get to steal who we are. Not anymore."

For the first time in who knows how long, I wasn't just a tool following programming.

I was Vincent Dodd. And *I* was choosing this. *Both of me.*

Dr. Blake yelled at the surg-bot. "If you can't do what I need, will you please get a hunk of synthetics in here that *can*?" She pressed her fingers against my neck.

My mind split in two. My bodies rejected everything. Oxygen was poison. Breathing was death. Light burned through my skin like acid.

A roar tore out of me, shredding my throat and tongue.

Glenn grabbed my arm and started typing on my chronolink, cursing and mumbling under his breath. His fingers slammed against my skin like stones against silk.

I felt *everything*. My clothing raked against my skin. Both the floor on Lumen and the table beneath in the lab on Prime pressed against me until they nearly squashed me flat. Glenn cursed again and tapped and typed. Then he squeezed my arm, the pressure exploding into my eyeballs.

"Thanks, old friend," Glenn said, voice thick with more emotion than I had ever heard from him. "Thanks for trying to save my family. Keep an eye on them for me."

He tapped the chronolink, and the air around Glenn rippled, twisting the gymnasium as if heat were bending the world sideways. His outline doubled for a split second, then collapsed inward. There was a soft crack, and he was gone.

Then suddenly Glenn was on Prime, materializing in the rejuvenation lab next to my table. Dr. Blake looked up at him, startled, and then set the compupad down on my chest. The pressure of the thin tablet was like a boulder, crushing my lungs and ribs. I gasped, unable to draw breath.

"There you are," Dr. Blake said with a sigh. "Surg-bot, tranquilize him."

Glenn raised his 600-year-old shotgun and shot the surg-bot, blasting it into tiny pieces. Karron Blake raised her hand. Glenn turned the gun on her and pulled the trigger. I recoiled, the sounds exploding inside my head. Drops of Karron Blake's blood pounded against my skin like a hailstorm, then finally ceased.

The floor of the school gymnasium was cool against my burning skin as the pain slowly subsided to a dull ache. I gasped, gulping in air, my lungs in both places functioning once again.

The dead bodies of the guards littered the gymnasium floor around me. They would be revived on Earth Prime eventually, but on Lumen, no one would understand why four people in strange uniforms had all suffered heart failure at the same time.

"Dr. Blake will be revived tomorrow," I rasped to Glenn on Prime, the words echoing across time. "She'll keep looking for you."

Glenn sighed, a huge rising and falling of his chest. "I know."

"She might still be able to find your family."

Glenn smiled, full of regret. "I couldn't let you die, friend."

Sirens echoed through the school walls, the local authorities probably responding to the gunshots. .

On Prime, alarms rang through the rejuvenation lab, and a copbot rolled into the room. "Time to go, Vincent." Glenn grabbed my arm, attempting to help me up, but my limbs were unresponsive. "Vincent. We're out of time. You have to get up."

On Lumen, the chronolink in my arm was dark, fried. On Prime, I had no chronolink at all, no way to jump. No way to run. I was trapped in both timelines.

I grabbed Glenn's hand. "I will watch over your family on Lumen. I promise."

"Don't be stupid. I'll carry you if I have to. We have to go." He tried to pull me up and over his shoulder, but stumbled, falling against the medical table.

"You just jumped six hundred years into the future. You don't have the strength. Go, before you fall into cardiac arrest. *Now*."

Glenn stared at me, his skin gray under the medlights, indecision at war on his face, then he struggled to his feet and limped off into the hall.

And I lay in both places.

One consciousness.

Two bodies.

Trapped on both worlds.

I am here. I am there.

I am Double Dodd.

END NOTE

Ren, maybe you can replicate the chronolink. Could be useful in tracking chipped individuals across splinters. I'll see what I can find on it; I'm heading time-side on this one. They appear to have tacos.

—Ms. Six

AN IMMORTAL'S LAMENT

By Kasey Selma McQueen

They promised us the universes
But didn't name the cost—
Now for every clone in which we wake
More of ourselves is lost.

Fluent in eleven languages,
But nothing left to say.
Our books, art, music—all mockeries
Of what real humans made.

No way of knowing what happens next.
No one to ask because
Where gods once reigned and the faithful prayed,
Now all we have is us.

Death—once solemn, somber, sanctified.
We play with it like ghouls,
Take the bodies and the wasted lives
And bring us back our souls.

Date: 2590-04-17 02:57:22
From: Green Kinsha
To: Torts El-Sayed, Anachronauts Supervisor
Subject: End of Report Batch / Thoughts / Also Cats

Well. You've read them all now.

I know. Take a minute. Have a cookie. Breathe into a bag if you need to.

Before I started, I figured most of the accounts and reports would turn out to be nothing but coincidence, the usual immortal meddling we document and file away. Instead, this week we've got a plethora of nexuses, time loops, supernatural powers, time loops, and at least one splinter where the entire population all collectively agreed to forget basic facts about reality. Which I really kind of respect. That takes commitment.

Here's what I think: these aren't just accounts of copies of Earth and what the immortals did to them. They're accounts of what the people on those Earth copies did anyway. Despite everything, they still fell in love. They still fought for each other. They still made art and asked questions and occasionally committed very creative crimes.

I think Nerrid is right and the universe is either pushing back, or the humans are. Possibly both. Gentor thinks this is mostly superstition. Gentor is also, as previously noted, a dodo.

We have more splinters to document, more accounts to collect, and the Space Cat Council has requested a full briefing, which I am going to delay for as long as bureaucratically possible because the last one took four hours and they kept interrupting to groom themselves. With respect to the Council, I don't think they fully grasp the urgency here. Or maybe they do and they just don't care, which, given the fact that they are moonbase-running Cats, is the best we can hope for.

The point is: we're not done. We're barely getting started.

Green Kinsha

Splinter Analyst, Anachronauts

Contributor Biographies

Writers

AJ Stevens

AJ is a Whitney Award finalist for her book *Mere Mortal*. She studied Microbiology with an emphasis in genetics at a university on planet Earth, but prefers writing to lab work, so that's what she does.

Ash Stevens

Ash is a Health and Kinesiology student at the University of Utah—though she still can't spell "kinesiology" without double-checking. Ash began writing poetry at eighteen as a way of coping with anxiety and depression, and it has become a source of purpose and creative freedom. When she isn't crafting emotionally devastating poems or buried in coursework, you can find her mountain climbing anything that isn't actively collapsing, reading, weightlifting, doing jiu-jitsu, and yapping her heart out with her girlies.

Boydell Bown

Boydell is a Realm Award semi-finalist for his book *Splinter's Edge*. As a software engineer by day, and a supervillain by night, Boydell finds it a challenge to spend enough time writing to let free the stories plaguing his soul.

Brandon B. Chambers

Brandon is an author and accomplished martial artist, with black belts in Taekwondo and three different variants of Karate. He recently opened his own dojo and enjoys balancing martial arts with his love of writing.

Elesa Hagberg

Elesa is a Whitney Award finalist for *The Dissection and Reassembly of Cohen Hoard*. She loves cookies, board games, collecting and remodeling travel trailers, laughing louder than other people, and hanging out with her family.

Esther Davis

Esther is the author of "A Dog, 3 Cats, and a Dragon," a collection of family-friendly speculative fiction stories. You can also find her sci-fi and fantasy works scattered across the internet, including "Frozen Heart" and "Scars" on T. Gene Davis's Speculative Blog, and "The Baboons of Mars" on Tall Tale TV.

Ethan Whitaker

Ethan is a speculative fiction/fantasy writer from Spanish Fork, Utah. He is a part-time student at Utah Valley University, where he is studying creative writing. "Into the Void" is his first published work, and hopefully not his last.

Faralee Pozo

Faralee is a Teen Readers Choice Award finalist and a Realm Award finalist for her book *Sorry, Humans (Especially Greg)*. In her spare time, she plays tabletop games with her family, reads, and tries to avoid cooking.

Jan Hassmann

Jan first studied and then taught English Literature at universities far from home. He has recently returned to Europe, where he runs an amicable poetry club in Plovdiv, Bulgaria. He's in *Seaside Gothic, Dishsoap Quarterly, WireWorm Magazine, Stone Circle Review, Sparks of Calliope, PoemAlone,* and elsewhere.

Jessica Guernsey

With twenty-seven stories in print, it's safe to say Jessica is obsessed with short fiction. Two of those stories are in coloring books! She reads the slush pile and crushes dreams by day and produces anthologies by night. Also, she was once hit on by Vanilla Ice. So that was cool.

Jessica Kendall

Jessica has a BFA in creative writing with minors in both English and History, and she is an editor for CookieLynn Publishing. Jessica is a self-proclaimed reading omnivore who loves to immerse herself in multiple genres, so long as there is kissing and/or stabbing. She lives in Idaho with her hunky, science-nerd husband and four brilliant, creative, and crazy kids. When not editing, reading, or writing, she bakes, beats her kids in Nertz, and binges shows like *Leverage, Buffy, Great British Bake Off, The Nanny,* and *Golden Girls.*

Kara Reynolds

Kara lives in Arizona, where it's almost always too hot. She works as an administrative assistant to Laura Rennert at Andrea Brown Literary Agency, and teaches at the Storymakers Conference in Provo, UT.

Kasey Selma McQueen—writer and artist

Kasey is a professional content writer for a marketing company. Two of her stories have won the Storymakers first chapter contest. She's a digital nomad, wandering the globe in search of delicious recipes to add to her repertoire and exciting new playgrounds for her toddler sidekick.

Kristina Atkins

Kristina's debut epic fantasy novel, *Feathers Sharp as Knives*, released in May 2023. It was an Honorable Mention for the 2024 Writer's Digest self-published e-book awards. She's had multiple chapters shortlisted in *Uncharted Magazine*'s Novel Excerpt Prize, and *Uncharted* also published her first short story, "Mercy Kill," a sapphic zombie story set in 1900 West Virginia. She received her MFA in Creative Writing from Converse College in 2012.

Kyro Dean

Award-winning poet and author of the *Rogue Royals* and *Fires of Qaf* series, Kyro also has works in various anthologies. She owns Eight Moons Publishing, the writing resource blog Vanillagrass.com, and is an experienced editor, book coach, and indoor plant enthusiast.

Matthew Cushing

Matthew is an American author of speculative fiction short stories and novels. He is a winner of the Gold Rush Literary Award for speculative fiction and a Finalist for the Roswell Award. An animal lover and trombonist, Mr. Cushing lives in Connecticut.

Paul Martz

Paul is a science fiction writer, technology blogger, and former punk rock drummer. He's published at *Amazing Stories, Creepy Podcast, Sci-Fi Lampoon*, and others. His awards include the *Uncharted Magazine* AI Flash Challenge and the Roswell Award. He recently published the nonfiction book, *Solve It! The Only Speedsolving Guide for Blind Cubers.*

Regan Wolfe

Regan is a fantasy and sci-fi writer, currently based out of Edinburgh, Scotland. Her short stories and poetry have been published in *Touchstones* and *Warp & Weave,* and she came in first in her heat for the NYC Midnight short story challenge. Regan loves discovering new places, finding hidden coffee shops, talking about death, and hearing people's life stories.

Russ Marcum

Russ is the co-creator of the soon-to-be published graphic novel, Sleeping Wizards. He is also the co-winner of Tucson Horror Fest Best Script. Father of four humans, two cats, and married to a wonderful hypnotherapist. He's currently in third term as the social media director of the Whitney Awards.

Shelley Thayer

Shelley Thayer has been writing since she was seven, starting with a story about a superhero potato. She holds a BA in Creative Writing and is editing her debut YA fantasy novel. She once appeared in the background of the Today show—just a few feet from Al Roker.

Taryn Skipper—writer and artist

Taryn's publications include picture books, activity books, poetry and cover art, as well as her debut novel for young adults, *Between Tungsten and Gold.* She has served on the Storymakers Guild board of directors and as president of the Whitney Awards for novels.

Artists

Asia Bushman

Asia got her first sketchbook at seven and hasn't stopped creating art since. Her art grows with her. She likes to create, whether that be nail art, painting, drawing, or cross-stitch. Art is her passion—she finds joy in anything that could be considered art.

Crow Spencer

Crow is an artist from Utah who is currently pursuing a BFA in Studio Arts and Art Technology from the School of the Art Institute of Chicago. They are working to become a game designer, with their projects usually focusing on memories, environmental storytelling, and birds.

Helix Arts

Helix Arts, otherwise known as Jefferson Hunter, is an aspiring young artist who has had art displayed and sold at the Springville Museum of Art. With an undying love for creating stories, Helix hopes to one day be a published artist in a weekly magazine.

Lydia Pozo

Lydia Pozo is an artist that loves any sort of paint, and is proud to have placed in a Springville Chalk the Walk competition. Aviator and reader, she is eager to explore this world and the fictional ones.

Mary Guerrero Gutierrez

Mary Guerrero Gutierrez has always loved making. From twist tie rings to elaborate oil paintings, Mary has done a little bit of everything in between. She started taking art classes at a young age and then began teaching art classes to even younger kids. Through the years, Mary honed her skills, primarily in realism. Now, this recovering perfectionist enjoys making art for the sake of making art. She loves exploring different mediums and styles and participating in creative play. Mary currently works in healthcare, but dreams of becoming a crazy old art lady someday (she's already got the crazy part covered).

Orpheus

Orpheus is a twenty-three-year-old philosophy student and artist. They work in multiple mediums, but they mostly do either acrylic on canvas or marker on paper when doing traditional art. They're an avid reader and aspiring writer, and have long loved anything fantasy, magic realism, or sci-fi.

Rebecca Sorge Jensen—cover artist

Rebecca loves telling stories and drawing pictures, so becoming an illustrator made perfect sense. She currently lives and works in Utah, creating art for children's books, magazines, posters, cards, and anything else people will let her draw on.

Regan Turley

Regan is an Art & Design student at Utah Valley University with a love for visual storytelling. She aspires to write and illustrate her own comic books.

River Koenig

River is a nineteen-year old artist and musician. She loves creating art in various formats, and shares her time between the American southwest and Norway, where she hopes to attend college.

Sydney Whitaker

Sydney has loved drawing since she was little and has always had a creative spirit. She enjoys using art to express her ideas and imagination. Sydney is excited to be part of this anthology and hopes her work brings a little joy and inspiration to others.

A special thanks to our amazing backers:

Adam Dickstein, Albenita, Alex Harlequin, Amanda Sedivy, Angela Mathers, Anja Hassmann, Anne Bown, Anthony Pieper, Becky Saldivar, Benton Marcum, Bookdog, Boydell Bown, Brandon Regan, Brian Hart, carlos pozo, Cassi, Corey Votta, Craig, DeAnn Peterson, Diego Riley, Eight Moons Publishing, Eric Farmer, Eric Miller, Faemarie Whitaker, Gina Denny, Grace Nicholson, Hannah Gibbs, Hannah Sorensen, Hazarod, Ian, Janelle Carolyn Youngstrom, Jared, JC, Jessica Springer Guernsey, John Lamar, Josh Symalla, Joshua McGinnis, Josie Pozo, Julia Libby, Justin Lindsay, Kasey McQueen, Keith Teklits, Kelly McQueen, Kimberlee Vantine, Kristina Atkins, Kyle Williams, Lillian Elliott, Linda Bolander, Luis Cordova, M&M, Marion Boyd, Mark Heinze, mdtommyd, Meshia, Michael Doty, Mike Saldivar, Monica molina, Nancy Boyd, NPHarris62, Owen Johnson, Paul, Paul Martz, Raeven Hohsfield, Randall Barfield, Raphael Isla, Rebecca Sorge, Rob Mayer, Rob Skidmore, Rusty Marcum, Samantha Keil, Sarah, Sarah Rogers, Sue-Rae Rosenfeld, Suzanne Lambert, Taryn Skipper, Teixeira, Thomas Karlinsey, Timo Hassmann, Todd and Letitia Williams, William Funderburk, Yvonne Rode

www.ingramcontent.com/pod-product-compliance
Lightning Source LLC
LaVergne TN
LVHW041103080826
845145LV00007B/1673
9781960108234